## About the Author

Amanda Crowe lives in Ontario, Canada, with her husband, Patrick, her son, Wyatt, and their two dogs. She has a bachelor's degree in creative writing from West Virginia Wesleyan College, which she attended on a soccer scholarship. She currently works as a Dog Guide Instructor at Dog Guides Canada, training dogs in the Diabetic Alert Dog program. In her spare moments, she is often lost in her own mind sorting through various stories, plots, and characters. It is a great joy to be able to bring one of those stories to life.

# Chase

**Amanda Crowe**

Chase

Olympia Publishers
*London*

www.olympiapublishers.com
OLYMPIA PAPERBACK EDITION

Copyright © Amanda Crowe 2023

The right of Amanda Crowe to be identified as author of
this work has been asserted in accordance with sections 77 and 78 of
the Copyright, Designs and Patents Act 1988.

**All Rights Reserved**

No reproduction, copy or transmission of this publication
may be made without written permission.
No paragraph of this publication may be reproduced,
copied or transmitted save with the written permission of the publisher,
or in accordance with the provisions
of the Copyright Act 1956 (as amended).

Any person who commits any unauthorized act in relation to
this publication may be liable to criminal
prosecution and civil claims for damage.

A CIP catalogue record for this title is
available from the British Library.

ISBN: 978-1-80074-450-9

This is a work of fiction.
Names, characters, places and incidents originate from the writer's
imagination. Any resemblance to actual persons, living or dead, is
purely coincidental.

First Published in 2023

Olympia Publishers
Tallis House
2 Tallis Street
London
EC4Y 0AB

Printed in Great Britain

## Dedication

I dedicate this book to my mum, thank you for teaching me how to be brave.

# Acknowledgments

To Patrick, my best friend and hubby. So much of what I do is because of you. Thank you isn't enough, but it is a start. You are the most selfless person I know, and I adore that about you. Thank you, I love you.

To my mum, dad, brother and sister, thank you for being my biggest cheerleaders and pushing me to be my best.

To my friends and family, thank you for always believing and supporting me.

To Amanda Dobson, you are the best writing partner out there! Thank you for always lending your eyes to read over my stories and energizing me to keep going.

To my Dog Guides family, you all inspire me every single day. I hope you know how amazing each and every one of you are.

To my professors at West Virginia Wesleyan College, thank you for creating an environment where creative minds, like mine, can learn and grow.

# Chapter One

Lana slowed her pace to a slow jog as the small peak of the cabin came into view. It was still probably a kilometer away, the edges of the framework becoming more distinct with each step. "Thank God!" she huffed to herself. No matter how many times she trained out here, there was no better feeling than seeing the finish line. Her feet tapped the ground in a methodical movement as she stepped into the small heart shaped clearing. She smiled feeling the full sun on her face for the first time all day. She breathed a deep breath and hesitated a moment allowing the warmth of the sun's rays to fill her body. A small pain shot up her leg and averted her blissful moment. She twisted her lean body, her long brown hair tumbling off her shoulder to find a small gash in her calf. "Ughhh," she groaned, yanking off her pink buff to wipe at the trail of blood down her leg.

She looked back at the forest with a scowl. As if the trees could interpret her annoyance. She thought back on her run, and tried to remember if she had stumbled or kicked anything. *Nope.*

"Probably a thorn," she mumbled to herself. It wasn't deep, just the top layer of skin. Still, it vexed her. She had yet to make it out of the forest without any kind of injury, torn clothing, or dirt smeared on her. The bleeding had pretty much subsided now, and was replaced by a familiar irksome stinging, like the burn of a papercut.

She stood back up and glanced back at the trees. For fourteen years that forest had been her playground, and it still never took it easy on her. I guess that was a testament to its unpredictability and formidability. She closed the gap to the cabin in an easy walk. She wasn't going to jog in today. The early spring air was thinner than usual and that run had really kicked her in the butt.

She swung the backdoor of her cabin open and kicked her shoes off. She made sure to drop them outside the door, if Aunt Alice found them inside caked with dirt and leaves she'd never hear the end of it. She leaned over the kitchen sink to chug some water, splashing some of it on her leg removing the last of the dried blood.

Her breathing was already almost back to normal, walking back to the cabin greatly aided in that. She wiped at the sweat beading along her forehead and she scoured the kitchen cabinets for food. It was kind of like a ritual after her daily run. She plopped her iPod on the table, and climbed onto the counter to look onto the top shelf. She cringed hearing it slap against the hard surface. "Shit," she said, reaching for it and turning it over ever so slowly.

She blew out a relieved breath, "Phew, still in one piece." Not that it really mattered, the thing couldn't hold a charge anyways. It barely lasted more than an hour into her workouts. She didn't even know why she brought it any more. She should have asked for a new one about four years ago, but it seemed to lack importance, and since hers still technically worked, she figured it was easier to just stick with it. Her aunt had better things to focus on than getting her a new iPod.

"Aunt Alice," Lana yelled, still hunkered on the counter, "I'm back," she said, slamming the final cupboard shut. "Aunt Alice?" she called again, jumping off and trotting over to the stairs that led to the kitchen. She swung on the railing to the second floor waiting for a response.

She heard a sound then, but it wasn't from upstairs. She stilled listening harder. It was from outside. Her ears perked and quickly distinguished the sound of car tires struggling up the road. She trotted over to the front window just in time to see a large black all-terrain vehicle pass the narrow opening at the end of their driveway. The Rocky Mountains weren't exactly easily managed terrain, even less so at this altitude. There was pretty much one road up and down the mountain and very few cars passed by. If they did, it was almost always one of three; campers, hikers, or hunters. The expensive all-terrain vehicle gave these guys away, they were hunters.

"Oh, Lana dear, you're back?"

Lana turned to see her aunt hobbling into the living room, her short gray hair half pulled back into a ponytail. "Hey auntie, I called out when I was home," she said, watching her frail aunt carefully sit herself on the edge of the couch.

Lana pinned her arms to her side to resist the urge to help. The last six months had been a major turning point in their relationship, Alice's health had majorly deteriorated. Lana often cursed herself for not catching on sooner, but there weren't any outward signs for her to catch; no lesions, or coughing, or pain. The signs were much more discreet, but much more worrisome.

Alice wasn't Lana's biological aunt, in fact she was more akin to a grandmother than an aunt. She had no blood relation to her. That didn't mean they were any less of a family. Well actually, Alice was her *only* family. It had been just the two of them for the last fourteen years, ever since her parents were murdered.

That was a whole other story. One she knew equally little about. Just like the dementia she saw in her aunt. It wasn't an illness that she could solve or even treat for that matter. She felt—

helpless. She had read every book she could get her hands on and most of them said the same thing. Keeping them in a routine in a familiar environment would help, and certain spices and herbs like turmeric were said to be helpful. All of which Lana had implemented right away.

She bit the inside of her cheek to distract herself as she listened to her aunt recount to her *again* how much her late husband, Earl, had enjoyed his dinner last night.

"Steak and potatoes," her aunt mused, "your uncle said the cook was perfect. Isn't that lovely?"

Lana smiled and nodded. There was no point in correcting or unraveling her illusion even though they'd had a cashew stir fry last night. Meat obviously wasn't super easy to get up here unless you caught it yourself. It was rare that they would ever get to have a steak. No, the steak was a memory from another timeline. One that she lived with Earl. One Lana hadn't even been born for. That was another thing the book had said, sometimes it was easier to just let the scene play out.

Alice's typically only lasted a few minutes. The odd time, she did correct her, mostly when she lost her patience or let her frustration get the better of her. Every time, her aunt always seemed to get more confused, sad or angry. It was easier to just let it be. For the both of them.

A part of Lana knew that was only the beginning, but she often pushed those thoughts of the future as far from her mind as she could manage. "Day by day," she reminded herself. Her aunt was the only person she had in the entire world. She couldn't even think about losing her. She didn't even know who she was without her aunt.

Lana was only five years old when her parents were killed, only five years old when her entire world was ripped out from under her feet like a '70s shag rug. The memory of that night tugged at her mind and she tried to push it away, biting back the tears that threatened to follow. The closet that her mother had hidden her in did little to mask the gun shots that took the lives of her parents. It was so long ago now, but the shots still reverberated in her memory like a never-ending echo.

Lana rubbed her temple, forcing the memory back and refocused on the old woman sitting in front of her. She leaned her long-toned frame against the wall and tucked her wavy brown hair behind her ears. *It's not all a tragic tale.* She thought to herself, the hint of a smile appearing on her face. *That's the same day I met Aunt Alice.*

Lana didn't remember a lot about that day, but she did remember Aunt Alice. The power of her voice as she fended off reporters, the ferocity with which she shielded Lana's body cupped against her own. She would have taken Lana away to the cabin that night, but she had to be vetted as her legal guardian first. After a few weeks in a local hotel, when everything was sorted, her aunt wasted no time in whisking her away to this cabin, pretty much in the middle of nowhere. *Well—that's not completely accurate,* Lana thought. *The cabin is somewhere, but it's somewhere that's extremely well hidden from society.*

The cabin had its own personal, and completely natural, cloaking mechanism. The thick Canadian forest of the Rocky Mountains. It comprises of some of the most majestic and difficult terrain in North America. Lana of course had grown up in the woods, and there was nowhere in the world she felt more at home.

She'd always assumed her parents' murder was the reason behind her aunts reclusive and paranoid nature, but as the years went by, It just became part of who her aunt was. It didn't take very long for Alice to instill those same behaviors and distrustful habits upon her. After all, it was a learned behavior that soon just became a habit. She was untrusting and she was careful, which weren't terrible qualities to have.

Lana adjusted her shoulders against the wall and cringed as she watched her aunt sit forward and reach across the coffee table to grab her journal. The old woman's hands shook as her long spidery fingers wrapped around the brown leather of the well-worn book.

That was the other downside. Her aunt's body was simply not as strong or capable as it once was. However, in her moments of clarity, she was also still very proud and would rather stick a sewing needle in her eye than ask for help. How do you tell someone that has cared for you your entire life, to slow down? How do you tell them not to do things they have been doing forever.

"Don't give me that look," her aunt said, "I'm fine." She nodded, setting her journal in her lap.

Lana raised her hands in surrender, "I didn't say a word."

"You didn't have to, your eyes said it all. I don't want your pity dear. Age is a part of life. I don't need you shadowing me all the time."

Lana smiled. This is the no muss no fuss aunt she was used to. Her stomach growled loudly and her aunt looked at her curiously. She hadn't found anything to snack on after her run and her body was protesting. Lana hopped up and checked the time on the stove flashing 1.33 p.m.

"I'm going to head down to Ayiana's. It's Friday so she should be there for a few more hours. I'll see what I can get to restock our shelves. I'll put in an order for next week too. You have any cravings for anything?"

Alice shook her head. "No, get whatever you want dear, I don't mind."

"OK, well," Lana said, "I better get going if I want to get there before she leaves."

"Mmhhmm," her aunt said, her attention seeded in her journal. Lana hurried through the back-screen door and slung her leg over the quad runner.

"Say hi to Juney!" her aunt yelled, as the door swung shut.

Lana laughed out loud. Her aunt knew her so well. Ayiana had been importing supplies to this region for the last ten years or so. Her heli drops had greatly increased the ease of Alice and Lana getting supplies and groceries. Before Ayiana, it was a solid four-day trip to get those things.

She wasn't there all the time though, she split her time between three locations in the mountains for the best productivity. She originally learned to be a pilot for her own first nation territory, but when she saw the need elsewhere, she didn't hesitate to lend a helping hand.

It was Ayiana who brought her all the books she requested when investigating Alice's condition. It was also Ayiana who had consoled her when she came to terms with her aunt's diagnosis. She was pretty much the only other person in her life besides her aunt.

Lana pushed her foot down on the gas and twisted the handlebar. She had one stop to make before Ayiana's. She tore down the path that she'd used so many times before ducking under every outstretched branch and curling around every uprooted tree. It was a well-practiced craft for her. She felt the wind whip around her head, blowing her hair freely behind her. She smiled appreciating the wildness of that feeling. A joy tingling in her stomach.

Thirty minutes later, she made a sharp turn into denser wood. This path was significantly less traveled. Lana meant for it to be. She didn't want strangers to stumble upon it and disturb Juney. She dismounted the vehicle, popping her helmet on the seat. She took off on foot muscling through the difficult terrain, her anticipation whirling as she made her way closer.

She came to the rocky outcrop she was looking for and approached the jagged cliff face. "Juney? Juuunneey?" she called, scanning the area. "Where are ya, Juney?" she asked, crouching down to peer into the small cave dwelling in the base of the rock. "Come on, Juniper," she said again, searching the rocky terrain. "Juniperrrr," she called again, cupping her hands on either side of her mouth.

She heard a chuffing noise from above and stiffened, her heart dropping into her stomach. She tilted her head up slowly. A long yellow form hanging in the tree above her, lounging casually on an outstretched branch. "Shit." She hadn't done a sweep of the trees before moving in closer. *Rookie move Lana.*

The massive animal pushed itself up onto its haunches and launched itself at her. She only had a moment to prepare her body for the impact. The creature thumped down onto her sending her breath from her body in an outward huff. Her body crashed down onto the solid rock beneath her. She gasped and grappled with the animal twisting this way and that, squirming-kicking-punching-anything to get it off her.

The cougar adjusted to each of Lana's blows with ease and almost annoyance at her effort. He grabbed her by the back of her shirt collar and chuffed his breath shooting down her back.

Lana let out a long groan. "OK, OK fine, Juney you win. Get off."

The large cat chuffed again, this time in satisfaction and slid off his target. He bent his long body in a yoga-like stretch. "Hi Juniper, how's my boy doing?" The tan colored cat trotted toward her and ran his muscular body underneath her hands. He straightened his long angular frame and wrapped his massive paws around her shoulders. He licked his rough sandpaper tongue on her face. Lana laughed and stroked him.

Juniper was the closest thing Lana had to a pet. She'd rescued him from a poacher's trap when he was just a cub. His mom had unfortunately not been as lucky. He'd lived with Lana for about a year while she rehabilitated him and tried to teach him how to be a cat and not a person. He came by the cabin every now and then, mostly when he was too lazy to hunt. He'd settled in this den shortly after it was far enough away to have his own space, but not too far from his people.

Lana had named the large cat after the Rocky Mountain Juniper Tree, a special evergreen-esque tree found in this very forest. It seemed fitting for him. She rubbed the cat and talked to him as if he were a human. She always felt uneasy when she saw hunters in the area.

"—so, hang around here for a few days, OK? The last thing you need is to get caught in another trap."

The cat laid across her lap purring contently. "I can't stay Juney, I have to go see Ayiana." He let out a low grumble. "Hey!" she chuckled, whacking him in the side. "None of that. I'll come back soon."

Lana left her big fur ball with a smile on her face. He sometimes came down to Ayiana's with her, but she didn't feel like risking it today. Not with those hunters nearby. She revved up the quad and gunned it toward the clearing where Ayiana landed her Heli. She skirted around the corner just as Ayiana was closing the boards of her shed. She looked back, her arms crossed over her chest, daring Lana to approach. Her long black hair whipping wildly around her. "Closing time is three p.m., Lana."

"I know, I know, I'm late—again. It's aunt Alice she—*never mind*—it's not going to change the fact that I'm here—right now." She pleaded, clasping her hands together dramatically, "Can I grab a few things to hold us over?"

"Oh, go on." Ayiana waved. "Like I would say no to you."

Lana winked and smiled, slipping into the small wooden shed. She pulled a bun out of a sealed bag and jammed it into her mouth. "Not even going to wait until your home *abinoojiinh?*" Her First Nation tongue ringing in Lana's ears like it always did. There was something about the sing-song melody of it that always calmed her. Lana knew the word was one of adoration, like child, in her Chippewa language. She knew a couple of words from her dealings with Ayiana, but not as many as she would like to know. Lana grabbed a couple boxes of pasta, canned tomatoes, bread, and a box of granola bars.

"I think that's good, and just put in our normal order for next week."

"*Akina, akina,*" Ayiana mumbled, nodding and waving Lana off. "Go before you run out of light abinoojiinh."

Lana piled her haul on the back of her quad and clipped her helmet on her head. Ayiana was getting ready to board her helicopter. "Hey Ayiana."

"Yes?"

"Pretty sure, I saw a hunting party headed up the mountain, if you see them heading near the cabin, or Juniper's rock, can you send a heads up?" Ayiana answered with a thumbs up, and that's all she needed to kick her quad into gear and head back up the mountain.

\*\*\*

It was nearly dark by the time she reached the cabin again. An instant worry ignited in Lana's chest. Aunt Alice always seemed to be worse in the evening. She hesitated a moment staring at the cabin, her hand resting on the goods sitting on the back of the quad. The wood paneling was really starting to wear at the edges. A sign of its age—and good use. There had been a bear or two in the past that tried to use it as a scratching post. Lana smiled, remembering just such a time and how like always Aunt Alice had made it a teachable moment.

*"Stay calm, Lana. I want you to make as much noise as you can and walk into the kitchen. You will get the air horn and the bear spray from under the sink. The spray is just precautionary. Now, peak outside the window, what do you see?"*

*"I can see a black bear right by the door,"* her breath barely more than a whisper.

*"How many?"*

*"Just one."*

*"All right dear, get close to the door, but tuck yourself behind something. If it comes through that door be sure to have your bear spray ready."*

Lana obliged, as she always did with Aunt Alice. She curled herself behind the kitchen counter and waited. Aunt Alice nodded to her. *"When you're ready, press the air horn for as long as you can manage."*

Lana did without hesitation. Her ears stung from the shrieking assault of the air horn. She could only hold it for a few seconds before she felt like her ears were bleeding. They both stayed silent for a few moments and Lana clenched every muscle in her body. She craned her neck closer to the door listening for any sound.

"All right," her aunt cut in. "I want you to look through the window again."

Lana nodded. She took a deep breath and shakily crept from her huddled position to peer over the windowsill. "I don't see it. I think it's gone!" triumph rang clear in her voice.

"Excellent, well done, Lana," her aunt commended coming around from behind the dining table. She put her arm around her shoulder and gave her a small squeeze. "Now, I need you to walk the perimeter of the house."

"Wh-what?" she stammered, not wanting to venture out where a bear had just been.

"You have to work through your fear. If you let it, it will prevent you from achieving many things." They swept the perimeter of the cabin together that night. As they walked her aunt elaborated on her previous direction with the bear. She took every opportunity she could to teach Lana something, and after fourteen years she somehow never ran out of things to teach.

"Black bears are only violent when spooked, cornered, or with their young. The best way to prevent an attack is to make as much noise as possible so they are aware and can make the decision to go elsewhere. If the noises had frightened the bear and it charged through the back door or window, you would have used the bear spray. If it pushed through that, then we would have used the airhorn and retreated to the second floor."

She had it all figured out. In the seconds that the interaction took place she had figured out every possible outcome and their solution to it. Lana idolized that about her. She was always ready with plan A-C and sometimes D. Thankfully, the air horn was enough that night. She smiled and chucked her boots aside as she came into the cabin, shoving her stockpile on the counter and calling out for her aunt.

No answer, she called again, no answer. She walked into the living room... nothing. She checked the bedrooms and bathroom—nothing. A slow rising panic kindled in her gut, a simmering pot of water bubbling its way through her body.

She called for her again, one time, two times, three times. She looked out her bedroom window. A shadow in the front yard caught her eye. Lana's heart leapt in her chest and she charged down the stairs, swinging her body around the banister at the bottom and throwing herself toward the front door. She stumbled out, almost moving too fast to coordinate her limbs, "AUNT ALICE!" she yelled.

The old woman turned, she was holding a feather duster, standing outside in her bare feet, her sweater half hanging off her shoulder. Her eyes were glazed over. She turned back not registering Lana's presence. "Go on, GET!" she yelled.

Lana reached her side to see what she was fussing over. She stood toe to toe with a possum who was playing dead at this point. Lana sighed deeply and wrapped her arm around her aunt's' shoulders. "It's OK, auntie, it's just a possum. I can take care of it. Let's get you inside."

"Did you see the size of that thing! Did you see? It came out of nowhere, right up onto the porch."

Lana nodded, half listening to her aunt's' tales, rubbing her shoulders as they walked. Her body was cold to the touch. She'd been outside for a while. Lana was familiar with that possum, *Georgio,* her aunt had affectionately named him. He came to the porch every night where Aunt Alice normally fed him a carrot. He must have gotten the scare of his life tonight.

Lana tucked her aunt in bed and sat on the floor by the doorway. She leaned her head against the wall and squeezed her eyes shut to fend off the tears pushing to the surface. She breathed a deep shaky breath and swallowed hard. The ache in her chest was undeniable. A dull clenching pain that seemed to grow stronger every time her aunt had an incident.

## Chapter Two

The next day was the same as before. A myriad of training, exercising and time spent in the forest. She pushed the backdoor of the cabin open after her afternoon run, kicking off her shoes. The muffled sounds of voices startled her. They never had company here; it wasn't common for people to find this place, or for her aunt to wish to interact with anyone. She crept a little closer decisively placing her feet along the sturdiest floorboards so they didn't creak.

"There you are, dear," Aunt Alice cooed, as Lana sauntered into the living room. A young man and woman sat across from her aunt, sipping tea silently.

"Lana, this is Claude and Annette Carson, the poor dears— their car broke down just a mile down the mountain and they're just waiting here for the car service." Aunt Alice said, squinting at the couple through her black rimmed glasses.

A piece of Lana's long brown hair fell into her face and she tucked it behind her ear before responding. She analyzed the couple in front of her, ever so discreetly taking in their disheveled appearance and seemingly kind faces. She was suspicious. Like always.

"Nice to meet you," she sang, faking a smile. "It's not often we have visitors here." She continued, pretending to be weary from her run. That was a lie. They *never* had visitors up here. It wasn't an easy place to visit. The man smiled and placed his teacup on the table. He was characteristically handsome, blonde hair tousled on top of his head, a strong flexing jawline and trim physique. "I was just telling my wife that I could not believe how lucky we were that you all live way up here. We were sure we wouldn't find anyone to help us," he said dragging out the words in a distinctive southern twang.

"Yeah, aren't you lucky," Lana mumbled.

Aunt Alice excused herself from the room, mentioning she wasn't feeling well. After a moment of silence between the three left in the living room, Lana followed her aunt to the kitchen. She wasn't a great conversationalist to begin with, now you add some random southern strangers to the mix? She'd follow her aunt's lead on this one.

"What's going on, auntie?" Lana inquired, watching her putt around the kitchen as if in search of something. "Nothing deary, the young couple just needed a phone, they would have been stranded without my help. I just suddenly got this queasy feeling," she said, placing a hand against her stomach and tugging on the fridge door with the other. "Do you know where the gravol is?" she asked, her hands shaking as she spoke.

Lana sighed and steered her aunt away from the refrigerator and toward a kitchen stool. "The gravol isn't in the fridge, auntie," she said, trying her best to hide the disappointment in her voice.

The last six months had been hard. Almost every day Lana was seeing more and more of these changes in her aunt's attitude and memory. Six months ago, she would never have allowed strangers into her home, no matter what their circumstances were. "Are you sure you're OK?" Lana asked, fear coloring the ends of her words.

"Just feeling a little under the weather dear, no need to worry," she waved away Lana's concern and attempted to stand again. "You are eighty-five years old, even if it's nothing—you're going to lie down," Lana demanded. There was no way she was going to risk anything happening to the one person she had left in her life.

She quickly maneuvered around her aunt and helped her up the stairs. "OK, auntie, I'll just shut the drapes and be out of your way," she stated, kissing Aunt Alice on the forehead. The old woman was asleep as soon as her head hit the pillow. "That's strange," Lana thought to herself, "she usually puts up more of a fight."

Lana moved to the drapes, but something caught her eye before she could pull them closed. Down on the front lawn was the woman, Annette? Lana squinted trying to make her out. There were three burly men with her, trying to hide in the shadow of the trees. Lana's heart thudded in her chest. A million thoughts raced through her mind. *This was not normal. Why were those men hiding? Who are these people?* There was clearly more going on here. Lana drew the curtains back further to get a better look.

The woman's hands were raised in reassurance. She was trying to convince them of something. She reached her hand out to accept an item being passed to her by one of the burly men. She pulled the back of her shirt up and placed a small handgun in the back of her jeans. Lana's heart beat faster in her chest, panic started to cloud her every thought. The floorboard creaked behind her and she spun on her heels to see Claude.

"Everything OK?" he asked, clearly faking concern.

"Yeah, yeah—" Lana stammered. Her mind raced for an excuse, "I was just putting my aunt to bed. She isn't feeling well," she answered, desperate to find a way out.

"Oh, should we give her some privacy then?" He offered, backing out of the room.

"Actually," Lana jumped, trying to buy herself more time. "I uh, I think I dropped my phone in here somewhere, can you help me look?" Skepticism flashed across his face; his eyes narrowing slightly. "I know I had it when I came in here, but can't seem to find it."

Claude slowly came back into the room and attempted to look for the phone. *It's now or never.* She needed to act fast. She pretended to look for her phone dipping her head behind the dresser. She slyly unplugged the metal lamp standing there and clamped her fist around the stem; her grip tight enough to turn her knuckles white. She took one last look at Claude; he had his back to her now. This was her chance. In three swift steps she crashed the lamp upon the man with everything she had in her.

Aunt Alice was a light sleeper and normally she would wake at the smallest hint of wind, but the loud commotion didn't budge her. There was only one thing that would keep her aunt asleep like this. The realization struck Lana like a freight train. Her aunt had been drugged. She crept to her aunt's aid and shook her frantically. "Please, wake up auntie," she begged, continuing to shake her. "Please, please, please," she cried, "do not make me do this!" Lana flashed back to the lessons her aunt had drilled into her for the past fourteen years.

*"Now, remember Lana if it ever comes down to it, you must always run and never look back!" she instructed across the kitchen table. A classic sternness in her voice.*

*"But auntie, I could never just up and leave everything, or leave you," Lana replied, setting her hot cocoa down on the table.*

*"ALANA. You listen to me very carefully," her aunt breathed. You are the only thing that matters, and you must take care of YOURSELF. Do not worry about me, I will take care of*

myself."

Lana's brow creased in concern; her aunt continued before she could interrupt.

"Dear, I promise you that I will do everything in my power to protect you, keep you safe, and prepare you for survival, but if there ever comes a time when you have to choose between me and your safety, you must always RUN," she said, placing a hand over Lana's and bending down to look into her eyes. "Now, promise me dear, promise me you will always run." There was no disobeying Aunt Alice, or reasoning with her for that matter. She nodded.

A tear streamed down Lana's cheek as she tried desperately to wake up her aunt.

"Claude?" She heard a woman call from downstairs. Lana's head snapped up, adrenaline shooting through her so ferociously she was practically shaking. *Shit. She's back in the house and now she has a gun.*

"What's going on, Claude?" The woman called again, impatience nagging at her words. Lana heard her starting to climb the stairs. She whipped back to her aunt and exhaled a shaky breath.

"I love you," she said, "I'm not going to say goodbye because I will see you again!" She grabbed her aunt's hand and squeezed it one last time before dashing out of the room. She ran for the bathroom, one of the only rooms in the house with a lock. She searched frantically for something to defend herself with.

"What the hell happened?" Annette screeched at the man. "I thought you said you could handle her?" His response was too muffled for Lana to comprehend. The bathroom lay in disarray as she had been through every nook and cranny trying to find a weapon.

'Bam-bam-bam!' The door vibrated with the force of the knock. Lana's heart threw itself against her ribcage, sweat dripped from her forehead. "Come on out, sweetie, we just want to talk to you." The woman sang calmly from the other side of the door.

"In my experience" – Lana seethed – "people that carry handguns, don't only want to 'talk,'" she said, as she opened the window and began to pop the screen out.

"That is just precautionary," the woman answered.

Lana needed more time to make her escape. She had to make them think they were talking her down. "Oh yeah, I can see how one girl could cause so many precaution," she answered, sarcasm dripping from her words. She hoisted herself out the window, her hands holding the frame for support.

"Well, clearly you have already forgotten how you brutally attacked Claude for no reason," Annette continued, jiggling the door handle as she spoke.

"Oh, I had a reason," Lana whispered to herself. She didn't hear the rest of the woman's argument, she had lowered herself out the window, now hanging by her fingertips. She hesitated a moment before letting go, there was still about a twenty-foot drop to the ground below, but she had no other choice. She bit back her fear and dropped.

Pain exploded through her shins and feet as she laid in a ball on the ground. The grass itched her face and the slick dew provided little comfort. Her bare feet throbbed from the impact, and she gritted her teeth, groaning loudly from the pain.

"HEY! There she is! In the back!"

Lana turned to see the three burly men running toward her. She set her feet beneath her toned body and took off into the forest. Her forest. She pushed herself further and faster with every step. She could feel the rocks and twigs beneath her tearing at the bottoms of her feet like knives cutting into soft fruit. The sound of her heart drowning out all other sounds. She ran, dodging trees and rocks. She ran harder than she'd ever run before. They would never find her in here. This was her home.

She quickly scaled a tree scraping her hands along the rough bark. She climbed until the branches got too weak to hold her. There, tied to a branch was one of the survival kits her aunt made her hide out here years ago. She tugged the knapsack down letting out a long calming breath. "It's go time."

# Chapter Three

Lana crouched in the highest of tree branches, unable to be sighted from below. The camouflage backpack was about thirty pounds and carried everything from a sleeping bag to energy gel packets. They would help keep her alert. It had taken her five years to know this forest inside and out and eight years to become familiar with the plant and animal life. She knew that by following this tree line east for three miles she would end up at a cave where she could shelter for the night. There were four other backpacks in this massive forest that would help her survive.

From time to time she heard a branch snap below and froze in anticipation. Her entire life had been preparing her for this moment. All the relentless, agonizing training had prepped her for this. A feeling of satisfaction rose within her. One that was coupled with curiosity. It's true, she was prepared for this, but the question remained, why did she *have* to be prepared for this? She began unloading the survival kit, looking to fashion herself some make-shift shoes.

"I can't believe I didn't pack shoes in this thing."

She scrambled through the bag letting her mind wander sorting through countless questions. How long would these people search for her? Were they even searching, or had they given up? How soon would she be able to go back for her aunt? She pulled out the white medical tape from the small first aid kit, reaching back in search of the Polysporin. She dabbed some of the clear slick liquid on her open, dirty gashes and layered gauze overtop.

She fumbled with the medical tape nearly dropping it off her branch. "Shit," she exhaled snagging the tape with her finger. She pushed her back against the rough bark and stretched her feet in front of her. The movement sent a burning sensation through her torn and bloody feet. She assessed her handiwork. Her feet looked like they'd been bandaged from a burn, a patternless wrapping of tape halfway up her ankle. "This won't last forever," she said, changing her position to lean against the trunk of the tree and crossing her legs in front of her. She needed a plan…

Her best option—wait for nightfall and then try and rescue Aunt Alice, assuming, however, that those people weren't at the cabin. "That's unlikely," she mumbled, chewing her lower lip thoughtfully. "I at least have to make an attempt to save her, whether they are there or not." Lana again searched through her backpack until she found a three-inch dagger, normally she would tuck it into her boot, but seeing as she had no shoes, it would have to be taped to her leg.

Only one of the five survival kits hidden out here contained a gun, they weren't easy to come by, and sitting alone in a vast Canadian forest, a gun would be a very valuable weapon. Lana had never liked guns. Aunt Alice had taught her how to shoot, and reload, but it always felt too risky and obvious. Everything in her preferred to be covert and quiet, the exact opposite of most guns.

Plus, her skills were built around surviving, not hunting. Her reflexes were unlike the normal person. She reacted quicker and was more agile than most others, she attributed that to her training. She definitely worked out more than anyone she knew, and she had done so since she started living with Aunt Alice.

Lana hugged the tree waiting as long as possible before she

moved. She didn't want to bring any unnecessary attention to herself, but she had to start moving soon because the sun was starting to set.

As much as she wanted to go back for her aunt, she knew it wasn't rational to go tonight. Whoever those people were, if they were sticking it out, they were willing to wait at least a day. She would wait a little longer, until she was sure they were gone, and then she'd go back.

She climbed down the tree, careful not to snap any of the thin branches. She dropped to the ground, cringing at the raw pain in her feet. She sucked in a short breath, "Ow!" and hobbled around for a few minutes before she got used to the new pain. It only took her twenty minutes to make it to the cave east of the cabin.

She approached slowly, tossing a rock inside first to see if any live animal came scampering out. The rock landed with a hollow thud. She nodded to herself as if acknowledging that was all she needed to hear. She didn't plan on sleeping, but the cave at least provided some protection from the elements. Even though it was mid-spring the temperatures dropped fast at night. It wasn't out of the ordinary for it to get to freezing or below.

Her gums ached and she wished she'd had time to grab her medication before dashing into the woods. She'd had an oral condition for years now, she took meds for it every day. It had something to do with the alignment of her teeth pressing against her jaw. She didn't really know, she just wished it didn't happen.

Her hands and feet were throbbing and she rubbed them absentmindedly blaming the pain on the adrenaline. Lana sat uncomfortably in the cool, dank cave. Well, she did so purposely so she wouldn't fall asleep. All she could think about was her aunt. She had to leave her. She didn't have a choice. If she had stayed what then? Not only would her aunt be furious with her, but they would have both been at the mercy of those strangers. Still, her rationale didn't lighten the guilt. She bit her lip to keep from crying. It was the right decision she knew that but that didn't make it hurt less.

A memory tugged at her mind. It was a familiar one, actually one of her most familiar ones. She remembered hiding in a closet, twelve years ago, sitting as still as possible, barely breathing. It was hours before she heard her name being called, but still she didn't move. She remembered seeing Aunt Alice for the first time through the crack in the closet doors. She didn't dare move toward the stranger calling her name.

*"Alana?"*

*"Alana? It's Aunt Alice? Are you here? Come out please, we have a long trip ahead of us."* Still Lana didn't move. *"Come on now, your parents wanted me to take care of you, Alana."* She crept toward the closet and Lana scrambled away from the door. Her movement highlighting the location of her hiding spot. She found Lana hiding behind a hamper, shaking and crying. She scooped her up into her unlikely strong arms, and hurriedly rushed out the door.

***

*Years later…*

"But why can't I go to normal school? I don't want to train any more, I want to be normal—"

"Lana, I'm sorry, but you are so special that this is the only way for you to be successful. And that's all I want for you, is to be successful. So, you need to keep training and be ready"

"Be ready for what!"

"When the time comes, you'll know. I am sorry, Lana, that's

*just the way it is."*

A light crunch in a tree nearby jolted Lana out of her reverie, she peeked out of her cave to see the sun shining overhead, she watched the Blue Jay that had awoken her drift into the sky and fly away. She sat there for a moment, enjoying the peacefulness of it. Just a moment until the events of yesterday flooded her brain like the rising of a tide.

She shuffled to her feet and carefully checked her surroundings. She had to move to another location. She tore open one of the gel packs feeling her stomach grumble in anticipation. It was watermelon flavored which sounded incredibly appetizing but she was starving any flavor would have sounded satisfying. Lana gagged.

"Ugh," she grumbled nearly spitting it back out. She pinched her lips together and forced herself to swallow. She knew she needed the nutrients. She turned the packaging over and read the label, *incredibly tasty food supplement* – she snorted; "Well, that's false advertising." She was not looking forward to eating another one of those.

Lana spent the next three days doing much of the same. She never spent a night in the same spot, staying as close to the ground as possible. She didn't like to be off the ground, everything in her body wanted to be crouched, grounded and ready to run. However, there was a significant aerial advantage of sleeping in a tree, so she'd convinced herself to perch in one last night. She could watch for any signs of people and hopefully get a better idea about the cabin people.

She'd stopped by a pond on her second day loaded with arrowhead. She hated arrowheads. They were disgusting to eat, but it could be dried and stored and eaten raw. So, she'd just suck it up for now. She'd taken as many as possible before heading to a freshwater creek for drinking water. Her clothes were ripped and torn and she probably would have frozen if it weren't for the aluminum blanket in her backpack. She was lucky that she had only encountered a few deer, a badger, and a porcupine. The bears were the real danger in these woods.

Lana touched her gums tenderly, pulling away a red-tipped hand, she sighed, frustrated. Her gums had been bleeding every morning for half an hour and then at random increments throughout the day. She spat a couple times but couldn't rid her mouth of its metallic flavor. She kicked dirt over the pool of saliva making sure not to leave any indication that she was there. If these people had dogs, she didn't need to leave them a trail. Lana also knew that without her medication the bleeding and pain would only get worse. She had to go back to the cabin.

According to Aunt Alice, Lana had a rare oral condition that caused agitation, pain, and bleeding in her gums. She needed her medication to prevent the pain as it sometimes became crippling – and crippled was something she could not afford to be right now.

She moved through the forest making her way back to the cabin. She hadn't seen any signs of humans since the first night and she thought, with any luck *Claude and Annette* had moved on. She'd been able to avoid eating another gel pack, as the backpack also had a few energy bars in it. That coupled with the arrowhead tubes had been her main sustenance thus far. Lana stayed hidden in the thick brush, maneuvering quickly and agilely through the trees. The terrain was far from easy, but she had spent her entire life training and running through these woods.

She was only about a hundred meters from the cabin now – but something was wrong. Lana couldn't see the tan colored wood of the cabin through the tree line. She should be able to see it from here. Her brain searched for an explanation, her heart rate steadily increasing with each foul thought. She scanned every vantage point trying to see the familiar pointed roof, or reflective window. *Nothing.*

"Please be OK, please be OK," she repeated, creeping forward to find a better angle. Her heart dropped into her stomach as she took in the forest opening where the cabin had once been, there was now open ground, covered with a dry black substance. She stared in disbelief; *How can it just be gone? It was a two-story cabin? It's not easy to completely demo something like that in the middle of a forest. Why? Why is this happening?*

All she wanted to do was curl in a ball and cry, but her instincts prevented her. Lana knew she had to move and move quickly. But something held her back. She couldn't make herself leave. An insatiable urge to get closer to see it first-hand tugging on her heart. If there was no cabin, she had no idea where her aunt might be. That was another problem all together.

She waited to see if there was any movement, huddled in the tree line for a few hours. There wasn't. She sucked in a deep shaky breath and tucked her hair into the back of her shirt to give her some disguise and to keep it out of her face. Vulnerability swept over her immediately as she stepped into the opening. Everything in her screamed to take cover again. She fought her mind and pushed. She had to see it. She had to face what she had done. The mess she had left behind. She needed to be sure there was nothing left.

The black substance coated the ground and every so often would blow up into the neighboring wind. Lana traced its path upward, the fluffy white gray substance unmistakable. "Ash?" She scanned the clearing. "They burnt it down?" Lana's eyes watered, she wiped at them before the tears could fall. *Not now,* she determined. *I won't let this beat me.* She walked through the ash, her jaw clenched. She couldn't stop the feeling of emptiness from washing over her. It sunk into her stomach like a pit. This home was everything she knew. It was her safe place. Her constant. Her childhood. Without it… "What the hell am I going to do now?" she whispered.

She kicked through the ash, moving through miscellaneous pieces of wood and metal. Her foot caught something and she winced as it hit one of her cuts. It wasn't just a random hunk of metal though, it was the picture frame that had adorned the kitchen cabinet. The one that held a picture of her and Aunt Alice, covered head to foot in paint. It had been taken a few months after Lana had moved in, they were re-painting the house and she'd let Lana do a wall on her own. After all, she had said, this was her home now too. This time she didn't try to stop the tears from falling.

"Please don't be dead," Lana begged, dropping to her knees in the debris. "I can't lose you too!" she chuffed, yanking the knife off her leg and using it to pop open the picture frame. The picture was badly burnt, barely recognizable, and no bigger than Lana's palm – but that didn't matter. She folded it and stuck it in her bra. She had left her backpack just inside the tree line.

"This isn't over!" she whispered to the ground. "I'm going to figure this out," she affirmed, standing up and dusting the ash off her legs. She dusted the remnants of the only life she'd known.

Lana felt a sharp pinch in her shoulder blade and crippled over in pain, "Ow! What the fuck?" The sensation felt like a bee sting but enhanced about ten-fold. She had experienced her share of bee stings including the time she accidently knocked a hive out of a tree and had spent the night covered in ointment, and ice. However, none of those endeavors felt quite like this. The stinging pulsed through her shoulder blade and down her side.

Her eyes blurred and she staggered to the side. She reached over her shoulder and felt an odd metal tube sticking firmly upright. Lana grabbed the object as best she could and ripped it out of her skin. The pain surprised her, and she gasped, tightening her grip on the foreign object. She rolled it between her fingers. It was a clear cylindrical tube spearheaded with a syringe on one end and blue tail feathers on the other.

"A dart?" Realization filtered into her mind. "Holy shit!" Lana spun on her heels and assessed the tree line that formed an easily concealable circle around her. She noticed movement coming from the north side. That was all she needed, she took off as best as she could manage in the opposite direction. Her vision steadily decreased and a heaviness weighed on her muscles. She ran as fast as her legs would allow, but the resistance increased with every step.

"Come on, just get to the trees. You can make it in the forest," she mumbled, shaking her head in an attempt to clear her vision. She felt like she was treading water in a hurricane. She wasn't stupid, she knew she could only fight the effects of the dart for so long. They would catch up with her soon. She just needed to get far enough away to hunker down and hide. She might be OK then. "Almost there," her lower back exploded in pain. Her legs stumbled underneath her and she fell to the ground. Any attempt to stand was made impossible as she lost all feeling in her legs.

Lana pushed herself onto her back grunting with the effort it caused. Her breathing was too short and ragged to lie on her stomach. The movement almost caused her arms to give out. She lay on the grass immobile, letting out a small whimper from the pain. The second dart had clearly hit a nerve cluster in her spine. She felt the numbing sensation spread into her arms, and down through her elbows, starting to creep up into her neck.

A shadow fell on her face. She didn't have to see clearly to know it was a person. She wanted to run, to fight, to hide, but her body muted every effort. She was completely trapped in a motionless body. A slow feeling of terror started to consume her. It was one thing to be attacked and it was another to be unable to fight back. She willed her body to obey, to get up, but the response was empty.

"Get away from me!" she rasped, her voice slipping.

The person standing above her chuckled; "She's still conscious," he called, there was a resounding patter of feet before four more shadows fell across her body. She could only see shapes at this point; she wasn't going to last much longer.

"Shit, I've never seen anyone take more than one dart," a male voice announced, holding a camo dart gun in the air.

"Better give her a third, just to be sure she's out and stays out!" A woman's voice this time. Lana recognized it. It was the same one that had been in the cabin, but it was slightly different. She couldn't figure out how, her mind was foggy. One of them pointed a gun at her, not taking the time to line up his sights.

Lana had no idea where that one hit her. She was just relieved she didn't feel it. The effect was immediate this time. There was no fighting it. The wave overpowered her and pulled her deeper and deeper from reality. Her eyes fluttered twice before she finally let go.

# Chapter Four

Lana came to, finding herself in a seated position. She moaned softly and blinked to clear the blurriness out of her eyes. She had a very bad headache. Every time she shut her eyes they begged to stay shut. "Welcome to the land of the living," a male's voice boomed. Lana cringed and squeezed her eyes shut. Everything was amplified right now. She sucked in a deep breath and attempted to steady her sensitive body. Her brain searching to remember how she got here.

She peeked through her lashes. A rectangular wood structure sat directly opposite of her, its mahogany coloring was eerily similar to her desk at the cabin. A male figure blurred into frame behind it. Lana realized where the voice had come from. She blinked away the rest of the fogginess and focused on bringing the man in front of her into focus.

He was smiling at her, his dirty blonde hair perfectly styled on top of his head. If not for the white bandage tapped across one side of his forehead, Lana would have considered his appearance quite attractive.

"Ah yes," Claude nodded, following Lana's quizzical gaze.

"That bandage is a direct result of a lamp being struck across my head," he acknowledged, pointing to the bandage. "A piece of glass nicked me right above the brow."

Lana couldn't help but feel like a schoolgirl sitting in her headmaster's office. For someone who'd never attended public school it felt silly to make that comparison, but it's all she could come up with. She looked away from him and instead pretended to be incredibly fascinated with the floor.

"Nothing to say then?" he continued. Lana's ears perked up. He sounded different. His tone and mannerisms were the same, but his voice was different. His accent was different. He elongated his words in a sophisticated drawl. Not like the sing-song way of the American southerners, but more akin to the hard, quick mouth of a Brit.

"If you're expecting an apology, you're going to be waiting a while," Lana grumbled, pushing her shoulders back. She assessed the room. Only one door in and out. Her wrists clinked with the movement. She looked at them for the first time to find each wrist fastened in a pair of handcuffs to the arms of the chair.

"Now we're getting somewhere," Claude announced, clapping his hands together.

Lana pulled against her restraints feeling the metal chaff at her wrists.

"Those are just in case you decide to morph during our session, those and this," Claude chimed, placing a silver gun on top of the mahogany desk.

"Let's not waste any more time then, what's your morph?" Lana slitted her eyes at him. The words seemed to bounce around in her brain, not finding an answer. *What the hell is he talking about?*

Claude sighed dramatically. "We know you are a very rare morph, we just don't know what it is, so if you would be so kind as to inform me."

"I have no idea what you're talking about," Lana answered, again tugging at her restraints. How long had she been unconscious? How far of a run was it to her forest? Could she make it there without being caught? She scanned the room again, but there was no exit except for the singular door right beside Claude. She would have to wait him out.

"Alana, please don't test me. We can get along, trust me."

Lana stiffened. He knew her name. Her full name. She thought back to the cabin. Her aunt had most definitely introduced her as Lana. This wasn't a random kidnapping. They knew her. "Trust you?" she spat. "You lied to me, tried to kidnap me, drugged me and now you have chained me to a chair. A chair that is welded to the floor and you want me to trust you!"

"You have every right to be upset and scared—"

"Where am I? What do you want? Where is my aunt?"

Claude shifted uncomfortably in response to her last question. The reaction was miniscule, but enough to prompt Lana further.

"Where is she?" Lana asked again, her long, brown hair falling into her face.

"Lana, I have been very patient with you and if this will motivate you to answer some questions then I will agree, for every question I answer, you too must answer one of mine."

Lana bit her lip, she wanted to run away, she wanted to cry, she wanted to fight, but most of all she wanted answers. Her heart raced. She hated the idea of giving this man what he wanted. She wouldn't give him any more than he asked for.

"OK, how long did you live in that cabin?"

"Fourteen years."

Claude scribbled her answer down on a notepad and raised his head expectantly.

"What happened to my aunt?"

Claude nodded, sat back in his chair. "I should have known that would be the first question you would ask, but all right fair is fair." He paused and placed his pen down on his desk. "She died, Lana. She was a very old woman and her heart could not take the strain of losing you."

That was it. The answer she feared was coming. The answer she somehow knew was coming, maybe not today, and maybe not by this man, but it had become an ever-consistent thought in her mind for the last few years.

When Lana started to recognize the signs of aging, one plaguing thought clawed its way into her brain and never left. Her aunt was aging and she would die at some point. She would be left all alone. Her stomach clenched and her heart thudded with a dry ache. She clenched her teeth to fight back the tears and ripped her gaze away from the man. She stared at the ceiling and blinked rapidly. His coolness about the situation made one thing crystal clear, these people were dangerous.

"Lana, do you remember your parents at all?"

Her head snapped up. That was wildly intriguing. She had never discussed her parents with anyone except her aunt, and even then, it was rare and bare. Most people didn't know about them, or what happened to them, and yet, somehow, these people did? Just like they knew her name. Could they know something about her parents?

"No," she lied blatantly.

Claude pursed his lips as if he knew she was lying to him, still he scribbled down her answer in his notepad.

"Where am I? And what do you want with me?"

"That's two questions, Lana."

"Fine," she bit down hard. "What do you want?"

He drummed his fingers on the boards of his desk, a smile stretching across his face. He answered as if it was a rehearsed slogan. "We believe you are a unique individual who could prove both a danger and an asset. The outcome is up to you." He pushed himself out of his chair and walked around the desk, leaning himself against the front of it.

Lana recognized the move of intimidation almost instantly; she'd seen it a hundred times in her aunt's old VHS movies. He dropped his hands into his lap and intertwined his fingers. "What is your morph, Lana?"

Lana rolled her eyes. "I have no idea what you are talking about. There has clearly been some mistake so if you will please just let me go," she said, pulling at her hands bound to the chair. As if in response to her anger, the door of the room was thrown open. It crashed against the wall, with a suddenness that made Lana flinch. Claude jumped up as a familiar petite blonde woman stormed in. It was the woman from the cabin. The second half of the stranded couple. It was clear that had all been charade. These two were not in a relationship. Neither of them were wearing wedding bands, but there was something between them, some kind of familiarity, she just hadn't figured it out yet.

"Claude! Have you gotten ANY information?" she screeched.

"Yes, I—"

"Oh, shut up," she said, stepping in front of him. She turned her ice blue eyes toward Lana. A permanent scowl adorned her face. "Enough. No more babying of the little girl! What is your morph?"

Lana watched her for a moment before answering, both in curiosity and defiance. "I don't know what you're—" red hot pain flashed through her cheek. She sucked in a sharp breath soaked in shock, and pain. Annette's hand was red from where it had struck her. The woman stood in front of her trembling. Annette leaned over her chair and Lana breathed in a mouthful of her pungent perfume. The strength of it was overwhelming.

"Answer me, Lana."

Lana turned her head to take an untainted breath. After a moment she answered, "I told you I don't know what you're talking about." Again, Annette slapped her. This time Lana bit her lip to stop from crying out. She tasted blood before she felt it on her lip. *Not now, Lana thought, please not now. I can't show weakness now.* There was no stopping it, her gums started bleeding.

The woman scoffed, "I didn't hit you that hard."

"Don't flatter yourself," Lana spat. "This isn't because of you," she clarified, leaning forward to wipe away the blood with her restrained hands. Annette stared at Lana, her eyes wide, chest pumping quickly. A second later she turned sharply on her heels and barked at Claude, "In the hallway, now!"

Lana welcomed the silence. She was alone. *Finally. How the hell do I get out of here now?* She could hear muffled voices on the other side of the door. She stilled to try and make out their words.

"Maybe she doesn't know what she is?"

"Did you see her eyes? Don't be so naïve, Claude! Of course, she knows. How else would you explain it, if you were morphing?"

"Maybe she's not."

"What?"

"Maybe she's not morphing," Claude repeated.

"You're trying to tell me that we have spent fourteen years looking for her, and she might not even be a Mutt?"

*Fourteen years,* Lana thought. Did she hear that correctly? They had been looking for her since her parents were killed? *And did they call her a Mutt? Like a crossbred dog? What the hell did that mean?*

"No, that's not what I'm saying," Claude added, "but maybe she's a late bloomer."

Lana pulled against her restraints. She pulled every direction, up, down sideways, forward back. They were not budging. They just cut deeper and deeper. Her wrists were starting to bleed now and as much as she tried to wriggle and squirm the chair was not moving from its spot either.

Frustration edged at her mind, adrenaline building in her veins. She would normally revel in it. Allow it to fuel her. It always worked wonders in her training, but this wasn't her training. Right now, she was strapped to a chair, held captive by people she didn't know, for a reason she didn't understand. Right now, her adrenaline was spiking all the wrong emotions! A strange panic laced itself with her emotions and worked through her body like an Olympic sprinter.

*What the fuck is going to happen to me?*

"How am I going to get out of here if I can't even get out of this goddamn chair!" she exclaimed, slamming her back against the frame of the chair. She could feel the tears welling in her eyes. She squeezed them shut and forced herself to take a long-controlled breath. "Get it together, Lana."

It wasn't long before two men, dressed identically in navy blue shirts and beige khakis came and unfastened her from the chair. Her arms were immediately cuffed in front of her. Her head swirled with the movement; her entire body ached. She immediately missed the stiff rigid chair covering her back side. She was less exposed in it, less vulnerable.

One of the men reached to grab her arm and she immediately tried to wrench it free. His grip tightened in response. He wasn't letting go. She was moved quickly, with little space between her and each guard. The one on her left pinching her skin every time he adjusted his grip. Her stomach lurched with every step and she was suddenly thankful that it was empty.

She felt the cool hardwood floor beneath her feet. There was a familiarity about it that comforted her. It felt like the cabin. The heaviness of that hit her in the chest with an unexpected weight. She'd never feel that homey-ness again. She'd never curl up in her own bed or read a book on the worn living room sofas. She'd never get to sit and have tea with her aunt again—*Stop. Don't go there. You cannot let them see you break.* She refocused on something physical. Something concrete. Her feet. A searing burn stung every time she took a step. There was no repositioning them in a different way because every angle agitated a different gash, or scrape.

"This way, Mutt," the guard on her left grunted and tugged her roughly around the corner. *Mutt*? That was an odd word. Especially for everyone to be using it. It must be something to them. But what? There was a familiar note to it. Something other than the colloquialism for man's best friend. Something that was peaking in her brain every time it was said. She'd heard some semblance of it before. She allowed her guards to drag her this way and that while her mind searched for the answer. *Mutt.* She repeated in her head. Why did it seem so familiar?

Her mind searched through the many lessons Alice had given her over the years. It felt like her mind was flipping through pages of information, like fanning through an encyclopedia. W*ait? What if it's not an English word?* She thought. That's it. That's why it was familiar to her, but she couldn't place it right away. *Mùth*, pronounced *[Muh-t]* or *[MUT]*. It was Gaelic. Although its translation didn't give her *any* answers. *Mùth* could generally be translated to *change, alter*, or *mutate*. For the first time, she appreciated the various language lessons her aunt enforced.

*It must have something to do with them. They kept saying morph too. Morph, obviously means to change or adapt shape. So, very similar to Mùth.* The question remained, what did that have to do with her?

Lana was escorted down two eerily similar hallways and up a flight of stairs all of which were completely void of people. They rounded a corner at the top of a carpeted stairwell and entered into a small foyer. The foyer had had three identical doors equal distance from one another. The man holding her arm pushed her to the one closest; he opened the large metal door and thrust her inside.

The second guard followed her inside. He was considerably younger than the other guard with a much kinder looking face. He smiled at her reassuringly and unclipped her cuffs, "Don't worry, it gets better," he whispered, keeping his eyes fixed on the cuffs.

"TODD!" the other guard barked from outside the room. The young man jumped and dropped the cuffs on the floor. He quickly scooped them up and stumbled out the door. He closed the door and Lana heard a deadbolt slide across the exterior. The door had been locked from the outside. She couldn't help herself from reaching for the handle. Her hand swept through the air, and she stumbled forward. She hadn't been looking where to grab. She'd just reached out of habit for the handle. She looked down now, her palms flat against the door where they'd caught her fall. There was no handle on this side of the door.

"You've got to be kidding me!" she yelled, kicking the door hard. She gasped and cradled her foot in her hands as pain exploded through her toes and into the ball of her foot. "Shit, shit, shit!" she screeched, her jagged cuts throbbing angrily. She pinched the bridge of her nose and bit back the pain. "That was my own stupid fault."

Her feet were still haphazardly bandaged but a fresh ache rang through them. She didn't waste any more energy on the door. She often saw it in movies. The victim screaming and relentlessly pounding and scratching to be 'let out.' She didn't want that. She didn't want those people back and supervising her. She didn't want to be 'let out' she wanted to 'get out.' If she'd been smart enough to assess her surroundings first, she would have realized there was no door handle. The door was not going to open for her no matter how hard she tried. It was built to keep people in.

She turned to face the room and groaned loudly, "Be smarter about this." She wanted just one victory in this wretched place. She looked around the room for the first time. It was slightly larger than her room in the cabin, though much emptier. Lana wished she had seen more of where she was, but that was probably intentional.

"Obviously, the less I see, the more dependent I am on them and the more difficult it is for me to escape." Bitterness rang through her voice. She looked around the plain room; there was a bed, a desk, a small window and a dresser. The room sort of resembled a cross between a dorm and an insane asylum, with a beautiful stale, musty fragrance to top it all off. It was evident no one had been in here in a while.

There was a window in the middle of the back wall almost out of reach. Lana managed to grip the bottom of the ledge and pull herself up. The glass was shrouded in a frosted cover. She couldn't see anything through it. She traced the edges of the window with her fingers hoping to find a corner to peel off the frosted panel. Her fingernails scraped along solid glass, again and again. The frosted pane was on the outside of the open-less window. "Clever," she scoffed. It let light in but nothing out.

Lana tried breaking the glass with her elbow, nearly falling to the ground. The ledge wasn't quite big enough to fit her comfortably. She tried again pressing her left hand down on the ledge for support. It was no use; the glass was reinforced, 'figures,' she mumbled, climbing down from the windowsill.

She sank down to the floor, feeling an overwhelming urge to cry. Tears pushed themselves closer and closer to the surface. Tears of anger, desperation, devastation. Tears of pain. She wiped the dampness from under her eyes. "NO," she said, sitting cross-legged, with her back against the wall. "Don't give it to them. Hold it in," she squeezed her eyes and let her mind find her breath. Focused on it. The ease of it. In and out.

The tidbits of the conversation she overheard slipped into her mind, the words bouncing around trying to find an anchor. *Late bloomer, Mùth, morph? They all had to be connected somehow.* There was an importance to them, she was of some importance to them. She circled back to one consistent thought. One thing she couldn't stop from rising to the surface. The one thing that had always been a question in her life. *My parents.*

Fourteen years. Was it just a coincidence that was exactly how long her parents had been dead? Could they have something to do with this? Were there maybe answers here for her? "None of it makes any sense," she huffed, slamming her palm against the floor. The pain rang through her hand, pulsating through her bleeding wrists. "Goddammit!" she cursed cradling her hands.

She sat there for a while, staring at nothing in particular. Her mind swirling the same questions to her on repeat. Her eyelids started to fall, a heaviness settling in her body. Exhaustion was starting to set in. She looked at the bed beside her and ran her hand along the wire frame. It looked very appealing. Especially so, after spending three days in the forest. She pulled her hand back and balled it in her lap. She turned her head away. If she didn't look at it, it would be easier to ignore. She wouldn't climb into that bed. She wasn't going to roll over and just accept her fate. She'd been taught better than that. Her head was still pounding, her wrists and feet ached, and she could taste blood in the back of her mouth.

"How am I going to get myself out of this one?"

# Chapter Five

Todd leaned against the wall beside the metal door he was guarding. He wondered who this girl was and why she was so important. They only put the really powerful Mùths up in these rooms. He wasn't even sure if there was anybody in the other two rooms. Usually, they were used as solitary.

Todd had been awake for the past twenty-four hours. The other guard, Locust made him take the night shift. *One of the many benefits of being the rookie* he thought to himself bitterly. He ran a hand through his brown hair and took to rehearsing his ABC's to keep himself awake.

A repetitive clacking sound stirred him from his rehearsal. He slowly lifted his head to see Claude striding toward him. Todd straightened immediately, flattening out his rumpled shirt and standing to attention. "Good morning, Mr. Armstrong," Todd chimed nervously.

Claude nodded at him in response. Todd was nearly the height of the door frame. He dwarfed over most people including Claude, but there was no denying the difference in status. Wherein Claude was refined, agile, and intelligent, Todd was clumsy, slow, and novice. "Open the door, please."

"Yes, sir," Todd said, quickly turning and fumbling with his keys. He opened the door with a loud clank. The person inside, who had been sleeping in a ball on the floor, raised her head. Todd couldn't help the feeling of sympathy from creeping up from his stomach. How could he? The sight before him was heart-breaking. A young girl sat in front of him. Her long brown hair falling past her shoulders. She pushed herself up into a seated position. Her wrists bruised. Her feet gashed and bloody, dirt smeared across her torn clothing and face. *What happened to you?*

A finger tapped him on the shoulder. Todd jumped aside realizing he'd been blocking the doorway from Claude while he stared at this girl like an idiot. "Miss Chase," Claude said as he walked into the room. "Why, may I ask, are you on the floor?" A flicker of annoyance in his tone.

The girl hadn't moved an inch. If anything, she seemed almost more firm in her position on the floor. Quite defiant. It was not something Todd was used to. Not here and especially not around Claude. The girl rubbed her eyes and looked over to the bed and then back at Claude. Silence filled the room quickly.

"So, we're going to play that game again, are we?" Claude huffed, crossing his arms over his chest. Todd stood just behind him, his curiosity getting the better of him. He inched forward and watched her shake her head back and forth. A few long strands of her brown hair falling around her face. Todd could practically feel the tension in the air between them. The girl drew her eyes up at Claude. She stared at him hard. Her eyes unblinking.

Todd squeezed his hands together, the apprehension rising within him. No one stood up to Claude like this. *Who is this girl?* She was brave, there was no denying that. Typically, when Morphers first arrived they were a mess of tears, screams, and fear. This girl, whoever she was, she was doing none of those. She was quiet and resigned, and from what he could see, disobedient. He had never seen anyone disobey Claude before. The silence was waning thin, he wondered who was going to break first. The tension grew thicker as the seconds ticked by. Todd held his breath as he saw the young girl smile at Claude, a physical answer to his question. *She's taunting him?* This girl was on a whole other level.

***

Lana knew smiling at him would piss him off. It's probably the reason she did it. She felt the tug at the side of her mouth and gave in to her instincts. She smiled snarkily at her captor. He was displeased she didn't sleep on the bed, that she showed defiance. He had no idea what he was getting himself into. She was not going to roll over and play nice. No fucking way.

"You find this funny?" Claude asked, his voice rising a little too high at the end of his question. Clearly agitated.

Lana licked her lips and debated her answer. She stared at Claude. He was dressed perfectly again. Not a crease in his shirt. His black dress shirt tucked neatly into his black dress pants, like somehow he thought dressing professionally made all of this okay. He was attractive. There was no denying that. His crisp blonde hair was tousled appropriately atop his head. His posture was straight and his speech well mannered. It was hard to find a physical fault in him. Which just made him even more sinister. She wished for a moment that he was ugly, like the woman. It made things less confusing. There was an inherent charm to him, paired with his attractiveness that made you want to trust him. It definitely made things more difficult for her and easy for him to lower peoples defenses.

"I think," she said, pulling her hair out of her face. "It's funny that *you* think this is a game." She reached over to her wrist for a ponytail to tie her hair up but scratched the raw skin instead.

She gasped, not expecting the searing sting that hissed through her arm. She let her hair fall back down across her shoulders. *Fuck!* She clenched her jaw hard, embarrassment and anger zipping through her. She didn't want to show any signs of pain or discomfort that could be counted as a victory on their end. She would have to be more careful how she moved in order to mask some of her injuries.

"Well, you can sit here all day," Claude said, spreading his hands wide to gesture to her bare room. "Asking yourself a series of unanswered questions or you can cooperate." He tilted his head, his question hanging in the air between them. "Come with me for a much-needed shower, clean clothes, and food. Then you may have the answers you are so longing for."

Lana wanted to say *no* more than anything. She wanted to sit in her cell and watch them fall apart. But her stomach was groaning in protest and she could not deny her yearning to have a shower. She had to play this smart. She wasn't going to learn anything by sitting in her cell all day. She needed to know more, about where she was, why she was here and most importantly how to escape. "Fine."

"I'm starting to see a pattern here, Lana." Claude chimed, looking over his shoulder to see where the guard was.

"Yeah, what's that?"

"You only give, when you get something in return."

Lana stood up, brushing her hands against her running shorts, "And who in the hell would give something to you without getting something in return?"

Claude paused. Lana could have sworn she saw anger flash in his eyes. He covered his discontent with a smile, "Shall we?"

Lana followed him out of the drab, empty room into the obnoxiously bright corridor. It looked the same as it had yesterday. Lana analyzed the yellow wallpaper, its faint flower patterning. It reminded her of something you'd see in a retirement home. It was simple yet comforting. She trailed along down the stairs; her arms free of restraints fell casually at her sides. It would make most people feel more at ease, and calm. An assurance that you were earning some trust. It had the opposite effect on her. She knew it was a strategy. A way to slowly manipulate her. A technique often associated with Stockholm syndrome. She may have been tempted to believe this *'newfound trust'* had it not been for the guard literally breathing down her neck. She shook the urge to speed up as they came to the bottom of the stairs. She kept pace with Claude, who was entering the room at the end of the hallway.

"Holy hell." Lana breathed, despite her best efforts to keep quiet.

The room nearly took her breath away. It was so unexpected from where they had just come. The grand foyer opened up to her with an enormous silver chandelier hanging high in a vaulted ceiling. There were several pictures of London, Paris, and Vienna adorning the immaculately taupe and cream-colored walls.

Four hallways branched off the foyer all decorated with white trim. The walls were paired brilliantly with soft elegant couches and chairs nestled in the rounded corners. Lana felt outclassed; this room was of a higher caliber. She couldn't take her eyes off of the chandelier; it cast beautiful patterns across the walls and floor. Her eyes drew her across the room to every corner before they finally rested on Claude. His smile made her stomach churn. "I take it you fancy our breezeway?" Claude asked, spreading his arms wide to encompass the room.

"Your what?"

"Breezeway," he answered, without missing a beat. "It is

what we call this foyer. It is the center point of our residence and connects nearly every entrance and exit."

"First things first," Claude continued, before Lana could speak.

"Follow me, we have a lot to get through today." He spun on his heels, his shoes squeaking with the movement and turned down one of the hallways. He came to an abrupt stop at the first door and checked his watch impatiently.

He swung the large wooden door open to reveal a beautiful bathroom. The room was tiled from floor to ceiling. The floor carried a dark gray color that faded as the tiles reached the ceiling. At the far end stood an elongated rectangular shower, large enough to encompass the entire back wall. Bright blue cotton towels sat folded on top of a wicker basket and a brand-new toothbrush lay on the porcelain sink. Lana noticed the colorful clothing atop the towels and assumed those were her new, clean clothes.

She turned to face Claude, hoping he didn't think she was going to shower while he watched. He seemed to read her mind. "I have a few things to get organized. You have half an hour to do what you need, and then Todd will escort you to me."

Lana looked in the large floor length mirror beside the sink. She almost didn't recognize herself. Her clothes torn, a textured blend of dirt and blood spread across her body, her hair a tangled mess. Claude cleared his throat, Lana turned. "What about food?" she asked, feeling her stomach grumble underneath her fingertips. Claude smiled.

"There is just no pleasing you. Yes, you will be able to have lunch when we finish our meeting and you are mildly behaved."

"What's that supposed to mean?"

Claude shrugged heading out the door. "Whatever you need

it to mean."

Lana stood stone faced for a few minutes unsure of what to do next. She heard a creak from the other side of the door. She didn't hesitate another moment for risk of losing this opportunity. She longed to wash away the memories of the last few days, and with it, she hoped, some of the pain. At least, she wouldn't be carrying a constant reminder of the terrifying events that led her here. She jumped into the shower, as she heard another floorboard creak outside the door. She tore her clothes off in one movement. She didn't want to give them any excuse to come in.

# Chapter Six

She let the hot water roll over her muscles and carry her anxious thoughts away down the drain. She pulled her fingers through her knotted hair and breathed in the hot steam. She let it fill her pores as it fogged the glass doors. She scrubbed nearly every inch of her body. Her feet were extra tender. She saw them for the first time unbandaged and mud free since before she was taken. She sat down on the shower floor and investigated the gashes. They were all superficial and had started to scab over. She scrubbed her feet hard, tearing off any scabbing that was there. The last thing she needed was to get an infection. She wiped at her feet, clearing away the last of the soap.

She sat there for a while. It was her first peaceful moment in a long time. She heard a light rap on the door followed by Todd calling a five minute warning. She dried off with one towel and wrapped her hair in another. A piece of paper sat folded in the middle of the floor and Lana, confused, picked it up. *Did someone leave me a note? Is someone on my side?* Hope made her heart race. It was soon replaced with a crashing blow of despair and guilt like a wave tumbling to shore. It wasn't a note. It was the picture of her and her aunt. A lump formed in her throat, tears welled instantly in her eyes. *It must have fallen when I jumped in the shower.* She touched her side where it had been pinned under her sports bra. She hugged the picture to her wet body, taking a deep shaky breath before folding it up again. She never had a chance to put it away after finding it in the cabin's ashes. Tears tickled the back of her throat. She couldn't think about that right now. She couldn't let that distraction in.

She picked up the clothing sitting on the extra towels. The material felt soft against her palms. It weighed delicately in her hand. She had never owned anything made of this material, it felt... "Expensive," she said aloud. Lana scowled at it. It was a dress. She had never been a *dress* kind of girl. They weren't practical because she was always training. She couldn't do the things she needed to do in a dress. "You've got to be kidding me?" She seethed, scouring the room for an alternative.

It didn't take long for her to realize how useless that was. There were no other options. Of course, there weren't. This wasn't a clothing store. She groaned looking at the fabric once more before squeezing her eyes shut and tugging it over her head. It fit perfectly around her slim, toned body. The dress was off white in color, with light pink and yellow flowers. The colors complemented Lana's sun-tanned skin. She assessed her appearance in the mirror detangling her wavy hair and setting it to one side. The dress was a halter top, fastening behind her neck. It had a deep open back stopping a few inches above her butt and a gray satin ribbon was situated just under the chest accentuating her small waist.

There were a pair of gold gladiators atop the wicker basket and Lana scoffed at *the wanna-be* shoe. Was there anything that was going to be somewhat her style? Those thin flimsy sandals were completely inappropriate. They provided no protection or support. "How am I supposed to run or climb in these? I'm not," she whispered, answering her own question. She fastened the open sandal onto her feet. "Well, if they're trying to make me feel out of my element," she breathed an annoyed breath. "They are succeeding."

Lana pushed on the heavy wooden door, to her surprise it swung open with ease and nearly flattened her guard in the process. He skirted away from the door, his cheeks flaming red. Lana assessed the tall boy. His limbs were much too long for his body, making him look rather lanky.

"This way," he motioned down the long hallway. Silence enveloped her; all she could hear was the slapping of her sandals against the wood floor. The stillness felt eerie and irregular. She felt incredibly exposed in this short dress. It barely covered any skin, not to mention she didn't really know how to move in a dress. She felt the material sway away from her with every step making her feel more and more uncomfortable.

Lana came to a stop at the end of the hallway, it was a dead end. A large brown wall stood in front of her, a strip of wood paneling separated it at the center. The lower half decorated in a geometrical wallpaper. She spun on her heels to face her guard. "I don't know about you, but I'm not overly fond of walking into walls."

Lana watched the briefest of smirks flash across his face. He brushed past her and placed his hands on the wall in front of her. She scrunched her face in annoyance. *Is this guy for real? He's going to push a wall?*

The guard gripped a small round handle camouflaged by the color of the door and slid the frame away. A portion of the wall slipped away much like a glass door. It opened up into a very ordinary staircase. Lana turned back and flashed Todd an unimpressed look.

"Another staircase," she mumbled, peering into the small room. It had much the same appearance as the one that led to her cell. Were they going in circles? She looked upward seeing the structure wrap around three distinct times.

"What?" he asked, leaning forward.

"Nothing," Lana grumbled not realizing she had spoken aloud. She strained her attention on ascending the stairs in her annoyingly short dress. She gripped one hand around the dark brown banister and followed the slightly winding staircase to the top floor.

Her heartbeat sounded loudly in her chest. She was almost certain that this guard, what was his name again? *Todd, that's it.* She was almost certain he could hear it. She had no idea what to expect next from this place. She was walking into this meeting blank. She hated having such a massive disadvantage. The bottom of her sandal caught on the carpeted stair. Lana dropped forward catching herself on the railing.

Todd placed a hand on her back. "Are you all right?" he asked, a sweet kindness in his voice. Lana stayed where she was a second before spinning around to fix her shoe. He might be her best shot. He was sympathetic. She could see that in his eyes and hear it in his voice. He might be able to give her something to go on

"May I ask you something, Todd?"

*No answer.*

"I'll take your silence as a yes," she said, standing back up. "You have clearly been assigned to me and this—" she waved her hands around her. "This is most certainly some kind of facility. So, tell me, why am I here?"

"Mr. Armstrong will answer all your questions in a few short moments."

"That's all fine and dandy, but I am asking you. What do they want with me? Who are they? Where am I?"

"Please, if you just follow me, all your questions will be—"

"Look," she interrupted calmly. "I don't know who you are

or what your story is, but I happen to be pretty good at reading people and I have to believe you have some kind of compassion in you. You cannot leave me empty handed. I have to go into this *meeting* with the people who drugged, kidnapped, and confined me to a cell." She threw her hands up in the air. "After everything I've been through the least you can offer me, is one answer."

Lana perched herself on the edge of the step. Her eyes boring down into his a few steps below. If Todd didn't tell her something, she would have the lower hand. He stood there for a moment, unmoving. A moment passed and he swallowed hard and nodded, "Just one."

A quick shot of elation flew through Lana's body. It worked. She honestly wasn't expecting it to.

"But I get to choose the question," he interjected before Lana had a chance to speak.

"You asked where you are."

He paused for a moment. Lana could see the strain in him. "You were correct that this is a facility." He spoke very slowly and carefully. "It is fortified inside and out." Lana opened her mouth to interrupt, but he cut her off. "Before you ask," he said, waving away her eagerness.

"*No*, you cannot escape. There is only one way in and out of this place, and that is by helicopter."

"Helicopter? Why helicopter."

Todd bit his lip. His eyes shining with conflict. His shoulders sank, "I'm sorry, that's all I can say," he said, shaking his head. Lana wanted to push for more but she could see assertiveness in him. He straightened his back, his lips pinched into a tight line. Almost like he was physically preventing himself from saying any more. She replayed the information in her head. What did she know already? She knew they were remote. It's the only way they could hide this place. Only way they could kidnap her with no one knowing. It would also be why they needed a helicopter to reach it. But why only a helicopter? Surely there were roads. Unless the terrain was difficult or it was located at a higher altitude—but even if they were high up in the mountains, there were certainly vehicles equipped to handle that kind of ascent. No, there had to be another reason. Lana stopped dead in her tracks, as if the answer had halted her entire body with a jolt.

"Lana?" Todd asked, touching her arm lightly. "It's just through this door here." He said pointing to her left, thinking her sudden stop was because she didn't know which way to go.

"It's an island," she whispered.

"What?"

"It's an island," she said again, turning to face Todd, "isn't it?"

His face paled. "I never said that—"

"You didn't have to."

"An island would need to be accessed by helicopter. A boat would suffice, but if the location was remote enough it could take days for a trip by boat. A helicopter would cut that time down significantly."

Todd said nothing. His jaw flexed from biting down. Lana could see he was trying desperately not to say anything more. He stepped in front of her and held the door open. She turned to follow, her eyes catching his for a fleeting second. In that second, he gave her all she needed. In the most minor of movements, he dipped his head forward in a nod.

*It's an island.*

Todd led her into another striking hallway. The corridor mirrored eight doors on either side, like a hotel. There wasn't anything unique or distinctive about them. Lana could hear muffled voices escaping from the cracks in the doors, light and shadows peeking out from underneath. Her heartbeat quickened again. Her uneasiness increased with each step. *What is this place?*

They entered a large round room at the end of the hallway. Three doors stood opposite her. They were very different from the others. They had large elegant wooden frames and heavy cedar doors. They were delicately accented with gold metal around the trim and handle. There was a myriad of couches and lounge chairs placed around the grand room. It had the odd appeal of a waiting room. Claude emerged from the door to her right.

"Lana, dear, you look lovely," he said, smiling.

Lana had almost forgotten about her flimsy attire. Claude's eyes raked her body from foot to head. She crossed her arms over her chest and resisted the urge to tug at her hemline. She was uncomfortable enough in this clothing without having to be assessed like a cow for auction. He smiled again. His smile was unwittingly attractive. It highlighted his light eyes with a handsome crease and dimpled in his cheeks. He was by no means an old man. He was probably in his early thirties, if she had to guess. It was a well-rehearsed move. Lana could see that. He knew his smile was misleading. It was charismatic as hell. It could easily make you lower your defenses, but Lana could see something underneath it. Something unsettled. Something sinister. He ran a hand through his blonde wavy hair and extended his arm. "Let's get started then?"

Lana looked from his extended hand and back to his face. She drew her eyebrows together. *Seriously?* A hand offered as if from a knight to a lady. *He thinks I am going to accept that?* He clearly didn't know her at all. She could not be swayed that easily.

*Trust,* she reminded herself. *He is trying to build my trust.* She swallowed her fiery retort and smiled sweetly instead. She brushed past his outstretched hand and into the room.

The space wasn't what she expected. One wall was covered from top to bottom in filing cabinets and the other held what looked to be a blacked-out window? At the center of the small room sat a wooden table. Annette leaned against the wall behind it. An immediate heat of distaste shot up from her stomach and into her throat at the sight of her, lingering there like the staleness of bad breath.

"Please take a seat, Lana." Claude said, tapping his hand on the table. "We want this to be as fast and painless as possible." He pulled his chair out and sat down slowly. "Why don't you tell us what you know, and we'll go from there." He tucked his chair under the worn table and folded his hands together on top.

Lana sat herself in the chair opposite Claude, silence slipped over the small space. The room felt like it was well used. The chairs were dull in color, the paint on the walls faded and marked, even the filing cabinet looked as if it had seen better days. Whoever these people were, and whatever they were planning, one thing was abundantly clear, they'd done it before. Lana leaned back in her chair. She smiled cheekily at Claude. "I don't know anything."

Claude sighed. "Lana—"

"Oh no, wait," she interrupted, smacking her hand on the table. "I do know something," she said, excitedly. "I know that I have been kidnapped and held prisoner against my will, which breaks about a dozen provincial and federal laws, but who's counting?" she said, flipping her hand like it was no big deal.

Claude waited a moment before responding, seemingly chewing on his answer. His eyes scanned the back wall, "Lana, I have been fair with you," he breathed. "I have been patient and reasonable, but you must not forget that you are not in charge here. My attitude toward you can change very quickly and that would be most unpleasant for everyone here."

She wanted to come back with a sarcastic remark, she had about five lined up in her head ready to go. But she didn't want to escalate him too far. She still didn't know exactly what he was capable of. She'd have to play this a little more on the safe side.

"OK." She nodded. "I'm Lana Chase, nineteen years old, orphan, home-schooled."

Claude smiled. "That's it? That's all you know?"

Lana answered him smiling. "You mean besides the fact that this facility relies on helicopter transportation due to its remote location. It's clear it's meant to hold more than just me judging by the number of floors and locked doors. The logos on these brutes' shirts—" she jabbed a thumb toward Todd standing in front of the door. "This is some sort of company or organization," she finished, leaning back in her chair.

She savored the look of surprise that crossed Claude's face and thought she heard Todd shifting behind her chair. The attractive Englishman watched her, his surprised look slid into one of intrigue. "Your deductions are impressive. There are not very many of our morphers that are privy to that information right away." He ran a hand over his chin. "I'll be sure not to underestimate you, Miss Chase."

"Now then," he said, clapping his hands together. "Shall we get started?" He looked at Lana, his eyebrows raised to emphasize the rhetorical question. Lana nodded slightly. Claude sat back. "What do you remember about your parent's murder?"

Lana's head snapped up. A coolness slipping down her spine. "My parents?" she asked, forcing the words from her mouth. She was right. That inkling deep in her stomach. That hesitation that her aunt had been hiding her from something. Something that had to do with her parent's death.

"Why do you want to know about my parents?" she asked, her voice spiked. The back of her throat itched, like it always did when she thought about her parents. The same sensation that followed whenever she tried to hold back tears.

"Answer the question, love."

Lana shook her head, her long brown hair sweeping across her shoulders. She dropped her head to her lap and pressed her folded hands together. She felt the tears welling in her eyes. Even after fourteen years, she still felt the grief like a raw emptiness. She didn't remember much about her parents, but she always felt like she was missing something. The feeling bombarded her like a reoffending wave upon a buoy. She was never quite able to get away from the weight of it. "Nothing!" she said finally, "I do not remember anything," her voice rising.

Claude leaned back in his chair, a statement of impatience. He licked his lips and let out a long breath. "Lana," he breathed, leaning forward on his elbows. "I am just going to cut to the chase," he paused briefly. "What is your morph?"

"Again, with this morph thing?" Lana rolled her eyes and tossed her arms in the air. "I have no idea what you are talking about!"

Annette slammed her hand against the wall, silencing everyone. "Goddammit, you conniving little shit!" she screeched. "YOUR MORPH! WHAT IS YOUR MORPH?" Lana opened her mouth to speak, but Annette yelled over the top of her.

"WHAT ANIMAL DO YOU TRANSFORM INTO?"

Claude glared at the blonde woman in annoyance. This was

clearly not the way he wanted the interrogation to go. She returned his glare with one slightly icier. Lana looked from the screaming woman and back to Claude. Her eyes slitted. "What?"

The woman let out a feral groan and started across the room. Claude caught her by the wrist. She spun on him with a twitching fury. "Let go!" she yelled. Claude nodded and released her wrist. He stepped toward her and placed a hand on her back turning her away from Lana.

"Patience, my dear sister," he whispered, his voice eerily calm. "She is under our control. Let us be sure to exhaust all other options before we resort to violence." He paused and wrapped his arm around her shoulder. "Yes?" he asked, his voice inflecting with the question. The cold woman nodded in response. *Sister.* That was it. That was their relationship. They were brother and sister.

Claude reseated himself at the table. The woman took a moment before turning back around. She flicked her hand at Claude to continue. He smiled thankfully at her, flashing the same smile toward Lana. It twisted in her gut. She knew it was a ploy, but the sweetness of it definitely simmered her defenses. "Well?" he asked. "What is your morph, Lana?"

"You're serious?" she asked, searching his face. *This is a joke. They cannot actually think that is possible? An animal? This isn't a supernatural TV show. This is real life.* Her eyes darted between Claude and Annette, she waited for that moment of revelation, but there was none. They believed what they were saying.

"Oh my God," she whispered. *These people truly think that I*—the words stammered together in her head unable to take root. *I don't understand how—*

"Lana?" Claude encouraged.

Lana stared at the table in front of her. Her chest rising and falling more rapidly every minute. "You think I can *transform* into an animal?" she whispered. A laugh tickled the back of her throat. She let it tumble forward, "You are insane," she said. "Both of you! You are genuinely, and clinically INSANE!"

Claude rubbed his eyebrows in agitation. "Lana, I'm going to take a shot in the dark here and say you have no idea what Mùths are, or that you are one of them. I'm also going to assume that you don't know that it's *why* your parents were murdered."

Her heartbeat slowed, "What?"

"Let me finish." He held up a hand. "I'm going to tell you a few things and it's probably going to be hard to swallow, so bear with me." He repositioned himself to lean on his elbows. "Your parents were from an ancient breed of humans called Mùths, or Morphers. They were hunted because of their incredible abilities and eventually exterminated because they refused to submit. Your father possessed an incredibly rare Morph, that of a Canadian Lynx, and your mother," he paused, choosing his words carefully. "We believe she carried the Mùth gene from an incredibly old lineage. A morph that we've never seen before. The genetics of your parents make it." He sighed. "Well, they make the likelihood of you, not possessing a morph, to be nil." He paused, his eyes finding hers. "There's also this" – he raised his index finger to his eyes – "your eyes, they are a dead giveaway."

"My eyes?"

"The gray-silver pigment is a genetic trait of all Mùths. So, the question for us isn't an if, it's a what?"

Lana heard the words and tried to grasp them as they floated around in her head. Her mind reeling from the insinuation about her parents. She'd so desperately sought any crumb of information about them for her entire life. She savored any titbits she could get her hands on. Her aunt had always been so tight lipped about them. The tangled web of words somehow found her lips, "I don't remember," she answered, her voice barely above a whisper, her eyes blank.

"What's that?" Claude asked, leaning forward.

"I don't remember," she repeated.

"You don't remember what, Lana?"

Finally, the swirling in her head came to a stop. She took a deep breath and reminded herself how outrageous this *actually* was. Even if she wanted to know more about her parents. It wasn't this. It wasn't completely concocted stories like something out of a comic book. "I don't remember them ever *magically* turning into wild animals," she said, sarcasm dripping from her voice like a wet sponge.

Annette's cold blue eyes cut across the room like daggers. They somehow tightened the air in the already cramped space. Lana pushed away from the table, her chair squeaking with the movement. She stood up and almost reached for the door. Todd slid into her line of sight reminding her that he was there and blocking the exit.

"Alana, sit down!" Claude yelled, standing to lean his hands on the table. His dark eyes bore down into hers, sending a chill through her body. This was the real Claude. The presence of untapped anger shrouded beneath a personable, charming façade. A warm pool of fear dappled in her stomach, growing larger with each breath. She moved back to her seat slowly, feeling her heartbeat in her ears.

"You captured my attention in our first meeting when you appeared uninformed about Mùths. My curiosity got the better of me and I thought there were only two viable conclusions." He spoke, stepping aside from the table. He put his hands behind his back and stared at the black window in front of him. "Number one: You were an extraordinary liar. Which seems unlikely seeing the absolute isolation you came from. Number two: The more probable theory; that neither your aunt nor your parents told you."

Claude began, his accent pulling at the ends of his words. He turned and leaned his back against the window and folded his arms over his chest. He gazed at the space between them and crossed his ankles casually. "That would answer the history question, but not the Morph. Your Morph would have manifested in adolescence. As such, the only possible way for you to be this bare" – he drew his eyes up to hers – "is if your aunt gave you something to stunt your natural Mùth instincts."

*Gave me something? Gave me what? Like a medication?* Lana's eyes widened, a bitter taste trickling down her throat. *Oh my God—my medication! My meds for my gums.* She could feel her breathing get faster and shorter. Her chest rising and falling quickly in the same rhythm. *Could this be real?*

Lana watched the small smile creep across Claude's face. He knew he was right. She could see the acknowledgment in his eyes. He didn't need a verbal answer. He wasn't expecting one. He simply read the reaction on her face. No matter how minor. "It's no matter," Claude said. "We will just have to wait for the drug, whatever it is, to fully exit your system. Your morph will soon take light."

*No, no, this still can't be. It's not possible. He's trying to get in your head.*

"Look, as convincing as your story sounds," she interrupted, fumbling her hands in front of her. "What you're saying is impossible! It is scientifically, genetically, biologically *impossible,*" she breathed, sweat turning her trembling hands clammy.

The words somehow felt false to her. There was something in his story. Something that felt certain. An answer she didn't know she had been searching for, but more than that, there was something about it that felt familiar. The information didn't terrify her as it should have. It nestled in her mind, seemingly outrageous, but also somehow *OK*?

"Not all things can be defined by science, young Alana."

Claude nodded to Annette. The woman smirked a maniacal twisting of her lips. She flipped a small black switch just right of her shoulder. The black window in front of Claude came to life. The fixture had a silver trim along its wide rectangular frame and reminded Lana of her bathroom window. She looked through the glass. It didn't look outside, like she was hoping, but rather into another room.

The room resembled a surgical suite. The furniture hard and metallic. The cabinets along the back wall stark white. There wasn't much else in the room except for him. A small boy who sat cross legged on a rectangular stainless-steel table in the center of the room. He was facing them, his head tilted up to stare at the ceiling. His mouth moving slightly. The oddity of it struck Lana. How could he be so calm in such a place? How could he not be the slightest bit concerned about people observing him. His mouth continued to move, Lana noticed his hand tapping against his thigh, his head bopping every now and again. *He's singing.*

Claude knocked twice on the glass and the boy looked over expectantly. He started to undress, and Lana felt immediately uncomfortable. What the hell was this? He stripped down to his underwear which were a charcoal gray with blue lining. They looked more like spandex shorts than boxers. The boy closed his eyes almost immediately. His chest expanded, his shoulders pulled back his breaths long and deep. Lana watched, not realizing she'd left her chair to stand beside Claude at the glass.

She tried to blink back the blurriness in her eyes, but it only seemed to make it worse. She couldn't bring the boy into focus. She nearly wiped her hand along the glass in front of her, when Claude shifted beside her. She glanced at him quickly, his tall muscular frame clear as day. He wasn't blurry at all. She snapped her head back to the boy now, random streaks of orange dappled into the fuzzy picture.

*It's not my eyes. It's him. He's blurry.* No, that wasn't the right word. He was in a way vibrating, no—humming, humming with a mesmerizing sort of energy. Before she could speak, a red fox sat where the boy had once been. It cocked its head to the side curiously and curled its bushy tail around its slim, agile body. Lana placed her hand on the cool glass needing to feel something definite beneath her fingers. She thought she heard Claude murmur something behind her, but she couldn't be sure. Her mind was spinning.

*This is impossible,* she thought. As if in response a picture of a quote flew to her mind. The one her aunt hung above the fireplace. *"Everything is possible. You just have to find a way to make it so."* Lana gasped, bringing herself back to reality. Her eyes immediately filled with tears. She squeezed them shut and took three deep breaths. The ache in her chest raw and throbbing. Her aunt. She hadn't yet allowed herself to mourn the woman who raised her. And now, now she was supposed to believe that her aunt had knowingly kept all this from her. She opened her eyes, the ache in her chest turning into a hot, slicing pain. It lingered there burning more intensely with each fleeting emotion. Disbelief, grief, shock, despair, and anger all flashed through her mind, none of them finding a base. She wasn't sure what to feel right now.

She watched the door open on the other side of the glass. There were voices speaking behind her, but she couldn't bring them to the surface. She stood feeling like her mind was on the edge of insanity. How could she believe any of this? Todd entered the room on the other side of the glass, with a long red rope. His eyes connected with hers for a second before slipping the leash around the fox. The fox hopped off the table lightly and walked out of the room.

Lana stood breathless, looking into the empty room. *It just can't be possible, can it?*

# Chapter Seven

Lana scratched her nail against the dull concrete wall in her room. There wasn't much else to do. Claude told her he would come to get her after he dealt with a few things. She wondered if leaving her here, by herself, was part of their plan to break her. All she could do was sit and think, think about everything they had said. Think about how many questions burned inside her one after the other on repeat. Think about her parents and their possible involvement. Think about her aunt and her potential dishonesty.

"I'm not going to cry," she whispered, stretching her legs upward against the back wall so she could lay on her back. It was a position of habit. One she usually did after a day of hard training. It was supposed to help drain the lactic acid out of your legs, but Lana only did it because the position relaxed her. It had been at least an hour since her meeting with Claude and impatience had set in. She had taken to playing the drums on every object in her room with her hands, but the latest fascination was making different sounds with her mouth to hear the echo in the room. It wasn't long after that her large metal door shifted open, and Todd faced her. He smiled when he saw her lying on the floor, her body twisted to accommodate her long legs.

"Come on," he instructed, trying to keep the door open with his foot and hand at the same time.

"Come, where?" Lana asked, assessing his awkward frame once more. Lana shrugged, "I think Claude is full of shit. So, I'm going to stay right here."

"I guess that's your decision, but if you want to stop that whale music you might want to actually listen for a change." He snapped his mouth shut like he'd spoken out of turn. Lana slitted her eyes, "Whale music?"

Todd nodded, pointing at Lana's stomach. She smiled, a real smile for the first time since she'd been here and tapped her hand on the floor. "OK, you got me. If you're going to use the phrase whale music to get my attention, I guess I can cooperate for a few minutes." She thought she saw a hint of a smile tug at his mouth before shutting the door behind them. Claude was standing in the grand foyer, clapping one of her guards from earlier on the shoulder. That damn smile on his face.

"Lana," he said, walking over to her. "I'm a man of my word even though we didn't learn as much as we would have liked to this morning, I am still going to honor that promise."

Before she could answer, a large boy with black wavy hair sauntered into the foyer. He looked from Claude to the guard, a cocky smile stretched across his face. "Ello Govna," the boy chimed, mimicking Claude.

"That's Mr. Armstrong to you, boy," the guard grunted, scowling at him.

The boy made an exaggerated effort to mock the scowl, his face scrunched, eyebrows furrowed, "What's the matter, Locust? Run out of puppies to drown?"

The guard started toward the boy. He grabbed him by the collar and slammed him against the wall. "Wanna get smart with me?" The guard huffed, thumping him hard against the wall.

"Enough," Claude commanded, his voice cool and calm. He walked over and placed a hand on the guard's shoulder. "Release him, Locust." The guards fist tightened around the boy's shirt collar. He tugged his head forward toward his shoulder. He held him there long enough to whisper in his ear. The whole action was less than a second, but Lana could see the satisfaction on the guard's face as he stalked away down the hall. The dark-haired boy remained unfazed by the remark. *Is he acting, or is he really that indifferent?*

"Well, Mr. Emmerson, it seems you are tardy for lunch, yet again." The boy re-adjusted his shirt, and pulled a piece of lint off the shoulder, seemingly invested in its cleanliness, unbothered by Claude. Lana noticed him wince as he did. So, clearly the guard had caused more damage than he let on.

"One more and I'm afraid you'll have to visit the Underground."

The boy laughed, his voice carrying around the circular foyer. He stepped forward, thrusting his hand into his pockets, "Oh Claude, is that a threat?" Claude's eyes darted to Lana and back to the boy. He smiled, clasping his hands in front of him.

"No, Mr. Emmerson, it was simply an observation. One more tardy and you will be escorted to the Underground. Are we understood?"

The boy's impossibly light silver eyes assessed Claude, "Understood el cap-i-tain." He nodded, saluting him and continuing on down the corridor next to us. "Oh, by the way, Mr. Emmerson," Claude called after him, waiting until he spun around before continuing.

"This is Miss Chase. She is new to our facility and needs a *gracious* host to show her how everything works." Lana watched as the boy looked at her for the first time. There was nothing in his eyes, not even a hint of curiosity. "I am appointing *you* to be that host." The boy rolled his eyes and started again down the hallway, waving at her to follow him.

Lana hated that she had to scurry to keep up with the dark-haired boy, but his stride was much larger than hers. Her mind hurled a million questions forward, but she bit down on her tongue, she got the distinct feeling this kid wasn't very chit chatty. The boy looked over his shoulder as he came to the door at the end of the hall. He kicked the bottom with his boot and waited. There were a couple of clicks and a gravelly sliding noise and the door swung open. Inside stood yet another guard.

"How many of you are there?" Lana said under her breath. The guard's head snapped up, surprised by the communication. He clenched his jaw and the dark-haired boy slipped past him with the briefest of smiles on his face. Lana could only think of one word to describe the room she stood in. *Pavilion*. It was a large semi-circular room with a clear plexiglass roof and exterior wall. Fresh air bombarded her, nearly knocking her over, a ground level earthiness mixed with salt. They were outside, *kind of*. Glass wrapped around the spherical room like a bubble. A series of symmetrical round holes stamped in the glass on the vertical wall. *Airflow,* she thought. *That's where the saltiness is coming from. Saltwater is nearby.*

The area was carpeted in a rich green grass. Lana could see the wild trees, and plants on the other side of the glass. The enclosure reminded her oddly of zoo animals. A contained environment, meant to keep its patrons in.

She stood just inside the door on the only area in the room that wasn't grass. The wood beneath her feet angled off to her right to a small corner-sized deck. Her eyes darted back to the greenery opposite her. It called to her soul, the sight and smell of it perked her mood, and tingled warmly at her heart. She looked to the dark-haired boy who was studying her reaction. "Yeah." He nodded. "We all get that feeling, but this is as close to the outdoors as you're going to get."

Lana felt her head tilt back as she traced the edges of the glass. *It's right there on the other side.* This was the closest she'd been to any kind of freedom.

"It's meant to," the boy said.

Lana looked at him curiously. "It's meant to make you feel free," he explained, gesturing to the room. "They literally call it our free development room. We call it, the Oval." He turned to face her. "Here's all you need to know." He pointed to the area on her right, the wood deck. "That's where you get your food. You can eat wherever you like, and however you like so long as it's in the Oval. You cannot take any food back through those doors. If you try" – he paused, then shrugged – "there will be consequences."

He continued before Lana could interrupt, "You get to spend a few hours here every day for meals, social time and what we like to call grass time. I'm sure you know how crazy it would get in here if we never got to go outside." He scanned the room, Lana did too. She saw the various groups of kids huddled together on the grass, some lying down, others propped together in conversation, others engaged in minor games like cards, and one duo throwing a frisbee back and forth. The boy turned to face her again, "OK," he said abruptly. "That's it. I hope you enjoy your stay on the island." And with that he walked past her to the food.

# Chapter Eight

"Are you just going to stare at it or are you going to pick something?" a small voice piped up from behind her. Lana turned to see a boy, no older than twelve standing there. His strawberry blonde hair was starting to grow down in front of his eyes and he had to flick his head to move it out of the way. His eyes were slightly too big for his face, and they looked a little buggy on his small oval head. It was his eyes that she noticed first. Exactly like hers, light gray. She had never seen anyone with her eye color before, but she never considered it strange. She just figured it was rare. Now, in a matter of minutes, she had met two people with similar colored eyes. Claude mentioned it was a genetic trait, and now she began to see some truth in that statement. The boy smiled at her and nodded toward the counter to which Lana was looking at absently. "You're new, aren't you?"

She looked at the boy and nodded slightly before turning back to the table. She made a gesture with her hand for him to go ahead of her, but he shook his head vigorously from side to side. His long hair swung back and forth across his face, "No, this is seconds for me. You should go first."

Lana turned and grabbed the first thing she saw and stalked away from the counter, slightly agitated. She held her plate firmly in her hand and scanned the open area. She hadn't exactly been given much direction. She inhaled deeply letting the fresh air fill her lungs and calm the uneasy feeling that was making her heart race.

"It can be a little overwhelming at first," the small boy said, popping up in front of her. When she didn't say anything, he continued. "You know the whole new home, new life, new friend's situation," he continued and nodded for her to follow making his way toward an empty picnic table.

Lana forced herself to keep moving, to follow behind this boy, especially when her feet touched the grass. The cushion of it underneath was comforting in a way she hadn't experienced before. She'd always enjoyed her cabin and its surrounding beauty, the cool forest air, the fresh scent of pine mixed with an earthy hue of dirt and bark. She'd never been completely removed from it before. She refrained from dropping to the ground and rolling in the grass like a freshly bathed dog.

"Nothing, eh?" the boy asked over his shoulder, checking to see if Lana was still following.

Lana shrugged as they reached the table, "I don't really know what to say."

"Woah. She speaks!" he proclaimed, dropping his plate onto the wooden table. Lana rolled her eyes and looked at her plate for the first time. In her hurry to get away from this boy, she'd grabbed a plain bagel and a single dill pickle. The boy watched her, his large eyes curious.

"What?"

He cocked his head to the side and studied her more intently, "I'm just wondering what you plan to make with a plain bagel and a pickle." Lana was too embarrassed to tell him she'd grabbed it in a hurried accidental maneuver and instead ripped the bagel apart and placed the pickle inside.

The boy scrunched up his nose. "Interesting," he said. Lana waited a few minutes before asking the question that popped into her head the moment, she laid eyes on him. The moment she saw his distinctive strawberry blonde hair and large eyes. "You're the fox, right?"

He was in the middle of chewing a large bit of his grilled cheese sandwich. He smirked. "Well, I mean, I am pretty good with the ladies but I wouldn't say I'm a fox."

Lana rolled her eyes again and stood up from the table. She was in no mood and she wasn't going to play any more games, not with Claude, and definitely not with this kid.

"Wait!" the boy called, reaching out for Lana's arm. His fingernail caught on her raw wrist and she cringed. "Sorry, I was just kidding," he said quickly, his face pinched apologetically. "Just trying to lighten the vibe." He gestured around the room. "I don't have very many friends either. People tend to keep their distance from me because I am often Mr. Armstrong's guinea pig." He groaned. "So, to answer your question, yes my morph is a fox. I'm assuming you were in the look-through today."

Lana sat back down. "Look through?"

"Right." He nodded with a mouthful of food. "The look-through is the two-way mirror room." The boy swallowed a large piece of his sandwich and chugged back his chocolate milk. "You know where you can see on only one side," he continued mistaking Lana's silence for incomprehension.

"I know what a two-way mirror is," she said. "Yes, that was me and you—"

"Yeah, that was me. Weird though, they don't usually use the look-through for that sort of thing. It's more for tests not morphing."

Lana reluctantly took another bite of her bagel and pickle. She cringed at the strange and bare combination. She really wished she'd grabbed a grilled cheese, like the boy in front of her. The smell of it made her mouth water. "I'm Riley," he said, in between bites. "I transition easily, that's why they used me for your... demonstration."

Lana's brow furrowed. She tucked her hair behind her ear and adjusted her dress underneath her on the picnic table. It barely covered her ass when she sat down and blew away from her legs when a breeze passed by. A look of surprise crossed Riley's face and impossibly, it seemed that his eyes bulged out of his head even farther. "Really? You're that bare?"

"Pardon?" she chewed.

"Sorry," Riley blurted, smacking himself on the head. "I forget newcomers aren't used to our terminology. *Bare* means like you don't know a lot about our lineage, or Mùth legend." He sputtered, ripping off another piece of his sandwich and speaking mid-bite, "It's really uncommon. Our history is usually passed down by parents, siblings, cousins, and obviously when you start morphing it's pretty hard to ignore."

Lana placed her sandwich down on her tray. *Well, that explains why I don't know it then.* Her expression pushed Riley forward. "Are you OK?"

Lana swallowed. "Just peachy."

"You're being sarcastic, aren't you?"

Lana smirked at him.

"Well, will you at least tell me what your morph is?"

Riley cocked his head to the side. Lana's mind flashed a picture of a small red fox making that same head movement. Her mind stringing together similarities. As the moment, she'd seen in the look-through replayed in her mind. It was as if her mind was starting to believe Claude's words. Showing her irrefutable signs from her own encounters. Lana shook her head. *No. Stop it!*

She still didn't want to believe what she had seen earlier.

There wasn't a part of it that made any definable sense. And yet, there was still a part of her, something deep down that pulsated with a warm liquid fury. It ignited in these moments. It begged her to believe, to dive into the hullabaloo and let it absorb her, like a weight sinking to the ocean floor. The temptation of that relief was agonizing. She could just give in. Accept everything and get on with her *new* life. Play the game. It would be so much easier than fighting them every step of the way.

The other part of her chastised her for even hinting at their baseless, unfounded stories of what she could only describe as lunacy or witchcraft. The rational part of her that was ripped away from her peaceful, practiced life and thrown into this world so drastically different than her own. She wiped her hand over her face, exhaling a breath in frustration.

"I really wish people would stop asking me that."

Riley sat there quietly for a moment. When Lana finally looked up again, she found him staring at her, his head tilted to the side again, his eyebrows drawn together in concentration.

"You don't know, do you?" he whispered.

Lana looked at him again. She said nothing. She didn't have to.

"My God, you really are bare."

Lana's heart started to beat faster in her chest, an answer to the anxiousness building within her. His reaction unsettled her. She watched the realization flash behind his bright eyes. She folded her hands on the picnic table and swallowed hard, biting down hard on her cheek to bring her mind back to the moment. "Don't worry," he stumbled, "sometimes there are people that live alone and never actually see their morphs. I mean it's super rare, but it has definitely happened. Next time you're with Mr. Armstrong, morph and then you'll finally know what you are."

Lana snapped before she could stop herself, her anger getting the better of her. "I guess it would help if I knew *how* to do that." Riley dropped his chocolate milk, the small bit that remained spilled over the table and slipped between the cracks of wood.

"Wait. What?" He leaned across the table, his shirt dipping in the freshly spilled milk. "Are you saying you have *never* morphed?" he whispered, his hand cupped around his mouth.

Lana leaned forward to meet him. "That is exactly what I am saying."

Riley sat back again. His face inquisitive, not comprehending. "Then what are you doing here?"

Lana sat back and crossed her arms over her chest. "That's a great question."

Riley sat back and let Lana eat the rest of her meal. Silence floating between them. He perked up a couple times as if to speak, but sank back down almost as quickly. Finally, he said, "Well, is there anything you have questions about?" His gaze met hers. Lana gave him a salty look, but Riley took it in stride.

"OK, well, here's some basics. There are pretty much two rules here. Number one: Do what you are told, and number two" – he hesitated, his eyes dropping away from Lana's – "prove a valuable morph," he said quickly. Before taking a breath, he rushed, "If you do those two things you can live a relatively normal life. Well, as normal as all this can be." Riley gestured to the plexiglass oval. He smiled at her, a fake attempt at reassurance, Lana could see through it. He was worried.

Lana rubbed her now clammy hands against her bare thighs. Her dress wasn't nearly long enough to cover them in a seated position. Riley didn't outwardly say it, but he didn't have to. *If I'm not able to do what they want me to do, I'm of no use to them.*

"Have there ever been people who *never* morph?" she asked hesitantly, hating the feeling of fear that was creeping up her spine. Riley's big eyes sought hers and in them she saw nothing but sorrow.

"Not that I know of. But there are stories, not just of people not morphing, but of people disappearing. Mostly uncooperative people. That's all I know about it though, if you want some more answers, I suggest asking Bennet. He's been here the longest, but he can be a bit prickly."

Before Lana could ask who Bennet was, a yellow light above the heavy entrance doors flashed three times. Riley sighed, long and dramatically. He flicked his hair out of his face.

"Time to go."

Lana sat there for a few moments watching everyone in the pavilion herd toward the now open doors in a synchronized blur. Her mind not focusing on any one person, *what's going to happen to me if I don't get out of here?* When Lana turned back around she was met with empty air. Riley was already gone. "Oh."

"Crap," she said, jumping up from the table. The boy was gone. She looked around feeling a little lost. She hadn't realized how much the little boy had made her feel at ease. Even though the information he provided was unsettling, there was an innocence to him that made her feel, somehow, safe.

# Chapter Nine

"Hey, Rook," a rough voice called from behind her. She turned to see the dark-haired boy approaching her. He was a large boy, easily six foot tall, lean and strong. Her gracious host. "Here's a tip," he said, raising his index finger toward his ear. He flicked his finger from his ear to the ceiling. "When you see everyone else leaving a room, you should probably follow suit." He circled in front of her. He stood in the middle of the breezeway now, the sight of which still made Lana feel inferior. A quite foreign emotion for her, and equally unsettling. She pushed it out of her mind just as the boy started to speak again.

"All right, Rook," he said, clapping his hands together in front of him. "I'm supposed to give you a *tour*," he said, using air quotations, "but I'd rather not waste my free time guiding a spoiled preppy little girl around our concrete island prison." He gestured around himself. "You'll learn everything you need to know as the days go by because" – he laughed – "well, you'll have nothing else to do and—" He took a breath and whispered, "Nowhere else to go."

"Is that supposed to be funny?" Lana's voice squeaked louder than she hoped. Her fear starting to etch into the edges of her words.

"Nope." He smiled cheekily. "Enjoy your life, princess." He turned to walk down the corridor behind him. Her fear turned to anger. She couldn't stop it, like water floating into steam. Screw this. She was already completely out of her element. Vulnerable, alone, and not in control. Getting a tour, and more information from this guy was going to be the best part of her day. Information that would at least give her a better picture. Something she could turn into a positive. Something that would help her escape.

She yelled after the brooding boy, "You can't take two seconds to be a decent human being? You selfish—"

"Call me whatever you want," he answered, already a few feet away from her. "It doesn't change the fact that I have *zero* interest in escorting meek little girls around or assisting Claude in his collection of obedient puppets."

*—Fuck this!* Lana felt the last of her patience drop away, like the snap of a dry spaghetti noodle. She lunged after the boy and wrapped her fingers around his arm. Before he could protest, she yanked him hard and he stumbled backward. *Meek? What an asshole!* Her anger burned satisfyingly within her, paired with her ranging adrenaline.

She didn't waste a second. She knew exactly how to capitalize on an opponent's hesitations. He started to shove her off, but she countered, digging her nails into his arm. She dipped down and swung her outstretched leg along the ground, knocking his ankles out from under him. She pulled tighter on his arm and pushed forward, slamming him to the ground with a loud thump. The air audibly exhaling from his chest.

Lana dropped onto his torso. Her dress flew away from her body, the movement of it annoyed her. She resisted the urge to tuck it underneath her leg while she pinned the boy. If she took her mind off her opponent, that was a moment they could overtake her. She ignored the dress even though she had probably just flashed everyone in the vicinity. She pressed her knee into the boy's chest, "Stop being such a dick!" she growled. "You think you're the only one who has shit to deal with? Take a number you arrogant—"

"What is going on here?" A familiar British voice boomed across the round foyer. Lana froze, her leg still pinning the boy to the floor. Her hair a wavy fury around her face.

"Well?" The voice inflicted with impatience. Lana rolled her eyes and begrudgingly stood up and stepped away from the boy. She clenched her jaw, her tendons flexing on the side of her neck. She stared back at Claude silently. She heard the boy get up behind her and brush his hands along his pants.

"The rookie here," he said, taking a step to pat her on the back. Lana stiffened underneath his hand, her shoulders taunt. "She was just showing me that she's not a *weak* little girl." He paused, purposefully dipping his head into her line of sight. "Nah." He laughed. "Just a temperamental one."

Lana reacted before she even knew what she was doing. She turned on him and threw her fist forward, forcefully connecting with the boy's cheek. He cried out in surprise and fell back against the wall. The same wall the guard had pinned him to earlier.

Lana's fingers exploded in sharp biting pain. She grimaced and shook it at her side. "Goddammit."

Before either of them could do any more they were separated by guards. Thick fingers dug into her shoulder and wrenched her backward. The hand lingered there as Claude came forward. The pain in her hand felt strangely good. Satisfying. It calmed her increasing anxiety, like sand to a fire. The coals were still there, and still hot, but they simmered under the sand slowly dying out. She felt a large portion of her anger slip away after striking the boy. A physical release to her inner turmoil. There was a small part of her that felt a little guilty that this boy was on the receiving end of a lot of pent-up emotions. He happened to push the wrong button, at the wrong time.

On a normal day, she probably wouldn't have cared at all about what he said. He was acting out, that was clear. She'd normally see right through that and take the high road. But, at that moment, he'd redirected on her, as she had on him. The brunt of that hit wasn't meant for him, but rather the frustration of the last few days. She would give anything to spar with these people. Show them what she was truly capable of. She smiled thinking of how good it would feel to strike Claude in the face.

*I'll take what I can get,* she thought gratifyingly.

"Enough," Claude interrupted, standing between the pair. "I should have known better than to pair you with Bennet." He looked between the two. "That's my mistake. Pede bring him to the Underground, I think he's earned a few minutes." Claude flicked his finger to elicit the guard's motion, "Todd, please escort Miss Chase to my office."

Lana yanked her shoulder forward out of Todd's grasp and gave him a warning look. She hadn't even realized he was the guard who had separated her. He sighed and led her, without touching her, to Claude's office.

***

Lana sat in the same chair she had yesterday, without restraints this time. She waited impatiently, her teeth grinding together. Even Todd's hovering presence bothered her. "Just tell him what happened," Todd whispered. "It'll go better for you. The truth, that's it."

They waited for a few more minutes. The silence was starting to wear on Lana's stillness. She felt her fingers start to fidget with the wood underneath her fingertips. The very same chair she was shackled to. Somehow that already felt like a very long time ago. Claude entered, agitation flashing quickly across his face, but as always, he covered it fluidly with a quaint smile. "We have rules here, Lana," he began, seating himself behind his desk. "One of those rules *being* no violence, of any kind. No matter who the recipient is," he breathed, and adjusted himself in his chair. "Usually the punishment for breaking one of the rules is severe—"

"Wait a second," Lana said, raising her hand to interrupt. "You are not seriously implying—"

"Let me finish, Lana," he spoke overtop of her, like a condescending parent.

"Our rules here are serious. However, since you have yet to fully *learn* those rules, I am granting you a pardon." He paused and looked her dead in the eyes. "Do not mistake graciousness as weakness. Do not mistake it as favoritism. I am nothing if I am not fair." He leaned back in his chair.

He adjusted one of the buttons on his dress shirt and continued, "We have two paramount rules here. The most obvious one, of which you are already aware, is to cooperate and behave. The second is not to overindulge. We give all Morphers the same opportunities. There's no extra food in the dorms, or personal memorabilia that has not been provided by counsellors. For instance, if one person wants a poster in their room, then all Morphers will receive the same opportunity. It's important to provide a sense of equality amongst your kind." He breathed, and shook his head. "Negates a lot of arguments, hostile emotions, and yes" – he nodded toward her – "even violence."

As convoluted and heinous as this place seemed to be, Lana couldn't deny the rules made sense. There were only so many ways to control a large group of hostile people. These simple rules allowed for a system of harmony in an inescapable holding. Sure, there would still be uproars, but on a much more manageable level.

"Now," he continued, tapping his hand on his desk. "We can consider you informed about our regulations. Should you, Miss Chase, choose to disobey one, a punishment would follow." Lana couldn't stop the smile from spreading across her face. *Punishment.* It was meant to sound foreboding, but it came across preachy and cartoon-villain like.

Claude's eyes flicked between Lana and Todd, her smile off-setting him. "Something funny?"

She looked up at him, a smile still on her face. "Not at all." Her sarcasm seemed to irk him. "I'm just trying *not* to interrupt, like you asked," she said, smiling again. "You know, like rule number one—obey."

"Watch your tone, love." Claude growled. "I am a fan of witty banter when it is appropriate. I will be clear in stating that it is not appropriate right now." Lana sat back and drummed her fingers along the arms of the chair.

Claude continued, "For most cases, a simple removal of free development time in the Oval is enough to punish the wrongdoing. The second comes only after a pattern of acts, after the third you will spend time in the Underground. If you wish to know about the latter, I suggest you ask your fellow Morphers." He paused, his eyes cutting across the room. "Are we understood?"

Lana sat stone faced in front of him. She resisted the urge to roll her eyes. The chastising tone of his voice grating on her ego. She swallowed back the tumble of colorful words that wanted to spring forward. There was something in him, in the way he held himself, the intense unchallenged look he was giving her, something that told her, this was not the time. If she was going to get out of here, she needed to be somewhat compliant. It was the only thing she was going to learn and earn some trust.

He leaned forward, expecting an answer. "Yeah," she grumbled, crossing her arms over her chest. "Got it."

"Brilliant," Claude said, tapping his hand on his desk. "Now, to find you another host, preferably one that you will not injure."

"Then just give me someone less irritating."

Claude smiled. A beautiful and sinister thing that Lana felt tingle in the base of her spine. His eyes lingering a little too long on her bare legs before drawing up her body to meet her gaze.

"I think I can make that work." He nodded toward the guard at the back of the room. "Todd, you may leave us now, thank you." Lana had nearly forgotten about the broad lanky guard standing behind her. He excused himself without a word. Claude picked up a black rectangular object on his desk and held it to his mouth. Lana realized it was a two-way radio. "Locust, copy?"

A gruff voice answered him, "Go fah' Locust."

"Please bring Mr. Churchill to my office."

There was a brief pause. "Churchill? The older one or the younger one?"

"The younger one."

*The younger one? Oh God, do they have entire families in this place?*

There was some kind of acknowledgment on the part of Locust before Claude put his radio back onto the desk. He didn't say another word, just watched Lana, a slight twist in his lips implied his content. She wanted to say something to break the silence, break the somehow controlling silence he had created. But she also had no desire to speak with him. So, she battled him in this game of wills, sitting completely silent. She did toss him a well-earned sneer every now and again.

It was at least ten minutes later that Lana heard shuffling feet padding along the hallway. As it turned out her new host was actually Riley. The small bug-eyed boy from before. He smiled brightly when he saw her and waved enthusiastically even though he stood only about a foot away from her. Claude remained seated behind his desk. "You have two hours, Mr. Churchill. Then it's practicals until dinner."

"You got it, Mr. Armstrong!" he said, saluting him excitedly.

\*\*\*

"So, there are basically four approved Morpher sectors," Riley began, enigmatically. He gestured wildly with his thin arms. "The dorms are on this mostly, but there is a small wing over there." He pointed and moved on before Lana could even follow his direction. "Then there's the offices—where we just left, the media room, the exam corridor, and the practical rooms. I guess if you include the Oval and the Underground then there are six sectors." Riley glanced back to see the look of aggravation on Lana's face, "Sorry, I'm not making much sense to you, am I?"

Lana bit back the sarcastic remark stinging at her tongue and nodded instead. *He is not the reason you are angry,* she reminded herself. Her hopes of escape were slowly starting to feel more futile as the tour went on. The place was well thought out, well-guarded, and so far, she'd only seen one entrance or exit—however you wanted to classify it.

"OK, think of it this way." He bubbled, spinning in front of her. "If you had a compass, you have north, east, south, and west, right?" He didn't wait for her to respond. "The foyer, you know the super fancy one, that's like the center of this place. You can use that to figure out where everything else is. So, the foyer is like the compass face, then the Oval for instance would be north. We're heading toward the exam hall now, which is southeast. Then there's the practicals right beside it, east. On the other side, the media room and dorms." They were zigzagging between halls so quickly Lana was grateful for the comparison. She quickly envisioned a compass in her head and used the foyer as its center, the map slowly fell into place in her mind.

"There are also a lot of dead ends here, so you really can't go anywhere you're not supposed to. There are more layers to this of course but we don't have access to them. They are purely for the guards and Armstrongs. And counsellors."

"Counsellors? Like therapy?"

Riley sputtered a laugh. "No. They are kind of like teachers. Most of us still need schooling, high-school or university. We get some of that outside of training. You won't start that right away though. They'll give you time to get settled in first."

"Super," Lana droned, the sarcasm clear in her voice.

"You'll notice we only passed one door. That's the only one I know of, and it's guarded and locked with a digital passcode."

"Are you giving me a tour or trying to infer how difficult it would be to escape?"

He seemed surprised by her comment. "Huh. I guess a bit of both. I think describing this place in detail lessens the judgment from new morphers."

"Judgment?"

Riley turned to look at her. "I get it, you know," he said, dropping his gaze to the floor. "It's weird to see people like me so at ease with this life. So willing to follow along and play the good boy. When I make this place sound big and ominous, then perhaps it's a little more understandable why we do, do that." He shrugged and led her down another hall. "We're not weak or submissive or anything like that, we're just outclassed and a lot of us realized that pretty early on."

He stopped in front of another wood door. Identical to every other they had been to so far. "But you—you came in with so much gusto," he said, swinging his arm in front of him like Popeye emphasizing the word. "It's hard not to compare yourself. And when you do we seem quite docile."

Lana couldn't hold back her smile. *Gusto? How old is this kid, forty?* "That was never my intention," she said, placing a hand on the boy's shoulder. She was unsure what to do after that, and awkwardly dropped it to her side.

"Oh, I know." He smiled brightly. "It's just who you are. Which is totally badass by the way," he blurted, swinging the door open. "But in the pattern I have seen here, you often get farther with honey than you do with salt."

Lana's face pinched. "What do you mean?"

"The Islanders seem to diminish rebellion rather quickly, through uhm—various routes." Lana poked her head into the room. It was a small rectangular room with a large oval table in the center. It had eight leather chairs circled around it.

"Boardroom," Riley said flatly, before closing the door again, and shuffling her farther down the hall.

"Speaking of the Islanders, I guess I'll give you the big *schpeel*," he said, stopping in front of yet another door. "The media room is a private room, which means you have to have permission to be in here. They keep files on each of us, detailing everything they know about us, and our kind. Which," he added, raising a finger for dramatic effect, "we are allowed to review, with permission of course. You'll also be supervised in this room at all times." He paused and pushed on the door knowing it would not budge.

"See, it's locked. And" – he rapped his knuckles against it, a thick metallic thud responding – "it's not wood, it's metal. It's one of the only rooms on this floor that cannot be easily accessed."

"Anyways the reason I'm telling you this is because the Islanders believe in a *tell-all-share-all* policy. Which is a fancy way to say no secrets. They won't treat you like a prisoner; they'll treat you like a human being and always let you know what's going on. They find it provides a happier and healthier living situation."

*"Or that's what they want you to think."*

"Hmm?" said Riley, turning back to her.

"Nothing," she answered, waving her hand at him. If this room held files on each of them, there would have to be one on her. But how? How could they know anything about her and her life? She didn't even know anything about her life. And she'd spent three quarters of her life quite literally living in the woods. This room though. It could have some information that she had longed for her entire life. The small droplets of information she yearned so strongly for, the same information her aunt refused to share. Information about her parents.

"How do you get permission for this room?" she asked, avoiding his large eyes and continuing to stare down the hall, feigning curiosity.

Riley brightened, excited by her sudden interest. "Two ways, you earn it through good behavior, or you ask Mr. Armstrong and he'll tell you how you can *earn* it." Riley frowned, "Oh, I guess that's really just one way."

Lana tried not to let the disappointment show on her face.

"Oh," was all she said. She pulled at her hair, sliding it out of her face and over to one side of her head. It was getting increasingly annoying falling into her face.

At the end of the hall was what Riley described as the practical rooms. Four identical rooms, equal distance from one another. They were large and rectangular in shape. The ground was separated into sections of green plastic grass, and black rubber mats. There were objects stationed around the room—*no not objects instruments.*

The room was probably half the size of a soccer field. There was a large steel structure with different levelled platforms scaling toward the ceiling. There was a large treadmill in the far corner. A set of large silver rings in various sizes, leaned up against the back wall. Three gray punching bags hung along another wall all with jagged rips across them.

"These are practical rooms 1, 2, 3, and 4. You train in here and have tests."

"Tests on what?"

"Your skills as a Morpher."

Lana groaned, and Riley dipped his head in front of her at the sound. So, these were like training rooms. Training rooms for whatever these Morphers thought they were. She followed Riley back into the main foyer.

"That's about the gist," he spun animated. "Do you have any questions?"

"Hundreds," she breathed in one exhale.

Lana wasn't exactly sure where she was supposed to go when Riley left her for his practical. She stood in the hallway, hands pressed against her eyes, absorbing all the information. She replayed the rooms she'd seen and where they were, marking them in her mental map. One thing that certainly took precedence there was the media room. She might not know how to escape from this place yet, but while she figured that out—maybe she could also get some information about her parents.

*Just play the game Lana.*

# Chapter Ten

Todd headed toward the practicals. He was late. He was supposed to escort Lana back to her dorm half an hour ago. He walked as quickly as possible without looking panicked. He lengthened his stride and kept his head down. He cursed himself for closing his eyes on his break. He meant to just take a twenty minute nap, clearly he was more tired than he realized. The last thing he needed was to get reprimanded. He had just been promoted from junior minder, to guard. The Armstrongs were not particularly forgiving. He essentially jogged into the breezeway, his heart gaping with relief at the sight of her.

He wasn't sure how to summon her, Lana, Alana, Miss Chase, Miss Lana Chase? She was leaning against the wall, the palms of her hands pressed against her eyes. He wondered if he should give her a moment or if he should make a sound to alert her to his presence. He stood there awkwardly for a second too long.

"You have a thing for looming, huh?"

Todd swallowed hard and tried not to let the embarrassment color his face. "I—uh, I'm here to collect you and escort you to your dorm."

She lifted her head and flicked her gray silver eyes toward him. A slight vulnerability dappling through the surface. She blinked it away quickly and pushed herself off the wall. Todd forced himself to look just above her eye line, avoiding the bareness of her legs and chest. Claude had dressed her this way purposefully. It let Lana know who was in control, and it was something he didn't mind looking at. It was a little strange actually, Claude normally didn't show much interest in the new recruits. He was rarely as involved as he had been the last two days, before her arrival. The first few days with new morphers was tedious. A lot of tears, and tantrums, Claude never had the time of day for that. And Lana, she had been a whole new challenge since she was keeping her morph from them. She was spirited and determined. Todd was surprised she hadn't made a run for it the first moment she was alone.

He walked her back into the main foyer. "What were you doing?"

"Hmm?"

"Just now, against the wall, what were you doing?"

Lana stopped, her head cocking to the side, "Why does that matter?"

"I just figured" – he shrugged – "that if you had the opportunity and you were alone, you'd try to escape or something."

Lana smiled at him, her eyes squinting slightly, her cheeks dimpling. Todd could feel the soft flutter in his stomach. It was an anxious feeling. There was no denying his attraction to her, but this was something more. Something sweeter, something about her that tickled the inside of his stomach. He dropped his head to his watch, feigning interest in the time. Anything to quiet the stirrings inside him.

"You don't give me much credit, do you?"

"I'm sorry?" he said, his head tilting back up with surprise.

"I would never just" – Lana threw her hands up – "run around like a lost dog trying to find a way out." She smiled cheekily at him. "I like to think I'm a little more calculating than that."

Todd nodded, the rationale seeming almost embarrassingly obvious. Of course, she wouldn't just try to escape without a real plan. She was smarter than that. Before he could divulge an apology, his radio crackled at his hip. Locusts' distinct gargled tone came through, "Todd, copy?"

"Go for Todd."

"Annette wants the Lana girl upstairs in the mirror room."

Todd paused, a slight hesitation before responding, "Right now? Over."

"Did I ask you a question or give you an order. Do it. Over and out."

\*\*\*

Todd barely made it to the door before Locust stormed out. He dismissed Todd with barely a look and turned toward Lana. He grabbed her by the arm and threw her into the same room she'd been in this morning. She fell on the ground hard, the air leaving her chest with an *umph*. She pulled herself up using the metal table and took a step away from the ugly man. A tumultuous blend of anger and fear colliding within her. Her heart rate matching the rising tide of her emotions. Screw him for being so unnecessarily rough to assert his power and position. Lana hated men like that. Not even just men, women as well. She bit down on her lip, smothering the insults she wanted to hurl his way. She compromised by giving him a hard-unimpressed look.

His walkie talkie crackled then breaking the silence.

Lana leaned herself against the back wall, farthest away from Locust. She crossed her arms over her chest. It was unnerving that he'd left the lights off. Something about this situation felt off. The guard reached down to his waist and twisted the small nob at the end of his walkie talkie. Lana heard a soft click.

*He turned it off? That's weird.*

He smiled at her. An ugly broken tooth smile of hunger. His eyes drank her in. He licked his bottom lip, "Looks like it's jus' me 'nd you—you know that's a very pretty dress you got on." Lana's eyes shot to his, hers shining with disbelief.

*No!*

Her heart threw itself against her ribcage. He took a step forward and Lana pushed herself harder against the wall. She could feel her heartbeat in her ears, the blood rushing to her cheeks.

*No, no, no, no, no, no!*

Lana's mind screamed at her to say something, but fear vibrated louder, and left her frozen. Locust lunged forward crossing the small room in two quick strides. He pinned her against the wall with his meaty hands. He was strong and burly, built like a wrestler. His muscles were thick and heavy, and easily controlled Lana.

She would have to be smart about this. It wasn't going to be like sucker punching the cocky boy earlier. She felt her voice ripple up her throat, she let it forward screaming in his ear. She kicked out, her foot connecting with his knee. She felt it buckle inward. He dropped forward, his face now inches from hers.

"Come on now, darlin', don't be shy."

"Don't touch me!" Lana screamed.

He had a hand around her throat now, he reached behind his back with the other one and Lana jumped at the opportunity. She swiped at the hand restraining her by the neck and thrust her knee upward into his chest. She was about to run past him when he held out an outstretched arm, a long black rectangular object grasped between his fingers. Lana would have thought it was a walkie talkie if it weren't for the blue electrical current stemming from the end of it.

"Thas' it now. Les jus slow it right on down."

She froze. If he teased her she'd be incapacitated, and she definitely didn't want to be left defenseless right now.

"Why don' you go ahead and take that off?" he said, nodding toward her dress like a greedy hunter.

Lana's eyes widened. "No!" she said draping her arms around her shoulders, hugging herself tightly. She slowly sidestepped as he crept closer. He watched her movement and didn't hesitate, he moved quickly now closing the space between them. He pushed his thick, heavy body up against her pinning her between him and the wall.

"STOP! GET OFF ME!"

"Shhh," he said, his hot breath filling her nostrils. He reached for the hemline of her dress and yanked it up.

Her gums screamed with the increased blood flow and she tasted the familiar metallic tinge in the back of her throat. His hand was under her dress now, making its way up her thigh. Lana thrust her hips forward catching him off balance. He slammed the taser down on the counter beside him and grabbed her neck with both hands. That's exactly what she needed. Lana pushed her hands in between his squeezing her neck. She felt her heart accelerate looking for oxygen, the corners of her vision blackening. She pushed her arms up and out as hard as she could, smacking his hands away. He fell forward. She thrust her palm upward to catch his nose. She felt it crunch satisfyingly against her hand.

"FUCK!" he yelled.

Lana kicked at the same knee she had earlier, and he went

down hard. Locust grabbed at her ankle, "I'm not done with you yet, girlie."

"Fuck you!" Lana spat. She picked up the taser off the table and jabbed it into his side. The guard convulsed on the ground for a few seconds, but Lana didn't stick around long enough to watch the end result. She scrambled to find her feet beneath her. Her hands shaking uncontrollably. She wanted to scream and cry and laugh all at the same time. But she didn't. She didn't scream, or cry or laugh, she closed the door behind her and ran. She ran knowing she had nowhere to go and knowing she couldn't really get away. She ran because it was the only thing she could do. She ran because she just wanted to put distance between her and that sick excuse of a human being. She ran through the halls and down the stairs, she ran until she ended up in the foyer again.

"Fuck," Lana said, rubbing her clammy hands against her dress. "Fuck, fuck, fuck." She balled them into fists to try to stop them from trembling. *Get yourself together Lana.* She felt a drop of water roll down her arm. She wiped at her eyes obsessively hoping to stop to the tears. She was trembling with adrenaline and rage. "Breathe, Lana," she said aloud, her voice quivering. She paced back and forth in the large circular room.

"Deep breaths, one… two… three…"

She rubbed at her eyes again and noticed a red tinge on her palm. "Blood?" She rubbed her face again. "Definitely blood." Lana thought back to the struggle and tried to recall a moment when Locust struck her. She couldn't. She rubbed her face again and found the source. Her mouth. Her gums were bleeding again, and if it weren't for the adrenaline the pain would be nearly crippling.

"Miss Chase?"

Lana jumped and spun, her hands tightened into fists to face the familiar British voice. *Claude.*

"Why are you not—"

"Get away from me!" she said, backing away her voice shaking.

Claude stopped; his head cocked slightly to the side. His eyes narrowed, assessing the situation. "What—"

"Get the *fuck* away from me!" she warned again.

"Watch your language, Lana." He took another step toward her, pausing as he read her reaction. He raised his hands in a friendly sign of surrender. "What is going on? Why aren't you in your dorm?"

Lana growled, her chest pumping. She slammed her hand against the wall beside her. "Your fucking sidekick tried to rape me. *That's* what happened."

The color drained from Claude's face. "Todd? He tried to—"

"No, not Todd!" she yelled, her voice falling at the end. "Locust," she whispered. "The goddamn guard. He had a taser, I couldn't—he's probably still up there." She pointed down the hallway. Her words coming breathy and jumbled. "I just ran. I didn't know what else to do." Lana felt herself crumbling. She couldn't formulate the words she wanted. Her chest was heaving, tears flowed down her face. She leaned a hand against the wall to help hold her up. She forced herself to breath a controlled, steadying breath.

"It's OK, Lana. It's OK," Claude said, his voice calm and low, as if approaching a wounded bear. He moved toward her slowly. "You're all right." He stood just in front of her now. Lana reacted, she lashed out thumping her fists against his chest. He was too close, and he grabbed her arms easily.

He pulled her into his chest and held her tight. Lana felt the tears streaming down her face. "NO!" She bucked and writhed but his grip was unrelenting.

"Let me go." He kept hold of her wrist with one hand still pinned to his chest and wrapped his other arms around her. He didn't say anything more. He held her tightly, his muscles flexing underneath his shirt. Lana's nose filled with his cologne; she felt her body start to relax. He was strong, his body firm against hers, and his holds practiced.

He squeezed her tightly and Lana felt the comfort in it. He simply kept repeating, "You're all right." Until he felt her body relax. He gently released her and moved to stand in front of her again.

She met his eyes for the first time, anger and betrayal seething from within her. Her gums ached with pressure but for the first time she saw a flash of anger in Claude's eyes. An anger that wasn't directed toward her but for her. Claude shook his head. His perfect blonde hair shaking out of place.

"Lana, I have no idea how this happened, but I can assure you, it will not happen again. As much as you think we are the bad guys because we removed you from your home and previous life, we are not. We want you to feel safe and at home and this, this is beyond inexcusable." He stopped, and looked her dead in the eyes. "And I am incredibly and holistically sorry."

He had his hand on her shoulder now, like a father comforting a daughter. Lana swiped at his arm before he could feel her trembling and took a step away from him.

"Just leave me alone, please God, just leave me the hell alone!"

Claude bit his cheek and took a long deep breath. "Lana, I am not going to defend what Locust did. But neither can I tolerate disrespectful behavior. I will escort you back to your dorm and you can be assured I will take care of Locust."

# Chapter Eleven

Lana sat wide awake in her room. She should sleep. She knew that. It had been a crazy day, and she realized it had only been a matter of hours since she'd been sedated. Her body could definitely use the rest. But, she couldn't. She couldn't turn her mind off. She'd been here less than twenty-four hours, at least she thought it had been less than twenty-four hours, she didn't know for sure. She didn't exactly have a watch she could reference. She thought back to the Oval, where she had her pickle sandwich. She wasn't even sure what time of the day that was. It could easily have been lunch or dinner, but honestly it could have even been breakfast. The foods offered were more commonly associated with lunch or dinner, hence how she had made the earlier deduction, but she could easily be wrong.

She pressed her back against the concrete wall, forcing her posture straighter. She wanted to curl up and sleep, for hours, just sleep and forget everything just for a little while. But, there was another part of her, a stronger part of her that was waiting. She wasn't one hundred percent sure what for. Was she waiting for Claude to come up and apologize again? Waiting to be escorted somewhere? Waiting for Locust to sneak in to try and finish what he had started, waiting for sleep to overtake her? She didn't know. She was just waiting.

She tried to distract her thoughts from tumbling toward Locust, his hot breath and cruel tongue, his large meaty body pressing against her. She jumped up and walked around every time her mind started to pull along that thread. It happened more than she would like, but sitting in this room only gave her so many topics of distraction. She paced back and forth shaking her hands out at her side. Her finger brushed the edge of her hemline swiping gently across her skin just beneath. She jumped, her mind forcing an image of Locust with his hand on her leg, sliding its way up toward her—No. "Stop!" she said aloud to herself. Her voice louder than she anticipated in the empty hollow room. She wanted to squeeze her eyes shut but anytime she did that, she just saw him again, heard his breath in her ears. She pulled a hand through her hair, her body trembling. She tilted her face toward the ceiling and breathed a shaky breath quelling the tears threatening to fall.

"No," she breathed again. "You can do this, Lana." Pacing around wasn't working any more, she needed something more. Something more physical, she immediately started doing jumping jacks. One thousand jumping jacks, five hundred burpees, three hundred sit-ups, two hundred push-ups. She cycled through them until light started to peek through her window. For some reason, that settled her. She'd made it through the night. Locust had not returned and she hadn't crumbled under that *new* threat. The light made her feel a little safer.

She could deal with everything else, the craziness of the Islanders' beliefs, the consistent threats of violence and isolation. All of it. What she had not expected, what she was not prepared for, was the sexual assault. In twenty-four hours, she'd been kidnapped, drugged, caged, lost her aunt, and then, well, Locust. She needed to give herself some credit for that. *No, I haven't figured out how to escape and normally I'd be pretty pissed at myself for that, but right now all things considered, I think I'm doing okay.*

"Little victories," she assured herself. "They count just as much." *It counts.*

She finally sat down again, her body nearly falling to the ground with exhaustion. The adrenaline had kept her going, but now it was beginning to subside, which meant she was going to crash soon. She curled up on her side, her head resting on her arm. Sleep found her the moment her eyes closed.

\*\*\*

The knock on her door came much too soon. Again, this was a time she wished she had a watch, at least then she would be able to tell how much sleep she had gotten. Before she had even rolled over the door opened.

A long lanky frame stood in its emptiness. The same guard from yesterday. Todd. She was beginning to think he was personally assigned to her. She'd seen several 'guards' stationed around the building, even on her tour with Riley, and outside the Oval, but they never associated with her, it was always Todd.

There was something different today though. It wasn't just Todd. Normally, she would expect Claude behind him, or maybe even Annette, but a dark, red-haired woman stuck her head in the room.

"Miss Chase?" she asked, as if expecting a different answer.

Lana pulled her hair back out of her face, it was probably a messy fury after her fitful night. She pushed herself up so she was sitting, her back against the wall. She pulled at the hemline of her dress tugging it further down her thighs from where it had bunched in her sleep.

The woman nodded as if Lana had answered her. "Right, well, are you ready?"

Lana's face pinched. She looked from this strange woman to Todd who was still in the doorway.

"Huh?"

The woman looked back over her shoulder now, Todd only shrugged in response. "Did you not know you had a session this morning?"

Lana stood up and stretched her arms against the wall. "Does it look like I have any idea what you are talking about?"

"Ah." The woman nodded again. "I was warned about that."

This got Lana's attention. She turned crossing her arms over her chest, "About what?"

"Your temperament," she stated matter-of-factly.

Lana dropped her hands to her side, a small, exasperated laugh escaping her lips. "My temperament," she repeated to herself. "Because *I'm* the crazy one," she said, again speaking to herself.

"That's not what I meant," the woman interjected, adjusting her large rectangle glasses. "Poor choice of words," she said, waving her hand toward Lana. "I simply meant, your reactivity is fortuitous. It is uncommon in these circumstances. Not bad or good, but uncommon."

Before Lana had a chance to respond, the woman nodded, "Right." She walked over to the dresser opposite her. She pulled out an emerald green piece of fabric, a thong, and bra. She tossed them to Lana, "No point wasting any more time," she said, before curtly walking out the door. "Five minutes," she called over her shoulder as the door shut with a clank.

Lana stared at the soft silky fabric between her fingers, still trying to piece together the strange interaction. The woman was well dressed in tapered pants, and a black flowy top tucked in. Her hair hung around her shoulders with blunt bangs across her forehead. A word came forward in her head, something Riley had said yesterday. *The Armstrong's* "Claude and Annette", *the guards,* "Todd and everyone else I've seen in that same navy-blue polo and beige khakis" but there was one more, *counsellors.* That's who this woman was. A counsellor. It had to be.

As much as she wanted to rebel in every way possible including tossing the new clean clothes aside, she could not refuse her desire to be rid of her dress and its tainted hold on her. She changed into the emerald green suit, which happened to be a romper. She'd never worn one of these before, similar to the dress it lacked practicality. She liked it more than the dress though. At least this was similar to wearing a shirt and shorts albeit fancier. It made her feel less out of her element.

The romper had thin spaghetti straps draping down into a V on her chest. The fabric cinched around her torso accentuating her waist, but didn't have a belt. She thought that was odd. There was a coiled band within the fabric instead that formed to her waist, the rest fell away from her in breezy waves.

The dress though, the one she could practically see the outline of Locusts' hands on, was lying in a ball at her feet. She swept it up into her hands and pulled at the bottom drawer of her dresser. It was empty. She stuffed the dress inside and slammed the drawer shut, kicking it with her foot. "Fuck you," she said, with the action.

It wasn't *at* the dress. It was just a piece of fabric. She knew that. She cursed instead at the way it made her feel. At what had happened to her while she was wearing it. She cursed at him.

The door opened again, this time without a knock. She jumped and turned, wiping the scowl off her face from her argument with the dresser. The red-headed woman stood there. "Great" – she nodded to her outfit – "follow me," she clipped quickly passing through the door.

Lana waited a moment in surprise. There was typically more explanation than that. The counsellor had not even given her the opportunity to object. She'd simply left. *I shouldn't go,* she thought to herself. *I should plant my feet here and refuse. They need to know, I'm not just going to give up and fall in line.* Her body took a step toward the door in defiance of her mind. She could see out the door now. *Yep, she is definitely gone.* There was no sign of the red-headed woman. Lana looked back at her room, the thought of staying there, cooped up with nothing but her thoughts made her sick. An immediate icky warmness plummeted in her stomach, like the nose-dive drop of a rollercoaster.

*Staying here is not going to help me.* She took a deep breath and entered into the corridor. She nearly jumped out of her skin when she saw Todd leaning against the wall next to her door. He scrambled upright at the sight of her. "Oh," he blurted. "I wasn't expecting—" He shook his head. "Never mind." He swung his arm forward. "Miss Mason went this way."

\*\*\*

"Would you like to sit down?' the red-haired woman, Mason, asked. Lana looked around the room, she wasn't sure *where* she meant. There were several options, there was a high-top rectangular table with four chairs on one side of the room. A three-seater beige leather couch, accented by a large gray chaise lounge on one side and small, stiff looking chair on the other. A large coffee table separated the couch from a small desk nestled against the wall nearest to her.

"Anywhere you like," the woman answered as if reading

Lana's internal dialogue. Lana chose the chair next to the chaise lounge, closest to her.

"Interesting," the woman said, she picked up a laptop off the coffee table and sat herself on the floor in front of it. Her fingers quickly typing something.

*That was a test. She's testing me.*

"So." She started looking up from her computer. "Miss Chase." She nodded at Lana. "My name is Abigail Mason; I am one of the counsellors on the island." She paused, allowing Lana a moment to digest the information before continuing. "It is my job to care for your mental health and education while you are here."

Lana said nothing. Her eyes flicked to Todd who was standing by the door silently. She thought it was discreet but the counsellor's head popped up and then back down, typing away again on her computer. *She's taking notes.*

"How long have you been here, Miss Chase?"

"This is a test?" Lana answered not missing a beat. Miss Mason looked up from her computer. She smiled slightly, not at all confused by her unrelated answer. "What do you mean by that?"

"Exactly what I said," she repeated. "This is a test."

"Mmm," the counsellor mused, an eyebrow raised. "I am going to have to get used to that brashness," she said, typing again on her computer. When she finished, she looked at Lana again.

"Why did you choose that seat, Lana?"

"What?"

"Why did you choose that seat?" she asked again, gesturing around the room. "There are plenty of options, why that one?"

Lana felt an incredible sense of unease wash over her. She

knew exactly why she had chosen this seat. It wasn't a random pick. Nothing Lana did was random. She'd picked this chair for a reason, she just hadn't expected someone to notice that.

"All right," the counsellor interjected, "I'll tell you why I think you chose it. Let me know if I hit the nail on the head at any point." She leaned back from the keyboard. "You chose that chair because it is one of two sole seats in the room. Which means you won't have to sit next to anyone. That chair" – she nodded toward Lana – "and the chaise lounge. But the chair you chose has a direct path to the door. No obstructions." She hooked a thumb behind her. "Out of all the very comfy options available, you chose the least appealing, which means you don't want to get comfortable."

She paused pushing onto her knees and placing her elbows on the table in a casual lean. "Am I getting warm?" she pushed, that small smile curling on her lips again.

Lana sat there for a moment. She was right. All of those scenarios ran through her head when she chose this chair in the room. Finally, Lana nodded. "Yeah," she clipped, "but that doesn't mean you know me, it doesn't mean anything."

"On the contrary, Miss Chase," the counsellor interjected, typing again. She paused and folded her hands in her lap. "It tells me that someone taught you all that."

"So?"

"Don't you find that interesting?"

"That I know how to protect myself?"

"Yes," the woman laughed. "Yes, precisely, but more than that." When Lana said nothing she continued, "That someone trained you to do that."

# Chapter Twelve

Days passed with the same routine. She'd even been given a printed copy of the day-to-day itinerary. It was now one of the only items posted on her bare dorm walls. She had not hung it there, Miss Mason had, but she wasn't bothered enough to remove it.

6.30 a.m.: Counselling session
7.30 a.m.: Breakfast
8.00 a.m.: FDA (free development time)
9.00 a.m.: Practicals
12.00 p.m.: Lunch
12.30 p.m.: FDA (free development time)
1.00 p.m.: Free time
3.00 p.m.: Counselling session
4.00 p.m.: Practicals
5.00 p.m.: Dinner
6.00 p.m.: FDA (free development time)
8.00 p.m.: Curfew

Her counselling sessions were a mix of questions, some completely unrelated like what her favorite color was, others were more poignant. Questions about her childhood and upbringing. She avoided most of the latter. Not only because she didn't want to give the Islanders any information, but also because she didn't want to touch on any subject related to her aunt. She hadn't fully processed that loss yet, and she feared if she started to get into that, she would crumble very quickly.

Miss Mason also asked her to complete various tests, nothing physical, just written tests. She'd done algebra, English writing and science competency tests. She figured they were trying to understand her knowledge level. She'd been home-schooled her entire life, she wasn't sure if she was above or below the average person for her age bracket.

But what she did most, was watch. She watched Riley morph over and over again in his practicals. Each time feeling her hold on defiance slip farther and farther away. It was hard to deny the Mùths' existence when she sat front row for a demonstration day after day. Maybe that was the point. The slow interception of her own beliefs and conversion to theirs.

Lana watched Riley jump through hoops for the Islanders. *Literally,* big black hoops stationed at different heights throughout the room. She hadn't seen Claude since her encounter with Locust. It been a few days now, if not more. She felt her mind draw back to the day trying to recall how much time had passed. She saw Locust, his ugly face and thick sweaty body, she could smell the stench of his breath. She shivered and pulled her mind away. *NO. Don't go there.*

Claude on the other hand. She was somewhat surprised he had not appeared yet. This was by far the longest she'd gone without seeing him. It made her feel both anxious, and calm. It was an interesting concoction. A part of her enjoyed the separation, the moments to herself to breath, and the other part of her knew she would see him again and just wanted to get it over with.

"He's either avoiding me or giving me space."

She'd unloaded this paranoia upon Riley many times to which he usually just shrugged. It felt good being able to talk to someone again. Her aunt had been in such a decline lately, they had not been able to have a real, thoughtful conversation in months. She forgot what it felt like. She'd forgotten what a release it could be.

It was strange how much she trusted Riley, especially considering the brief amount of time they'd known each other. Somehow, she really trusted him. He'd reluctantly agreed to help get her into the media room. It had taken some convincing as he preferred to keep his little brown nose out of trouble.

If it was up to her, she would have already been in that stupid room where they were keeping her files, but Riley had convinced her to wait. He said the guards had a ten-minute lapse on Fridays where they all had a brief meeting with the Armstrong's. It would be her best chance to get in and out unseen. That also happened to be today. They would have an extra fifteen minutes after dinner, where all Mùths have time to return to their dorms. They would have to be in and out, in order to make curfew.

"Here he goes again," Lana said aloud, interrupting her own thoughts.

"I'm going to do it this time!"

Lana nodded, waving him ahead. He stood with his back against the wall, in a blink he morphed. He stood there for a few minutes adjusting himself to the transition and then the little fox took off full speed across the length of the room.

Just before he met the opposing wall he leaped into the air, nearly seven feet. His body arched with the momentum. He stretched his small body so that he looked like a flying squirrel. He caught the third highest ledge and hung off the end with his front paws. He dangled for a moment whining in aggravation and scrambled up onto the platform. He'd been trying to reach the final perch for a few days which was two higher than he was now. He whipped his head around looking for Lana.

"I'm on it," she announced, crossing the room to stand underneath him. "Go ahead, I'm right underneath you, but if you scratch me again, I'm going to drop you on your big nose. Got it?" She heard a high-pitched whine in response. Riley leaped off the ledge and Lana caught him with an *oomph*.

"Zero for twelve, Riley. Maybe you'll get it on number thirteen." He pushed away from her with a small growl and dropped easily to the floor. He trotted back to the other side of the room and lined up against the wall.

"Again Riley? Really?"

He gave her a look that was meant to be fierce but simply made Lana giggle. He took off again.

After a few more unsuccessful attempts, Lana finally convinced Riley to give up so they could go to dinner. They were already late, and didn't have much time left for the meal. It had become Lana's favorite time of the day just as Riley had predicted. Her mouth salivated at the wafting smell of hot food. She ran her tongue over her gums, they were tender and achy. She wished she had her medication. It was a persistent bother now, something that split her focus when she definitely didn't need it to.

Her attention turned back to Riley, who was speedily rambling about something, *the grass? Bugs? The food?*

"That's why Spiderman is the best," Riley said, matter-of-factly as he pulled a spoonful of spaghetti onto his plate. "Do you agree?" Lana tuned back in. She had no idea what he was talking about, but she didn't care enough to ask. There was something else that had her attention.

Riley poked his head in front of hers. "Earth to Lana?" he said, waving a hand in front of her face.

Lana shook her head returning her focus to the boy. "Hmm,

what?"

Riley's eyes scrunched together. "What was so interesting—" he stopped himself, his eyes finding what had distracted her moments before. "Oh" – he shrugged, pulling another scoop of spaghetti onto his mound – "he's back."

The dark curly headed boy sat alone at one of the picnic tables in the farthest corner of the Oval. *Bennet.* She didn't know how long it had been since she'd seen him or well, since she struck him. Probably about the same amount of time since she'd seen Claude.

He looked different. Noticeably different. His face pale and creased as if in pain. His shoulders hunched and his plate untouched in front of him. His dark bruised eye caught hers and gave the slightest of nods. Riley quickly grabbed Lana's arm and steered her toward a table in the opposite direction.

"I wouldn't," Riley advised.

"I'm not going to hit him again."

Riley squinted his eyes in a disbelieving look. "Mhmm, come on, let's sit over here," he said, gesturing to an empty table.

"I just want to talk to him."

"I wouldn't."

"Why not?"

"Because he's still recovering from the Underground. It might not be the best time to *talk* to him," he said, using air quotes for emphasis.

"The Underground?"

Riley bit his lip, his eyes bugging out of his head, "Nobody really likes to talk about it."

Lana rolled her eyes and pushed herself up from the table, "Then why did you bring it up?"

"Lana—"

"Relax, Riley." She quipped as she made her way over to Bennet's table. There was something Riley had said that still weighed on her. There were far too many unknowns about this place. She was tired of simply adding more questions to her unanswered list.

"Bennet?" she asked, touching him lightly on the shoulder, so she wouldn't startle him. He dropped his shoulder away from her touch and turned slowly, his face cringing from the movement.

"Look, Rook, I'm really not in the best shape for a tussle—"

"Not why I'm here," Lana countered, waving away his remark. "I just wanted to ask you something."

A flicker of surprise crossed his face. He leaned back as if assessing her, weighing her honesty versus malfeasance. After a moment, he nodded. "All right."

"I heard that you've been here the longest."

He titled his head to the side, his eyes curious. A gentle smirk sprawling across his lips. "Do you have a question, Rook?"

Lana slid onto the bench beside him. She turned to face him, one leg on either side of the wooden bench. They were seated in the far-left corner of the Oval. Everyone else was in front of, or beside them. Lana sat with her back to them all. A clear position of vulnerability. She was exposing her back side to a room full of people she didn't know. Bennet noticed it immediately. A display of trust.

"How long would that be?" Lana said, her back rigid. Noticeably uncomfortable in her position.

"I don't know," he shrugged, "I stopped keeping count. Feels like forever."

Lana lowered her voice. "Have you ever heard of someone not morphing?"

Bennet's head swiveled; his brows drawn together in confusion, "What?"

She leaned forward, her voice still low. "Someone not morphing—has it happened?"

"You know where you are, right?" Bennet asked, his hand gesturing around the room. "They don't bring you here unless you are a Mùth."

Lana rolled her eyes. "Hypothetically," she hissed. "If someone didn't morph, what would happen to them?"

Bennet took a few seconds to answer. He fiddled with the spoon on his tray, "Nothing good," he said in a soft exhale. Riley popped up in front of her then making her jump. "Jesus, Riley. A little more warning next time."

"Time's up, princess," Bennet said, pushing himself up from the table. His teeth clenched in pain. He walked toward the flashing yellow light.

"Sorry!" Riley Squeaked. "I was just coming to let you know oval time was over."

Lana smiled and swept a hand through his long copper hair. "Not many people can sneak up on me."

"It's in my DNA," Riley said, poking her with his elbow.

"What?"

"Because I'm a fox," he said, his hand pointing to his chest as if she didn't know who he was talking about. Lana lifted her eyebrows, her face pinched in incomprehension.

"You know, sly as a fox?" he pressed. "You've never heard that?" He cocked his head to the side. "Really?"

"No, I can't say that I have," she said, her brain searching its history for relevance. Finally, she shrugged. "That's quite an inaccurate analogy."

"What? How?" Riley stammered, his tone wavering on

offended.

"Foxes are agile, quick, light and intelligent. I would not classify that as sly."

Riley rolled his eyes. "All right, all right, next time I'll whistle, OK?"

Lana chuckled and gave him a shove.

\*\*\*

Riley whipped the card out and slid it across the reader, the plastic barely touching the metal mechanism, and pulled it back to his chest. The lock flashed red. A look of panic washed over him, his large eyes widening. "I swear this is the right card," he said, his eyes flicking back over his shoulder nervously. They were standing outside the media room. The guard had just finished his rotation which meant they had ten minutes before the next guard arrived, and only fifteen before they needed to be back in their dorms.

"Hey ninja," Lana said, reaching her hand out. "Can I try?"

Riley pulled the card closer to him. "I can't risk anything happening to it—"

Lana snatched the card from his fingers before he could finish. She raised her finger against his lips to silence his objections. Riley ducked his head, cringing at himself and checked over his shoulder yet again.

"You see," Lana said, placing the card against the metal lock. "If you leave it long enough for it to read the card" – the lock flashed green and made a satisfying click – "then you might just be successful." She smiled and passed the card back to him.

Riley scurried through the door like an escaping cartoon. "Come on," he said, ushering her inside, the door barely ajar.

"Come on, come on!"

Lana could feel the slow prick of Riley's anxiety creep into her energy. It pressed on her chest, and steadily pumped her heart. Its rhythm increasing every second like the beating of a drum. Riley turned frantically toward the room, his eyes wider than Lana had ever seen them. She reached for his arm before he ran around the room like a frightened mouse.

"Riley, stop."

"We don't have much time." He panted, trying to pull his arm from her grasp.

"We won't have any time if you do not *calm down*." She dipped her head down in front of him and slid her hand up to his shoulder. "Listen to me for a second," she said, her voice low and smooth.

"If you panic, your mind will be working overtime. You won't be able to think clearly. You most likely won't find what you're looking for because you are so worked up." Lana could see the boy's chest start to rise and fall more slowly as her words sunk in. She gave his shoulder a reassuring squeeze. "Besides, if we get caught. I'll just say I threatened you," she winked, and almost immediately felt his muscles release underneath her hand. His lips turned up in a small smile.

"OK," he whispered, turning back to the room. It was a lot smaller than she'd imagined. She'd pictured something more akin to a newsroom, busy with papers, computers, printers, and all sorts of technological machinery. This room, on the other hand, quite resembled a library.

It had four shelves reaching nearly to the ceiling. They were stacked with beige file folders intermittently mixed with the odd book here and there. The disorganization of it was oddly unsatisfying. There was something comforting about the crisp cleanliness of a library. Their clean vertical and horizontal lines of neatly positioned books and symmetrical adjacent shelves was appealing. This library lacked that comfort. The room was poorly lit, just like every other room so far except for the Oval, with no natural lighting. A couple of floor lamps were positioned around the room, and one overhead light hung above a scattered row of rectangular tables.

She found Riley's eyes watching her, waiting for her to make the first move. He was probably too scared to do anything right now. Lana nodded toward him and headed into the aisles of files. Thankfully it seemed to be alphabetically categorized. She found *C* quite easily. Cabell, Cabrin, Cace, Cecil, Chase.

Lana yanked the beige file folder out of its slot, nearly spilling its contents on the floor. She grabbed at the paper flying away from her and held it firmly in her outstretched arm, like a mannequin frozen in position. What if this was it? What if these were the answers, she'd been hoping for her entire life? Answers about her parents, who they were? What really happened to them, and maybe even how they were intertwined with this place.

"Lana?" Riley whispered, peeking around the corner. "Are you OK?"

Lana remained frozen, the paper still in her outstretched arm. "Lana?" Riley pressed, moving down the aisle to her side. He placed a hand on hers and gently pushed her arm back to her side.

"Are you OK?"

"I don't know if I'm ready," she said, her voice a breathy whisper.

Riley cocked his head to the side, his bright eyes clouded with confusion. A moment passed, "Whatever you want to do Lana, is OK." She breathed a shaky breath and looked at the small boy beside her. "Remember what you just told me?" He flicked his hair out of his face. "Well, it might be in a different way, but you can use the same advice."

Lana shook her head. He was right. *Jesus.* She'd just lectured him about not panicking and she had let a single piece of paper throw her for a loop. She took a breath and nodded toward the boy.

"You're smarter than you look, you know?"

She opened it to find one single sheet of paper. On it was written:

Mùth Information Sheet:
  Name: Alana Claire Chase
  Born: 13 September 1997
  Morph: Unknown

  History:
  Mother: Claire Chase
  Died: October 29, 2002
  Lineage: Unknown lineage

  Father: Logan Chase
  Died: October 29, 2002
  Lineage: Canadian Lynx

  Guardian: Alice Emerson
  Born: 25 December 1926
  Died: 25 April 2016

  Notable Remarks:
Alana lived with her guardian for fourteen years after her parents' death. Referred to Ms. Emmerson as *Aunt Alice*. Alana was unaware of

her relation to Ms. Emmerson. Awaiting her morph. We expect a rare and explicitly valuable transition.

Lana felt like dropping to her knees. Her eyes welled with tears and she crumpled the worthless piece of paper in her hands. Disappointment pulled at the bottom of her heart, sinking deeply into her chest. It wasn't all consuming though. Somehow, she felt the prickle of relief pump through her with every breath. It wasn't the information she was looking for, that was clear, but it also wasn't the information that she feared.

Her parents. Their involvement. She wanted answers, but— she realized, she wanted her answers. She wanted proof that they weren't Mùths, that her aunt wasn't a liar, that she didn't know about Mùths' existence, and that her presence on the island was *indeed* a mistake. But, as much of her that wanted to believe all that, there was another part of her that doubted it.

"Are you OK, Lana?"

Lana smoothed out the piece of paper and slipped it back into the folder.

"It's OK to be disappointed you know. You don't have to hide it," Riley said, leading them out of the aisle.

"I'm not sure what I'm feeling right now."

"Well, whatever it is, you can talk about it. You don't have to tuck it all away," he said crouching to the floor every few feet to pick the tiniest little fibers.

Lana paused, her face scrunched. She could hear her aunt's words ringing in her mind, *"Emotion only weakens you and strengthens others."*

Riley stopped now, he stood next to one of the rectangular tables. "What?"

Lana shrugged, "Expressing emotions gives people insight

into your vulnerabilities. It is mentally fatiguing, and easy for others to manipulate."

"For some." Riley nodded in agreement. He nudged the table beside him an inch, as if that made the room look somehow less conspicuous to their trespass.

"But not when they are your friend. A friend can help you carry it, instead of struggling with the weight alone."

# Chapter Thirteen

The window in her room didn't give her much of a view. However, it did occasionally let her feel the warm sun on her face... She sat uncomfortably, in the small crevice, her mind lost in a flurry of thoughts. She pulled at the threads as they came up and followed them until they dropped off into another.

The most unbelievable part about this entire place seemed to be the one thing she could no longer refute. Morphers existed. Plain and simple. She'd seen Riley shift *far* too many times to dispute that. She'd had way too many conversations with his fox form, well not so much conversations as words from her and squeaks from him. She rubbed at her eyes, the lunacy of her normal starting to pound behind her eyes.

She groaned as her mind tugged at the thread that had been wrapped around her brain since she got here. It gave a little squeeze every now and again to remind her it was there. *Why?*

*So morphers exist? So what? Why did they need to be rounded up and held here? Was it for control, for personal gain, for service, for what?* Every time she was taunted by an answer, she was smacked in the face with another question. She thought back to the worthless piece of paper she'd discovered with Riley.

There was no way that was *all* they knew. The Islanders would not have just magically stumbled upon her *intentionally secluded* cabin in the forest, armed and ready for extraction. No. They came with a team, a plan and a target. You don't do—you can't do that with the information in her file.

"There's more" – she nodded to herself – "there has to be."

Whether it was another file hidden somewhere or maybe on a hard drive, they knew more than what was contained in that file. The more she thought about it, the more it made sense. Riley had said some morphers earn supervised time in the media room. Those morphers would have ready access not only to the computers but their own files. Claude could easily use that as a bargaining chip against many.

"If you behave, you can see your file," she said aloud, mocking his British tone.

"It's probably tempted so many." She sighed. The answer of a long missing relative, which seemed to be common amongst morphers, or else the assurance that whoever they left behind was okay. A gentle warmth surrounded her heart, like socks on cold feet. A fleeting moment of comfort and satisfaction. Had Claude dangled that above her head like a bone to a dog, she may have leapt for it. Now, she removed that piece from his game board. What's better? He didn't know it. She'd seen the file, and she did it without a guard breathing down her neck.

Lana squeezed her eyes shut. The images flooded her mind before she could stop them. She saw Locust, his hungry eyes drawing up her body. His dense weight pushing up against her. The hot smugness of his breath filled her nostrils once again. Lana punched her fist against the window silencing the raw images slicing through her mind like a knife through butter.

She fell out of her window crevice and into a heap on the floor. She pushed her palms against the cool concrete letting its firmness calm her. For once, she allowed the tears stinging in her eyes to drop to the floor. She made no attempt to wipe them away.

The sound of her door being unlocked pulled her back to reality. She pressed her palms to her eyes and breathed three short breaths. *Emotion only strengthens them.* The figure in the door actually gave her a breath of relief. She smiled and watched him struggle to look professional.

"Uh, Lana—Alana, I mean Miss Chase, would you follow me." He said, frantically patting the wrinkles in his shirt.

"Where are we going, Todd?" she asked, pushing herself up off the floor.

"The mirror room to see Mr. Armstrong."

Lana walked over to the dresser. Six sundresses and one pair of shorts and a tank top left.

"I need to change, Todd. Can you give me a second?" A look of horror flashed across his face and he stumbled trying to back out of the room and close the door at the same time. "Of—of course, sorry. So sorry," he stammered. He gave up and settled for tucking himself behind the door.

Lana bit her lip to keep from laughing. She pulled on the tight red khaki shorts, and deep blue tank top and knocked on the slightly ajar door. He poked his head around and Lana flashed him a thumbs up, her face pinched with sarcasm. They walked in silence, side by side. Lana kept dipping her head into his view, but he avoided her eyes. His cheeks were slightly pinked and he walked a little too quickly. His long strides, equaling two of Lana's.

They exited the stairwell, and Lana could see their destination at the end of the hallway. The three symmetrical doors plucking a tender string in her chest. She felt the bile tickle the back of her throat. She saw Locust again—*NO.* She shook her head. *Don't let it in. Don't let it in.*

She steered her gaze away from the door. Her legs still tingled from the phantom presence of his hands. She felt her pace dragging as they got closer, the lump in her throat pushing higher with each step.

"Good morning, Alana," Claude said, emerging from the central door. "This is Dr. Otazzi." He gestured to a small, dark haired Asian woman standing behind him. "She will be examining you this morning."

He nodded toward the door, prompting them inside. Lana followed, her teeth clenched in annoyance. Claude stood just inside the door, his black dress shirt tucked perfectly into his beige khaki pants. It had been a while since she'd last seen him. She'd nearly forgotten the ease of his charm, and how disarming it could be. The doctor remained outside.

Lana turned. "Examining me for what?"

Claude smiled. "Nothing to worry about Lana, just routine."

Lana slitted her eyes toward him, and crossed her arms over her chest. "Well, that's intentionally vague."

Claude erupted in a loud boisterous laugh that consumed the room. "You're right." He threw his hands up in the air. "You're being examined to determine your likelihood and timeline for morphing." He shrugged and shooed Todd out of the room with one finger. "Good luck," he whispered, ushering the doctor inside. He sent a wink toward Lana before slipping through the door.

This room was smaller than its twin. It was still rectangular in shape, but this one was styled like a medical suite. It consisted of a metal table wrapped in crinkle paper, a set of metallic drawers, a small stainless-steel countertop and accompanying steel table. There was also a large rectangular mirror behind the table. Lana pulled herself up onto the table and pushed her back to the mirror. She'd never been on this side of it, but that didn't mean she was going to give them an easy show.

"I'm going to start by taking some of your vitals," the small doctor asserted. Her voice squeaky and timid. After the usual flashlight in the ears, tongue depressor and reflex check Dr. Otazzi took three vials of Lana's blood.

"How much do you need?"

The doctor looked surprised by the question and referred to her clipboard.

"It says they want five. For testing."

"Well, they'll have to survive with three," Lana clipped, yanking her arm back.

"No, no you don't understand, I have to take five, that's what the instructions say."

"—and I don't particularly care what your instructions say."

The doctor paused for a moment. Her brown eyes quizzically assessing the situation. She threw herself forward, wrapping her little brittle fingers around Lana's wrist.

"I just need—"

"Get off me." Lana bucked and jumped off the table, the paper tearing underneath her. She grabbed the doctors outstretched arm and spun her around twisting it behind her back effortlessly. The woman was weak and clearly unpracticed in these maneuvers. She cried out in pain and dropped to her knees.

"I said no more." Lana growled. Heat pulsated through her and she could feel her heart pounding in her ears, adrenaline surging through her body. It twitched in her fingers and legs. She breathed a satisfying breath, like a drink to an alcoholic. The door swung open, and Claude stood there. Lana expected him to be mad, yelling, frustrated or angry. He wasn't. He was calm, completely and utterly calm.

"Lana, please release Dr. Otazzi, as she said, she was just following instructions."

When Lana didn't move he continued. "We won't poke you

with any more needles today, I promise." Lana released the woman and took a step back. The doctor gasped and fell to the ground. Lana whipped her head around to glare at Claude. She resisted the urge to pull her hair out her face and instead stood there as defiantly as she could manage.

"Dr. Otazzi," Claude said, his eyes never leaving Lana. "I assume you are capable of completing the physical without any further altercations?"

Dr. Otazzi pulled herself to her feet, and shakily adjusted her blue polo shirt.

"Yes, Mr. Armstrong."

"Good." And with that Claude left the room again.

The doctor did her best to look unphased, but she did an exceedingly poor job of it. She barely spoke, her hands trembling with every movement. Her small dark eyes darted from the window to the door every few seconds, her shoulders flinching every time the room creaked or groaned. *She's terrified of him.* Lana realized. *She doesn't want him to come back.*

Lana felt bad for a moment. She wondered who this lady was and if she was here by choice. *She could be just like me.* She shook the thought from her head immediately. *No, we're not the same, I would never help them.*

The rest of the exam only took about ten minutes. The doctor shuffled all her papers and piled them together on her clipboard. She scooted toward the door as quickly as she could without losing some and left. Lana fought the urge to look at the mirror behind her. She didn't know what she was supposed to do at this point, but she hated the idea of looking at Claude for direction or permission.

She hopped off the crinkly paper and took two short strides to the door. She felt slightly empowered. A little more herself. It might have just been from the adrenaline, but it didn't matter. She felt good.

Her victory was short-lived. The door was locked.

"For fuck sakes." She breathed.

# Chapter Fourteen

Claude stood on the other side of the two-way mirror, his hand clasped behind his back, his eyes never straying from the girl on the other side. The voices behind him droned on in a monotonous rumble, he'd barely listened to a word. There was something about this girl that simply fascinated him. She was lying on her back on the examination table tossing a rubber band ball up and down over her head.

Her behavior was so different from any of the other Mùths. In most cases a combination of fear and manipulation was enough to secure an obedient subject… and yet, those same tactics had not broken Lana. He'd been doing this for quite a few years now. The response varied slightly from Mùth to Mùth, but the outcome was always the same. *Acceptance.*

"Claude, are you listening?" A shrill voice pulled his eyes away from the mirror.

"Hmm?" he said, turning to face the two women in the room. Dr. Otazzi stood just inside the door, her hand nearly resting on the door handle—ready to leave. Annette was pacing in the opposite corner. Claude hooked a thumb toward the mirror, the guard moved without a word and stood in front of the mirror watching Lana on the other side.

Claude flashed his sister an easy and relaxed smile. He watched her tightly wound body start to release a little bit. He pulled a chair from the table between them and offered it to her. Annette sat, and he swung around to the chair on the other side.

"Go ahead, doctor," Claude said, waving his hand in front of the other empty chair.

The petite woman blinked rapidly and shuffled forward into the chair. She flipped through her papers, "I—uh, I'm not sure what you want me to tell you. Her vitals are strong. *Very* strong actually. From what I can tell she does appear to be in extremely good health. I haven't tested the blood yet, but I—uhm, I can't imagine that there will be anomalies."

A small, satisfied smile drew across Claude's lips. The doctor had not stopped shuffling her papers the entire time she was talking. "Doctor, are you nervous?"

The woman squeaked and laid her papers down, her chest rising and falling rapidly. "No. I am a professional," she asserted. Claude knew the assertion was more for herself than anyone else.

"Then please continue" – he waved his hand over the table – "without the paper stacking."

The woman paused. She looked between the two people seated before her. Her discomfort was evident. "I am a professional, and I did what you asked of me. I just don't know what you want *me* to tell you."

"JESUS! Do we need to fucking caudle you?" Annette screeched, slamming her hands down on the table. The doctor nearly jumped out of her seat. Claude put a reassuring hand on his sister's arm and hushed her with a look.

"Annette, love, perhaps I should deal with Dr. Ottazzi alone?" he suggested, his voice peaking with suggestion. Annette nodded, her eyes wild with excitement. "I'll be in the corridor." Claude smiled sweetly at his sister and waited for her to exit before continuing. The doctor was gripping the table so tightly her knuckles were white with pressure. She squeaked and flinched in one movement, Claude smiled again and placed a hand over hers on the table.

"Love, I am not going to hurt you. Sometimes, you have to release the hot air from an engine before it pushes you off track." He gave her hand a reassuring squeeze, his head dipping down into her sightline.

"Doctor, all I need to know is if the girl's body can withstand some," he paused, his lips pursed, "heinous and extreme conditions."

The woman's eyebrows drew together, eyes wide, a mixture of fear and confusion dappled on her face. "Pardon?"

Claude nodded, he realized his wording carried a misleading connotation. "We are not going to do anything to her," he said. "It is more akin to something she will do to herself, and we simply want to *help* her," he said, his words dripping with double meaning. It's true, they weren't going to abuse Lana like his earlier comment mistakenly alluded. However, they weren't exactly going to make her life sunshine and rainbows.

Claude was good at this. He could use versions of the truth and spin them in ways where he wasn't lying, but also wouldn't be held accountable for someone's own inference.

"Do you mean she is going to hurt herself?" the doctor whispered, her eyes flicking to the mirror across from her.

Claude shrugged. "We just want to keep her—"

"Safe?" the doctor interrupted.

Claude leaned back in his chair, a devilish smile splayed across his face. He pulled a hand through his tousled hair, "Exactly."

His sentence had been finished at '*keep her*,' but like he'd intended, the doctor made her own inference.

The doctor glanced back at the window one more time before referring to her notes. "Her health is good. It's way above average. The only minor discrepancy I charted was a minimal amount of swelling in her gums. Other than that, she is probably one of the fittest and healthiest individuals I have ever examined."

"Thank you, doctor. That is all I needed to know." Claude nodded toward the guard.

The small woman stiffened. "Go ahead," he said to the guard.

"Wait!" the doctor screeched, as the burly man started toward her. "Wait, don't—please don't!" The guard reached behind the woman and ripped one of the filing cabinets forward. It slammed against the table with a significant bang. The doctor screamed, and jumped away from the table. Claude pulled a thick book off of one of the shelves and tossed it to the guard who threw it against the door with incredible force. Tears started to form in the doctor's eyes, her body shaking.

Claude strode over to her. "It actually works to our advantage," Claude said, flicking his hand through her hair. "That you already had a tussle with Lana." He pulled at her scrubs to make them look disheveled.

"It is in your best interest to go with it." He gestured to her body. "My sister isn't the forgiving type."

He swept his arm toward the door. "She will escort you to the lab where you can run a full diagnosis on Lana's blood samples. After that, you will be fit to leave."

The doctor's cheeks were wet with tears, her eyes widening as her mind slowly put the pieces together. The woman hurriedly scooped up her papers with both arms and pressed them against her chest. She nodded slightly in Claude's direction and slipped out the door.

He caught Annette's eyes through the gap for only a second.

But in them he saw what he had hoped for and what he'd expected. A sweetly satisfied smile.

Claude stood there for a moment unmoving and silent. He watched the guard shift his weight in front of him, his mind snapping back to the present. He'd almost entirely forgotten about Lana because of his charade. He plucked the book off the floor and tucked it back onto the shelf.

"What do you think?" he asked the guard, whose body was back in front of the glass.

Claude joined him, peering through to the girl on the other side. She was still lying on the table, but she was now pulling all the elastics off the ball and tying them together. Her tanned and toned body was curled into the shape of a C with her long brown hair hanging off the table.

"Sir?"

"Do you think she's playing us, Pede?" he asked, his head tilting to the side. "Do you think she's known her morph this whole time, and is just an exceptionally stubborn thespian?"

The broad chested guard clenched his jaw and tried to hide the look of embarrassment from his face. "Thespian, sir?"

Claude smiled and clapped him on the shoulder, "Yes, as in actress," he clarified. His tone cool and quiet.

The guard looked back to the glass, assessing the young girl on the other side. "I don't know, sir."

Claude sucked his teeth. "Very well, very well." He pushed his hands into his pocket and leaned his shoulder against the glass facing Pede. "I just haven't quite figured her out yet and it's both incredibly annoying and fascinating."

Pede said nothing. Claude nodded to himself, "Please escort Miss Chase to the Oval for dinner. She'll be able to make the tail-end of it if you hurry." The guard nodded and left the room.

Claude waited and watched as Lana's body jerked upright at the sound of the door. The elastics falling to the floor. The muscles in her arms tense and still.

*Preparing for a fight perhaps?*

Pede appeared in the doorway, and Lana hopped off the table, her body resigned and stiff. She sent a fierce and prolonged look at the window. Claude took a step back wondering if someone had flipped the translucent switch on him.

He reached for the switch and felt its familiar downward position. No, it was off. She simply just *knew* he was still there. "Just so fascinating," he mumbled.

\*\*\*

"She's quite unique," Abigail said, crossing one leg over the other.

Claude watched her from behind his desk. Her skirt nestled just above the knee. She sat across from him and sent him a sultry smile in response to his lingering attention.

"Would you like to elaborate on that?"

Abigail shrugged. "She is a lot of things," she said, drumming her fingers along the arm of the chair. "But a liar is not one of them."

"So, you believe her lack of a morph, or knowledge of it is truthful?"

Abigail nodded, a stray red hair coming loose from her bun and falling across her eyes. She tucked it behind her ear, her big doe eyes rich with suggestion.

Claude licked his lips, a playful smile on his face. "That's what I was hoping you would say." It was always like this between the two of them. He wasn't going to complain. There weren't any other women available to him on the island. It was common for him and Abigail to hook-up. It was a great stress release. He was sure she wanted more, but she was his employee, he wasn't going to let it go farther than what it was. Which was sex. Plain and simple.

"I have a recommendation if you are open to it?" Abigail said, standing up and leaning herself against the red mahogany of his desk. He turned the lock on the door handle. His eyebrow raised curiously.

"Suspend her sessions for the time being."

He pursed his lips considering her words. She slowly pulled her hand up to the buttons on her dress shirt. Plucking at them one by one so the shirt started to fall open. "Silence can be a useful tool. She is not divulging any information during our sessions." Claude closed the distance between them.

"Give her some time to think," she said, smiling with his advance. "It will allow her to sit and stew, have some time to herself, it might help her open up later on."

He was inches from her now. "OK." He nodded. "No more sessions then." He tipped his head down to her ear. "Now, enough work talk."

# Chapter Fifteen

Lana was exhausted by the time she got to the Oval. It had been a long day. She didn't even want food. She just wanted to feel the fresh air on her body and grass underneath her feet. She suddenly missed the warm, crisp smell of her forest. The comfort it held immediately soothed any anxieties or trepidations. She'd wandered into its leaves many times over the past few months to help bear the increasing pressure of Aunt Alice's dementia.

It often provided the breath she needed to reset. Lana walked straight toward the grass finding an empty spot against the glass. She peeled her sandals off and felt the cool soft grass under her feet. She ignored all the confused and peculiar glances thrown her way. She took a deep breath, expanding her lungs to their full capacity before blowing out again. She tasted the salt in the air and crouched down, her back against the glass, taking a few moments to just breath. She felt a smile on her face and leaned her head back, her eyes closed.

"Where have you been?" a voice asked, cutting into her short reverie.

Lana couldn't help but smile. She couldn't be mad at him for interrupting her tranquil moment. The innocence, and fragility in his voice, sprinkled every word. It would be like yelling at a puppy. A big, doe-eyed, bouncy puppy.

"Hello to you too," she said, her eyes still closed.

Lana suddenly felt the heat of another person's body, her nose filled with his familiar pine fresh scent, like someone who had scrubbed too hard with soap. "I thought something happened because of our little... you know, adventure."

She felt his breath on her face and her eyes flew open. She immediately pushed him back, her hand splayed against his chest. His eyes were wide, she could feel his heart hammering beneath her fingers. "You know, the other night—" he suggested, his voice squeaking.

"Riley, first do not get that close again. You only do that for two reasons. When you're going to hit someone, or kiss someone." She pulled her hand off his chest. "Got it?"

Riley rolled his big gray eyes and crossed his arms over his chest. "Fine," he grumbled, "will you tell me where you were just now?"

Lana patted the grass beside her. Riley smiled and excitedly sat himself next to her. "I got checked," she mumbled.

"Did you just say you got checked? Like in hockey?"

"No," she laughed, her heart lifting with the expression. "As in check-up, like a physical exam with a doctor."

"—oh, what for?"

Lana turned her head and pulled her hair out of her face. The tail end of a breeze sent it whispering around her with an evening chill. The sun had gone down. Lana raised her eyebrows, her eyes wide with mocking annoyance. "Oh—you know." She shrugged and plucked a few blades of grass beside her. "To see if I'm fit for a triathlon coming up in the next month."

"OK, quit it with the sarcasm," he snapped, his tone taking Lana by surprise. It seemed to surprise him as well. He bit his lip and shook his head, his voice dropping to a whisper, "Sorry, I'm just scared."

Lana felt the guilt sink into her gut. Of course, this little goody-goody was petrified about potential consequences of their little rendezvous. Lana saw the slight purpling underneath his eyes, his noticeably muted personality, and irritability. He probably hadn't slept at all.

Lana laid her hand on his leg and smiled. The maneuver softening his stiff position against the glass. Lana explained the last few hours to Riley. He ate it up, his big eyes drinking in every detail. All he needed was a bag of popcorn and a large cola drink.

"I can't believe you attacked the doctor," Riley whispered, shaking his head. "That kind of thing can get you sent to the Underground."

"Me? She attacked first."

Riley shrugged, sticking a long blade of grass in his mouth. "That usually doesn't matter."

Lana groaned. "Time to go." Riley sang in response to the flashing light.

"See ya in the morning, Lana." He saluted her and ran off toward the door. God forbid he be the last one through those doors.

\*\*\*

Lana looked at her bed. She wanted to sleep in it. She desperately wanted to let the soft cotton sheets hug her body and momentarily take her away from this place. Even if it was just for a little while. She wanted to slip away in a slumber so deep the last few days would drift entirely. She stopped, her hand laying atop the metal rail headboard. She'd moved without even realizing it, her body overtaking her mind.

"No," she whispered, her hand dropping back to her side. She leaned her back against the wall and slid down slowly. She sat there just underneath the window; it was her favorite spot in the room. Maybe because it was the furthest from the door, maybe because it was closest to the window and by relation closest to some sort of freedom. Maybe she liked it for no other reason than it was a clear defiant alternative to the bed.

She laid on her side, her legs pulled up in front of her stomach. She rested her head on her arm and felt a tear roll down her cheek. She didn't particularly know why. It probably wasn't one singular thing. One was followed by another, and another. She didn't sob, or hiccup or heave. She simply laid there and let the tears roll down her face, collecting in a pool underneath her cheek. She would be better in the morning of that she was sure. But for now, she let her body react the way it wanted to. The way it *needed* to.

"You can do this, Lana."

The next morning came too quickly. Lana groggily pushed herself into a seated position, her head leaning against the cold cement wall. She yawned and pushed her long arms above her head in a satisfying stretch. It was this fleeting moment of peace that she craved every morning. The moment before her brain fully registered her situation. A moment where she was simply waking up and nothing else. They ended almost as soon as they began, peeling away like the dry outer rim of a fruit, to reveal the truth laying inside.

*Her cell. The island. Morphers. Her aunt. Claude. Her parents.* They flew into her mind like a flurry of busy gnats, barely resting long enough before another came in. Another thought resurfaced, as it had many times over the past few days. *There has to be another file.*

Lana closed her light gray eyes and drummed her fingers along the concrete floor beneath her. *Where would it be?* The question pounded in her mind, louder and louder with every repetition. She felt like the answers she longed for were floating in the air right in front of her, but they were just out of her reach. Frustration pricked at her mind, and she let out an agonized groan.

She could hear her aunt's soft voice in her ear, calling her mind back to a memory.

*"What are you doing?" her aunt called, her foot propping open the back door. A damp tea towel wrung between her hands. Lana laid on her stomach on the ground, she lifted her head and felt the sun spill across her face, she rolled herself onto her back with a grunt.*

*A shadow fell over her eyes. She didn't need to open them to know who was standing above her. She opened one eye at her aunt. "What is the problem, Alana?"*

*Lana pointed to the five stainless steel bars in a lateral structure, six feet above her head. Her aunt followed her finger and nodded. "Yes, I noticed you were working on the monkey bars, but that does not answer my question. Use your words please, Lana."*

*"You know they're my weakest point." She pushed herself into a seated position, crossing her legs in front of her. "I was trying to push past my personal record but I keep falling 3 rungs before," she said, smacking her hand on the grass in frustration.*

*Her aunt nodded and squinted up at the bars. "Why is it that you chose to test yourself on your weakest skill today?"*

*Lana stared at the grass between them. She shrugged, "I don't know, I just wanted to beat it, I guess."*

*"You wanted a victory?"*

*"Because those newspapers you requested from Ayiana about your parent's death did not provide you with the answers you were looking for?"*

Lana's eyes widened. She'd been so careful about that. She only had Ayiana bring her a few newspapers from the time of their deaths, and she kept them hidden in an airtight bag back in the woods.

"You don't think I have noticed your runs seem to be taking you an extra five, ten, fifteen minutes longer than usual?" her aunt pushed.

Lana's cheeks flushed red, a swirl of embarrassment and guilt tumbling down her throat.

"I'm sorry," she blurted. "I know you don't want to talk about it."

Her aunt narrowed her eyes slightly, then softened, a small sigh escaping her lips. "Alana, you are correct that I do not enjoy speaking of your parents, their loss still haunts me. However, it is also dangerous for you to be looking into that kind of information. It can lead someone right to you."

"I just wanted to see if I could learn something, some reason as to why—"

"Your curiosity about your parents is completely natural." She crouched down and placed a hand on her shoulder. "But I need you to respect the boundaries I have given you."

Lana bit her cheek and nodded silently.

"Now, you decided to accomplish something to make yourself feel better. In control? Yes?" she asked, her voice questioning.

Lana nodded.

"But you set yourself up for failure," her aunt corrected. "The rungs of those bars are still slick with morning dew, no amount of chalk is going to change that…" Her aunt picked her chalk bag off the ground and handed it to her.

"You've given yourself two unattainable goals. Answers

*about your parents, and a PR on your weakest element first thing in the morning."*

*"I wasn't thinking."* Lana shook her head, a few strands of hair coming loose from her bun. She knew the bars were slick this morning, but she thought she could power through and have an even greater victory. The foolishness of it now fluttered in her chest with embarrassment.

*"Precisely,"* her aunt responded, in a concise tone, indicating her resolution.

Lana stared at her blankly. Her aunt waited a few minutes to see if Lana would draw her own conclusion. Finally, she sighed, *"You did not think. You did not use your head. You used your heart. You chose to satisfy your craving instead of following through on a methodical sensical plan."*

Lana felt like a child again. Aunt Alice had scolded her many a time for her decision making, and letting her emotions get the better of her.

*"Refocus that limitless energy of yours into a positive outcome,"* her aunt called, as she walked back toward the cabin.

*"What do you mean?"*

*"Do you feel sad right now?"* She turned her voice slightly raised.

Lana dropped her gaze again and whispered a small, *"Yes."*

*"Then this is the perfect moment to retrain your mind. Instead of feeling sad, go outside and do a full circuit. Run harder than you have before, move quicker and more agilely. It doesn't matter if you start to feel tired, push past that. Refocus that energy into something worthwhile.*

The small, pale haired woman pointed to the mountain ridge in the distance. *"Give yourself something attainable. Circuit three, to Elkner mountain and back. You have two hours, starting now." She smiled, tapping the watch on her wrist.*

*Lana looked up at her aunt in disbelief. "Don't give me that look Alana. Get out there and retrain your mind. No distractions. Focus on the physicality of it alone. You better get going, your time is slinking away."*

*Lana jumped to her feet, a fierce smile fresh on her face. She took off toward the tree line. She would do it, absolutely she would and she'd do it in less than two hours.*

The memory washed over her like a tub of ice-cold water, both shocking and relieving. She'd almost forgotten about that day. It was before Aunt Alice started to lose her memory. Lana was probably only thirteen or fourteen years old at the time.

She knew what her aunt would say about her parents. That she couldn't change the past and there was no point putting any of her energy into something that wouldn't benefit her in any way. She knew that. But there was still some part of her that longed for those answers almost as much as she longed to escape from her captors.

The opening of her door brought her back to reality. She opened her eyes and saw Pede standing in the entrance. He was a large man, with dark tanned skin and a bald head. Her heart dropped a little. She had been expecting Todd. The reaction surprised her. She hadn't realized how much she appreciated the kind, lanky guard.

"Breakfast," the man gruffed.

"Aye, aye captain." Lana saluted, and followed the guard down the hall.

"Mr. Armstrong wanted me to inform you that you will have a practical session after breakfast."

"—Wait what?"

The guard harrumphed and pushed Lana toward the large

entryway to the Oval.

Lana sat across from Riley and pretended to listen to the long, elaborate story he was telling, but her mind was elsewhere. She made a few noises to satisfy his attention. Her stomach twisted, a cold nerve sliding up her throat. She wiped her sweaty palms on her dress.

*Steady Lana... steady.*

"You haven't touched your eggs, Lana."

"Hmm?"

"Your eggs? You haven't touched them. Are you all right?"

"Yeah, I'm fine, just distracted I guess." She avoided Riley's large inquisitive eyes. She feared he would unravel her quite quickly. She felt a heaviness in her chest, like a cinder block pressing on her. The nerves were not something she was accustomed to. She twisted her fingers together in her lap. A knuckle cracking every now and again. She counted the seconds until the end of the breakfast period.

Lana thought about herself morphing—imagined it, for the first time since she arrived on the island. She wanted it, and yet she didn't. Morphing meant that she would be connected to her departed parents in a way she never imagined possible. She would get to share a part of her life with them, something she didn't have a chance to do before. Morphing also meant she was off the Islanders 'dispose of' list. Not that she wanted to get comfortable here, but there was some part of her that longed to feel safe again. To feel in control.

The flip side was just as complicated. She knew that if she morphed she would be giving the Islanders exactly what they wanted. An outcome she simply could not tolerate. She could already picture the smug, sickly smile plastered across Claude's face. It lit a raging fire within her, burning through all her nerves.

"Lana? Are you all right? You've barely said anything," Riley squeaked. "Is it something I did?"

Lana shook her head and turned to look at the light bulb above the door. "No, Riley. You didn't. I am just waiting for something."

# Chapter Sixteen

Lana laid in a star-shape on one of the gymnast-type mats in the center of the practical room. It was the same one she'd visited with Riley so many times before. Oddly, that made her feel a little more at ease. A lot of things ran through her mind. Mainly a list of *what ifs*.

She'd been waiting for at least two hours now. She distracted herself by counting the colored spots on the ceiling tiles. *567, 568, 569.*

"Miss Chase?" A crisp voice interrupted.

Lana raised her hand and answered without hesitation. "Present."

She heard a soft chuckle and adjusted her position slightly to take in the large lanky figure standing in front of her. Todd! Her heart lurched. She dropped her arm back to the mat with a thud and shot him a flashy grin. "Hey, comrade."

He smiled, only slightly. But enough for Lana to see it.

"Miss Chase." The same voice called from behind Todd, there was no mistaking it's cool, concise quip with Todd's. "Are you ready to begin?"

The boyish guard pulled Lana to her feet and pointed her in Claude's direction.

"That depends on what you think is going to happen here."

Claude stood next to the door. His perfectly blonde hair was styled slightly different today. It was shorter on the sides and longer on the top. Lana hated that she noticed it. She hated even more that it made him *even* more handsome. His pristine white dress shirt was pressed into his fitted black pants, without a single crease or crinkle. There was not a hair out of place.

"We'll start with the treadmill," he said, nodding toward the machine in the far corner. The session didn't stop there.

Lana trudged from element to element exhausting every muscle in her body. Claude barely spoke except to tell her when to move from one machine, or object, to the next. Her lungs screamed after an hour on the treadmill at the highest speed and that was only the warm-up. She was immediately transitioned into sled pulls. She could feel her muscles stretching, weighing heavier and heavier with every step. She'd done lots of training before, but nothing like this.

She didn't know how much time had passed, she could barely remember the previous exercise. Her mind just as labored as her body. She hung from the medal rod ten feet in the air, her body shaking with exhaustion. She waited for the whistle to blow indicating the start of another pull-up repetition. Sweat ran down her face and arms, her muscles screaming for relief. He was doing this on purpose. He was trying to push her limits. She remembered her aunt, and that day with the bars at the cabin. She squeezed her hands tighter, the memory fueling her grit.

She held on and tightened her grip on the bar for what felt like the thousandth time. She let out a hiss as the newly formed blisters on her hands rubbed raw against the steel bar. Blood trickled down her wrist and onto the mat beneath her. Claude stood stoically in front of her. His eyes never leaving her body.

"Todd, would you leave us for a moment?"

"Sir?"

"Leave. Now." He breathed without hesitation.

Todd gave one last sympathetic look in Lana's direction

before slipping out of the door on the other side of the room. Lana let out a small cry as she repositioned her hands on the bar yet again. More blood ran down her arm.

Claude watched her. His head tilted slightly to the side. He raised the whistle to his lips slowly, never losing sight of Lana's eyes. He blew it. Lana's chest rose and fell quickly as she summoned the strength to pull her chin above the bar. Her legs kicked out at the empty air beneath her and she exhaled short quick breaths. It wasn't enough. Her grip loosened and with one last momentous effort she slammed to the mat below.

"FUCK!"

She didn't mean to say it. She didn't want Claude to know he'd hurt her. He could obviously see the physicality of it, but she'd just let him know her mentality as well. She crouched on the floor panting. Her body resting on her hands and knees as she stared at the godawful blue mat. Her vision swam before her eyes and she swayed slightly. *No—don't pass out, Lana. Don't!*

A pair of polished blue shoes spun into her vision. She tilted her head to look at the perfectly prim man standing over top of her, like a lion championing his meal. He said nothing. The only sound was Lana's labored breathing. He raised his eyebrows in expectation, urging her to say something, to challenge him. She wanted to. Her mind screeched at her to get up, get in his face, tell him to fuck off. But for the first time in a long time, her body failed her. She couldn't move.

Claude's eyes swept over her body from top to bottom. A small cheeky grin tugged at the corner of his mouth. He took one step closer and crouched down in front of her. His peppermint cologne clogged her nostrils and she swallowed against the gag reflex pushing forward. He cocked his head slightly, and flexed his jaw, the heat of his body radiating over her. His presence loomed, dominating in every way. He waited there for what felt like an agonizing amount of time, but Lana knew was probably only seconds.

"Progress," was all he said.

He left her alone in the room shortly after that. Lana punched the mat beneath her and felt a well of tears rush down her face. She couldn't stop them this time. She couldn't do anything. Frustration, agony, defeat, fatigue, anger and inadequacy washed over her all at once. It was too much. So, she let the tears fall. She let them pool on the mat and soak her shirt.

***

When Lana finally pulled herself up about an hour later, she noticed Todd standing silently next to the door. He looked over at her in surprise at her movement. They made eye contact and his cheeks flushed red. He took a step toward her as if he wanted to help but stopped. He stood cumbersomely by himself.

Lana almost smiled… almost. She slowly and achingly made her way over to him.

"Are you all right?" he asked, before he could stop himself.

"Never better," she grunted, gingerly feeling the palms of her hands.

"Where to now?"

A look of surprise flashed across his face. "Dinner, of course."

Lana's brow furrowed and she sent her mind searching for how much time had passed. Had it really been an entire day?

"It is four thirty p.m." Todd answered, before she had a chance to ask and placed a reassuring hand on her shoulder. Lana felt like she was in a daze. Four thirty p.m.?

Todd quickly pulled his arm away realizing that wasn't exactly *guard* etiquette. "Your session was four hours."

Lana said nothing, she was attempting to add the time in her head. Breakfast ended at nine. Then she waited at least two hours for Claude, *eleven a.m.* She laid on the mat afterward for at least an hour, which would bring them to three thirty p.m. So, her practical had lasted four and a half hours. Which was absolutely insane!

"I'm not supposed to say this," Todd whispered, "but I'm sorry." He led Lana through the halls. "I've never seen anyone go through a practical like you had today. It was insane, Mr. Armstrong, he—he wouldn't stop. He just kept going. Those routines and circuits—that's normally a week's worth of practical's, and you—he made you do them all. I just—what I'm trying to say is, I'm sorry." He exhaled a hard breath. "I'm just sorry, you had to go through that." He looked over his shoulder to make sure no one was approaching.

Lana felt herself slipping. She didn't really *hear* everything Todd was rambling about. His voice was more of a welcome rumble. Her bright eyes glazed over and she felt her knees wobble as she stepped... Her body crumpled forward. Todd managed to catch her by the waist before she hit the ground. "Lana?"

Her body was limp in his arms. Her rich brown hair spilling out behind her in a tangled mess.

"Shit, shit, shit. Lana—hello? Lana wake up, please," Todd cooed, his voice dropping off as the words folded into one in her mind. Blackness enveloped her and she let herself fall into it.

# Chapter Seventeen

Todd found himself acting a little too efficiently. It was sure to draw notice. *Just relax. You've done nothing wrong.* He nodded his head in recognition as he walked past Pede, one of the guards he regularly switched off with.

He quickened his step to avoid a conversation. Although, with Pede the extent of it would be "Any trouble? No?" and then a grunt and nod to say continue on. Todd made it to the media room where he was to meet with guard superior. The highest-ranking guard was in charge of scheduling, duties, and reviews. He wiped his brow, a few small beads of sweat lingering there.

"Todd, you're ready fo' your test?" a distinctively rough voice asked. He looked across the room to see Locust sitting at the table. "Come on Toddler, we don' got all day!"

Todd choked back the surprised stutter on his lips and shuffled into the room. He bent his tall lean frame to fit through the short door. Locust was, for lack of a better word, a brute. Todd avoided interactions with him whenever possible. He was unpredictable and rash which was not a clever combination. He was also *not* who Todd was expecting. He was not guard superior, or at least he hadn't been, unless this was a very recent move.

Todd couldn't stop the discomfort from sliding into his stomach. If Locust was guard superior, that was going to make things *much* less enjoyable, for everyone… not just morphers. Locust grumbled something that Todd didn't quite catch and motioned for him to sit down. He was standing shoulder to shoulder with Quito hovered over the desk positioned between them.

"Me and Wig have switch'd duties fo' now," he said. "Somethin' happened and we—he's taking more of a traditional role and I'm a be doing more behin' the scenes work for a little bit," he said, his eyes never leaving the desk.

"What happened?" Todd asked, leaning forward. His curiosity getting the better of him.

"Girl couldn't take a compliment." Locust snarked and nudged the guard behind him, who responded with a soft chuckle.

"Anyways," Locust continued, "'cording to Wig, you have to have like a test every coupla' weeks," he said, flipping the page to what must have been a book.

"Evaluation."

"What?" Locust gruffed, his eyes sliding over to him for the first time.

"Wig always called it an evaluation. To, you know, see how I was performing—"

"Do you ever stop talking?" Locust countered, his attention snapping back to the desk.

Todd stopped and bit down on his tongue. A surge of embarrassment heating in his cheeks. He waited for the conversation to shift toward him. He waited somewhat patiently adjusting himself in his chair every now and then to remind Locust and Quito he was there.

He leaned forward slightly and caught the thin colored edge of a page as it turned. It squeaked with the pressure of Locust's chubby flinger sliding against its polished page.

*OH,* he thought to himself. It was not a book they were enamored with. It was a magazine. Todd didn't have to see the whole thing to know what kind of *magazine* it was.

He felt even more uncomfortable than he had a moment ago, as if he was intruding on a private moment. Although, Quito and Locust were anything but private. They had no shame about the X-rated content or where they enjoyed its temptations.

He swallowed hard and dug his fingers into his chair. He focused on that, on his fingers digging into the chair and after about twenty minutes, Locust seemed to finish greedily flipping through the pages. He dragged a chair around and sat across from Todd. The chair scraped along the floor with an awful metallic sound that made Todd's ears ring.

"First question, have you broken any regulations during your shifts?" Todd's mind flicked back to Lana. *Just relax, they don't know what happened. Just answer the question as simply as possible.*

"No."

Quito made a note on his clipboard. "Second question, hav' ya had any inappropriate conduct with a Mùth?"

Again, Todd thought about Lana. His conduct had not been inappropriate, but he knew it could be more *guard-like*. He pushed the thoughts from his mind and answered sternly. "No." His heart-beat increased steadily with every question. He kept his hands firmly wrapped around the bottom of his seat.

"Have you been tempted to help a Mùth in any way?"

Todd paled. He wondered if these questions had been explicitly selected. He wondered if they *knew* what he had just done. How he had, *indeed*, just broken the rules.

*Don't over-react, this is just a procedure.*

"No."

"Do ya believe Mùths are dangerous?"

Slight hesitation. Then, "Yes." It wasn't the answer he wanted to give but he knew it was the right one. They were grooming him, making sure that he would turn out to be a big-brainless enforcer like the rest of them, like Locust. He didn't argue. He knew he couldn't. This was the only option for him.

The evaluation only took about thirty minutes. The questions were pretty much all the same in variations of the first few. Todd knew that was purposeful. It was to see if he would slip up and provide a different answer. Locust and Quito grumbled to each other for a few minutes before stalking toward the door. Quito took a minute to clap Todd on the shoulder,

"Toddler ol' boy, take my lookout shift for me, would ya?"

Quito didn't wait for an answer before the door closed behind him. The question was rhetorical, Todd knew that. He was often delegated unwanted shifts from senior guards.

He held still for a minute, waiting for the thunk of Locust and Quito's boots to soften down the corridor before finally releasing his grip on the chair. He bit his lip and slowly uncurled his fingers, his palms and forehead slick with sweat.

His thoughts came crashing back upon him, no longer distracted by the evaluation. *Lana. Shit!* He had definitely crossed the line of guard etiquette. He just hoped no one found out about it.

"Stop it!" he said aloud, cringing immediately at the volume of his voice, though it was barely raised. The small room was sparsely furnished with a singular rectangular table, six chairs, and Keurig machine sitting atop a stool in the corner. Todd shook his head at his own jumpiness. Apprehension vibrated through him. It raced through his heart like a deadly poison winding deeper with every beat. It made him uncharacteristically jumpy.

He pulled open the door standing just beside the coffeemaker. The adjoining room was even smaller than its counterpart. His eyes scanned the pixelated screens that stacked five feet tall in a semi-circle around him. He scanned and scanned until landing on the one he was looking for.

*24-A*

He dropped himself down onto the single swivel chair and stared at the keyboard in front of him. His fingers hovering over the keys. Todd typically didn't mind the extra work. It made the days go by faster. It was a distraction, of sorts. But this, this particular shift was of paramount importance to him.

Todd had originally planned to just hang around the break room a little too long… long enough for someone to shirk their shift onto him. He hadn't anticipated Quito's readiness, but did not question it either. It was exactly what he needed, to be alone in the lookout. The odds of the universe were in his favor today. He wasn't going to tamper with that. He took one last look at the screen just above his eye level, he took a deep breath and pressed the button.

***

Lana pushed herself up onto her elbows. She gasped at the sharp pain that ripped through her side. She clutched her aching abdomen, gasping again as her raw and ripped hands held by her side. Everything came flooding back. She slowly pulled herself up, every muscle weighted with a heaviness only exhaustion could bring.

She brought her eyes to focus, blinking away the bleariness that lingered there. The fog that urged her to slip back down into a peaceful slumber. She was lying on the floor as usual but, there was something different. Lana pinched the blanket draped over her body between her fingers. Its cotton fibers soft and warm beneath her tender fingers. She looked from the bed beside her, and back to the blanket. It was most certainly the accompaniment to the bed.

*But why is it on me?* her brain slowly trudging through the fog of its memory. *I wouldn't have taken the blanket, would I?* Lana groaned and pinched the bridge of her nose.

*What is the last thing I remember? I was in the practical, Todd and Claude were there. I was doing chin ups and then Claude left. That's it.* Lana replayed the same few scenes over and over again in her head trying to push further. She growled in annoyance, "There must be more."

Lana peered around the room, searching for some kind of clue. It felt stupid, but her mind was like a puzzle missing various pieces. Lana grabbed a fistful of the blanket covering her legs. No matter what happened last night, she didn't need to add to Claude's victory by letting him catch her using the small comfort.

"Fuck that." She tossed the blanket. It pathetically made it only halfway. Its other end spilling down toward the floor. Lana sneered at the blanket as if it was its fault that her fatigued body had failed her. A flash of white caught the corner of her eye underneath the blankets' fallen edge. She pushed the rest of the blanket onto the bed, peering below at the object. *A bowl?*

Almost as soon as she saw it, she could smell the savory scent of garlic and spices spiraling up into her nose and down her throat. It immediately sent her stomach into a fury of growls and grumbles.

She slid the plate out, gritting her teeth to muffle the cry of pain, stinging in her freshly blistered hands. There were two pieces of bread and a heaped portion of what looked and smelled like chili.

"What in the worl—"

Her mind snapped back like a ruler hitting a desk. *Todd.* The fogginess cleared away like the sun peaking on a summer day. She remembered Todd coming to get her after the practical. She remembered that, but she still couldn't remember getting back to her room. Her eyes darted to the camera in the corner of her room. The green light was not flashing. *It's not on?*

*Todd.* She could hear his voice in the back of her mind. His strange reassurance like a soft melody between her ears. She couldn't fully pull the words forward from her memory. Todd had taken her back to her room. He'd also gone out of his way, and broken various islander rules to bring her some dinner. Not only that, but she assumed he had also somehow turned her camera off. Lana didn't quite know why he hid the food under the bed when the cameras were off, but she didn't care.

She smiled to herself, and bit into a piece of bread.

*Why would he do that? Does he feel bad for me?* Or perhaps, he could be the link she was hoping for. The link she could easily expose. *If he doesn't fully believe in what the Islanders are doing—or if she could convince him to help her maybe—maybe he is a chance for her to get out of here.*

Lana ran through her next course of action, her mind busy while she ate. She'd be left alone until the morning at least. The gloomy shadow cast from her window told her it was the middle of the night, or early morning. She would have time to rest her body. That was good! She didn't want to add to Claude's ego by appearing hurt and sore... even if she was.

*If Todd turned these cameras off, he might be able to do it again.* Lana chewed her lip as she debated her chances of converting Todd "to the dark side." The thought almost made her laugh.

"How the hell would I even do that?" She shook the thought away and focused on another. It was too risky without knowing how *on-board* he was with the islander life.

"I'll have to figure that out. Test him somehow."

As soon as she said it, she knew it was the right thing to do. She just needed the right circumstances. She stretched her arms out cringing as her muscles corded beneath her skin. She let out a long breath and then repeated the stretch with her legs. She hoped beyond all hope that she did not have another practical tomorrow. She did not fancy her chances of making it through another one like that.

"One day at a time, Lana. One day."

Her gums throbbed and she cupped her mouth and waited for the blood to come. The bleeding had been getting worse. Her medication may have stunted her morphing, but it also really did help with her sensitive gums. She leaned her head back against the cement wall and closed her eyes. She pulled at the blanket again and held it up to her mouth to absorb the blood. She hated swallowing blood. No matter how many times she'd done it in the past, she never got used to the metallic overture tickling her throat.

She slept easily that night, for the first time in a long time. She didn't know if it was from exhaustion or the fact that she finally had some resemblance of a plan. It didn't matter. When the light started peeking through her window, she was up like a shot. She was ready and waiting. The light on the camera was green again. Her brief period of privacy had come and gone. No matter. She knew what her next step was.

Uneasiness weighed on her as the hours crept by and no one came to her room. Not a guard to bring her to breakfast, nor Claude to taunt her. The pressure stacked in her stomach, the levels building upon each other like a beaver's dam. For now, it was bearing the weight, but the branches were splintering.

*What was he playing at? Why would he practically torture me one day and leave me completely isolated the next.*

"He's testing me," she said aloud. "Son of a bitch," she swore, slapping her hand against the wall. "He knew I'd be preparing for another physical practical—so instead he's playing the mental game."

Lana huffed and growled as she paced back and forth. She felt the annoyance slide up the back of her neck and tighten in her shoulders. It was so simple. A classic hostage tactic.

"He doesn't care which way he breaks me. He just wants to break me."

Her theory was quickly proven to be correct. No one came to her room, not with food, not with clothes, not even to talk. She was alone. Isolation was something she was utterly familiar with and yet it had never felt quite like this.

The exhaustion in her body combined with the lack of food lead her thoughts toward delirium. That was dangerous. If she didn't hold out until they brought her food, she wasn't sure what state she would be in. The time ticked away, bringing her closer and closer to her snapping point.

## Chapter Eighteen

She wasn't expecting the visitor that came to her room. The light slap of approaching footsteps sounded almost foreign to her now. She pulled her hair out of her face and ran the back of her hand over her clothes, flattening the creases. She was extra careful not to twinge the blisters on her palms. If it was Claude, she was not going to look like a complete bum. He would be too pleased about that.

She had been fading in and out for hours and had absolutely no idea what time it was. She glanced up to the window, there was a muted light coming through. It was daytime, but its faintness was harder to determine. It could be either early morning, or late evening.

The heavy door pushed open a crack. "H-hello?" a timid voice asked. A familiar petite black-haired woman slipped inside the door.

Lana's eyebrows drew together, her mind puzzled. "Doctor Otazzi?"

The doctor fidgeted with the clipboard in her arms. She pressed her shoulders against the heavy door, standing as far from Lana as she could. "I uh, I'm here to go over a few things."

Lana pushed herself up, using the wall for support. The doctor jumped like a shotgun had gone off screeching wildly, her body jolting against the door, sending her papers flying in the air. She spun and scratched her nails against the handless door behind her with frantic breaths.

Lana jumped, startled by the unexpected shriek and placed a hand over her quickened heart. "Shit!" she cursed annoyed at her own startle reflex.

The woman kept scratching at the door, her voice a whimper as it remained firmly shut.

"I'm not going to hurt you." Lana breathed, her voice agitated.

The doctor froze, her hand still on the door.

Lana groaned. "Look, I'm sorry about the other day. I shouldn't have lashed out at you. It wasn't your fault." Lana sputtered in an attempt to make the doctor more at ease. She was definitely not the one to be afraid of in this place. Lana sighed loudly. "Can you just turn around. I'll stay against the wall here. I promise," she said, patting the wall behind her so the doctor could hear where she was. After a few seconds she finally turned around, her face was as white as a sheet, her small mouth quivering.

"Let's just get this over with, OK?" Lana said. She felt herself sway from the effort of speaking. She was exerting too much energy.

*Dammit! Just stand still and keep your eyes open. You are wasting energy by trying to make her more comfortable.*

The woman nodded quickly and adjusted her stethoscope around her neck. She didn't make a move to pick up her papers still scattered on the floor around her. "I wanted to tell you that your results were conclusive. You are completely healthy."

Lana scrunched her face, "OK?" she said, her brain not understanding the relevance.

The doctor pushed herself further against the door.

"That's all you had to tell me? That I'm healthy?" Lana scooted herself into a seated position. She didn't trust herself to stand any longer. She wrapped her arms around her torso to muffle the grumbles of her stomach.

"Well, yes, that uhm, your tests are in-line with the other patients here."

*Patients? Did they refer to us as patients when talking to this doctor? Or did they tell her something different entirely.*

Lana nodded her head, the answer coming to her clearly. *She doesn't know. She only knows what they have told her, and that's definitely not the whole picture. I'm sure it's difficult to get doctors here in a truthful manner. Withholding key information like the Mùth lineage and an island full of captives, would certainly make things easier. It also meant that the Doctor could return to her regular life afterwards.* Lana's eyes flicked up toward the Doctor. *The Islanders definitely wouldn't appreciate people leaking information about their organization to unwanted ears.*

"Did you hear me?" the doctor squeaked. "Your tests match the other patients completely."

Lana quieted her internal dialogue, refocusing on the woman in front of her. "You line up with them in every aspect." the doctor continued, mistaking Lana's silence for incomprehension. Lana swallowed hard, allowing the words to take root in her mind. She matched. Which meant she carried the same gene. The Mùth gene.

A slight sensation of relief washed over her taking her by surprise. She felt a small branch dislodge from the dam of her anxieties, allowing for a small trickle of water to pass through. The thought of being '*disposed of*' had clearly been affecting her more than she realized.

She would morph. That was good, but at the same time it was bad. *Shit.* A loud knock on the door interrupted their brief conversation.

A shrill voice called, "Doctor Ottazzi, we need you in the foyer for a moment."

Lana heard the familiar slug of the door unlocking and the doctor scurried around the room picking up her papers and flew out the door.

The hateful blonde woman stuck her head in the door. Lana felt her own repulsion twitch in her lips. "Hello, Lana," she said, a wild smile on her face. "She will be back in a couple of hours. In the meantime, I'll get one of the guards to bring you some breakfast." Her voice taking on an uncharacteristically sing-song tone, floating from word to word. She spoke in such a kind British fashion that Lana almost had to remind herself who was speaking to her.

Annette smiled, a similar smile to the one her brother boasted. The one that looked sweet and conniving at the same time. It made the hair on her arms stand up. She glared at the woman unsure of what to make of this... newfound compassion.

"Be back in a jiff." She smiled.

It was Todd who finally showed up with food for Lana, and he was a very welcome sight. His arms were piled high with different dry goods and a cup of oatmeal. He nodded to the bed when he came through the door and Lana needed no further explanation. She shoved her hand under the cot and pulled her plate and bowl from the day before. Todd dropped a handful of berries into the bowl and put it on her bed.

Lana looked at the tall lanky boy and couldn't hide her thankfulness. She smiled at him, mildly impressed. He'd figured out a way to get the dishes out without causing a fuss. Lana plunked herself down onto the floor and started spooning mouthfuls of the oatmeal into her body. The warm liquid slid down her throat in a gloriously satisfying fashion. She shivered with fulfilment.

Her consciousness increased in vividness by the second. It was amazing what a simple amount of sustenance could do. Todd leaned against the desk, the corner of his mouth turned upward in the tiniest of smiles.

Lana had consumed the food in record time and sat quietly. She knew what she wanted to say next, but propelling the words out of her mouth was harder than she'd anticipated. She felt the steady increase of her heart matching the nerves tingling in her fingers.

*This is my shot. I might not get another when no one else is around. I have to do it now. I have to test him.*

"Todd?"

He lifted his head, the smile still there.

"The other day when you turned the *camera's off*," Lana said, mouthing the last two words. His eyes turned wide and he snapped straight. His head swiveled between the camera in the corner and back to Lana. His hands flapping wilding in a hushing motion. Lana bit her lip to muffle her giggle.

"Relax," she said, his hand now close enough, she grabbed it and squeezed. "I know they are back on." Lana shook her head. Her brown hair shaking over her bare shoulders.

"I don't care about that," she said, tucking her hair behind her ears. "Well, I do, that was awesome, but that's not what I was getting at."

Lana dropped her eyes to the floor. She couldn't look at him for this. "OK, I'm just going to say it." She took a breath. "I morphed," she said and squeezed every muscle in her body as she held her breath.

She waited for his response, but heard nothing. After an

excruciatingly long thirty seconds, she finally lifted her head. A startled look of pure incomprehension crossed his face. He caught Lana's glance and adjusted himself appropriately, he cleared his throat, "Mr. Armstrong will be pleased to hear—"

"He doesn't know," Lana interrupted.

Todd pulled a shaky hand through his hair. His chest rising and falling quickly. "Wha–what do you mean?"

"I think you know what I mean. I morphed, Todd, after my practical. Right here in my dorm." Lana exhaled and gestured around her.

"And the cameras were—" he gasped, the answer taking shape in his mind. He spun around and looked to her for confirmation. She nodded slightly.

"Oh shit. Oh shit, shit, shit! This is not good. Shit!" he sputtered and paced back and forth. He covered the room in two strides before turning around again, and again, and again. He stopped suddenly and turned to Lana. "Wait, if you—what are you?"

"I didn't exactly have a mirror."

Todd nodded and started pacing again. "Right, of course," he mumbled.

Lana nodded, folding her hands in her lap. "I can tell you what I did see? Will that help?"

He didn't answer, just continued pacing. Lana pulled the lie forward she had fabricated last night. "I had this short sandy-colored snout, these like huge, huge paws and only a stub for a tail." A vague enough answer. It could be several different things.

He mumbled something Lana didn't quite catch.

"What?"

He turned to face her, "Bobcat?"

Lana stayed quiet and let him come to his own conclusions.

*It doesn't matter what he thinks I am. It matters what he does with that information,* she reminded herself.

"For fuck sakes." He threw his hands up in the air. "How am I going to get myself out of this one?" He stopped in the middle of the room, his shoulders hunched, eyes drawn. "I have to go," he whispered, heading for the door.

"Wait—" Lana called after him. "What are you going to do?"

He turned to her, his eyes full of remorse. "I'm sorry, Lana. I am so, so sorry."

Her heart dropped into her stomach with the resounding thud of the closed door. She felt the weight of her realization crash down upon her, pummeling her like a wave crashing against the sand. *He's going to tell Claude.* His loyalty was not as easily swayed as she had originally thought. Which meant he's not going to be of any help to her.

"Shit!" She smacked the floor.

"Well, back to square one. Now Claude is going to think I've morphed." She had mis-read Todd's character. She hadn't really spent much time considering the consequences of her little tale. "Fuck, that backfired, didn't it?"

She spent the next hour drumming her fingers along the concrete floor. She was getting used to her little room. It oddly reminded her a lot of her room in the cabin. Simple, impersonal and plain. She remembered asking Aunt Alice for pictures and keepsakes to decorate her desolate bedroom but the answer was always the same. "The more you have the harder it is to walk away and the more distracted you become with unimportant things."

Lana groaned as the words rang as loud as a church bell in her mind. As if Aunt Alice had just spoken to her. The reminder sent an unholy ache through her body. Not a physical one. An ache of longing, loss, and absence. The longest amount of time she'd ever spent away from her aunt was three days. This was a level she was entirely unaccustomed to. She wished more than anything she could talk to her again. See her face, see her wobbly shuffle-like walk. Lana realized with a start what she was doing. It was a feeling she hadn't felt in a very long time. Fourteen years to be exact.

"Grief, my old friend, it's been a while." She'd felt this pain before when her parents were killed, but this was very different. She didn't remember much from that time, only certain titbits stood out. She remembered missing her parents. She remembered crying when Aunt Alice told her they were in heaven. She remembered she had a hard time sleeping for a little while. But, she also remembered that it got better. It hurt less and less every day until eventually it stopped hurting and their absence became normal.

She couldn't imagine the same thing happening to Aunt Alice. She would miss her forever. She'd never be able to get used to it, of that she was sure.

Boredom seeped into her mind like the silky threads of cotton sheets. It poured into the crevices of her brain getting heavier and darker with each passing moment. She fidgeted with anything she could get her hands on, groaning loudly when that object finally lost interest to her. Her body ached, and she caught herself moving quite gingerly so as not to aggravate her sore muscles.

She followed Todd's lead and began pacing her room. Something had her incredibly anxious, antsy and agitated. It tugged at the bottom of her stomach impatiently. An unrelenting flicker like the flame of a fire. She knew the doctor would be back, but she still didn't understand why. She didn't even want to think about Annette. What she wanted, what her angle was. The ambiguity pressed on her mind, the fire burning stronger as her thoughts fanned the flames.

She was pacing again when the large door pushed open. Lana approached with a stilted step. The petite doctor walked in followed sharply by Annette.

"Thank you for waiting, Lana," she chimed. "Go ahead, Doctor Otazzi."

The doctor didn't lift her head. She kept her eyes glued to her little clipboard. Her hands gripped the plastic with a tightness that turned her knuckles white. Lana felt bad for attacking this woman, a slight inkling of guilt and regret mixing together. This woman who was so clearly just as much a victim as herself. Maybe not in the same way as Lana, but this doctor definitely didn't feel safe, and that violation alone was enough to ignite Lana's sympathy.

"I have come to the concise conclusion, based on your results, and the information Miss Armstrong most recently presented to me, that you have no reason to not be morphing."

Annette looked at Lana expectantly. Lana's eyes widened with surprise. She looked from the doctor and back to Annette. So, she did know about Mùths. *Well, that dissipates some of my sympathy. No wait—she said recently informed, so she didn't know before, but she knows now, why?*

Her mind jumped back to Todd. *Did he already tell the Armstrongs, is that what she's getting at? They think I morphed. Fuck!*

"Well, do you have anything you would like to tell us, Lana?"

Lana could feel the panic rising from her stomach. She quickly forced the spiraling worries from her mind. She didn't have time to unwind those intricacies right now. She forced an eye roll at Annette and leaned herself against the wall, under her window. "Tell you? Like what?" she said, attempting to look disinterested.

"Oh, I don't know maybe that you have been capable of morphing this entire time and that you're just remarkably apt at controlling your shifts," Annette sniped, rounding her thin lips around every word with devilish conviction. Lana's heartbeat grew louder in her chest. The panic itching its way forward again. She swallowed hard, pushing it back down. *Todd definitely told them my story about morphing.* Annette was too sure of herself. She was oddly content about something. "And," she continued. "That you have been lying this entire time."

Lana remained silent and pulled her chocolate brown hair out of her face.

"You might have my brother convinced, but I do not fall victim to those big doe-eyes of yours," she said, her voice slowly reverting to its signature screechy vibrato.

"I don't know what you're talking about."

"Oh, I think you do. So, I am going to ask you this one time," she hissed, "after that, the consequences are on you. Do you understand?"

Lana said nothing and crossed her arms over her chest, a slight jab of disobedience toward the hateful woman. Annette pursed her lips, a moment of anger flashing across her face. "All right," she quipped, "Lana, what is your morph?"

Lana exhaled and rolled her eyes dramatically, she summoned as much conviction as she could manage and responded slowly, "My answer has not changed since the last time we had this conversation," she said, her mind avoiding the answer she knew Annette was searching for. The fake answer she'd mistakenly told Todd.

*It doesn't matter what she thinks she knows. It's not true and the only way to get out of this is to tell the truth.* "I don't know."

Fire gleamed behind Annette's eyes, a sick smile twisting across her small face. "You know Lana, for once, that is just what I was hoping you would say" – she licked her lips with satisfaction – "Quito, could you come in here, please."

The large guard lumbered into the room, he stood silently behind Annette and awaited her command, like a watchdog waiting to be released. "You remember what we talked about, Quito?" The guard bobbed his head in acknowledgment.

"Go ahead," she said, turning to look at the camera in the corner of the room. "The cameras are off."

Lana took a step back hating herself for giving in to the fear creeping up her spine. Her heartbeat lunging deeper with the passing seconds. The guard jumped and Lana would have dodged it, *quite easily,* but he didn't jump at her.

He tackled the doctor to the ground and slammed his fist into her head. Lana froze, shock overtaking her body. The doctor let out a terrible scream. It consumed the small angular room and echoed off the walls at an excruciating decibel. The guard didn't falter, he continued to punch, and knee the woman on the ground.

"What the hell are you doing?" Lana screamed, taking a step toward the woman. Annette responded with her own step. She matched Lana's and faced her head on. The angry women held out a taser, the metallic end pointed squarely at Lana's chest.

"Make a move, Lana, I beg you. Make a move."

Lana stilled. Her heart racing. "WHAT ARE YOU DOING?" The doctor's screams were so loud Lana could barely hear her own words.

The guard pulled the now limp woman to her feet and dragged his fingernails across her cheek in one long drawn-out motion. Lana couldn't help herself, she lurched forward in the woman's defense.

"STOP IT, YOU'RE GOING TO KILL HER!"

Pain exploded through Lana's torso traveling through her

body with the force of a small car. She screamed and fell to the ground, her body convulsing and spasming uncontrollably. Lana's long brown hair sprawled out on the ground beneath her and she felt her consciousness slip. A black fog pushed at the corners of her eyes. She knew she couldn't hold on much longer, especially with Annette's death grip on the electrical current. She let herself fall into a deep darkness, but not before she watched the guard drag the doctor's battered body out of her dorm like a forgotten rag doll.

\*\*\*

Lana came to lying in a heap of hair, drool and sweat on the floor of her dorm.

"Eh hem," a woman's voice sounded.

Lana did her best not to cringe. She tried to speak, but her voice came out gravelly and catching. She dropped her head and cleared her voice before speaking again.

"Don't bother," Annette said, "I don't care to hear whatever you have to say. It's my turn to talk." She tossed a pair of black spandex shorts and sports bra at her. "Put those on."

Lana took them with a look of incomprehension. *She's dressing me now? What is this woman playing at?* The spandex clothes were a matching set, jet black with a metallic blue outline. It glimmered slightly in the faint light of the window. She turned her back to Annette and started taking off her clothes.

"Wipe yourself off with this." The woman spat, tossing a wet towel at her and drumming her fingers along the desk impatiently. Lana pulled the clothes on, it took her longer than she wanted. Delightfulness and intimidation spewed from Annette like a noxious gas. Lana tried not to look uncomfortable, but it was difficult, her limbs were aching and heavy. She kept her sundress on and slipped the pieces on underneath, which only made it more of a struggle. But she wasn't going to just fully undress in front of this tyrant. She didn't hold that much power over her body. Not yet anyway.

She noticed her name, *Chase*, scrawled across the right thigh of the shorts and left shoulder strap of the bra. Annette's arms were crossed over her small chest. Her breath coming and going with complete ease. The sight unnerved her greatly. This woman was rarely calm. She reached her hand out expectantly.

Lana raised her eyebrows in confusion. *What does she want now, a high five?*

"The dress, dear girl." Annette sighed, her arm outstretched.

Lana bit down on her tongue to muffle the curses she wanted to let fly. *I don't need to aggravate her any more. She's armed and clearly has no apprehensions about using it.* Lana pinched the hemline of her dress and pulled it over her head. She tossed it to Annette's hand.

"So, Miss Chase, I have some bad news."

Lana waited, trying her best to look unaffected by everything that had just happened. She couldn't help but feel vulnerable in this outfit. It showed more skin than her bathing suit. She stood tall and faced the woman down. *I won't give her the satisfaction. I won't let her see that I am uncomfortable. That's exactly what she wants.* Lana's core flexed with every breath, her lengthy muscles tight and ready to fight.

"You have had your third strike."

"What?"

"You know very well what I am talking about, dear. You attacked that poor doctor who was on her way home. She only came to give you an update and you flat out attacked her without cause."

Lana's chest tightened. Her pulse quickened. "We cannot tolerate this grievous offense, and so, Miss Chase, my darling, you will be going to the Underground." A slow smile spread across the woman's tiny face. It sickened Lana in every way. An immediate sense of dread washed over her. *Whatever makes her THIS happy, is not good for me.*

"You set me up?" Lana breathed. "Why?"

"Oh, dear naïve little Lana. Did you think you were the only one who could play your little game? I believe you know your morph and that you've known it all along. You have been exceptionally well trained I'll give you that, but I am no longer following your ruse. This is my game now. I hope you are ready to play."

Annette turned on the last word and left the room. Two guards were there in an instant. Lana thought about fighting them, but the act wouldn't change anything. She was already going to the Underground and she didn't fancy her chances in a fight. Her body was severely fatigued and malnourished, before she'd even been electrocuted. Any effort now, would be minimal and probably hurt her more than help her.

She pushed her shoulders back. She would go, without a fight. She would go calmly and without the slightest inclination that she was afraid. Which was easy because she wasn't afraid. Oh no, she was terrified.

The Underground, much like her morph, had a big unending question mark hanging next to it. She did know, however, that out of everything that went on the island, the one thing that all the Morphers had in common was an intense fear of the Underground.

That thought didn't bode well for her now.

# Chapter Nineteen

Claude sat in the helicopter adjusting his position so he could show the pilot where to put it down. They never wanted to get too close to a city or town, it would draw too much attention.

"Just to your left there, mate." Claude crackled into the mic attached to his headset and pointed to a grassy park. The pilot nodded and pulled on the controls in front of him slightly. The large metal machine banked left and started descending into a perfectly secluded valley. He had scouted the spot earlier in the week on some area maps back on the island.

Claude flipped through the pages in front of him studying more of the material that he already knew by heart. He was an efficient man. He liked to have his corners tight, tucked and pressed, even so he never liked leaving the island. Or rather, he never liked leaving someone else in charge.

It is for that reason that Annette typically captained the recon efforts. She was capable of many things but keeping her emotions in check was not one of them. Since they'd exited the womb together thirty years ago, she'd been his responsibility.

He was a shadow of sorts. An ever-consistent hovering presence. He provided her with the conscience that she was born without. Annette was blissfully unaware of her own irrationality, something that had proved both beneficial and detrimental at very different times in their lives.

She often found him to be a nuisance, an overprotective brother. Claude let her believe that. She had no idea that without him she would have probably ended up in jail, a psych ward or dead. He remembered the conversation his mother had with him when he was only a child. The memory sliding to the front of his brain.

*"It is your job, Claude, to protect her and keep her calm." He puffed out his small boyish chest proud of the responsibility his mother was entrusting him with.*

She explained how Annette was different, her mind worked differently and that she could easily lash out without warning. *"But remember, you are not to tell your sister any of this. She wouldn't be happy if we told her. You want her to be happy, don't you, Claude, my love?"*

The young boy nodded eagerly. His ear-length blonde hair bobbing along with him.

*"That's my good boy. She needn't know she's any different than you or I. If she did, I fear she would succumb to her abnormalities, and sweetie what would the neighbors think if I had a daughter who was a socio—"* The pretty woman cleared her throat abruptly. She shook her head and threw her son a sinfully sweet smile.

*"I think you understand, love. Be her guardian."*

Claude exhaled a long breath and pulled a hand through his perfectly styled blonde hair. It wasn't easy. She had come quite close to some disastrous decisions over the years. He'd learned a long time ago that giving her the reins in small carefully selected doses was an easy way to satisfy her need for control and dominance, without causing a disaster. Such was the case with allowing her this opportunity to oversee the island while he was away.

The pilot had just set the chopper on the ground and gave him and the crew the thumbs up. Claude ducked his head and jumped out, the blades thumping loudly over his head. He waited for his team to assemble in front of him. They had been briefed before take-off so they didn't need much direction now.

"All right!" he shouted. "About two miles south of here is the town of Charles. We're looking for a girl by the name of Levi. Says here—" Claude pointed to his papers. "Eighteen years old, offspring of the Leung clan. If you're not familiar with the clan, the morph is an Osprey."

The team of guards nodded in response and headed off down the road. Claude turned and gave the okay for the helicopter to take off again. It soared out of sight seamlessly. Claude hunkered himself down on a park bench nearby and continued to finger through his files.

After a while he pulled out his radio, "Team Strong, update?"

The response was immediate. The members of his "Strong team" pleasing his desire for efficiency, although, that is why they were selected for this position. It was one of the most coveted on the island. A five-person strike team of sorts. They performed their own training and had their own ranks within the unit. Since implementing the superior tactical team the successfulness of their extractions had increased ten-fold.

"Guard central reporting. We are approaching the town now. About to begin recon detail."

"10-4. Update with progress."

Claude sat back and closed his eyes. This was the first peaceful moment he had in a long time. He tried to clear his mind and appreciate the silence, but it kept traveling along that familiar string. *Lana.*

He didn't want to think about her, she was probably one of the biggest proponents of his stress. Any time he felt like he was making progress with her she would do something that sent him flying backward.

A woman jogged passed him following the trail he was sitting near, up toward town. She slowed as she passed him smiling brightly. Claude nodded in response and returned to his papers. He was used to the attention. He knew women were easily attracted to men that looked like him. Trim, fit, and handsomely well groomed. Lana though, his charm never quite seemed to sway her.

It had not failed him with the other girls on the island. His charismatic attitude was often enough to convince them to conform. It was easy enough. The right combination of attention, kindness and protection in a fearful situation, usually garnered positive results. As shallow as that might sound, it was a formula that had proven its worth, over and over again. Yet, there was something so wonderfully unique and devilishly frustrating about this girl.

Claude considered for a moment the legend surrounding her bloodline. Her father was a lynx, an extraordinarily rare morph, if Lana flipped that switch, it would be monumentally lucrative to the Islanders.

Big cats were incredibly uncommon morphs mostly because the forebears of the Mùth bloodline originated the race with an unbreakable bond between human and animal. It is said when the animal's died the emotional separation was too great, and so the spirit of the animal re-joined with its human counterpart.

The problem was that cats were such independent and solitary creatures that formulating a Mùth bond with them was pretty much unthinkable, not to mention dangerous. The increase in poaching and game hunting drove populations so low, that it is nearly impossible to find a still-existing Mùths with that morph.

Claude tipped his pen toward his mouth. He chewed on the

cap, his thoughts sliding from one to the next in an easy manner. Lana could also take another route, as her mother's heir.

The Islanders began when a collaboration of a private firms and governmental agencies and funding came together to form one entity. They had existed for about sixty years now, spanning roughly two to three generations of morphers. The mystery behind her morph was simply because her ancestors were able to evade capture for those years.

There had been many different facilities over the years, but each one came with its own list of problems. That was until Claude's father purchased Zefreth Island eight years ago. The Islanders really started to flourish then. Especially under Claude's new command.

Claude flipped to the one page in his folder he had looked at one thousand times before. The one tracing Lana's lineage. He had spent hours compiling the information for her file, and the lack of detail irked him greatly. Abigail Mason's notes were added now. Some idlings about repressed memories, strong defiant personality traits, and a calculated intelligence. He skimmed over the last page, the one tracing Lana's lineage.

If his meanderings were correct, Lana's paternal bloodline originated in Rankin Inlet, Nunavut and her mother's originated in the mountains of Idaho. He had the puzzle pieces, he just had not quite figured out how they fit together.

The radio crackled, and Claude quipped a reply. He turned his wrist to check the time. He had only been gone from the island for a few hours. How much damage could Annette possibly do in that short amount of time? He shook the thought from his head. It felt like a jinx.

"I should never put restrictions on her. I know her better than anybody."

***

Lana faced a concrete wall, standing in between the two guards, Pede and the guard Quito, from earlier. He had tattoos covering both his arms, somehow making him more intimidating. They weren't restraining her, but they did keep an eerily close distance, their arms brushing her shoulder every now and again.

She could not remember how many flights of stairs they'd descended to get here. The walls reeked of mildew and dampness and sound echoed through the short tunnel with alarming volume. Unlike the rest of the facility, there was no artwork hanging here, no paint, and no cheerily fake attempts to make the space look like anything other than what it was. It unsettled Lana greatly.

The Islanders were always so keen to maintain a good first impression. They liked to present a flashy and warm exterior so that you would not discover the callus and uncomfortable interior. There were no distractions down here.

Discomfort rose within her. She was acutely aware of how far she was from the earth, from outside, from the grass. She was surrounded in layers upon layers of man-made hardened sludge, and it weighed on her.

Aunt Alice had warned her about that. The weakening effect of her body separated from the one thing that gave it light, strength and hope. Lana had undergone some isolation training, but not a lot. It was hard to find a space suitable and she avoided it when she could. The effect was so strenuous, like someone slowly draining the blood from her body.

She wished now that she had spent more time focusing on those things. On her weaknesses, instead of exploiting what she was already good at. She was good at running, why did she spend so much of her time doing it?

The answer was simple, and her heart knew what it was. As soon as she started to notice the change in Aunt Alice's behavior, she had altered her training so she could take care of her. She ran because it was easy, it was quick, and required little thought. It gave her ample time to exercise her body and yet, not leave her aunt alone for a prolonged period.

Lana heard Annette's heels clicking against the floor behind her, approaching quickly. The sound reverberated off the walls much too loudly. The frail woman placed a bony hand on her shoulder and Lana bit her lip to stop from cringing. She dug her nails in and ripped Lana around to face her.

"I'm sure you've heard of the Underground, Lana," Annette said, pausing before she continued. A well-rehearsed speech licking from her thin lips. "Normally, Mùths only spend a few hours down here and a couple of days in recuperation. However, due to the extent of your grievous action and the terribly unprovoked attack upon the doctor, I think a couple days might suit you better."

Lana felt the cold liquid dread slink down her throat. She clenched her jaw tight, keeping her face as blank as she could manage. She did not want Annette to see her fear. Quito snapped his head up. He stammered out a few incoherent syllables before Annette's shrill voice cut across the corridor like an out of tune siren.

"Don't ever speak out of turn, Quito. How dare you question my authority. Unless you would like to join Miss Chase in an equally torturous experience, I suggest you keep your stammerings to yourself." Before he had a chance to blink, she sneered, "Do I make myself quite clear?"

Quito clamped his mouth shut and made a small motion to

say he understood. Annette slid her finger over the keypad next to the door and flicked her finger at Pede to open it. A wave of nausea overtook Lana immediately. She entered the small square room probably only 12ft by 12ft. A lot smaller than she had imagined. A concrete base wrapped from the floor to the ceiling. The room was completely empty other than a small rectangular hole in the ground. It was about the size of a hot tub.

Lana fell to her knees, her breathing fast and uneven. She clutched at her throat. Her airway felt obstructed. Each breath she took ravaged the insides of her writhing body, slicing at her like a butcher wielding their favorite clever.

Heels clicked on the floor behind her, Lana felt her hair yanked backward. She gasped sharply and looked up into the ugliest pair of brown eyes she had ever seen. She wanted to scream at Annette, spit on her, fight her, something, but she could not move.

"Now, Lana." Annette gushed, her mouth salivating around every word like a hyena stalking its prey. Lana writhed under her grasp.

"Not only is this room filled with a special chemical compound called Venenum." She paused, and circled in front of Lana, who was on the ground on her hands and knees. "What we like to call Venom."

Lana squeezed her eyes shut, her stomach flexing hard with shortened breaths. Annette knelt down and pressed her thin lips against Lana's ear. "It makes every fiber of your being, every muscle, every nerve, every blood cell in your body want to morph. You will yearn for it, strive for it, and crave it more than anything in the world, but the Venom also prevents the transition. It's a fascinating little elixir we concocted."

As if on cue, Lana let out a horrifying shriek, and Annette

flashed her a sickeningly pleased smile. "Yes, just like that dear. I'm told it's quite excruciating." She popped up again and moved to the side. "Oh, there is also the added element, or should I say eliminated element of the earth," she said, holding her finger to her lip like a cutesy schoolchild. "Which really helps this room pack a wallop." She smiled.

Pede moved forward and dragged Lana into the pit. His hands pinching her around the arms. He secured her limp body with four heavy shackles, one on each hand and foot. The chains were long and heavy, and it was a struggle for Pede to lift them.

Tears streamed down her cheeks, the pain like fire coursing through her blood. She screamed again, this time long and agonizing. Her core flexed hard detailing the lines of her abs. Her thick hair matted around her as she twisted in anguish.

"Maybe after this, you'll be more *forward* with your morph."

Lana heard the heavy door sink shut after them but did not want to believe they were gone. Did not want to believe she would be stuck here. She screamed again, a sound she very rarely emitted. A defeating sound.

The pain was like nothing she had ever experienced before. The pain was not localized to one area nor was it one singular feeling. Unlike when you break a bone or scrap a knee where the pain is concentrated in one area. The air attacked her in an enthralling fashion.

Her throat burned like the tip of an iron fire poker. Hot and searing. The very breath that filled her desperate lungs also tortured her. The muscles beneath her skin twisted under a sharp piercing pressure. Similar to what pins and needles would feel like but dialed up to a thousand. Her skin burned cold like the bitter bite of a blizzard storm. It stung her flesh and tore at her body.

She could not formulate thoughts. She could barely summon the strength to breath. She could feel though. She could feel absolutely everything. She laid in a heap on the floor. She did not know if she was crying. She did not know how much time had passed. She didn't know if she'd moved at all since she'd been dropped here. All she knew was that she was screaming. She screamed until there was nothing left in her voice to scream. Then she collapsed.

She came to a couple times, only to pass out again a few minutes later. Every time followed the same pattern. She would try to scream a combination of panic, fear and pain crushing down upon her. Each empty scream felt like an old razor blade dragged backward along her vocal cords. The venom would flash across her body in a series of unrelenting tremors and pulverize her movements.

Lights out again, and again… and again.

# Chapter Twenty

Todd paced back and forth in the lunchroom. His thought spinning so quickly he could barely hold on to them. Anxiety crawled on his skin like the marching feet of a thousand ants. He could not shake the feeling that something was wrong.

As hard as he tried to push the thoughts from his head they came tumbling back with fire. He hadn't seen Lana for twenty-four hours which in normal circumstances would be no big deal, but these weren't normal circumstances. Annette was in charge, and conveniently the exact duration of her reign coincided perfectly with the time he had not seen Lana.

Well, that was a lie. He had *seen* her, or rather the back of her, as she headed down the east stairwell with Pede and Quito. That's what was bothering him. There wasn't anything down that way. Nothing, except the Underground. It had to just be a scare tactic, right? It had to be something in the Islanders playbook to get her to morph.

*Her Morph. The Morph she told me about. Did she tell someone else and this was her punishment? She hasn't been to any meals since then. She can't still be down there, right? Surely, she is back in her dorm by now.*

"Just relax, Todd. You barely know her anyways. No matter what happens it's not your fault. I mean, it can't be. Right?" He breathed out a shaky breath and wrung his hands out. There was a small knock on the door and Todd ripped it open to find Riley standing there, startled and wide eyed.

"Umm," the boy stammered surprised. "Hi?"

"Hey, Riley. Here, come in here, quick." He yanked the small boy by his shoulders into the lunchroom.

"I'm not supposed to be in here."

"Shhh, just tell me something quick and we'll go."

Riley took a step back, "OK, OK?"

"Have you seen Lana recently?"

Riley took a moment, suspicion climbing over his face. "No? I haven't, but that's happened before with Lana, she's always getting herself in trouble."

Todd shook his head, his hands shaking. "No, not like that. I think this time it's different." He moved to open the door and Riley slipped out as quickly as possible. Todd remembered the boy hated to be in any position where he could possibly get in trouble, and a pang of guilt shot through him.

Riley pointed to the bench outside the room. "We have a few minutes before dinner. Did you want to talk here instead of our usual walk? You seem jumpier than normal?" Todd nodded and chewed on his lip. He slunk his large frame down beside Riley. Neither boy spoke for a few minutes.

"So, what are you saying exactly?" Riley asked.

Todd groaned and ran a frustrated hand through his hair. "Lana told me something the other day that I think might get her into trouble if someone else found out" – he paused – "and might get me into trouble if they find out that I knew."

Riley's eyebrows drew together in a look of confusion. He took a moment. "By something you meannnn," Riley said, drawing out the last word. He followed Todd's gaze toward the east staircase. Todd watched the understanding filter into his eyes like shards of lights spreading through a window. He dropped his head into his hands and let out a long-pained groan.

"Oh."

"Oh, oh? all you have to say is oh?"

"You're referring to the Underground, right?" Riley sat back, "If something happened it would be her third strike."

Todd didn't respond. He peeled his fingers off his face and groaned again, more dramatically this time. Riley nodded and tapped Todd on the thigh. "You know this conversation might go a little smoother if you contributed more than gurgled noises."

Todd felt a smile tug at the corners of his mouth. Riley could always make him laugh. He shoved the small boy to the side. A few moments passed in silence before he spoke again. "God, this is so fucked up."

"Which part exactly?" Riley enthused. "The fact that we live our lives on a secret island? The fact that we can transform into essentially spirit animals, or that there's a medieval torture chamber in the basement?"

Todd sent Riley an unholy glare.

"OK, OK," Riley raised his hands in surrender to the piping look from the guard. "If Lana is in the underground, what exactly do you plan on doing about it?"

Todd dropped his shoulders, an inkling of defeat washing over him. "I don't know."

"Why is it that you care so much, Mr. Guard?" he teased.

Todd's cheeks flushed an uncomfortable bright red. "I'm just worried, that's all."

"Mmmhmm." Riley patted his leg. "Would it be kind of like a quickened heartbeat, thought consuming, can't take your eyes off her kind of worry?"

"Look, I don't have that answer for you right now Riles. All I know is that Annette has been in charge for about twenty-four hours, and Annette—well, you know how she can get. She's not rational."

"—and she's not fond of Lana," Riley added, his tone lower and concerned.

"Do you know how long Morphers usually stay in the Underground? I mean who's been down there the longest?"

A cold look passed over Riley's face. "I don't know really. No one really likes to talk about it."

Todd let out an aggravated noise. He patted his hands along his khaki pants. His patience waning. "I just want to know if she's OK that's all. But I have no frame of reference. She's been my first full time guard detail," He exhaled another groan, "I don't know what to do."

"I have an idea," Riley piped.

Todd turned his head slowly. "Please share with the rest of the class."

"We talk to someone who has been to the Underground."

"Do you have anyone in mind?"

"Just one, Bennet."

Todd's face fell. He crossed his arms over his chest. "Bennet will never talk to me. He hates guards, he hates the island. He won't tell me anything."

Riley sighed. "He doesn't have to tell *you*. He just has to tell me." Riley folded his hands in his lap. "It shouldn't be too hard. He's so incredibly personable and has so many friends."

"I think the odds of Bennet talking to you are just as good as the odds of him talking to me."

"It's worth a shot, isn't it? Or would you rather just sit here worrying all night long?"

\*\*\*

Bennet was sitting at the picnic table furthest from the doors and furthest from everyone else in the Oval. His shoulders hunched and his dinner sitting in front of him barely touched. Riley took a breath, and approached. "Eh hem," Riley cleared his throat. "Um Bennet?" he squeaked.

The dark-haired boy didn't turn around, he simply hunched his shoulders further in a quite determined 'go away,' movement.

"Bennet, could we have a moment please." Todd asked more firmly. The boy's back stiffened, and he shifted his head slightly to see Riley and Todd standing behind him.

"Well, if it isn't a lanky guard and his mini me. To what do I owe the intrusion?"

Riley skittered around the table and sat himself across from Bennet. Todd stood off to the side, his eyes sweeping over the morphers in the Oval. Bennet scrunched his face up and jabbed a thumb toward Todd.

"What's his deal?"

"We just want to ask you something."

Bennet tilted his head and looked from one boy to the other. "Ah, I get it. You're trying to make it look like you're on duty instead of talking to me."

Riley cut in before Todd could interject. "He has no problem talking to you. It's just the other guards might get suspicious."

"Oh well, pray tell, for you have captured my keen interest."

"It's about Lana."

Bennet stabbed a vegetable with his fork and pulled at it slowly with his teeth. "Who?"

"Lana, you know, the new girl. Long brown hair, gray eyes, about this tall?" Riley gestured.

"Sorry." Bennet shook his head. "There are a lot of people here."

"Oh, give it a rest, Bennet," Todd whispered.

Riley nodded vehemently, his irritability rising. "Yeah, come on. The girl who decked you in the foyer."

His face flushed pink and he stopped mid chew, "Oh, her."

"Yeah, her," Riley sassed.

"What about her?"

Riley looked at Todd who gave him a small nod of approval. Riley leaned forward, his strawberry blonde hair falling into his eyes. "Well, Todd here hasn't seen her in almost a day."

"And that matters to me because?"

"Well, I guess it doesn't but—"

"Great then we're done here."

Riley smacked his hand on the table. "Stop it. OK, just stop it. I get it you're the big bad Bennet who talks to no-one, helps no one and wants nothing to do with anyone. I get it, but Lana is my friend, OK? She is my friend and goddammit you will answer my question and then I'll leave you alone forever. Sound good?"

Bennet leaned back and smiled. "Well now, didn't mean to rile you up little fox. Go ahead, I'll be as helpful as I can manage without succumbing to my *better-than-thou* tendencies."

Riley rolled his eyes. "It's not just that she hasn't been seen for a day. And well, I'm sure you know Annette has been in charge and that's already bad news times two 'cause she doesn't like Lana. To top it all off, Todd saw Lana being escorted down the east stairwell. So, we're afraid that she might—"

"You think she's in the Underground?" Bennet asked.

Riley nodded, his eyes bulging with fear. "Well." Bennet shrugged. "What do you want me to do about it."

"Nothing, no. Not really. We just need to know how long…" Riley looked around and lowered his voice. "How long Morphers spend down there."

"You want to know how long sentences can be?"

"Yes!" Riley exhaled gratefully.

"There isn't exactly a chart, Riley."

"Right. Well, yeah I know that, but maybe you could tell us how long you spent down there?"

Bennet sucked on his teeth and pushed his food away from him. His nostrils flared and he blew out a long breath. "I don't know. It felt like forever."

Riley's shoulders fell. "What?"

"I didn't exactly have a clock with me and it's very disorienting. I still have no idea how much time passed. It took me a couple days to even be lucid enough to re-join daily activities."

"It took you *days* to recover?" Riley whispered, disbelief coloring his words.

Bennet nodded. "Yeah, little fox. I know nobody cares about, how did you put it? *The big bad Bennet?* So, no one truly notices when I'm not around." The boy huffed, shooting a glance at Todd. "Nobody should have to go through it. I wouldn't be surprised if it could kill a Morpher if they were down there long enough."

Todd went rigid. His heart hammering in his chest. *Lana.*

\*\*\*

By the time, the morning rolled around Todd was simply fitful. He hadn't slept all night. He had no idea if Lana was in her dorm, the Underground, or somewhere else entirely. His anxiousness surprised him. He hadn't realized how much he cared about the girl. Maybe it was because she was nice to him. Maybe, it was because normally a girl like her would never give an awkward guy like him the time of day. Mostly, it was because he didn't trust Annette and something kept nagging at him. Something telling him that Lana was in trouble.

News that Claude was back on the island, traveled fast. It felt as if everyone let out a collective breath that they'd been holding since his departure. All awaiting a detonation from the hot-headed, less-calculated sister. Todd was supposed to be at his post all day until his break at lunch. He knew he couldn't wait, but he also knew the severity of interrupting Claude.

"Sir?" Todd squeaked, rapping his knuckles on his office door.

Claude cast his eyes up from his papers, a look of irritation and surprise flickering. "Todd? I hope this is important."

"I believe—" he coughed and cleared his throat. "I believe it is, sir."

"Well, go on then."

"Sir, as you know I am Lana's assigned guard, and since your absence I have not seen her once."

"What are you telling me, Todd? Someone else took over your post and you're upset about it? Please take up these kindergarten affairs with guard superior." Claude flicked a dismissive hand at Todd, shooing him out of the room.

He wanted to turn and leave, scurry out that door like a mouse into its hole. Somehow, he stayed, his brain fighting his body's urge to leave. "No, sir, it's not that. I don't believe any guards have been escorting Lana."

"Good, that means she's acclimating." Claude chirped, his eyes glued to the mound of files on his desk.

"No, sir. I have reason to believe she may be in the Underground."

That caught his attention. His head snapped up, his eyes

narrowed. "Excuse me?" The lanky guard cleared his throat again and repeated the same words. Claude wiped an agitated hand over his chin and exhaled a long breath.

"Thank you, Todd. You may go." Again, he hesitated, "Todd, please do not try my patience. You have been dismissed."

"Sir, if I am correct, I believe Lana has been there since yesterday morning."

Claude hesitated a moment, his eyes looking somewhere past Todd. "Yesterday. You're sure?"

Todd dipped his head in acknowledgment before slipping out the door. He hoped that telling Claude was the right thing to do. For all he knew, Claude would leave her down there even longer. He blew out a long breath, his hands shaking. He would wait to see what Claude did about it, and if nothing happened, he would go after Lana himself.

"Fuck sakes."

# Chapter Twenty-One

Lana heard the first new sound in what felt like a lifetime. The muffled sound of voices trickled into her head as if in a dream. The diluted noise coming to her as if she were submerged under water. Distorted and unconnected. Her voice was gone. Her body too weak to feel pain any more. She laid on the concrete floor in a heap, her long brown hair twisted around her. Her wrists and ankles raw and bloody from the shackles. Her spandex wet with sweat. Her breath came in short-ragged spurts and she wondered if she might stop breathing all-together.

The blackness started to encroach on the boarders of her vision again, she willed herself to stay awake. She pushed her mind forward desperately trying to hold onto to the small bit of reality within her grasp. She was terrified that if she passed out again, she might not wake up. The voices were getting louder now. The sound called to her mind. She prayed that whatever, whoever was talking would stay. She needed something to focus her mind on.

Lana dragged her finger against the concrete floor wanting to push herself up. She quickly realized how futile that thought truly was. There was nothing left of her. The door swung open with an incredibly loud bang. A sound that would have startled her, had she been able to fathom such a response.

"Get out of my fucking way, Pede. I don't care what Miss Armstrong told you."

"You're not supposed to move her. We are under strict

orders—"

"Did I not just say I don't care? Move, before I move you."

Lana heard someone moving around in the tub beside her. She could see a large form tinkering with the chains that weighed her down. "Fucking hell."

"Lana? Lana can you hear me? Christ, look at your wrists. Lana?" The voice drifted through her mind without latching on. A hand pressed against her cheek and forehead then fingers on her throat.

"Fuck," the voice said again. Lana shivered and suddenly felt herself become weightless. She moaned softly as hard muscles pressed into her sides securing her in a cradle. She felt a new surge of pain crash through her body. Her hand squeezed her holder, tears streaming down her face dampening the stranger's shirt. The thick arms pressed her tighter to their chest. "It's all right, Lana. It's all right."

She felt herself slipping again. She pushed her head into the shirt of whoever was holding her and prayed for it to stop, prayed to feel like herself again. The inky black fog swam into her vision and she fell into a deep sleep, but not before she inhaled the distinct smell of peppermint.

\*\*\*

Claude was astounded by the state he'd found Lana in. She was a hair breath away from death. He was furious with Annette and had relayed that to her three times already since his return. She'd played the big doe-eyed innocent game that she always played, but Claude didn't back down, not this time. That didn't really bode well for either of them because now Annette was equally furious with Claude for not siding with her. Which consequently only put Lana in more danger.

He'd carried her limp body out of that room and up four flights of stairs to the infirmary only to find the doctor was not there. It was Todd who'd told him the doctor had been flown to a hospital yesterday afternoon. She'd been admitted under the false pretense as a victim of random assault.

Of course, Claude didn't want to believe that Lana had attacked the doctor and had he been here he's not sure if he would have handled the situation entirely differently from his sister. Lana may still have ended up in the Underground for her third strike, but she would *not* have spent over twenty-four hours down there. *What a stupid thing to do.*

He picked his shirt up off the ground where he'd thrown it in a fit of rage. He felt the dampness where Lana's tears had collected. Claude turned to see his profile in the floor length mirror across from him. He stood there, his hard body had perfectly sculpted after years of work. He fingered the long-jagged scar stretching from his hip to his chest. It was the most unfortunate part of his well-muscled body. He traced the scar over his abs and contemplated the happenings of the last twenty-four hours. He pinched the bridge of his nose unable to rid his mind of its incessant pounding. He let out a long breath.

He'd wanted to break Lana, break her rebellious nature, break her disobedience, defiance and insubordination. The same thing he'd done with pretty much every Morpher on the island. But not this way. He didn't want to break her spirit, that seemed to cross an unspoken line. It challenged the very morals he believed himself to exude. The act not only displeased him, but he also knew how far back this would set him with Lana. He'd been working to garner her trust, and although the trust was structured between king and subject, it was trust, nonetheless.

Lana had understood that Claude would do whatever it took to protect what was his, the island, the morphers, and the guards.

He rubbed a hand against the side of his head expecting to feel the length of his blonde hair. He'd forgotten that he was sporting a new haircut. The sides buzzed short with a long layer on top. He wasn't sure if he liked it yet. It seemed too modern for his taste. He tossed his shirt in the laundry hamper across from his bed. He pulled a crisp black button down from his closet and slipped it over his broad shoulders.

The bed creaked behind him and he turned to see the sheets shifting slightly. Lana's head flipped sides and she let out a soft moan. Claude closed his eyes, he could still feel the terror that raced through him when Todd approached him. It took everything in him not to bowl Todd over and go running after Lana in that instant. However, he knew better than anyone the effect and effectiveness of the Underground and the venom. He also knew the ferocity his sister was capable of.

He was out of breath when he reached the infirmary and laid Lana's body on the table. He didn't take a moment to compose himself this time, he yelled for Todd to grab Taurin. She'd been in a practical down the hall so it didn't take long for the thin beautiful brown-skinned girl to arrive.

"Oh my God, what happened to her?" she screeched seeing Lana's limp near naked body on the bare metal table.

"Miss Olivanté, if I remember correctly, you were a medical student, correct?"

"Well, yes but, I, I only finished one year of med school I can't—"

"You don't have an option. I need you to help Miss Chase, right now."

"I can't—sir, I-I don't know what to do."

"You know more than anyone else on this island right now and if you do not help her, she will die."

Taurin shook her head as she backed out of the room stammering. "Taurin," Claude yelled and grabbed both her hands in one of his. "If you do this. I will release you from the island." He paused watching her pupils dilate. "I swear to you."

The tall girl pulled at her dark black hair. Then she nodded. Taurin ran around the room, opening every drawer and cupboard. "OK, first I need to do an IV," she instructed herself as she tended to Lana's limp frame.

It was only because of the immediate sub-par medical attention that Lana had survived the next hour. The thought sent a new wave of fear crashing through Claude's body. He had come so close to losing an asset he'd worked so hard to gain. Loss was not something he was accustomed to. A knock on his door brought him out of his own head. "Come in."

"Wig said you wanted to see Mr. Armstrong?"

"Taurin, yes come in. I wanted to personally thank you for acting to save your fellow Morpher. If nothing else, I believe myself to be a man of my word so I will be releasing you from the island one week from today. You can take this time to say your goodbye's and assemble all your belongings. There is a strict exit program in place that you must attend over the next week before your departure. Other than that, you will be free to leave."

"I-I don't really know what to say. Thank you?"

Claude laughed. "No need for the fake pleasantries, Miss Olivanté."

Taurin nodded. "Can I ask how she is?"

"You may. She is still unconscious but looks to be recovering."

"OK, good." Taurin breathed as she placed a hand over her heart. "Good. That's what I was hoping you would say."

"That'll be all, Taurin," Claude quipped, dismissing the bright-eyed girl. He didn't want to see her go. Similar to Lana, every Morpher was an asset to him and to lose one... especially one with medical training, well it was a big loss.

***

*Lana dreamt of a simpler time. She dreamt of the garden in front of her cabin. The herbs and vegetables growing wildly. Aunt Alice humming behind her nudging each Rutabaga plant as she went. Lana leaned back on her arms, her skin black with dirt. She smiled feeling the sun beat through the trees. She breathed a satisfied breath.*

*"No slacking, Alana. Get the rest of those weeds."*

*Lana let her arms go and fell onto her back. "I'm not slacking, I'm just appreciating."*

*"Whatever you're doing, it's not productive. Come on tout suite."*

*Lana laughed and nodded. Her aunt had no patience, she was always up and on the go. Most times, Lana admired that about the old woman. Her aunt came around and critiqued her efforts... like always. Lana rolled her eyes and adjusted accordingly. Her aunt nodded in approval.*

*"You know dear it won't always be this easy?"*

*"What?"*

*"To readjust what you're used to doing."*

*"You never miss a moment to teach a life lesson do you."*

*"Notta one."*

*"All right, I'll bite. What do you mean?" Lana wiped her*

hands on her jeans.

"Sometimes life will throw new situations at you and your ability to adapt to them could be your saving grace."

"I get the feeling you're not talking about picking Rutabaga's now."

"No, not exactly. Just remember that your strength comes from your ability to persevere even in the most severe of circumstances. Take my correction just now. What ran through your head."

"Nothing, I just did it."

"Are you sure about that?"

Lana's brows furrowed, and she thought back to just a moment ago.

"When your shoulders hunched, and your eyes rolled, your mind told you nothing?"

Lana thought and then nodded. "OK, yeah, it did. I was thinking my way wasn't good enough... like usual."

"It was not a defeat Lana, in the negative way you interpreted it. Defeat is a wonderful thing. It gives us the opportunity to try again. To do better. To be better. To learn and to grow. Without defeat, we make no progress. Instead of succumbing to your negative thoughts, assess yourself and reattack. You'll be better for it."

Lana smiled. There was always a point to her musings, and they never failed to impress.

"What if I preferred my method?" she sassed, wondering what she could possibly come back with.

"Mmm. You've heard the saying, practice makes perfect?" Lana nodded, tucking her knees underneath her in a more comfortable position.

"Well, it's not true..." her aunt continued without missing a *beat, still assessing the garden vegetables. "Practice makes permanent. Practicing something the wrong way, will continually provide the same result. Let yourself experience defeat."* She stopped and turned to face Lana holding up a finger to correct herself, *"in small doses, of course."*

***

Lana squinted through her thick eyelashes. Light peaked through in a blurry streaky form. She could make out a dark form standing across from her. She waited for her vision to clear and watched Claude's trim form come into frame. Claude rolled the cuffs of his black dress shirt, fitting them a few inches above his wrist. Lana tried to push herself up and quickly fell back into a flurry of pillows. Claude turned at the noise, his dark eyes watching her intently. Lana opened her mouth to speak, but only a raw gravely sound emitted. Claude held up a hand to silence her.

"You probably won't have very much of a voice for a while."

He moved to stand over the top of her and for the first time she was acutely aware of the fact that she was still only wearing her two-piece spandex suit. She grabbed at the sheet around her and attempted to yank it up to her chin. The move was pitiful and she only managed to cover her lower half. It was as if her muscles had lost all strength, weighing her down instead.

"I wouldn't try to move very much," Claude interrupted, tapping his fingers along the wood frame of the bed. "You'll probably be sore for a while." His gaze lingering a little too long.

Lana looked at herself and then at Claude. Her chest rising and falling, vulnerability washed over her. Her cheeks colored with a slight pink hue, her eyes dropping away from his.

"You need not to worry, Lana," Claude said, taking a step

back from her. "My intentions are of nothing of the sort."

Lana's gray eyes darted around the room taking in the unfamiliar surroundings. The walls were a mixture of wood and stone. A classically beautiful fireplace was opposite her and cathedral ceilings gave the room an elegant feel. There was a small sitting area just beside the fireplace with two matching armchairs. There was a half empty glass sitting on the table between the chairs with a gold colored liquid resting in it. A small bookcase occupied the wall by the door.

Claude folded his hands in front of him and explained. "As you can see, you're not in your dorm. This is one of our suites, normally reserved for executives but as you are in a precarious position, I have granted you permission to use it for a while." He walked toward the door.

"We will talk about all of that, in due time. I have some matters to attend to. So first, some food, hot tea for your throat and fresh clothes." He opened the door and allowed a lanky form to duck in the doorway.

"Todd, I will be back in three hours."

Todd nodded and checked his watch. "Yes, sir."

The door closed behind Claude with a *thunk*. Lana swore she saw Todd exhale a breath of relief. He turned to face her, spinning so fast the tray he carried nearly toppled over. "Eek. Whoops. Sorry. Sorry. Last thing you need is hot tea spilt on you."

Lana felt a small smile tug at the corner of her mouth. She tried to push herself up again this time managing to get into a seated position. She breathed heavily with the effort. Todd was at her side in three strides. He placed a hand on her shoulder.

"Hey take it easy. Take it easy," he eased, kneeling down next to her. "Man, I was sure Annette had killed you."

Lana shimmied in her covers and Todd pulled the blanket

over her without her having to say a word. "I brought you some clothes, and the tea here is just steeping."

She tried to talk again and only emitted a small croak. She scowled at herself and looked around the room desperately. Todd's eyes grew big and he held up a finger. "Oh wait. I get it, I get it. Hold on." Todd pulled a pad of paper and a pen off the bedside table. "Here use this." Lana snatched the paper from him and scribbled down a question. She crossed it out over and over again deciding which question she wanted answered first.

*What happened?*

Todd watched over her shoulder as she wrote. He nodded when she pointed to the question she'd finally landed on.

"That's kind of a convoluted question... could you... could you be more specific?"

Lana licked her lips and drew her mind back to the beginning. What was the first question she needed answered? *Why? How long? How come?* Her mind seemed to ping as the answer rippled like a pebble thrown into a calm lake. Its waves lapping every corner of her brain. A pang of guilt dropped into her stomach.

*What happened to the doctor?* Todd seemed surprised by her question. "The doctor?" He looked to the door afraid someone might overhear. "Well, she was airlifted to a hospital. Her injuries were... I'm sorry, but her injuries were horrible."

Lana closed her eyes feeling that same pang drop into her stomach. She knew she had nothing to do with it, but it still felt like *her* fault. The doctor was the excuse Annette needed. Annette had no problem sacrificing an innocent person to get her way.

"Lana, there's something you should know about that." Again, Todd looked to the door. "There's no evidence to say you didn't do it. And while you've been unconscious and unable to tell your side, it hasn't stopped Annette from vocalizing her version of events."

Lana paled. Todd interjected. "Of course, no one wants to *believe* what she said happened, but she can be a convincing storyteller and... well, because you've attacked her once already... and you don't exactly have a spotless track record."

Todd was right. Lana was the perfect scapegoat for the crime. In fact, if Lana had been a random third party, she probably would have believed the story as well. She scratched a word onto the pad and turned it to face Todd. He smiled slightly. *Fuck.*

"My thoughts exactly," Todd said.

## Chapter Twenty-Two

Lana sat back for a moment. She took a long sip of tea. She wasn't sure what flavor it was, but it didn't matter. She savored the warm liquid as it slipped down her throat and into her stomach. She pressed her tongue against her gums feeling their ache vibrate through her head. The all-too familiar metallic taste rested in the back of her throat. It made the next sip of tea quite unpleasant. Not at all a flavor combination she would recommend. She snorted, finding the humor in it. *Would you like some blood with your tea?* No? *How about some torture instead?*

The word itself ignited a fury of flashes from Lana's memory; *lying on concrete. Chains weighing her down. Air choking her lungs. Her connection to the Earth pulled from her.* She shivered and clenched her teeth as the snippets intruded on her quiet time like an invasive beetle. Her jaw screamed at her in white hot agony. Her gums unappreciative of the new pressure, but she didn't relent. She savored the feeling, holding on to it to… using it to rid her mind of its current terrors. *The concrete, the chains, the pain... oh God, the pain... the arms that scooped me up...* her mind recoiled like an elastic band. She twisted in the bed rustling a familiar scent from its sheets. *Peppermint.*

The door swung open, and Claude strode in. Lana stilled and watched him. His agitation clear to her in his frantic movements. He noticed Lana watching him and composed himself almost instantly. He took a sip from the glass that had been sitting near the fire. His back to her. He stood there for a moment staring into the dying embers of the fire in front of him.

When he finally turned around, he was back to typical Claude. His shoulders back, face unreadable and stance confident. He opened his mouth to speak, his eyes catching on the end of the bed. He clamped his mouth shut just as quickly. His chest rising with a deep breath.

Lana noticed where his gaze had fallen. The clothes that she was *supposed* to change into sat at the end of the bed. Untouched. It's not that she didn't *want* to put them on, she did, more than anything she did. She wanted to get out of the damp reminders clinging to her body like an unwanted parasite *but*, she also knew that she *could* regain some control if she wore her stained spandex tiers with indifference. Indifference to what had happened to her. Indifference to the fact that she was barely clothed. Indifferent to the vulnerability she was *supposed* to feel.

Well, she did feel it. She had to fight the urge to tug the blankets up around her chest when she saw Claude's fire ridden glare tearing down her.

*He won't know that I'm uncomfortable. I won't give him that.* She clenched her teeth again, her jaw flexing and lifted her head to meet his gaze.

"I see you have decided *not* to put on fresh clothing," Claude quipped. "If that is your decision, then so be it." He finished, clasping his hands in front of him.

He stood there for a moment, silently. He sighed. "I'm going to be candid with you, Lana." He moved over to one of the chairs by the fire and rested on its arm. "The circumstances we find ourselves in, are not good. I normally would not divulge the following information to a Morpher, but the situation as I said, is unprecedented. So, it calls for unprecedented action." He waved his hands. "So, here we are."

He didn't wait for Lana to give any kind of acknowledgment. He simply continued. "While I understand the events of the last two days may *not* have unraveled in quite the fashion that Annette has been retelling them, I have found zero evidence to support a different claim." Claude leaned back and crossed one foot on top of the other. "Quito has also pledged on his honor that Annette's version of events is true."

Lana's chest rose and fell quickly. She squeezed her hands together in her lap. Tension rising.

"That being said, I also *know* my sister." He paused. "I know her better than anyone and it's entirely possible that she fabricated the event to… get *her* way." He paused again. His eyes meeting Lana's, eyebrows raised. "So, what am I to do? Her story has a supporting witness, and while I have not heard your version of events." He waved a hand at her, dismissing her urge to speak. "Which I'm sure is splendid. I can almost guarantee that unless you adamantly agree with my sister, your version probably contradicts hers in every manner possible."

Lana felt the color drain from her face. He was right. She didn't have any evidence to support what *actually* happened. Even if she told her side, nobody would take her word based on hearsay. She squeezed her hands together tighter. Her knuckles turning white.

Claude nodded as if hearing her entire inner dialogue. "Precisely. The predicament is quite severe." Claude licked his lips and ran a hand along the side of his head. "Unfortunately, I lost my head with Annette when I returned to the island. I was unaware of her imposed sentence. She is supposed to run things like that by me and—" he pursed his lips and took a moment to choose his words. "I'm afraid that I have only made the situation worse."

Lana shifted. She forced herself to unwind her tangled fingers and take a sip of tea, forced herself to hide the warm tendrils of terror slowly creeping up her spine. "I cannot control Annette. She is as much an Armstrong as I am and, *theoretically*, has as much power and influence. She will not be pleased that I did not support her sentence." Claude stood and crossed over to the bed. He leaned forward his hands resting on the footboard. "And so, the only way to make this work... to keep you safe is for you to take responsibility for what happened."

Lana dropped her tea. It spilt in the sheets around her, it burnt her thigh and crashed to the floor in a characteristically satisfying shatter. Lana didn't flinch, her eyes remained glued to Claude. *This had to be a joke.* Again, Lana opened her mouth to speak, and Claude simply shook his head.

"I have been over it myself. There is no proper way out of this. If you take responsibility Annette will not feel like she is under fire, or at risk of being proved wrong, and she may back off. I'm afraid, if you do not agree to this, she will go after you again."

His eyes sought hers, desperation filling them. "I can promise you that," he whispered.

***

Lana scooted forward as Taurin examined her. She'd only seen the tan-skinned girl one time before, on the way to one of Riley's practical's. She was older than Lana, but she didn't know by how much.

"Can I see your right arm, please?" Taurin asked. She secured the black blood pressure cuff around Lana's arm and started pumping. Lana moved to curl her legs inward into a cross-legged position. Taurin flinched. It was minor, but Lana noticed it nonetheless. Lana froze as if she'd done something wrong, one leg still stretched out.

Taurin flashed Lana an embarrassed smile. "Sorry. I just... Sorry." She mumbled, leaning over to undo the Velcro cuff. Lana noticed for the first time the amount of space Taurin was keeping from her at all times. If her hand needed to touch Lana, as it did right now, her feet were firmly placed almost a foot and a half away. The girl was using her long body to her advantage and leaning as much as possible.

*She's afraid of me.* Lana thought and pulled her outstretched leg in toward her as slowly and cautiously as she could manage. Her reaction made sense. Lana knew it made sense... and yet it hurt her. It hurt her in a way she was so unaccustomed to. It didn't bruise her, or sting her or make her bleed, which Lana usually relied on to classify pain. This was a whole new type of hurt. Similar to what she felt about Aunt Alice. A deep and guttural pain that pressed down on her heart and sent a numbness tumbling through her body. An emptiness that wanted to envelop her. Let her disappear. Her mind reeled. *She doesn't even know me. How can she be so afraid of me?*

Her questions were rhetorical... and yet she still wanted an answer. The desire to confront Taurin burned within her. She wanted to ask *How? How can you believe her?* Her fingers twitched with a sudden surge of adrenaline. Todd shifted his weight, Lana barely caught the movement in her peripheral. It was enough to get her attention. He looked at her, his brown hair falling into his eyes a bit. She watched him subtly express an outward breath his hands rising and falling with the movement. He nodded toward Lana.

She copied him without realizing it. She'd followed his

breath as her own, letting its deepness quell the adrenaline and desire burning within her. A few moments went by, and Lana grew more and more irritated every time Taurin took a step back to scribble notes on her clipboard. "I'm not going to hurt you." Lana scratched, her voice raw and gravelly.

Taurin's head snapped up surprised. "Oh no, that's not—don't worry I'm not—" She sighed and dropped the clipboard to her side. "I didn't mean to react like that. I just—I've heard stories you know?"

Lana nodded, and waved away Taurin's incessant apologizing. "It is entirely deserved." Taurin's eyebrows raised. "Your reaction I mean."

Lana made a decision in that moment. A decision that went against every one of her ethics. A decision based purely on survival, no matter how humiliating and self-defeating she found it. "I didn't mean for the doctor to get hurt." She breathed, her raw voice barely above a whisper.

Taurin's eyes widened. She took a small step forward like a child eager to hear a bedtime story. She seemed to catch herself and think better of it, scooting back to a safe distance.

Lana reached for her newly filled tea and took a long sip. Her throat burning from just those two sentences. "I didn't plan it. It just happened," she said finally.

Taurin left and Lana dropped back into the covers of the bed. She felt tears pushing on the corners of her eyes. She breathed, *in through the nose, out through the mouth. In through the nose, out through the mouth. In through the nose, out through the mouth.* Although, every word she'd managed to scrape out of her mouth to Taurin was *technically* true, she knew the girl would interpret them in a completely different way. The way Lana had intended they be heard.

There was a part of her that held onto the glimmer of hope that Taurin may understand Lana's meaning. That she would take Lana's words for what they were and create a flare of doubt. A tealight flickering amidst a hurricane. Taurin's reaction told her all she needed to know. Her story didn't matter. Annette had tainted their views.

"Well, I guess I only have one choice then."

## Chapter Twenty-Three

Claude oversaw the practical's progress from time to time. He heard the Morphers refer to the judgment as a trial. He didn't oppose the term, in fact it made sense since he often rewarded pleasing morphs, and reprimanded the opposite. It was a report card of sorts. What needs to be improved, what needs to be altered, how to decrease transition time... etc.

Locust and Centipede sat on either side of him, their backs rigid and faces expressionless. Locust cracked his knuckles and released an irritated grunt. Claude knew his tolerance was waning, he had the attention span of a toddler. A quiet unappreciated glance from Claude was usually enough to shut him up. It wasn't this time.

A small girl not four feet tall entered the room. Her feet padded along the hardwood floor with barely a sound as she made her way to stand in front of Claude.

"How much longer we gonna sit here, bossman?"

The tingling impatience crept up the back of Claude's neck like an irritating bug. His tongue flickered in his mouth like a snake, dancing over all the retorts he wished he could give. His eyes landed on the young girl in front of him and his priorities settled back in place. He let out a short breath.

"Sorry. Sorry—" Locust snickered, "Forgot I'm suppos' to be more formal now." He laughed and nodded at Claude. "Mr. Armstrong." He laughed again. Normally, Claude didn't mind the repertoire, but today his mind was elsewhere. He had enough going on without having to humor Locust.

A part of him wanted to make a snide remark about Locusts' own name but Claude's mind drew a blank. He thought about Centipede and realized he'd forgotten his real name as well. The guards had their own form of training in which he didn't interfere. The final chapter involved the appointment of a namesake. It was their responsibility to leave behind their birth name and everything that came with it. To assume the new role, they'd been given. He wasn't a fan of the insect genre they often attributed themselves with, but he also didn't care enough to say something.

"Mr. Armstrong?" a small voice piped. Claude was drawn back into the room and focused on the young girl in front of him.

"Yes, Nova?"

"Would you like me to start?" she squeaked.

Claude flipped a sheet on his clipboard and nodded toward her. "Whenever, you're ready love."

She stood in front of him, her straight light brown hair hanging just past her shoulders, with natural dark streaks peppered through and a slight crimp framing her face.

She gulped a large breath and nodded fervently. The image of her small body started to blur. No matter how many times Claude's eyes witnessed this, they never ceased to try and bring the blurred frame into focus. Even though he was acutely aware that he'd never be able to.

The blurriness increased and when Claude finally blinked a smile followed soon after. He leaned forward to assess the dog that sat in front of him. The embodiment of lassie the rough collie. Her beautiful brown coat, long slender nose, and trim frame stood stoically in front of him.

"Well done, Nova," Claude said, tapping his fingers along

his clipboard. "I am pleased. How is your exit transition?"

The dog's head dropped, her small almond shaped eyes cast downward. Claude nodded and motioned for Pede to escort her back to her dorm. He watched her trot out the door, moving ever so carefully so as not to slip on the polished floor.

Claude began pacing the moment the door shut behind them, his mind whirling. It was the same problem. The same problem repeating itself with every Morpher. The transition back. He couldn't get a handle on it. Most times they morphed back after falling asleep. So, he imagined it had *something* to do with the deceleration of one's heartbeat, but he'd made frustratingly little progress in the past few years.

"Locust, get me an update on the new elixir ASAP." He snapped at the sole guard left in the room. The guard hurried out the door without another word. Claude was surprised at the man's quickness. He was never one to make a quiet exit.

He shrugged. He's probably excited to be on the floor again. Claude continued pacing, his hands shoved in his pockets, his mind plucking along the same note like an out of tune piano. *The elixir.* He hoped it would solve some of his problems. A serum replicating the trance-like state of sleeping without the disadvantage of unconsciousness.

"Keep them lucid enough to see and feel what happens when they shift back—in theory it would teach them how to do it themselves." He plopped himself back down on his chair and stared at the floor underneath his feet.

"In theory," he whispered.

***

Claude had been back in his office for about an hour when Locust strode in. He set his coffee mug down and looked to the guard expectantly. Locust made himself comfortable in one of the chairs seated opposite Claude and smiled.

"Good news," he said, rubbing his hands together. His enthusiasm oozing. "The new elixir is in its final stages."

Claude leaned back in his chair, his head dipped with acknowledgment. "And tell me, what exactly are the final stages?"

"They just need your decision—on like—you know—how you want it done."

"An administering vessel, you mean?"

"Yeah, yeah exactly." Locust threw his hands up in the air, frustrated his use of words wasn't understood. "Do ya' wan it airborne like the venom or injected like the tranquilizers?"

Claude rubbed a hand over his chin. He was surprised to feel some stubble growing there. That was uncharacteristic of him. He paused with his hand there and tried to recall the last time he'd shaved. He caught Locusts' quizzical look and shook away the thought, dropping his hand to his desk.

"Well?" the guard gruffed.

Claude stood up and turned to face the large bay window behind him. He caught a glimpse of himself in its reflection. He looked like he always did, save for the stubble. His hair neat, his clothes pressed and tucked. His posture rigid. From the outside, you would never know the turmoil within. How little sleep he got and how each moment of progress was set back three strides by something else.

"Tell them I have another idea all together." Claude said without turning from the window. "A system we haven't tried yet."

# Chapter Twenty-Four

Todd waited for Lana to ask him something. Approach him. Look at him. Anything. She hadn't moved from her position on the bed since Taurin left. His heart ached for her. He knew Taurin's reaction had hurt her. The Morphers were supposed to be in this together, right? Them against the Islanders kind of thing. He could almost see the loneliness ebbing from her pale gray eyes. Like a ripple in a pond, expanding slowly at every moment.

He took a step forward and peered over the foot of the bed. He cringed hearing the flood board creak under his feet. Her body tensed, and he quickly retreated to his place in front of the fire. "I almost forgot you were here." He heard a soft voice say.

She sat up in the bed, cringing and squinting her eyes as she did. She faced him, her hair a tangled mess falling all over her shoulders. The circles under her eyes a deep purple, matching the cuff like bruises around her arms and ankles. This was the first time he'd really seen her. All of her, since her time in the Underground. No sheets, or pillows, or clothes to cover her. Simply her spandex uniform and the air between them.

He gulped a quick breath. Color rising to his cheeks. He wanted to look away, but he didn't want to make her feel uncomfortable. However looking at her half-naked could also make her uncomfortable. Her gaze met his full on. Her stare a little less fierce than usual. Todd submitted, breaking his gaze and casting his eyes toward the floor. "You feel sorry for me, don't you?" she asked.

Todd bit his lip, raising his head to meet hers again. He sighed and said nothing. He knew that wasn't enough. It wasn't what she wanted him to say. But he couldn't bring himself to lie to her. He couldn't tell her that, *hell no, he didn't feel sorry for her. Hell no, he didn't, because she was fierce and strong and brave*—he couldn't because he *did* feel sorry for her. He wanted to hold her, wrap her in his arms and comfort her. Tell her it would be *okay*. "You shouldn't."

"What?" was all he could manage.

"Feel sorry for me." Todd's eyebrows drew together, the confusion clear on his face.

"Well, I—"

Lana shook her head to interrupt him. "I lied to you." Her voice getting raspier with every word. "I told you I morphed." She shook her head. "I didn't."

Todd felt like he'd been hit with a baseball bat. His heart sank into his stomach like a weight dropped into a calm ocean. Everything that had haunted him the last forty-eight hours had been false. Anger flared within him. He stammered a few sentences, none of them reaching the words he wanted. Lana was sitting patiently on the bed. Her posture still. Her face unreadable. He felt the theoretical *knot* in his stomach crumble and sift away. The pressure of keeping that information had plagued his consciousness like a black spot on a piece of paper. It had twisted his mind, and entwined his nerves in a boiling pot of anxiety and trepidation.

The anger grew hotter inside of him, rushing through him like an out-of-control wildfire. It surprised him, but he didn't suppress it. She'd toyed with him like a plaything. What angered him even more is he'd allowed it. She'd used him, carelessly and blatantly and did not spare a moment to think about the immense risk she'd placed upon him, and his position.

She'd played him to her advantage. Completely. "You're not going to say anything?" she rasped. Todd shook his head, exasperation huffing out in his exaggerated breaths. He threw his hands up in the air. "You just—ugh, Lana. You just don't care about anyone but yourself, not even when it can affect—" he paused and looked her dead in the eyes. He didn't want to lash out at her. He was angrier with himself. *Don't get attached.* Guard protocol 101 he reminded himself. He nodded his head. Fine. He'd learned his lesson. Separate oneself from one's duty and actions.

"You know what?" he said. "No. I'm not doing this. You made your choice, Lana. The choice to put everything about me at risk for your own benefit. I'm making mine now." Todd said, slapping his hand on the back of one of the two chairs opposite the fireplace. He walked out the door without another word.

***

Lana sat in Claude's bed. She hadn't moved since Todd had stormed out. She assumed he was right outside the door. Not daring to abandon his post without Claude's permission, and even so, she waited and hoped that he would come back in that door so she could explain, but how? How could she explain it?

*I'm sorry. My mind normally only functions on survival mode. It was an instinctual decision not meant to hurt you.* But that wasn't true, not completely anyways. She knew it *could* hurt him. She knew the severity of it. How dangerous it was for him to know *that* secret, tell *that* secret, keep *that* secret. Every option increased his risk by an entire letter grade. Yet, she hadn't *really* cared how dangerous it was.

If Claude had found out that Todd:

1. Knew her Morph and didn't tell him straight away…

2. Was personally close enough to Lana to learn such information…

3. Debated his guard protocol and morals whatsoever…

Well—Lana didn't *actually* want to know what might happen to him. Her heart ached, and it bothered her more than the physical pains still simmering in her muscles and throat. A whole new kind of pain for her and she didn't like how much of it she was experiencing. It wasn't the kind of pain she could wrap a bandage around and apply ointment to. It was deep within her chest, hollow and chilling. Its icy hands hung inside her with a slow desolate drip. First Taurin, and now this. She was starting to understand why her aunt preferred to live in isolation.

She longed for Todd to come back. She wanted him to forgive her so that she could have an ally again. It was amazing how quickly people could imprint themselves onto your lives. She'd gone her whole life relying on only one person. Suddenly, in the span of a few weeks, she'd unwittingly let a handful of people affect her.

Hours went by, and Lana sat there quietly. Her mind whirling. Everything was pressing on her mind fighting for space, *Annette, her parents, her morph, her safety…Claude*. And yet one thought intruded on all her mental wavelengths like an unstoppable virus. She couldn't get rid of it. *Todd*. How she'd hurt him. How hurting him had somehow hurt her. She groaned loudly and fell back onto the bed.

She remembered a similar feeling from her childhood. The time she'd snuck into her great aunt's bedroom and tried to open a small box she kept hidden under her nightstand. She didn't even get the box open before aunt Alice found her. She remembered the rush of embarrassment and shame like it was yesterday. She swore to never let her curiosity get the better of her again. It seemed so minor compared to how she felt now. She was a child back then. She couldn't use that to excuse any more.

A small knock at the door brought her attention back. Her heart lunged hoping to see Todd walk through the door. There was a moment of silence before his lanky frame ducked into the room. Lana almost smiled at the sight of him. She wanted to slew together a string of apologies... *I'm sorry I was an ass, I'm sorry I put you in danger, I'm sorry*—his body language struck her and momentarily silenced her thoughts. Todd stood there, straight as a board, his jaw clenched, holding a balled-up piece of fabric in his hands. Lana opened her mouth to speak and was interrupted by a large form pushing past Todd into the center of the room. Lana felt her breath catch. She backed up further onto the bed. "Hello, princess. Av you 'ad enough time to lick your wounds then?"

The prickle of his voice made the hairs on the back of her neck stand erect. "Come on then. We got places to go." Lana didn't move. Her eyes slitted, her breathing short. She stared down the man that made her emotions meld into a concoction of fear and anger. Part of her wanted to play it cool, calm, and collected as if his presence didn't faze her in the slightest. Part of her wanted to curse him out and attack him, and part of her simply wanted to run away. Her mind stretched in so many directions she couldn't decide which angle to take. So—she remained frozen.

Locust took a warning step toward her. "You'll be comin' along then. Right now." He nodded toward her. "I won't be asking so *nicely* next time," he said, accentuating the word. "Oh," he added, ripping the fabric out of Todd's hands. "You'll be wantin' to wear this." He threw the sheer white material across the room. "O'course. I won't be making any objections if you decide not to," he said, his cold dark eyes raking her body from bottom to top.

Lana's mind was screaming at her, screeching for her to react. She felt numb. A high-pitched ringing sounded in her ears. She saw their mouths moving, but couldn't hear past it. She could see though. She saw Locust, she saw his eyes, she saw his gaze outlining every detail of her body. Her body responded, and she watched her arms sling the robe over her shoulders and fasten it at the waist. She felt like she was in a dream or, perhaps nightmare was a better analogy. It wasn't enough.

By the time she reached the hallway, Lana had somewhat regained control of her mind. *Don't be afraid of him. Stand up tall. Don't be afraid of him. You can do this,* she thought, as she followed him out the door. Her words failed to reach her. She was helpless to her body's reaction. The robe wasn't enough. She was acutely aware of how short it was. How sheen the white material was. She felt his eyes on her like the heat of a hot summer's days pressing upon her neck. It took everything in her not to scurry away from him keeping pace behind her. She cursed herself for not changing into the clothes Todd had brought for her. *Stupid stubbornness.*

Todd walked behind her other shoulder. She looked to him for a reassuring smile, or nod, something. He avoided her look, his eyes glued on the walkway in front of them. Lana's heart dipped a little bit, matched with a stumble of her feet. She was exhausted and thrown off by Locust's presence, coordinating her limbs was a conscious effort. Not to mention this was the most she'd moved in two or three days.

Her heart rate elevated, and she was nearly out of breath. She clamped her mouth shut and forced herself to breathe through her nose. She looked to Todd again hoping to get one of his small reassuring smiles, or else empathetic glances. Something to settle her mind, remind her where her feet were, but there was nothing there for her.

The large wooden door of Claude's office loomed over her. She heard Locust waning behind her impatiently. A weight dropped onto her shoulder and as if in slow motion she felt Locust squeeze and shove her toward the door. Lana recognized the dark corners of her vision push inward. She knew what was about to happen and she welcomed it. She dropped to the floor and let the blackness take over her mind. She passed out.

***

*Lana found herself in a dream she hadn't visited in a while. Her small body hidden under heaps of shirts and sweaters piled in a small corner of a bedroom closet. Mummy had said it was hide and seek. She was to be as quiet as possible until the game was over. The laundry hamper was pushed right up against her forcing her knees into her chest. She wished she could move it to get more comfortable, but she didn't want to ruin the game. Mummy would be sad if she did that. No, she'd stay there. Quiet as she could be.*

*She held her breath in stints for as long as she could. She passed the time by counting the seconds. She was up to fifteen so far. Her focus was interrupted by a loud banging. The noise startled her, but she dare not move. This was all part of the game. Her and mummy played this game all the time. If she waited in her hiding spot until Mummy came back, then she got a lollipop.*

*She liked lollipops, especially the red ones, they turned her lips red like Mummy's lipstick. The shouting was getting louder. Lana wanted to go see what was going on, but she couldn't stop Mummy's game. She plugged her ears and tried holding her breaths again. A loud crack vibrated through the house. Lana's body convulsed with a start. She took a deep breath to calm her racing heart. She didn't like thunder much. Even less so when it was that loud. She heard the front door close and waited for mummy to come and get her. She knew Lana didn't like thunder, so she'd end the game now. Her skin pinched around her face. Ouch. That hurt. Again and again she felt the pinching. The stinging zipped through her face and touched her mind.*

Her eyes fluttered open. Lana groaned and pushed herself up onto her elbows, nearly clashing heads with Todd in the process. He still had one hand on her cheek where he'd been pinching it repeatedly. The stinging made sense now. She pushed his hand away and felt an ache in her back from the hardwood floor. Lana recognized the ornate room immediately, *Claude's office*. The events of the last few minutes instantly charged her brain in a series of flashes. *Claude's bed. Todd. Clothes. Locust.* The scenes unloaded on her with increasing speed like a slinky toppling down a flight of stairs. She pressed her palm to her forehead and groaned again.

A blonde head waved into view her eyes taking a second too long to meld the colors together and make a shape. "Annette is going to be here any second. Get her into that chair. She can recompose herself from there." His voice snapped like the smacking of a ruler against a table. It was all Lana needed to bring him completely into focus. He flicked his fingers at Todd "Come on then, get a move on," urgency clear in his tone.

Todd scooped Lana up into his long arms and placed her gently in the chair in front of Claude's ostentatious red mahogany desk. Ostentatious. That's what she'd thought the first time she'd been in this office. The first time she'd sat in this chair. Her bare feet touched the cool floor and she shivered. Everyone was bustling about the room like worker bees in a hive. She could hear Claude barking orders at them, but his words hummed past her ears. A monotonous sound she wasn't tuned into. It wasn't directed at her and she found herself more interested in her chair. She tapped her toes along the floor and pushed backward. *Nope. Still bolted to the floor.*

A few minutes passed by before Lana refocused on the scene at hand. Claude had dismissed Todd and kept Locust and Quito. They were standing opposite each other in separate corners of the office. Quito's knuckles were slightly purpled from where he had pummeled the doctor. Lana understood their positioning immediately. She smiled. *They either think I'm super dangerous, or Annette is.* She looked at the guards placed on either side of her. *Protection and enforcement.*

She pushed herself upright in the chair, blinking a few times to wake herself up. A dull ached throbbed through her body centering around her wrists, ankles and gums. A flicker of annoyance shot across her face. She hated feeling weak, like she couldn't appropriately defend herself. The heaviness in her muscles weighed like tar, making a short jaunt down the corridor feel like an epic trek. It was a slow recovery. The aches in her body acted like flares intruding on her mind. They attacked her with a fresh fury of scenes from that day in the Underground, no matter how hard she tried to push it aside, it kept barging its way in. She ran her tongue over her swollen gums, swallowing a mouthful of salvia and blood. Oddly enough, this kind of pain she was OK with. Actually, Lana almost savored the feeling of it. It was familiar. In a way comforting.

The side door to Claude's office flew open with a loud whack. The same way it had the first time she had been in this room. Lana's body tensed, startled. The familiar sound sent her mind reaching for a memory. She pushed the thought away before it could find its roots. She focused instead on the small blonde woman sauntering into the room. Annette made her way to Claude's desk slipping in front of Lana as she did. She perched herself on the edge of the red wooden structure, her legs brushing Lana's as she crossed them in front of her.

Lana cast her gray eyes to the perfectly good chair sitting next to her, and back to Annette. Her face not masking her annoyance. She rolled her eyes and tried to look past the small woman to Claude. He'd seemed to notice her obstruction quite quickly and was already rising from his place behind his desk to occupy the empty chair. "So," Annette said, waving her arm in the air dramatically. "You wanted to see me, dear brother."

"Yes." Claude nodded and leaned back in his new chair. "There is a matter that the three of us need to discuss." Annette played with her fingernails and feigned boredom. She even let out an exaggerated sigh every now and again, much like an impatient child would do. "While I was away two things happened without debate. One: Dr. Otazzi was sent to the hospital with severe injuries. Two: Lana was sent to the Underground."

Annette swiveled her head around and looked Claude dead in the eye. "And?"

Claude sighed and folded his hands together in his lap. "And—you know I am supposed to be *involved* in those decisions Annette."

"Wait. Wait." Annette held a skinny hand to her mouth and chuckled. "Are you serious? Is that really what this is about?" She laughed, looking around the room for confirmation. Her expression changed on a dime when nobody met her careless energy. Her face grew tight, a scowl replacing her spry smile. "What has the little bitch been saying about me?" She screeched, the words turning to venom in her mouth.

She jumped off the desk and smacked her hands down on the arms of Lana's chair. She pressed into Lana's face savoring the entrapment maneuver. "Did she call me a liar then, little brother?" She cocked her head to the side. Her position unmoving.

Lana inhaled the overpowering stink of Annette's perfume and felt the heat of her breath on her face. Her mind was firing signals at her, *get out, get away, this woman is crazy, she's unpredictable, you're not safe!* Lana almost laughed at that. *Safe? When was the last time I felt safe?* She couldn't remember. Annette pressed closer. Her movements like a cross between a snake and the aggressive stalk of a jungle cat. "Did she call me a liar?" Annette asked, her frame still not breaking from Lana. Claude leaned forward in his chair. He mumbled something under his breath and walked toward Locust.

"What?" Annette yelled, her head snapping up. "Claude! What did you say?" Claude retreated to the back corner of the room and began pacing. Annette's grip tightened on Lana's chair one last time before jumping back and trailing after her brother.

Lana watched him pace away toward the back of the room. Annette following him in a matter of milliseconds. In that moment, Lana saw first-hand how crafty Claude truly was. He knew Annette would follow him like an eager puppy if he turned his attention from her. Her screeching was getting louder now. "What was it, Claude? Hmmm? What did she say? If she called me a liar, I swear I'll—"

Lana saw Claude's eyes flick over to her, his chest falling with the release of a breath. He manipulated Annette completely and in a way that probably only *he* knew how to do. Annette circled her brother and he raised his hands to quiet her. "If you would give me a moment to speak—"

"Oh PUH-LEASE," she interrupted, throwing her hands in the air. "Tell me Claude. Tell me that she called me a liar. Just say it."

"Actually," Lana interrupted, using the chair to help her stand. Annette's back snapped straight at the sound of her voice. She turned on her toes ever so slowly to face Lana. Lana fought back the light-headedness and took a deep breath. "He was probably going to discuss my—" Lana stalled searching for the right words.

"Discuss what child? Spit it out!"

"Discuss my terms," she blurted, and then nodded as if convincing herself along with Annette. "Seeing as attacking Dr. Ottazi was my third strike." Lana caught the smallest hint of a smile tug at the side of Claude's mouth. It was gone within a blink. What was it, relief? Pride? Appreciation? She didn't know. All she knew and all she needed to know was that Annette was no longer looking at her like a piece of meat. She wasn't even looking at *her* any more. Annette was staring at the space between them. Her mind probably racing. This was clearly *not* the outcome she was expecting from Lana.

Claude placed a hand on the back of her shoulder. "Well, now," he said. "Shall we begin. Annette, please join us. Your opinion is pertinent. I would like to know how this all unfolded. Lana clamped her mouth shut. She held her breath and counted the seconds like she used to do as a child. She yearned for this to end soon. She didn't want to push her luck with Annette. She was completely unpredictable. For now, she was enraptured by spinning her long tale about Lana. For now, she wasn't a threat.

*For now.*

# Chapter Twenty-Five

Todd laid on his bed in the guard's quarters. Their rooms were much like the Morphers' cells. Generic and plain. The biggest differences were that their doors didn't lock from the outside and they could come and go as they pleased. He pressed his palms against his eyes and filtered through the juxtaposition of emotions rapping at his mind, like hard knuckles against solid wood.

He was angry at Lana. There was no denying that. He *wanted* to see her differently. He *wanted* her to know just how reckless she had been. He wasn't going to stand for that. He was going to be tough. Be a man. Be a guard. He was going to separate himself from his duty. "Easier said than done," he said, pushing himself up on his elbows. She occupied more of his mind than he cared to admit, like a small sponge expanding itself in his brain with every encounter.

He stared at the gray brick wall in front of him. His room was smaller than most, windowless and dark. The short end of the stick, of sorts. The lowest on the totem pole got the least perks. He understood that. He didn't whine too much about it. He liked to imagine that one day if he did well enough he'd get upgraded. He'd get a room with a large bay window, like the one in Claude's office. He'd paint the walls blue to match the reflection of the water. He'd hang pictures of all the places he wanted to go. *Amsterdam, Dublin, Munich.* He'd never actually get to see those places, but at least this way he could feel closer to them.

His stomach let out a deep unsatisfied growl. The sound amplified by the desolate quiet space. He sighed and pulled himself out of bed. Claude had dismissed him from the meeting. He didn't know if it was because it was too high caliber for him to be a part of, or because he didn't want to set Annette off. Well, now that he thought about it, minimizing her interactions obliged the latter.

Either way, he'd been due for a break. He hadn't left Lana's side in roughly two-days. Even when he wasn't directly in the room with her, he'd been positioned outside. He didn't *have* to do that, both Roach and Wig had come to relieve him, but he'd insisted on staying.

Thinking back on it, he wasn't one hundred percent sure why he stayed. It's not like he could help her in any way. Her body needed rest. She needed to recover. He was an unassociated entity. Somehow, he'd convinced himself he needed to be there. He needed to check in on her and make sure she was all right.

He'd snuck into the room countless times just to make sure she was breathing. He'd slip out again before anyone noticed him missing. "I feel responsible for her," he said, his voice deep and husky like a freshly woken teenager. "Yeah. That's it," he nodded, saying the words aloud to convince himself. "I feel responsible for her because she's my detail." He exhaled a forced sigh and pulled a hand through his copper-tinged hair.

He stalked out of the room toward the kitchen, satisfied with himself. A glimmer of doubt flashed in the back of his mind like a wading life buoy. A reckless thought that threatened to push forward and crumble his new theory. He didn't just feel responsible, he felt—

"Time to eat!" he yelled to himself, in an empty corridor,

cringing at the sound of his own voice. He looked around to make sure no one heard him and ducked into the kitchen. He shook his head at himself, embarrassment rising. *I need to find a better way to silence my mind.*

***

"So," Riley asked, trailing behind Todd's long strides. "What did she do this time?"

"Huh?" Todd asked, raising his eyebrows dropping into a chair.

"Come on," Riley urged, leaning forward onto his elbows. "There's always something going on with Lana." Todd felt a small smile pull at his lips. Riley was right. Lana was always doing something dangerous, or *in* some kind of danger. Todd felt his shoulders drop, a breath releasing from his tight chest. "So?" Riley shrugged. "What is it this time?"

Todd unloaded the events of the last couple days to Riley. He didn't leave anything back. He let his mouth run like an unstoppable train. He needed to get it all out. He needed someone else to hear about *everything*. Someone who could bear the weight of it with him. "That's what you're mad about?" Riley gaped, open mouthed. "Well, that's dumb," Riley said, his face pinched in dissatisfaction.

"What?" Todd leaned back in his chair. "You're mad at Lana because she lied to you about morphing?"

"Well, yeah but—"

"What, are you in second grade?" Riley urged, crossing his arms over his chest. Todd clamped his mouth shut. His muscles flexing in his jaw. A moment of silence passed before Riley spoke again. "Todd, think about it. She's been kidnapped and held captive on an island full of people she doesn't know. She found out that she has the ability to morph into an animal, but has *yet* to do so. She's lost her independence. Her family. Her friends. Her home. She tells you one little lie, and you can't get over it?" Riley pushed himself out of his chair continuing before Todd had a chance to interrupt.

"You of all people should know what it's like *not* to fit in. Don't you think she had a reason for telling you this little lie? Lana doesn't do anything without a reason, or a purpose."

Todd was staring at his hands folded in his lap. He closed his eyes and cursed himself for being so stupid. An overwhelming feeling of guilt and embarrassment washed over him like a bucket of ice-cold water shocking him out of his self-pity. There were a lot of things rushing through his mind with no destination.

"Well?" Riley asked, dropping back into his chair.

"You're right, Riles," Todd whispered, unable to summon his full voice. He ran a hand through his hair. "A fourteen-year-old has better foresight than me." He shook his head. "How sad." Todd leaned across the round table separating them and rubbed a hand through the small boy's shaggy hair. "When did you get so smart?"

Riley laughed. "I've always been smart, but you know," he shrugged. "It helps when you're not in love with the subject matter," he said, batting his eyelashes and clasping his hands together flamboyantly. Todd shook his head. He should have expected that. He shoved Riley with one arm and sent the boy flying backward in his chair.

"Come on, we better get going," Todd said. Riley was right. Todd knew it, yes Lana had been cavalier with Todd's life, but what did he expect. Did he expect her to treat him like an equal when there were very clear lines defined between the two of them? She put him in danger, so? She was literally in danger every day. Or at least being threatened by Annette every other day.

Todd sauntered back to his barracks. He grew more furious with himself as the minutes ticked by. "Toddler!" a loud voice snapped. Todd jolted upright to see Pede walking briskly toward him. "Where have you been?" he snapped.

"Just on reprieve, sir."

"Well, if you're done taking your nap and eating your snack, it's time to get back to work."

Todd dropped his head to the floor. "Yes, sir." He bit his lip to muffle his snarl of frustration. It's not like he hadn't just worked seventy-two hours straight.

"Mr. Armstrong wants to see Taurin in his office." When Todd hesitated he continued. "That means now, Toddler." Todd nodded once more and set off in a trot to find Taurin. Pede was probably just too lazy to do it himself. He also knew he was the rookie. So, he had to put up with the other guards' shit.

\*\*\*

Claude sat in his oversized armchair, thrumming his fingers along the solid red wood of his desk. He listened to the methodical strumming of his fingers, his mind unfocused, his gaze fixed on a crooked ball point pen lying in front of him. His thoughts drifted seamlessly. A rare moment of uninterrupted tranquility. For a moment his mind wasn't drowning under a tidal wave of bureaucratic nonsense. A knock on the door snapped his focus back. He straightened his back in his chair and cleared his throat. "Yes?"

A tall, lanky frame ducked inside. "Mr. Armstrong." He

nodded. "I am sorry to interrupt you, Pede asked me to escort Taurin to your office?"

"Yes, yes," Claude answered, striding toward the door, "Allow her in." The beautiful tan skinned girl appeared behind Todd and slipped in behind him slowly, "That will be all for now Todd, thank you." Claude said, and patted him on the shoulder. Taurin waited with her hands folded in front of her, her eyes downcast. Claude smiled broadly at her and watched the tension melt away from her posture as he did. He could charm just about anyone, that was something he was good at. Something he knew how to use. He gestured to the two chairs sitting in front his desk, "Please Taurin, have a seat."

Taurin followed obediently, without so much as a breath in response. Claude sat himself down in the chair beside her. He ran a hand down his cleanly pressed black shirt and smiled sweetly at her again. He saw a delicate pink color rise in her cheeks. *Perfect.* He thought.

"Well Taurin, I just wanted to have a brief conversation with you," he said, leaning his back against the cushion of his chair. "How are your preparations coming since our last conversation."

A spark lit up in Taurin's eyes, like the yellow of a firefly. "Good! Really good. I've told everyone that I'll be leaving, and I've said most of my goodbyes." She smiled excitedly.

Claude nodded, "Very well." He leaned forward placing his elbows on his knees. "I would like to begin by saying thank you for stepping up to the plate with Lana. I know I put you under duress in that situation, but I must say you performed quite extraordinarily." Taurin dipped her head, a small smile of embarrassment pulling at her mouth.

"However," Claude continued, he rubbed a hand on his chin and sighed. "The issue, Taurin, is that since Dr. Otazzi is no longer on the island—I have no medical staff on hand." He paused, allowing the information to set in. Taurin's face pinched around her eyebrows and lips, confusion apparent in them. "So, I'm sure you can see the predicament that I am in, letting *you* leave us, with no one else on the island with any medical training."

"But I—" Taurin stammered.

"Let me finish, love," Claude said, holding up a hand to silence her. He stepped away from his chair and sauntered behind his desk, dragging his index finger along the tabletop. "I believe myself to be a man of my word, Taurin love. So, I will not force you to stay on the island as a medic." He turned to face her, watching a breath exhale from her chest. Her face bright with relief.

"However, I would like you to consider how—" Claude pursed his lips considering his word choice, *unpleasant*, it will be for all of your friends when I send them to the Underground, and they have no treatment available afterwards." Taurin's mouth fell open, gaping like a coy fish. "How tragic it would be if those friends of yours were to sustain injuries in their practicals with no one here to treat them."

"What are you saying, Mr. Armstrong?" Taurin asked, puffing out her chest. Her fingers gripped the ends of her chair, white at the tips. "Oh, come on now love. You're a smart girl. I think you can piece it together."

"If you're saying that you will intentionally hurt and torture my friends if I leave then—"

"—Then *what*?" He smiled and slunk around to the front of the desk, setting against it in a half sit, half lean. He slid his legs out in front of him, nearly touching Taurin as he crossed them at the ankles. "What exactly will you do?" he asked, folding his hands in his lap. A tear streamed down the girl's cheek. Her shoulders shaking slightly. She opened her mouth to speak, but no words came out. "That's right love," he whispered, leaning forward. "You're not going to do *anything* about it." He smiled, "Because you know *exactly* what I will do in reciprocation."

He pushed himself off the desk and took a long, calculated moment standing over top of Taurin. He patted the front of his shirt before circling back to his chair behind his desk. He ran a hand through his perfect blonde hair. "Do we have an understanding then, Taurin?"

The girl in front of him was a mere sample of the one who'd entered his office a few minutes earlier. Her body shook under her heavy sobs, tears cascaded down her cheeks with little reprieve. "I'm going to need an answer from you."

Taurin pressed her palms against her eyes and shuddered. Her emotions ravaged her body like a waterfall pulverizing the many layers of sediment lying below. A few moments passed before she nodded her head and squeaked out the tiniest, "Yes."

"Excellent," Claude nodded. "We will get you set up with some materials and manuals as well as a new dormitory near the infirmary." Taurin's eyes met his and Claude could feel the devastation in them. The fear, the desolation, the grief. He looked past it. He looked right past her actually. He nodded toward the door. "Off you go. You're going to want to start your move as soon as possible."

\*\*\*

Claude leaned against the back wall of his office. He was half listening to the monotonous voice droning over enforcement protocol. There had been a couple of slip ups in the last few weeks. "Lastly, we can install a secondary keypad outside the Underground to prevent" – the guard stuttered – "to uhm prevent—"

"—To prevent Annette killing someone." Claude snapped.

The guard stared wide eyed. Claude could almost feel him squirming under his stare, like an ant beneath a magnifying glass. He exhaled a breath, releasing some of the tension. It wasn't this guards' fault. "Couldn't we jus' get rid of the problem starters?" Locust interjected. Claude's head snapped up. The hackles on his back rising in the instant defense of his sister. "Choose your next words carefully, Locust."

"Ah bossman, I'm not talkin' 'bout Miss Annette. Nah, I mean the morphers. Get rid o' the troublemakers."

Claude's eyebrows drew together. He had less and less patience for his guards of late and their subpar intelligence. "Do you have some in mind then?"

"Well." He shrugged. "For starters, we could get rid o' the ones that don't even morph." He snickered. Locust clamped his hands over his mouth. "Whoops, sorry, I forgot you have a soft spot for 'er, don't cha?"

The room fell silent, the four senior guards seated around the table watching him closely. Again, Claude felt those familiar hackles rise on the back of his neck. Claude clenched his teeth, his jaw flexing with the exalted effort not to tear into Locust. He counted to ten in his head, bringing himself down with every number. The tension in the room grew. Roach and Pede sat closest to him visibly uncomfortable, Quito fidgeting incessantly with his pen.

"How long have you been waiting to say that then?" Claude breathed, pinching the bridge of his nose.

Locust sucked on his teeth and smiled. He shrugged, "Ah,

you know." Claude turned to peer out the window he'd been leaning against.

"What is it exactly that you are proposing, Locust? Release them back into society and risk being exposed? Release them back into society when they are a danger to both themselves and the world?"

"No, bossman, no, you got it all wrong. I'm not suggestin' we *release* them at all." He clapped his hands together. "I'm suggestin' we get rid of them, permanently. No muss, no fuss."

# Chapter Twenty-Six

Lana looked at herself in the floor length mirror standing across from her. She barely recognized herself. Deep purple and green bruises cuffed her wrists and ankles, equally purple bags sagged under her eyes. Her waist was thin, her body losing muscle from her lack of activity. Her hair was tattered and brittle at the ends and hanging lifelessly below her shoulders. She closed her eyes, the soft hum of voices in the hallway bringing back the conversation in Claude's office. She closed her eyes remembering every word like a song she couldn't get out of her head.

"I think a daily stipend spent in the Underground would be sufficient," Annette sang. Lana stiffened, fear pricking the back of her neck. Her heart dropped into her stomach. She balled her hands into fists, digging her nails into her palm. *Breath Lana, just breath. She wants to see your fear. Don't let her.*

Claude sighed. "I think that may be a tad aggressive." Annette shrugged her shoulders and flippantly pushed her hair off her bony shoulder. "Oh, I don't know. I think she can handle it." She turned smiling. "Right, Lana?"

Lana's fear quickly turned into anger. A simmering pot on the edge of boiling over. "You're a big girl, right?" Annette taunted, her tone mimicking that of a child. Lana squeezed her hands tighter and clenched her teeth. She didn't dare look to Claude for direction. If Annette caught the interaction she would know their game. She would know they had planned this interaction to appease her. Lana felt her breath shorten, a small notifier that her heart rate was steadily increasing. Her anger grew hotter inside her, firing through her veins like a liquid bullet.

*Fuck you. Fuck you. Fuck you.* She repeated in her head. She wanted to scream it and swear it. She wanted to launch her body across the room at the pathetically small woman and show her exactly how unmatched she was for Lana's physicality. Somehow, she remained seated. She wasn't sure what was keeping her there, but she didn't move.

"Annette, I think Lana has done her time in the Underground for this indiscretion. I propose we remove free time and seeing as she has no foundation for understanding her own heritage, she will be responsible for research about morphers. Hopefully, she'll gain a little bit more respect and understanding for what we do here."

Annette giggled. "Like detention." She clapped her hands excitedly. "Like detention for a grade schooler." Claude remained unfazed by her reaction. He pulled a red book from his shelf and flipped through its pages nonchalantly. "We can start with this one."

"I love it!" Annette piped. "Did you get that little Mùth, you're going to do all the grunt work for us and be drowning in a sea of paperwork for a heritage you swear doesn't exist. How sad for you."

Lana said nothing. Well, she said nothing out loud. Her mind screamed: *I HATE YOU!* She felt steam touch her face jolting her back to reality. She scurried to turn the shower down. It had probably been running for about fifteen minutes now. "Whoops." She whispered before slipping behind the curtain.

She was surprised no one had come to collect her. They

usually only had about ten minutes to shower. Maybe she was getting a little leeway, maybe they pitied her a little bit. Normally that would drive her crazy, but right now as the hot water slid over her body sending warmth to all her knots, bruises and cuts... she didn't care. For now, she'd take advantage of the pity. Because right now, it suited her.

***

She made her way toward the Oval for the first time in what felt like ages. She almost buckled at the feeling of grass underneath her feet. She stilled, breathing a deep breath and letting the air and earth wrap around her in a cocoon of happiness. She felt her long brown hair slip off her shoulders in the slight breeze. It traced the edges of her romper and found its way underneath to touch her skin. Goosebumps rose on her skin, her heart fluttering with pleasure.

She closed her eyes and allowed the fresh smells of grass and pine and crisp air slide into her lungs expanding them as much as her body would allow. When she finally opened her eyes again, the room had stilled. Almost comically, like a tableau. Two dozen sets of eyes were watching her, barely a breath disturbing the silence. Lana scanned the faces. A smile reaching her lips when she reached the one face grinning back at her. "Welcome back." Riley yelled across the room, purposefully disturbing the fishbowl.

As if on cue everyone else in the room seemed to lose interest in her appearance and returned to their huddles and outdoor games. Lana strode toward Riley's table. He was sitting across from a boy with dark curly hair. Surprise stirred within her.

"Lana!" Riley squealed, skirting around the table to hug her. Lana froze, not expecting the affection from the small boy. He seemed to feel her hesitation and stepped away. "Sorry, are we not the hugging type of friends yet?"

Lana laughed. The sound was foreign to her own ears. When was the last time she had laughed? She hadn't a clue. Riley took her laugh as a sign of approval and hugged her quickly again. He scooted back around the picnic table, "You remember Bennet, right?"

"Mm, quite clearly actually."

The boy's back snapped straight, chest puffing out in defense.

"Relax" – Lana waved her hand at him – "I'm not going to hit you, nor do I really care about what happened before."

Bennet's eyebrows pinched together, his light blue eyes gaping at her apologetically. "About that." He coughed, clearing his throat. "I was out of line before," he said, as Lana took up the seat next to him. "Sometimes I take things out on the wrong people." He adjusted his position on the bench to face her. "Friendly fire of sorts. You were just an easy target at the time." He shrugged and touched his eye. "Or so I thought."

All three broke out in a callous, rambunctious laugh. The kind that rumbled through your body and took your breath away. It was exactly the kind of healing that Lana needed. It lasted for a few minutes followed by a very poignant silence. No one knew how to ask her what had happened, or knew if she was open to talking about it.

"Go ahead Riles, I'm sure you're just about to burst with anticipation."

Riley didn't waste a moment. He leaned forward, elbows pressed down on the hard wood of the picnic table. "What happened?" he whispered and pushed his half-eaten sandwich toward her. Lana took a deep breath, a breath that ended in more of a sigh. "Sit back little man, cause this tale takes a few turns!"

Lana spent the next forty-five minutes explaining the whirlwind of the last seventy-two hours. Riley sat stunned in front of her. A blank expression on his small pale face and a large chunk of apple visible in his gaping mouth. "Riley, chew your damn food!" Bennet scoffed, tossing a napkin toward him.

"Let me get this straight." Bennet turned to face her. "You went to the Underground for over twenty-four hours. You almost died. You still haven't morphed. Annette pretty much wants you dead, so you need to watch your six. Claude clearly wants you alive or else he would have just let you die or left you to Annette. You were framed for hospitalizing the island doctor, and your punishment is grunt work about morphers?"

Lana nodded. "He also said he would remove my free time but Annette seemed to forget about that part, so I guess we'll see." Lana sipped from a bottle of water that Riley had passed her. "Damn," Bennet grunted. "You're almost having a worse time here than me."

Lana gave him a quizzical look. "Look, if Claude was going to serve me a punishment it definitely wouldn't be studying some books."

Lana nodded. She knew where he was going with this. "That's just the thing. Our Mr. Armstrong is much more manipulative than we thought. He knew that in Annette's eyes nothing was going to trump me being put on death row, other than something she saw as completely humiliating and demeaning to that person."

"I've always thought he played the good one," Riley interjected.

Both Lana and Bennet turned at that, their brows furrowed. "Pardon me?" Bennet said.

"You know like in movies!" Bennet looked to Lana for an explanation. She shrugged. "What are you talking about, Riles?"

"In the movies when they interrogate someone. There's always a good cop and a bad cop."

Lana and Bennet remained silent. Riley threw his hands up in the air in frustration. "In the movies, the cops are after the same objective, but one plays nice and the other plays mean." Riley took a breath and leaned across the picnic table again. "Claude's always been playing the same game as Annette. He just plays it smarter and better. He's more difficult to predict and harder to see coming." Riley sat back again taking a quick look over his shoulder. The closest people were well beyond ear-shot. "That's why he can get just about anyone in here to do anything he wants before even touching upon the fear and intimidation card."

A smiled pulled at the edges of Lana's lips. "Wow, Riles."

"What?"

"Not just a little kid there are yer bud?" Bennet tapped his hand on the table.

Riley laughed and mocked a hair flip. "I'm much more than a pretty face you guys. You should know that by now."

## Chapter Twenty-Seven

Todd paced back and forth in front of his bed. He swallowed back the lump in his throat and checked his watch for the fifteenth time in the last five minutes. If he procrastinated any longer he'd be late for his detail. "OK—" He breathed shakily. "It's fine," he whispered to himself in assurance. His steps falling in line with every breath. *Its-fine. Its-fine. Its-fine. Left-right. Left-right. Left-right.*

"You can do this," he said aloud as he approached the large arched wooden door. He stalled, taking one more deep breath and then rapped his knuckles lightly against the frame. When there was no answer, he cracked the door open. "Lana?" he called, not wanting to walk in on her if she was changing or something. "Lana?" he called again, this time louder. Still no answer. He pushed the door open fully, a part of him wondering if she was even there. Perhaps, Claude had come to collect her for something. He stopped short when he saw her lying in a tangled mess of sheets and pillows. A slight drip of relief dappling into his stomach.

He tried to call her name, but his voice failed him scraping out barely more than a whisper. He coughed to clear his throat, hoping that would be enough to stir her. It wasn't. He took another breath, this time filling his chest completely. "Lana?"

Again, she didn't respond. Not even a twitch in the sheets. He inched closer, calling her name several times, each time louder than the last. Still nothing. A slow icy strand of panic crept up his throat, like the growth of a plant. He felt his courage slip away like sand draining through his fingertips, replaced by his thundering heartbeat. *Fuck! Please don't be dead!* His mind screamed at him. Todd leaned over the bed, the panic within him flashing quickly from cold to hot. "LANA?" He shouted.

Her body snapped under the sheets rapidly. She jolted upright like a rattlesnake striking its prey, her head crashing against Todd's. Todd swore under his breath and staggered backward from the bed, a palm pressed to his cheek bone.

"Son of a—" he breathed. "Goddamn, ow!" Pain and embarrassment collided in his words. He felt both emotions similar to stubbing a toe. The instantaneous moment when you're more upset about the mere act of stubbing your toe, than the actual pain of it. A few seconds passed before Todd finally stopped fussing and remembered who his head had struck. His eyes snapped up and found Lana who was sitting cross-legged on the bed, a small smirk on her face. Todd dropped his hand from his face, heat rising in his cheeks.

"Well—" Lana said. "That was *quite* the reaction."

Todd opened his mouth to speak and closed it just as fast. He couldn't find the right words. *Dammit, why hadn't I thought of this before I got here?* The double meaning behind her words was clear. She was *clearly* not only referring to this very moment. He'd acted poorly the other day. A complete overreaction. He took a breath and exhaled loud enough for Lana to hear. "I wanted to tell you, Lana, that I'm sorry—"

"Todd, stop," she said, holding up a hand. She scooted herself to the edge of the mattress. "You don't need to apologize for anything. What you did wasn't *completely* unjustified. My aunt had this saying; *dwelling on the past brings nothing about.*" She took a moment to adjust some blankets in her lap, a small smile touched the edges of her lips. "So," she shrugged. "Let's move past it?"

Todd remained quiet for a moment. She forgave him? Just like that? What had he been so worried about? I guess he'd expected her to hate him. Yet another person who had let her down. She was watching him intently; he could see it. Her gray eyes amused. The only sound was the popping of wood from the fireplace.

"You know," he said finally. "I had to give myself a pep talk before coming in here today."

Lana smiled. A real smile that crinkled around her beautiful gray eyes. He had to stop himself from reaching for her face and tucking a stray hair behind her ear. He had to keep going. If he stopped now, he'd chicken out and never say what he wanted to say to her. "I know you want to move past it, but I think the reason I—" he groaned. "The reason I overreacted is because I care about you." He looked at her, his voice dropping to barely more than a whisper. "More than I should."

Lana's eyebrows drew together, her head tilted slightly to the side, her hair falling off her shoulders. Her lips parted in surprise. "Oh—" she said, sitting up straighter in the bed.

"It messed with my head and," he let out a tiny nervous laugh, "I don't know, I guess that's it." Todd could feel a surge of heat in his cheeks and ears. She hadn't moved, her face remained blank, her eyes vacantly staring at the floor space between them. He waited a few more seconds in a painfully awkward silence before turning on his heels and moving toward the door as fast as possible.

He'd do the remainder of his shift outside. It would be much less awkward. He wondered if he should have said anything at all? She was his first guard detail so he was still learning. *Maybe next time, don't get emotionally involved.* He thought to himself. That would probably make many aspects of his job a lot easier.

"Wait," Lana called, her voice still catching at the end.

Todd froze, every muscle in his body clenched at the sound of her voice. He squeezed his eyes shut and took one calming breath before turning to face her pity speech. Her words of reassurance that she cared about him, but in a different way, and they could still be friends. Now that he thought about it, that was probably the best outcome here.

He nearly rammed Into her as he turned around. Lana stood directly in front of him. Before he could say anything, she pushed herself up onto her tippy-toes and pressed her lips against his. He felt a surge of sweet heat course through his body, zipping from his lips down to his fingers and legs. It vibrated in him like an electric hum. His hand found the back of her head easily sliding into her hair. She pushed up into him harder. She felt so small in his arms, pressing her body against his.

After a while they broke away, both panting to catch their breath, both unsure of how to continue. It was clear that it would move very quickly from kissing to something else entirely. Lana stood in his arms, staring up at him. He wanted to kiss her like that again. He wanted to kiss her and never stop, but something did stop him. "Wait," he breathed huskily pulling himself away.

This wasn't the reaction he expected from her. Although, he wasn't really sure what he had expected. But this? Her feeling the same way? That was the farthest from his mind. There was one hiccup though. The very thing that halted them. How would this work? What was the plan? A secret relationship between the two of them?

*No, that's not possible. Not here.* He was a guard, and the island and Claude—it would never work. His heart thudded in his chest. He looked down at her, a tiny regretful smile on his face. Lana took a step back feeling the change in him, like a sudden drop in temperature. She was incredibly adept at that, "What?" she asked.

He knew the answer to his own question. It just wasn't the answer he wanted. They couldn't do anything or be anything. If anything happened to Lana because of him, he would never forgive himself. Just imagine if Annette found out. Lana just barely survived the last bout with her. If Annette got word of this it wouldn't be good.

"We can't, Lana," he forced the words from his lips.

Lana took a step back, a curious look on her face. She put some distance between the two of them, composing herself rather quickly.

"It's not because I don't want to," he started, biting his lip, "believe me I do—but..." He wasn't sure how to say this. He wanted this, he wanted her, but this would put both their lives in danger. "I'm a guard, this is my job." Todd gestured to his uniform and the small room they were in. He was desperate to find a reason good enough. Lana was quiet for a moment. She leaned herself against the desk in her room. "I get it Todd," she said, crossing her arms over her chest.

"I'm sorry, Lana, I wanted you to know I care for you, but I can't jeopardize—I mean I never expected you to—" he groaned and ran an agitated hand through his hair. It wasn't coming out the way he wanted. "It could get us both in a lot of trouble," he huffed. Lana sat back. She crossed her legs in front of her.

"Such a rule follower, aren't you?" she teased.

He lightened a bit at that, an inkling of relief blooming in his chest. "I've still got your back though," he said with a small apologetic smile. "Promise." He dipped his head toward her.

They stayed that way, on opposite sides of the room. For a while, neither of them spoke. It was as if they were both coming to terms with the fact that whatever was between them, would have to stay as it was. Unspoken and unacted upon. Nothing more could come of it. Not like what had just happened.

Todd knew it was the right thing, but in the moment it felt like the exact opposite. He was a guard, and she was a morpher, they had no chance. It was better to nip it in the bud now because it would be infinitely harder to do later on. "Still friends?" He smiled sheepishly.

Lana laughed. "I have so few." She nodded. "I can't really afford to start sacrificing them." He laughed at that. "Very true," he smiled.

***

"No, Lana—no don't press that one!" Todd groaned. He was hunched over a computer in the media room. "Look, you have to scroll down and click this one on the bottom of your screen."

"What the hell do you mean scroll? I don't see a scroll? There's NO SCROLL BUTTON ON THE SCREEN."

Todd took a deep breath. They'd been at this for two hours already. "I don't mean a literal scroll, I mean scroll your finger like you would down a book spine," he said, exhausted. Lana growled under her breath.

"This makes no sense," she said, pushing the mouse away from her. "Why can I not just take notes with pen and paper?"

"*Because*, this isn't the stone age, Lana. Besides, when it's typed you can be sure it's legible." He pointed to the bottom left side of the computer. "Now, right click on that icon there," he said. Lana rolled her neck from shoulder to shoulder, sighing in frustration.

"I'm sorry, but it's not like I had any of this" – she waved at the computer screen – "at the cabin. There wasn't exactly good reception."

Todd smiled, he'd never seen this side of her. It was cute. "It's OK, Lana," he said, his voice soft and reassuring. "I get it. This kind of stuff can be difficult for a lot of people." She smiled at that, a gratefulness sparkling in her eyes. "Well, mainly elderly people, but still," he teased, unable to help himself. He wanted to lighten the mood a bit. He'd never seen her give up on anything before and she was daringly close to doing so with the computer.

Her head snapped up, her eyes narrowed. For a moment, he thought she might have taken offense to that. She shoved her elbow into his side, falling into him slightly in a giggle. Todd stiffened slightly, he wasn't sure how to respond. Lana was acting no different than she had any other time. Maybe, it wasn't awkward for her. Maybe, she really was totally cool with it. That bothered him a little bit. Was he so easy to get over? He shook the thought from his head. *Don't go down that path.*

Lana set her fingers against the keyboard once again, striking the keys at an infuriatingly slow pace. Todd sat on his hands at one point to prevent from shoving her aside and doing it himself.

"OK good, you have a header now. So, refer back to your book here." Todd pointed to the leather-bound encyclopedia sized book, "And make some notes to go under your **ORIGIN:** header. Todd took a moment to stretch his legs, circling back every few minutes to check on her progress. He had to give himself a break, his patience was waning quickly.

ORIGIN:
– Dates back 3500 years

– First Eastern Morpher's lived in Damascus, and Athens.
– First Nations legends date back much further, specific regional origin unclear.
– Oldest Morphing families:
· *Smith*-North America
· *Eacho*-North America
· *Jones*-North America
· *Yenni*-Middle East
· *Alexopoulos*-Greek Islands
· *Wilson*-New Zealand
· *Taylor*-Australia
· *Williams*-Australia
· *Silva*-Brazil
· *Garcia*-Mexico
· *Zhau*-China
· *Mensah*-African Continent
· *Nakamura*-Japan
· *Henrikson*-Scandinavia
· *Miller*-Britain

Todd seated himself next to her again. His back hunched and eyes tired. He pinched the bridge of his nose to calm his pounding head. Lana sighed loudly and dropped her head into her hands. "I can't *do* any more." She growled, and shook her head back and forth. Todd's shoulders dropped in relief. He was exhausted. He bit back his celebratory words of relief and composed himself again.

"Well, there isn't a quota you have to reach each day, you just have to make it through these books," he said, gesturing to the small stack of books to his left. "Maybe we call it a day?"

Lana nodded slowly, "Yes please. My brain feels like

oatmeal."

Todd smiled, his headache instantly seeping from his brain. He stretched his arms over his head and yawned. He wasn't going to tell her how excruciating it was to sit there for two hours and watch her type one-page worth of content. He felt like a hamster who'd been running on a wheel for hours. An endlessly useless activity.

"I definitely wouldn't have cut it as a teacher," he mumbled, as he tracked to the back of the room to replace the books they had borrowed.

"What?" Lana called, from her seat near the computer.

"Nothing!" he called back.

# Chapter Twenty-Eight

Claude stood at the back of the room and watched Riley leap from one pedestal to the next, climbing his way to the ceiling. He waved at the little red fox and made some notes on his clipboard as the bushy tailed tyke obediently made his way back down. "That's good, Riley, that will be all for today," he said, flicking his finger at the doorway. A guard entered in response.

"Please take Riley back to his dorm." Quito nodded and attached a slipknot leash around the fox's neck.

"Oh, and Quito, please send Miss Chase in."

Only a few moments passed before Lana slipped through the large training room door. She walked into the room, her hair was tucked back in a French braid, and she wore a plain t-shirt and jean shorts. She reached the center of the room and looked Claude dead in the eyes. He smiled at that. He couldn't help himself. He admired her tenacity. Her unbreakable spirit. Her interminable desire to not break or be broken. It excited him in a way not many others did. He was not often challenged to this extent. He loved game, and Lana, she made the game infinitely more interesting.

"Miss Chase, good afternoon. If you would please remove your shirt and shorts, we will begin the session."

Lana paled, her body rigid. Claude held up a hand, his palm facing her. He shook his head slightly as he strode across the room to meet her. "Lana, love, I mean nothing of the sort." He gestured to her clothing. "I am expectant of your morph and your training suit is better for that transition."

He watched as the young girl took a deep breath and straightened her posture. Claude could almost see the willpower rising to the surface within her. She clenched her jaw and grabbed the bottom of her shirt, pulling it over her head and tossing it at the floor beside her feet. She unbuttoned her shorts and let them drop as well, kicking them aside.

Claude paused for a moment. He wiped a hand over his mouth and rubbed at the slight stubble starting on his cheeks. He walked over to the treadmill and tapped it with his pen. "Start with a warmup, love."

Lana followed without a word and stepped onto the treadmill. She wore her matching pair of spandex shorts and sports bra, her name written across in a blue font. The suits were a brand-new addition to the island. Their scientists had been working on a material that would morph with them, without looking like an animal wearing pants and a shirt. This prototype had been very successful thus far.

Claude ran her through a circuit, running, lifting; arms, legs, finishing with core. An hour passed, and Claude looked at Lana lying beneath him. She held her body in a plank position, her muscles defined with a glistening sweat. Her hair fraying along her back peeking out in wisps from her braid, her entire body shaking. The fatigue of her muscles blatantly clear. A deep puddle of sweat formed underneath her head. Claude knelt in front of her face. She squinted as sweat ran into her eyes and spit on the mat in front of her as it ran into her mouth. Claude could almost taste the salt in his own mouth.

He felt a smile pull at the side of his mouth, he waited until her eyes met his, until he saw the desperation in them. Then, and only then did he give her the slightest nod. Lana instantly dropped herself. She collapsed on the mat panting hard.

"That will be all, Miss Chase. I'll see you tomorrow."

She turned her head slightly and glared up at him from her splayed position on the floor. She took a few deep breaths and shakily pushed herself up. Her limbs slipping and sliding in her own sweat, before she made it to her feet. She clenched her teeth, clearly unimpressed by her ungraceful attempt to stand.

"Quito will take you back to your dorm." Claude nodded toward the door. He watched her walk out, before making his way out of the training center. He took a moment to scan the room, a smirk on his face. "I will do it one of these days, Lana. I will push you to your breaking point. I will force your animalistic nature to come out." He didn't hesitate a moment longer. He only needed that minor aside. He had a meeting to get to.

***

Claude held the small, clear pill between his fingers. It was no bigger than the average Advil, or Tylenol tablet. He could see miniscule silver balls within the pill, a stringed wire connecting them. A red band wrapped around its center.

A short fat man stood across from him. His eyes bulging behind his thick rimmed glasses, like a child waiting to be commended. "So, sir," he said giddily as he rubbed his hands together. "This is very exciting – *yes* – very exciting indeed. You were ingenious to suggest this method, if I can be so bold as to say that, sir, I—"

"Please, Francis," Claude interrupted. "Cut and dry. How does it work?"

"A chemical compound in the tube can be released by an electric pulse created by this gun." The older man nodded excitedly and shuffled to a drawer at the back of the room. He pulled out a black metal object and slid it across the stainless-steel table to Claude.

Claude looked down at the item. "Francis—" Claude said, annoyance clear in his tone. "This looks like an ordinary gun." The island scientist scurried over to his side of the table. "No, no." He panted, slightly winded by his short jaunt. "It is meant to mimic the appearance of a regular Glock pistol, but if you see this trigger here" – he pointed to a lever on the side of the barrel – "that activates the electric signal transmitted to the pill."

"So, point and shoot?" Claude asked, hesitant about how simple that sounded.

"Well, if you want to take it down to the absolute basics, then—yes, you can say point and shoot but, there is more science behind it, sir, and—"

"FRANCIS," Claude interrupted, his voice more stern this time. "Spare me the senseless jabber. Give me the black and white version of your endless storytelling."

Francis nodded his head up and down about three times before speaking again. Claude knew he was trying to prioritize his notes in variations of importance. He should be used to his frantic nature, but he was a very odd man. The man's energy didn't mesh well with his own. He'd been thrown out of various universities as a professor in years past. Which, conveniently, made him ideal for the island. He was maybe five feet tall, with a pot belly, balding brown hair, and short stubby fingers. "It will be inserted at the base of the neck," he said, tapping the back of his own neck. "It will require updating every eight months to a year depending on how often it is used."

"How long will they be out for?"

"That is difficult to judge, it would depend on the person. Anywhere from 1–5 hours."

"And they will be awake during that time?"

The scientist paused a moment. Claude could practically see

the gears turning in his mind as he chose his words, ever so carefully. "It would be more akin to a state of paralysis. The subject would not be able to move, so in one sense yes, they would be awake. However, to counteract the subjects falling prey to their own limp bodies, the electronic pulse will also counteract the body's natural melatonin levels and help to keep them *awake*," he said, placing air quotations around the last word.

"So, in theory, if I shot this at a morph, they will be lucid through their shift back to human form?"

"Yes indeed, sir."

"Well," Claude said, turning over the black metal pistol in his hand. He traced the groove on the barrel with his fingers, a tiny smile starting to form on his face. "That is *quite* excellent!"

"It will be fully operational in just over twenty-four hours. All the prototypes, including the one you are holding have all been successful."

Claude nodded, passing the pistol back to Francis.

"Sir, may I ask, do you know who the first subject might be?" he asked, the desperation in his eyes as hungry as an animal.

"Oh, I think I have an idea," he said, smiling a little bigger. "I have an idea," he repeated to himself in a whisper.

\*\*\*

Lana turned through the pages of the red leather bound book. Claude had allowed her to take one back to her dorm with her. She still had to take notes. For Annette, proof of sorts. She'd be able to type it up at her next session in the media room.

Morphers who descend from two Mùth parents have the ability to possess either parent's hereditary morph. The Paternal morph is exceptionally dominant. There are very few cases that exist where a child of two morphing parents carried the maternal morph. These cases only seem to occur when the maternal morph pre-dates the paternal.

Lana made a note on the pad of paper sitting to her right. She sat cross-legged on the floor of her room. Her back leaning against the frame of her bed. The large book sitting in her lap. She was actually semi-enjoying the monotonous task. It was easy, and it helped pass the time. It was better than just sitting in agonizing anticipation of the next time her door would open. She found herself somewhat missing the homey-ness of Claude's room. It had a warmth about it that was clearly absent in the morpher's dorm rooms. She also wondered why her sessions with Miss Mason had ended so suddenly. She expected they had only been suspended for a day or so, but they had yet to continue. Not that she was complaining, she didn't enjoy the woman's company. It just added another level of anticipation to her already anxious life. She returned her attention to the book beneath her fingers. "Focus, Lana," she reprimanded herself.

There have been several cases of orphaned Mùths, who, unaware of their inner nature, have injured and killed civilians. There are also unfortunate cases wherein the Mùths are unable to revert back to human form and remain in their morph for the remainder of their lifetime.

Lana placed her pencil down on her paper and set her book aside. She stared at the words on the page. Her eyes re-reading them over, and over again. Her chest pumped quickly, a nervous, uneasy feeling shooting down into her stomach. She pulled a hand through her hair and closed her eyes. She mentally pushed down at the billowing smoke of fear building within like an untamed bonfire.

"If I really am a Mùth, that might mean, that I—I'm never myself again?" Lana shook the words from her mind. She pushed her papers farther away, refusing to write those words down. As if, if she didn't write them, they weren't true. She could just forget she'd ever read it.

She stood up cringing at the ache in her legs from sitting too long. She grabbed at the bottom of her window and pulled herself up onto the ledge. She pressed her hand against the fogged glass and felt its cool condensation beneath her fingertips. She breathed in a long, controlled breath. She closed her eyes and focused all her attention on her breath. A breath to steady her pounding heart, a breath to quell the nerves tingling in her stomach, a breath to set her breaths pace.

Not long afterward Quito came to retrieve her for lunch. Lana couldn't hide the relief from her face. She needed to speak to Riley. She practically ran through the Oval's massive heavy door. She quickly scanned all the faces in the room once, twice, three times. *Nothing.* No Riley. "Dammit." She cursed under her breath. "The one time he's not here."

She considered just turning around and leaving, her stomach was in knots after all, it's not like she could eat right now. Just as she turned to leave, she saw a familiar black headed figure near the back of the room. She clenched her teeth, pushed her ego aside and trotted over to him. She slid into the picnic table, seating herself in front of him. He looked genuinely surprised to see her, pausing mid-bite of an apple.

"Uhm, hello?" he said. "I know we've made it past our differences, but we're not going to be like best friends now, right?"

Lana huffed and sent him a sarcastic smile. "Nice."

He shrugged his shoulder, unsure of how to proceed.

"Look, I wouldn't bother you with this, but Riley is my go-to and he's clearly been caught up being a teachers' pet somewhere."

Bennet put the apple down on the tray in front of him and nodded for her to continue. "I've been doing some research about Morphing and Mùth history, and I just wanted to verify something, when you—you know shift." She shrugged. "It's-easy-to-change-back-right?" She pushed the words from her mouth in a panicked jumble. Bennet took a moment and crossed his arms over his chest.

"Not always, no."

Lana felt the panic ignite in her core once again. "What happens if—"

"If you can't shift back?" he cut in. Lana didn't have to say anything to confirm, her pained face a clear indication of what she was thinking.

"It happens," Bennet shrugged. "It's not really a big deal. It kind of comes with the territory."

Lana's face paled.

"Look, it's not like the person is dead, they just have to live as their morph."

"Is there no way they can be turned back?"

Bennet paused. "That's probably something they're working on here," he said gesturing around himself. "The longer you stay in your morph, the more difficult it is to phase out of it. It's not impossible though, just more difficult." He sighed. "For some it is *too* difficult. It depends on the person, how strong they are mentally, physically and how *in-control* they are of their morph, things like that."

"I am assuming," Bennet continued, "that's not what you wanted to hear."

Lana shook her head. "I was hoping it was false information." She twisted her hands together in her lap. Her mind spinning.

"Lana, seeing as you haven't even morphed yet I wouldn't let it bother you. It may be something you never have to worry about."

Lana nodded, he was right, of course. She hadn't morphed yet, but that's exactly why she was worried. If she had done it, and come out of it, she would at least know a little more about the process and how she felt during it. Now, she didn't only have to worry about whether or not she would morph, but whether or not she would morph back.

"If it helps, it would be pretty difficult to stay morphed after your first transition."

Lana perked at that. "What do you mean?"

"Your first morph doesn't really last long, it's completely new to your body, and you basically pass out after only a few minutes because your body is completely overwhelmed and exhausted. Your body's default is to be human, not animal. After a few shifts that line can become blurred, and that's when it becomes more difficult."

Lana clenched her teeth together. She pressed down harder when she felt the searing spike in her gums. She tilted her head upward and swallowed the mouthful of blood.

"Are you all right?"

Lana grimaced at him and gave him a thumbs up. "Just peachy." She gargled.

"Your gums hurt, don't they?"

Lana's head snapped back down quickly, her hair spilling onto her shoulders. "What?"

"That's what you're doing, isn't it?" he said, taking another bite of his apple. "Clenching your teeth 'cause your gums hurt."

"How did you know that?"

"Because I used to do the exact same thing."

Lana felt her heart thud excitedly in her chest. She tucked her hair behind her ears and licked her lips. Her stomach twisting with anticipation. "You mean, you know what this is, why it happens?"

Bennet smiled, "It probably means you have a decent set of canine's heading your way."

# Chapter Twenty-Nine

Todd sat behind the flickering screen of a computer in the media room. He rubbed at his eyes, his vision blurring from fatigue. He quickly jotted down another note about Morphing history.

It was common for Morphers to be groomed as spies in ancient wars. It was especially popular in the Middle East.

Two pages of scribbled notes sat beside him, in an unorganized pile. Todd stared at them groggily, his eyes half open. He wished he'd been able to do more before exhaustion found him. He'd wanted to pump out some solid pages for Lana, but that proved more difficult than he anticipated because he was only able to use it after hours, which was post-midnight. He glanced down at his watch, 2.13 a.m. He told Lana he had her back and that apparently included helping her type up her notes for Claude. He sighed and started to sign off the computer. He folded up the papers and slipped them into his back pocket. He sluggishly erased every trace that he was ever there.

He gave the table a final wipe and heard the door to the media room bang open. His heart lurched and he dropped to his knees, shoving himself under the desk nearest him. He made himself as small as possible, which wasn't easy for a person his height. He pressed his palm over his mouth. His heart pounded so ferociously in his chest he was sure the person would hear it. He technically was not supposed to be in here at this time. He just hadn't expected anyone to find him here at this hour. A voice broke the silence, "I am well aware of the profitability," a charming English tone said aloud. Todd didn't dare move to get a better look. He didn't need to. He knew that it was Claude. His voice was extremely distinctive.

"Look, I don't know what else to tell you. I understand Annette made you a promise, but there is no morph yet. I can assure you I am doing everything in my power—" He paused, a moment. Todd could hear the muffled murmur of the person on the other line.

"No, I cannot confirm her morph," he stated. *More silence.*

"All I can tell you is that she comes from one of the oldest Mùth lines. We are certainly hopeful that—" a pause again, this time longer. "Yes, all relatives have been dead ends. It's a very secretive family. She does have one cousin, however their morph comes from the paternal line. He heard Claude pull a chair back and drop himself into it.

"I understand, and your contributions have been very generous. I will inform you of any progress." A slight pause, then "goodbye."

A heavy silence filled the room. Todd pulled his hand away from his mouth and pressed it against his chest, his heart was pumping so rapidly. A loud crash jarred him, he clenched his teeth in apprehension of being found. Claude yelled, an angry primal noise, and sent more things crashing around the room. Todd could just make out the edges of some books now laying on the floor.

"As if I haven't been busting my ass to uncover what her morph is going to be you bleedin' wanker!"

A small red file slid across the floor toward Todd. It had clearly been tossed in Claude's bout of rage. Todd recognized the file cover immediately. It was the same one they held for each of the morphers on the island, but slightly different. This one had a small sticker in the bottom right corner, the corner nearest him that read *Original.* He could just make out the last few last letters of the name on the cover—*ase.*

He knew without a doubt whose file it was. It was *Alana Chase*. A curiosity shot through him like the twitching of an unsettled cat. Lana had seen her file and it did not have an *original* tag on it. It had also been such bare bones information, even his own file contained more information than that. This file was clearly something Claude was working on himself. There might be more information about her family in that folder, there might be answers for her.

Todd spent another hour hunched under one of the desks. He hadn't adjusted himself so much as an inch. There would be no forgiveness for him if he was caught in here, after hours. He waited a solid twenty minutes after he heard the door close before peeking out of his hidey hole.

A momentous feeling of relief lifted from him, like cinder blocks rising from his chest. Claude had picked up all his books and papers shortly after throwing them around the room. Todd tiptoed toward the door. He pushed it open slightly and stopped. He listened for any sound on the other side. *Nothing.* He needed to keep going and quickly. He slipped out of the door and gently closed it behind him. He swallowed back the saliva building in his mouth and continued to tip-toe in a hurried fashion down the corridor. He paused at a large wooden door.

"Don't do it Todd—don't fucking do it," he whispered to himself. It made sense when he thought about it. If Claude had answers about Lana and her past, he wouldn't keep it in the media room where she could get to it. He would keep it separate, as a bargaining tool. Something he could bribe her with or use to sway her. He would keep that in his office, because no one would dare go in there without permission. "Fuck me," Todd whispered, placing his hand on the handle.

He opened the door much the same way. He opened it a crack and listened, before pushing onward. He could barely hear his own footsteps over his thundering heartbeat. His stomach clenched and unclenched as each step ignited a more threatening fear. He didn't have to go far. Claude was clearly tired and frustrated, he'd tossed all the materials on the top of his desk. Lana's red file sat like a beacon on the top.

Todd flipped it open. It wasn't what he was expecting. It was only two pages.

**Mùth Information Sheet:**
    **Name:** Alana Claire Chase
    **Born:** September 13, 1997
    **Morph:** Unknown

**History:**
    **Mother:** Claire Chase (Deceased)     **Lineage:** Unknown
    **Father:** Logan Chase (Deceased)     **Lineage:** Canadian Lynx

    **Guardian:** Alice Emmerson     **Location:** Tyndale home

**Notable Remarks:**

☐ Alana lived with her guardian for fourteen years after her parents' death.

☐ Referred to Ms. Emmerson as Aunt Alice.

☐ Alana unaware Alice Emmerson was her paternal biological grandmother.

☐ Alice married Evan Chase a non-Mùth. She had two sons during her marriage to Evan: Logan, and Richard.

☐ When Alice was pregnant with Richard and Logan four years old, Evan Chase left them.

❏ Alice reverted to her maiden name of Emmerson. Her son Logan maintained the surname Chase, but Richard unborn at the time of his father's departure took the name Emmerson. Logan Chase and Richard Emmerson respectively.

❏ Logan Chase married Claire Eache.

❏ Claire Chase, (formerly Claire Eache) derived from the ancient *Eacho* line. We have not seen a morph from this line in generations due to crossbreeding with non-Mùth.

❏ Claire's family crossbred for generations all of whom carried the Mùth genealogy but failed to produce the quality of offspring morphing required.

❏ Claire descended from the Eache Mùth gene, mated with another Mùth, Logan Chase of the Emmerson line. This can only result in Mùth offspring.

❏ The maternal morph is far older and therefore dominant over the paternal.

❏ We expect a rare and explicitly valuable transition.

Todd re-read the information before him three times before it settled in. "Holy fuck." He breathed. He dropped the file back onto the desk and quickly made his way back to his room. His mind spinning, not only did he get some answers for Lana, he'd found out one very important piece of information.

Her Aunt Alice was still alive.

# Chapter Thirty

Claude felt a mixture of anticipation and excitement twist in his stomach. It itched its way up his spine and down his arms. He felt himself being quite restless, constantly rearranging his position in the medical suite. Dr. Francis stood on the opposite side of the room. The short fat man was twirling the gun-like activation system in his hands, admiring it like a child.

Taurin swept around the room disinfecting a myriad of surfaces. She focused her attention on the dentist like leather chair bolted to the floor just in front of Claude. The obtrusive piece of furniture was brand new to the island, ordered as a special request by Dr. Francis. They had added some restraints to the chair. A nylon buckle sat on both armrests, another on the bottom to wrap around the feet.

Taurin knelt down in front of the chair, her back rigid. She peeked over her shoulder at Claude and he watched as she exhaled a shaky breath. She was clearly uncomfortable having her back to him. Claude felt the hint of a smile pull at his lips. He liked that. The intimidation his presence brought. It made him feel powerful. "How much longer Taurin love?"

Dr. Francis' eyes popped up for the first time. They widened nearly twice their normal size behind his large glasses. You could practically see him drooling with excitement.

"I'm almost finished. I just have to wipe down the headrest."

Claude nodded. He hoped this would be the answer he was looking for. The idea that it might be, was almost too pleasurable for him to consider. He should always keep his expectations low. He should know that after working with Mùths for this long. However, no matter how hard he tried, a part of him couldn't contain the tiny hopeful flutter in his heart. *This could work!*

"All right, we're ready!"

Dr. Francis yipped excitedly, and nearly ran around the large stainless-steel table between them. He placed the clear capsule with a thin red band around its center on the metal tray of medical instruments and flashed an ugly yellow tooth grin. The excitement spewing from him like a sputtering fountain. "It is up to you now, El-Capitan. When you're ready to make the call."

Claude paused for only a moment. He allowed himself to smile and patted the scientist on the shoulder. He pulled at the walkie-talkie on his hip, "Locust, retrieve and deliver the Mùth."

A moment passed. "10-4."

It was only about ten minutes later that there was a loud knock on the door. Claude opened it and Locust pushed his captive inside by the back of the shirt. "Here ya' go, sir," he gruffed. Claude found himself immediately agitated by Locust's brute use of force.

"That will be all," he said, clippingly dismissing him.

"Wha'?" Locust whined, "I don' get ta' stay for the fun bit?"

Without missing a beat Claude said, "Every person in this room has a purpose to serve. You have served yours, so as I said, that will be all, Locust."

The guard scrunched his face as if to say something, but Claude took a warning step toward him. Locust mumbled something under his breath and slammed the door behind him. Claude turned to see Taurin attending to the fallen morpher.

"Well now, are you ready to do this?"

The boy's big brown eyes looked to Taurin and then back to

Claude. He was afraid. His hands trembling. Taurin grabbed them in hers and pulled him to his feet. She wrapped one arm around his shoulder and guided him into the chair. Dr. Francis barely waited until the boy was fully seated before pulling the nylon buckles as tight as they could go.

Claude took a step forward, "I want to thank you, Riley," Claude said, looking into the boy's petrified eyes, "for being the first one to take this step." The young boy didn't respond. "Don't worry, it will be over before you know it, won't it, Dr. Francis?"

The doctor looked confused by the question. He'd been staring at Riley, like a dog with a bone. Claude shook his head, he didn't know why he expected something different from the estranged man. He had proven useful over the years, but definitely not professional or ethical. "Let's begin." Claude nodded.

Taurin put on a set of latex gloves and swabbed the back of Riley's neck with alcohol. She put a reassuring hand on Riley's arm and squeezed. "OK Riley, I'm going to make a small incision at the back of your neck, right here," she said, using her index finger to touch the spot. Riley flinched expecting pain. "It's OK, Riley," she reassured calmly, "not yet. It's important you try not to move. I will try to do it as quickly and painlessly as possible."

Riley puffed his chest out and clenched his teeth. Taurin nodded and picked up a scalpel. She carefully made an incision half an inch long roughly two inches underneath Riley's hairline. She dropped the instrument onto the metal tray with a clang as soon as she was done. A cue to Riley that that part was over.

Dr. Francis came around to Taurin cradling his creation in his arms. Taurin moved out of his way. She dropped in front of Riley and took his hand in hers. She gave him a reassuring squeeze. "You're almost through the worst of it." Riley blinked back the tears forming in his eyes, and squeezed Taurin's hand back. "You're going to feel a puff of air on your neck and a small shock—" Before she could finish, Dr. Francis placed the applicator against the incision in Riley's neck and inserted it.

The applicator looked like an epi pen. It was a small clear tube with a green button on one end and red one on the other. The pill sat in a compartment at the green end that was released with the compressed air, after pressing the green button. "Ouch," Riley squealed, before quickly clamping his mouth shut and looking to Claude apologetically.

"It's OK, Riley." Taurin assured him. "You're doing great!"

"OK," the doctor yipped, dropping the applicator on the metal table beside him with a clang. Taurin gave Riley another reassuring squeeze before slipping behind his head to close-up the incision. She wiped the area again and smeared an antiseptic ointment over the cut. She gently placed two butterfly bandages over the incision. "OK, all done," she said, patting Riley on the shoulder to let him know it was over for him as well.

"Thank you, Taurin. You may go have your lunch now." She hesitated for only a moment. Peaking back at Riley, who still had a painful look of fear bugging from his eyes. Claude pulled the door open and swept his arm wide through the gap. "Thank you for your assistance, Taurin love. Off you go now." Taurin ducked her head and hurried out the door.

"Now, Mr. Churchill." Claude smiled. "You are hopefully going to be a gamechanger in the efficiency of morphing. How would you like to give that a go?" Claude said, rubbing his hands together.

\*\*\*

Claude sat in one of the plastic folding chairs positioned against the back wall of the practical. He eagerly drummed his fingers along his leg as he waited for everyone to take their seats. Riley sat beside him chewing his fingernails. When Annette finally strolled into the room, Claude popped up from his chair and clapped his hands together. There weren't many in the room, Pede, Dr. Francis, and now Annette. If all went well, he'd have a grander showing for the rest of the guards. "All right! Riley, if you would join me up here, please."

Riley dropped his hands to his side and slowly met Claude where he was stationed in front of the row of chairs. "I'd like you to transition now Riley. Just as you normally would. Nothing out to the ordinary."

Riley frowned and motioned as if to say something. It fizzled in him before it reached the surface. He took a step back and closed his eyes. Claude watched as he always did as the shape in front of him began to blur. It took him a long time to dull his instinctual reaction to this. The incessant urge to wipe his eyes, or blink away the fuzziness. Anything to clear his vision. It wasn't his eyes that needed clarity of course and he knew that. The object in front of him was purposefully not in focus, and yet, no matter how many times he stood here, watching, it was always his first reaction.

A small red fox appeared before him, without missing a beat, it trotted over to the training gear, like he normally would in a practical. "Riley, not just yet." Claude called.

Claude stretched out his hand and Doctor Francis placed the pistol looking object into it. The fox immediately retreated a few steps, his head down, ears flat, hair erect. Claude knelt down and raised his palm facing out toward Riley. A visual cue to remain calm. "It's all right, Riley. It is not what it appears to be." He laid the pistol flat in his other palm and offered it forward to the animal. He encouraged him with a wave of his hand. "Come, see for yourself."

The fox took three small steps forward, hesitation clear in his pace. Claude remained still, the tip of his index finger still resting on the trigger. Riley took another step toward him. Claude swiftly tightened his fingers around the handle and turned his hand, pressing his finger down on the trigger.

Riley seemed to freeze in place for a second. Only a second. He swayed where he stood, his legs crossing over one another as they tried to get their bearings. He shook his head, once, twice, three times, before falling onto his side. The only movement now came from his chest rapidly rising and falling. Claude approached the morph, the anticipation vibrating within him. His heart rate matching its persistence. He reached down and looked into Riley's terrified eyes.

"I need you to calm down Riley," he said, running his hands through the fur on the top of the animal's head. "If you continue to panic you will exhaust yourself. There is a component in the insert that is meant to slow your heart rate. Don't fight it."

"We can make that stronger for the next trial," Dr. Francis piped from behind him.

"Just give him a minute," Claude assured. Almost on cue, he watched as the boy's chest rose slower and more deeply. "That's it," he whispered.

# Chapter Thirty-One

Lana looked at herself in the mirror of the bathroom. Her time in this elegant marbled space had come to be her second favorite time of day. The first being any time she was in the Oval. She gently ran her finger over her gums, flinching at their tenderness. She pulled at her cheeks and lifted her tongue, investigating further to see if there were any signs of canines. None. She dropped herself down on the toilet. A feeling of both relief and disappointment stirred in her. At least, if they were there, she'd finally have an answer. A reason to be on the island. Their absence just further taunted her belief in the morphing legend, and her captivity on the island.

She hung her head in her hands and breathed a shaky breath. "I don't even know what I want." A knock on the door brought her back to the surface. It was her five-minute warning. "Yeah, I'm coming," she answered. The knocking came again, more persistent this time. "Yes, I heard you, I am coming." Before she could finish her sentence, it came again, louder and faster this time. "I said, I am coming," she shouted, yanking the door open. A tall, lanky frame nearly fell on top of her. He pressed a hand against her mouth to silence her screech of shock.

"Shhhhh, it's me." He breathed in quickly. "It's me! Let me in quickly." He hushed as he fumbled the door shut behind him.

"Todd?" Lana breathed in a rush of confusion. "What are you doing?" She stood in front of him, her hands cinching her towel under her arms.

"I'm not—I just..." His eyes darting to her towel.

"Todd, if you look at me and not the ceiling that might be a good start."

"Sorry! Sorry!" He stumbled. "I just don't want to offend—"

"Oh my God!" Lana interrupted, rolling her eyes. "All right, here I'll put something on." Lana stepped into the shower and slipped into her floral romper. "I'm assuming you have a reason for being in here Todd?" she encouraged.

"Yeah, I—uh, I don't really know how, or where to start?"

Lana peaked her head out of the shower. "We're limited on time here, Todd," she said, a playful smile on her face.

"OK, well, to start things off, my name is not Todd."

Lana stilled, she drew her eyes up slowly. "What?" she said in a breathy voice.

"It's short for Toddler, it's the stupid fucking name they gave me as a guard. It was supposed to be something intimidating, you know like Locust, Pede-centipede, Roach-cockroach." He waved his hand. "The list goes on and on." He took a step toward her meeting her eyes for the first time. "My real name is Henry."

"Oh—"

"Wait, let me finish." He raised a hand. "That is not *even* what I came up here to tell you."

Lana stepped forward and sat herself on the edge of the tub. "OK, go ahead."

"Last night, I broke into Claude's office after seeing him with your file and not the abridged version that we found earlier. Your *REAL* file." Lana sat up straighter, interest peaking within her.

"OK." She nodded, elongating the word with encouragement.

"The file said that, well the main thing it said, is that your

Aunt Alice." Todd looked at Lana and sat himself on the toilet seat facing her. He shook his head and wiped a hand over his mouth. In one rushed breath he said, "She is not dead."

Lana felt her heart drop, disbelief attacked her brain like a hoard of bees. No words found their way to her lips. An ice-cold dread filled her insides, sinking in her stomach and tickling its way up her spine. She stared blankly at the space between them. Her mind unable to make the connection. How could she have trusted Claude's words so easily? How could she be so naive? Her heart rate accelerated, her breath coming fast and short. Her aunt had taught her so much better than that. She would be so disappointed in her. Doubt first, trust second. Another one of her many mottos. "Lana? Are you OK?"

She slipped down onto the floor, her lungs burned from the shallow breaths. "Lana, Lana, breathe!" Todd said, suddenly crouched beside her. His hand resting on her back. "You're having a panic attack. You have to breathe!"

She could hear Todd's words but she couldn't find the right pace for her breath. She kept gasping, desperately trying to fill her lungs. Her mouth seared red hot. She tasted blood as it slipped down the back of her throat. "Lana, deep breaths. Come on do it with me now," Todd said, "*In* one, two, three; *out* one, two, three; *in* one, two, three; and *out* one, two, three."

She closed her eyes, her hands starting to shake. She balled them into fists and bit down on her cheeks as tears rolled down her face.

"Lana, I need you to hear me." His voice drifted, feeling farther and farther away. "You are having a panic attack. Focus on one small thing in the room. Here," Todd said, moving in front of her. "Look at me, look at me." He pulled her hands into his and placed them on his chest. "Feel my heart. OK? Now breath with me. *In* one, two, three; *out* one, two, three. *In* one, two, three; *out* one, two, three."

Lana listened and felt the thumping underneath her fingertips. She breathed with his instructions and felt her heart starting to slow. She focused on the beats of his heart and slowly the shaking subsided. She sat on the floor, her hands still pressed against his chest. She didn't wipe away the tears, she felt them, let them shake her body in deep sobs. Todd wrapped his arms around her, squeezing tight. "I am so sorry, Lana."

Lana sunk into the embrace and let herself feel it all for a moment before pulling herself back. She used her palm to wipe away the wetness on her cheeks. "Shit," she said, touching a mark on his shirt. "I got your shirt wet."

Todd looked down at his shirt. "It'll dry, Lana," he said, unconcerned. He placed a hand over it to show her it was no big deal. He pulled his hand away, his eyes assessing his fingers curiously. "Lana," he said, his eyes still fixated on his fingers. "Look at me." He used that very hand and tipped her chin up toward him. He wiped at her lip, "You're bleeding." He looked down at his dark shirt again, pressing his fingers against the mark. They came away with a pinkish stain on them. Lana's hands fluttered up to her lips. She felt the tip of something firm underneath her fingertips seconds before it receded away. "Oh my God," she breathed.

"Lana, I think those were—"

"Canines," she said.

***

Lana waited for Todd to come collect her for breakfast. Her mind replaying the last hour over and over again in her head. They didn't have much time left after her panic attack. Todd or Henry *Fuck—what do I call him? I guess Todd-Henry until I get used to Henry.*

They'd quickly left the bathroom but Todd-Henry had run to get a new shirt. He didn't need another guard, or Claude, asking him why there was blood on his shirt. She knew he had more to tell her though. Their debriefing had been cut short by her panic attack, and canine interruption.

She wanted to focus on the new information about her aunt but there was one very clear thought that kept overriding it. One thought that kept pushing its way back in, unrelenting and unwilling to let her brush past it. She ran her finger over gums for probably the hundredth time in the last ten minutes. *Still nothing.* But, there had been something and that meant, well it meant everything and nothing at the same time. She might actually be a morpher, *yes,* but it did not in any way justify what the Islanders have done to her. Or what they have done to her aunt.

Anger and determination prickled along her arms, a gentle tingle similar to goosebumps. *I have to get out of here.* If she wasn't sure before, she was now. She'd lingered too long and she needed to get to her aunt.

The one hiccup with that was that in doing so she would have to let go of the hope of learning any more about her parents. She could criticize herself all she wanted for placating so long, but the truth was she wanted to know. She wanted to know if she was a morpher, and more she wanted to know more about her parents. There was a small part of her that believed she would find that here.

But she had stayed long enough. She didn't get answers she wanted, time to accept that and move on. She owed that to her aunt. *Todd-Henry* showed up finally and slipped quietly into her room. He sat down on her bed and asked her how she was holding up. "Just dandy," Lana sneered. She didn't mean to lash out at him. This wasn't his fault. He was just the closest punching bag for her torpedo of emotions.

"Lana," he began. "There is one more thing I needed to tell you before, you know." He pointed to his teeth. Lana nodded encouraging him onward. "I want you to be open-minded about it." He paused briefly. "Please," he whispered, dropping his eyes to the floor between them. Lana inched forward, curious.

"I was recruited to be an islander when I was twelve years old. They made me a deal. A really fucking good deal. They even promised to take care of my brother—"

He growled. "Our parents weren't exactly involved. We were bumped around from foster homes to group homes for about five years," he said, still staring at the floor. "The Islanders, they promised to keep us together, to put a roof over our heads and food in our bellies. Basically, all of the things I had been dreaming of providing for myself and my little brother." He paused, lifting his head, his eyes meeting hers, tears welling there.

"I had no idea that this" – he gestured around the room – "was the job." He stood up and paced toward the window. "I should have left when I found out, but how could I? My brother and I were finally safe. He was going to be cared for better than I ever could have."

Lana propped herself on the desk, crossing her legs in front of her. "It wasn't me that they really wanted," he continued, Lana could feel her heart starting to thump faster in her chest. "It was my brother. They played me to get to him. The thing is we're half-brothers, same mom, different dads. Neither of our dads stuck around long enough to make an impression and mom, *God*, she's a whole other story." He sat back down again on the edge of her bed. He wiped a hand over his face and sighed. "The island has been my home for eight years. I know the Islanders do some really shitty things sometimes, but they have stayed true to their word. They have sheltered us and kept us safe. I know that this— this information about your aunt is going to make you want to leave or rebel but, I-I really think you should stay and play this out."

Lana felt the chill rising from her gut creep up into her throat. Her eyes slicing across the room like the whisp of a dagger. She said nothing.

*Todd-Henry* wrung his hands out in front of him. He exhaled an anxious breath and dropped his head into his hands. "I'm sorry Lana, I know it's—" He paused, pulling his hands away to look at her. "I know it's not what you want to hear. But, this—this is my home and Claude…" He licked his lips. "He has been like a father to me." He popped off the bed and walked toward her.

She quickly jumped off the desk and backed away from him. Her head shaking back and forth in warning. *Todd-Henry* stopped, his face falling. "You don't need to be afraid of me." He retreated a step, to give her space. "Look, I don't think what they did regarding your aunt was just or fair, but I want you to be rational about it. I—" He stopped and threw his hands up in the air as he searched for the words. "I don't want *you* to get into any trouble or try to leave," he said, his voice barely above a whisper.

Lana still said nothing. She felt his words hitting her like an assault. She felt her ideas of escape slowly crumble in her mind. She'd needed *Todd-Henry* for all of them. She'd imagined him joining her, escaping with her, finding their way – together. He'd been her confidant and now, in the span of a few minutes he'd become one of them.

"Say something, Lana, please."

Lana rubbed a hand over her face. She exhaled a shaky breath. "I think you should leave." His shoulder sank, his tall frame becoming much smaller. He nodded, more to himself than to her. "OK. I just, I just need you to know that I'm not a bad person," he said as he reached for the door.

"No, you've just made a very poor choice," Lana said, only loud enough for herself to hear. The sound of the door closing crumpled her to the floor. She let go of everything that had somehow held her together for the last twenty minutes. She felt the heat of the tears sting her eyes and run into her mouth. She heaved on the floor, trying desperately to fill her lungs with enough air. The sobs convulsed her whole body. It was all too much. The canines, her aunt, and now *Todd-Henry*, whatever the fuck his name was. The crushing blow of his loyalty. For the first time since she got to the island, she felt truly defeated.

# Chapter Thirty-Two

Henry stormed down the hallway toward an unused dormitory at the end of the hall. He barged into one of the rooms and let out a feral yell. He threw his fist forward into the wall slamming it against the brick. He yelled again as a sharp pain shot through his hand. He never wanted to hurt Lana or betray her like he felt he just had. He didn't say anything bad, not really, but the look, the look on her face told him everything he needed to know.

Henry had felt drawn to her from the minute he first saw her as a bruised and bloody mess on the floor of her dorm. The pull to her, the pull away from the Islanders. The internal battle had been waging within him, like a page in a book split down the center, ripping farther and farther every day. A slow sting with only one plausible outcome. Betrayal. He had to betray Lana's trust, or the Islanders, and how could he do that to his home. The people that had raised him and given him everything.

Anything he'd asked for, Claude provided, from books to clothing to laptops. He should have been straight up with Claude about his feelings for Lana from the get-go. He could have been reassigned. He would have been able to keep advancing through the ranks and one day become Claude's number-two guy, but he didn't. His interest in Lana stopped him. "Fuck!" he yelled, turning to drive his fist into the wall a few more times. It wasn't until several minutes later that he was able to compose himself, his hand raw and scraped from the impact. He turned quickly and headed down the hallway.

He found Roach near the Oval. "Can you escort Miss Chase to the Oval for breakfast?" Henry asked. The intermediate level guard looked at him with a mixture of surprise and annoyance.

"Mr. Armstrong asked me to retrieve you," Henry continued without hesitation. He needed to be firm and confident for Roach to believe him.

"Why can't you do it, Toddler?"

Henry shrugged. "Mr. Armstrong asked for *you* specifically," he said, throwing his hands up in the air in pretend annoyance.

Roach stood up straighter at that. "Oh?" he inquired, his eyebrows raised with intrigue.

"Yep, I think she's proving difficult to handle and you have more experience than me so—"

Roach waved his hand at Henry, dismissing any further communication. "Yeah, I got it."

Henry bit back his smile and continued past him and headed straight for one of the empty practical rooms. He found the weights in the far corner of the room and started in. It was one of the only ways he could burn through his repetitive inner monologue of guilt and regret.

He stayed there for probably two hours. He lifted until he physically couldn't any more, until his arms dropped at his side like lifeless noodles. Riley came by curious, but Henry blew him off, rather aggressively. He didn't have time for the little boy right now.

He'd been taking advantage of the empty practicals a lot the past few weeks. Actually, now that he thought about it, about as long as Lana had been on the island. It was typically a long session and by the end of it, he usually felt a little less tension and anxiety. He was on his way back to his room when he saw Riley waiting outside his door.

He sighed and shook his head. An inkling of regret sliding up his throat from snapping at him earlier. It wasn't his fault, he was just in the wrong place at the wrong time and Henry took it out on him.

"Hey," Riley said, his voice soft and concerned. He clearly didn't know how Henry was going to react.

"Todd, is everything OK?"

Henry held up his hand. "Henry."

Riley's eyebrows shot up his forehead. "You told me not to call you that any more?" Riley's voice a whisper, afraid someone in the very obviously empty hallway would overhear them.

"It doesn't matter any more."

"What do you mean?"

"I told Lana."

Riley took a step forward. "You told her what? That your name is Henry Churchill or that you are my brother?" Henry thought back, well he definitely told her the Toddler part, but he couldn't recall if he actually got around to telling her Riley was his brother.

"I think both?"

"You think?" Riley said, astonishment pitching high in his voice. "It's pretty big news to not remember."

"There was a lot going on, OK, Riles. It all happened really fast." Henry unlatched the door to his room and sauntered inside. He dropped himself down on the bed with a huff. Riley hesitated in the doorway.

"Do you want to talk about it?" the boy asked, fidgeting with his fingers.

"Not at all."

***

Lana sat up, her tears had long dried. She'd been staring at the wall in front of her for at least an hour now. Her brain sorting through everything that had happened, and everything she needed to *make* happen. She had played nice for far too long. She was not meant to be here. Now that she knew her aunt was alive she had more motivation than ever to leave. Before, she wanted to escape, but she was conflicted about morphers, her parents and having nothing to return to. Although, she was still conflicted about the first two, she wasn't about the latter.

She pulled the papers from beside the bed, the same ones she was supposed to use for her *"homework"* about morphing. She leaned her back against the wall, and pulled her knees to her chest, propping the book on top of her knee. She started jotting down a very different kind of note.

She realized with an agonizing amount of frustration how compliant she had actually been. How part of her had actually trusted Claude. "How could I be so stupid? How could I fall so easily for their game?" She squeezed her eyes shut and breathed a deep breath of realization. But that was it though, wasn't it? That was his game. He played it over and over with every new morpher. A slow, long con and it had been working. Just like it had with everyone before her. The worst part was she had not even realized it. In a way this whole process made her invest in the island. She wanted to stay to see if she morphed. She desired to morph, so she could have an answer.

She opened her eyes again and scanned the elements on her list thus far.
- Island
- Reinforced exits
- Don't know where the exits are
- Don't know how big the island is
- *Todd-Henry* no longer an option

It's an island so by default there were only going to be two ways on and off, by air or by water. Now a boat would be the far more obvious and a probably achievable strategy, but also far easier to capture. She had no doubt that the Armstrongs had a fleet of boats that he could easily be unleashed to chase them. A helicopter though, that would be unexpected. Now, there was the small issue of piloting it, but she could figure that out later. She had yet to figure out how to actually get outside, every exit was very well reinforced.

But maybe getting to the roof *maybe*, that could be possible. Still, she'd need help. She groaned and folded her paper up, stuffing it beneath her mattress. She knew who she was going to ask. She just didn't like it.

There was a nervous tickle in her stomach as she walked into the Oval. She placed a hand against it as if that would make it go away. It was her mind that was creating it. A worry that if this didn't go well, she wasn't sure how else to make her plan work.

"Hey Bennet," Lana said, sliding into his picnic table.

"Is this going to be a habit of yours?" he clipped, gesturing to her position at his table.

Lana scowled in response, "I have a question for you." He raised an eyebrow at her. "Don't you always?" he answered annoyed, and stabbed his fork into a piece of broccoli.

"I want to get out of here," she whispered, stealing a piece of broccoli off his plate.

His eyes flicked up at her, narrowing slightly. She wasn't sure if it was at what she said, or because she had stolen his food.

"Yes, and?" He dragged, as if her statement was completely obvious. Which, now that she thought about it, it was. She assumed most people here wanted out.

"I have a way—" she said, lowering her voice and leaning in closer. "But I need some help."

Bennet sat back, his fork still pinched between his fingers. "I don't know what you are playing at, but it can't be done." He returned to his food.

"Let me ask you something," Lana continued. "How strong do you figure that wall is?" She hooked a thumb behind her, toward the plexiglass exterior of the dome. He followed her direction, squinting over her shoulder. She could see his mind working hard, trying to unravel what she had concocted in her head.

"Very," was all he said.

"Right." She nodded, turning her back to him as she scanned the room. "I take it there's no one in here with a large morph then?"

Bennet cocked his head to the side. His eyes lighter with understanding. He leaned across the table, a flicker of excitement gauging his interest. "Well, Timothy over there" – he nodded – "he just happens to be a bison." A wicked smile growing on his face.

Lana followed his glance. She found the petite Asian boy tossing a frisbee back and forth with another kid. "Him?" Lana asked skeptically.

"Mhhhmm," Bennet said with a smile. "I might put a pin in your balloon here, but you realize we're on an island, right?"

Lana swiveled back around to face him. "So?"

"So even if you manage to break out of here," he said nodding toward the plexiglass. "You have nowhere to go."

"I'm working on that," she said, scanning the room for the familiar strawberry blonde-headed boy.

# Chapter Thirty-Three

Riley stood in front of her, his eyes nearly bugging out of his head. "Are you crazy?" he whispered. "We can't break into Claude's office!" He grabbed her hand and pulled her over to one of the benches in the practical room. "Lana, we can't."

"Not we," she corrected, "you."

Impossibly, his eyes seemed to grow larger. His voice squeaked, "Me?" He dropped his head to the floor, picking a string on his pants anxiously. "Lana, I don't think—"

"Riley, you are the teacher's pet," she said, grabbing his wrist and giving it a squeeze. He seemed confused by that, clearly not understanding the correlation between the two. Lana rolled her eyes as if it was blatantly obvious. "You are the only one who will be able to get in and out of there without raising suspicion."

Riley leaned his head back against the wall and closed his eyes. He exhaled a long breath. Lana squeezed her hands together urging herself to be patient. She wanted to know his answer, but she didn't want to push him too far. This would have to be his decision.

He sighed and slowly opened his eyes, still not looking at her, "Is that a yes?" Lana asked, her voice quiet. She could see the fear and discomfort lingering in his eyes. She knew Riley cared about her. As she did about him. What she didn't know was how much. Would he put himself at risk to help her?

"I could really use your help, Riles," she said, giving his wrist another small squeeze. "But I'm not going to force you to do anything you don't want to do." It was true. As much as she needed Riley, he was her friend first. If he chose not to help her, she would be disappointed of course, but it was his choice to make. If she forced him or manipulated him into helping her not only would she hate herself for that, but he might resent her for it. She didn't want to lose him. He was one of the only people in her life who she actually cared about. Whatever his decision, she would respect it. She had to. He finally looked at her now.

"When?" he asked, his voice soft.

Lana's eyes lit up with excitement. "As soon as possible really." She rushed excitedly. She had Bennet and she had Riley. There was no denying it now. She'd made a plan, and it was starting to come together. She wasn't going to wait to see where things went or to see if she morphed. She needed to get out of here, but she would have to be very careful. If Claude got a whiff of her hope he would extinguish it fast, like a breath against a match. Quick and effortless. She needed to be cautious about that, cautious how her excitement might change her attitude and demeanor. If she was all of a sudden compliant and happy, he would know. He would see right through her. She needed him to keep on believing that she was assimilating as begrudgingly as she was a day or two ago.

"What do you plan to do with it?" Riley asked. Lana took a minute to unravel his question. She'd gone down such a rabbit hole in her thoughts in the past few minutes, she'd practically forgotten what they were talking about. She smiled slightly at the boy, "We're getting out of here obviously."

"Uhm, I'm not exactly sure—"

"Riley, stop." Lana raised her hand. "Look, I am not going to force you to come with us. I know you are comfortable here, but this" – she swept her arm across the practical room – "is only a fraction of what the world has to offer you. You can stay here and play along for the rest of your life, or you can come with Bennet and I and make your own decisions." Lana stood up and placed a reassuring hand on his shoulder.

"Like I said, I'm not going to force you, Riles. I'm not going to take the choice away from you—like they did." She tilted her head down to his level.

"Promise me you'll think about it at least?" Riley nodded.

"Oh, and Riley, you can't tell anyone about this," Lana said, standing to leave.

"What about Henry?"

Lana stopped, the name exhaling a breath from her body. *Henry?* How did he know that name? She stared at Riley, the puzzle pieces slowly sliding together. The same strawberry blonde hair, and lean frame. The same large eyes. "Henry," she repeated to herself in a whisper.

"Yes, my brother," Riley said, standing up to join her. She looked at him again, how could she not have seen it before. Now that she knew, she couldn't stop seeing the similarities between them.

Riley took a step back. "Oh." He breathed lightly. "I guess he didn't tell you."

"No," Lana managed to get out in a whisper.

"Don't worry he won't say anything," Riley squeaked, his eyes looking up at her expectantly.

"Riley, you can't tell him."

He pinched his eyebrows together, a concerned look on his face, he took a step back. "What do you mean?"

"He's a guard, Ril—"

"But he's my brother," he interrupted.

Lana groaned, "I know, but he's also a guard."

"You can't expect me to leave without him?"

Lana chewed her lip. Her mind torn in two directions. He was right, if Henry was his brother, then how could she ask him to keep this from him. She couldn't expect him to just leave his brother behind willy-nilly. But on the other hand, he was a guard, and he had made it clear he wanted to stay on the island. Telling him put their entire plan at risk.

"Lana?"

"I don't know, Riley. I don't know what the right answer is here."

He seemed surprised by that. "You always know what to do," he said softly, his eyes sparkling with worry.

"Do I?" she asked, doubt clear in her tone.

***

Lana sat across from Bennet at dinner. She hadn't touched her meatball sandwich on the plate in front of her. Her stomach was in knots. She hadn't stopped thinking about Riley. They had not really reached a conclusion. As far as she knew he could have told Henry by now, and if he did... what then?

She perked up as she saw that familiar shaggy head walk into the Oval. Lana smiled and waved him over. He stopped for a moment and gave her a small smile in return. Lana dropped her hand, that was odd. He was usually much bouncier than that. Riley turned and seated himself at a picnic table with some of the younger kids.

*Oh,* she felt a small dip in her chest, like a pebble dropping through water. She was so accustomed to that disappointment. Well—she was used to it in herself, but feeling it from another person, that was different and somehow harder.

"So, where are we?" Bennet asked, snapping her back to the present.

Lana bounced back. "Uhm." She blinked rapidly trying to pull information forward in her brain. She shook her head, ridding her worries about Riley. *Focus Lana. You can worry about that later.* "We still need some supplies, backpacks, or something that we can take out there,"

"I've been thinking about that," Bennet said, nodding at someone behind her. Lana turned to see Taurin approaching them. "Hey guys," she said, sliding her long legs along the same bench as Lana.

Lana looked between the two. She didn't want to say anything. She didn't know how much Taurin knew, or how trustworthy she could be. She wasn't exactly comfortable around Lana the last time they saw one another. So, she wasn't exactly chomping at the bit to divulge their secrets.

"It's all right, Lana," Bennet said, tapping his finger on the table toward Taurin. "She's cool, and she can get us some stuff under the radar." Lana turned to look at Taurin, she dropped her voice.

"I'm like the island medic now, so there are things in the infirmary that—well I'm sure they wouldn't notice if they went missing."

When Lana said nothing, Taurin leaned closer, dropping her voice even lower. "There are some satchels and two backpack-style bags. They are for the island doctor going off site." She paused for a minute, a tiny smile on her face. "Which this would kind of be, I guess."

Lana looked back to Bennet, a twitch to her lips. Impressed. "What?" Bennet asked in a defensive tone. "I have a brain, you know."

Lana shrugged. "This is the first I've seen of it."

"Yeah, yeah," he said, waving away her comment. "So, we're on board with the bags from Taurin? And whatever she can steal from the infirmary?"

Lana looked back to Taurin. "You want out?" she asked her.

"More than anything." Taurin breathed. "But I actually can't go with you."

Lana scrunched her face confused and looked back over to Bennet. He shrugged, this was the first he'd heard of this as well. "Claude won't let me leave," she said.

"Duh, he won't *LET* any of us leave, that's why we're not asking him," Bennet said, biting off the end of a carrot.

"No." Taurin shook her head.

"It's different," she said, tucking one of her curls behind her ear. "He was very clear, if I leave, he will hurt my friends." She looked over her shoulder back toward her group sitting in a circle on the grass. "I can't do that to them. My best bet is to help you get out, and hope you can do something about this place," she said, turning back around.

Lana nodded and took a breath, "We'll do our best."

***

Lana pulled her list out again. She didn't really need it. She made all the notes in her head, but there was something about writing it down that made it feel more real. It was comforting in a way to look at it and see a physical demonstration of her plan.

- Island-Helicopter
- Reinforced exits
- ~~Don't know where the exits are~~? Oval
- Don't know how big the island is

- ~~Todd Henry no longer an option~~ Bennet, Riley, Taurin.

That was it though. She didn't want it getting any bigger. It would be easier for someone to slip up, or be found out. She still didn't know what Riley was going to do, so she might actually have to make that list bigger. She didn't like that thought. The smaller they kept this the better it would be.

Of course, keeping it small meant she was leaving everyone else behind. Everyone else who, like her, had been completely uprooted from their lives. She had just barely come up with a way for her to get out of here. There was no possible scenario where she could get fifty morphers out, or keep them quiet enough that the Armstrong's wouldn't discover their plan.

There was still a good chance that she wouldn't get out. At least then it was only her neck on the line. If she got caught, it would just be her and Bennet taking the heat. She could handle that. Fifty morphers taking her word of escape and getting caught and punished because of her, that she could not handle.

She would think of something. Some way to take the Islanders down... if she did get out.

\*\*\*

Claude waited for Annette to join him as she typically did midweek for tea. It was their chance to step away and just enjoy one another's company. It had been less and less frequent as of late, but Claude had made an exalted effort for it to happen this week.

Annette sauntered through the main foyer to meet him, two to-go mugs in her hand. She held one out for him. "Orange pekoe," she said before he could ask.

"Mmm." He nodded. That was Annette's favorite. He was more of an English breakfast person. He nodded to Mantis, the mid-level guard blocking their exit. The guard hastily began the elaborate procedure of unlocking the thickly reinforced door. The doors were built like puzzle pieces. Each hinge, and lever needed to be positioned in an exact way, in an exact order for the door to open. It was an extra security feature. Mantis was further protection on top of that. There were only four external doors in the entire facility and for good reason. It was easier to monitor and keep the assets inside.

He held out his arm for Annette and she wrapped her small skinny arm through. They stepped out into the sun and fresh air. It was typically only thirty minutes, but he still looked forward to the time. No matter how erratic Annette could be, she was still his only family. Her presence comforted him in a way no one else could.

"So, what's new my brother," Annette chimed.

Claude shrugged, "Testing a new implant to improve the exit transition of the morphers."

Annette groaned. "Something less boring," she begged. "What about the girl?"

"Which girl?" Claude asked, blowing some of the steam from his mug.

"Don't play dumb."

"Let us just enjoy our tea, Annette, no use in getting in a tizzy."

She rolled her eyes, "I'm not in a tizzy Claude." She sucked her teeth. "You know I really thought siccing Locust on her would have unlocked her morph."

Claude turned, certain he hadn't heard that correctly, "Pardon?"

"Locust," she repeated. "Oh, come on," she said, mocking his surprised face. "You didn't think it was his idea to have a go at the girl?"

Claude could not hide the look of astonishment from his face. "Annette," he said, a cool tone to his voice.

"Come on, Claude," she interrupted, "you know it was a

good idea."

"A good idea?" he exclaimed in disbelief. "He tried to rape her?"

"OK," Annette dragged. "I obviously didn't tell him to go that far, but to just feel her up a bit" – she gestured with her free hand – "you know, make her uncomfortable."

"And you thought he would stop there?"

Annette shrugged, "I guess, I didn't think about it."

Claude placed his tea down and took a deep breath. "Annette," he said again.

"—Don't patronize me, brother." She clipped, a hot fiery warning in her eyes. He knew that look well. She was on the edge of losing control. He stopped and motioned to a bench near them. They were the only ones to ever sit on it. Neither the guards nor any of the morphers were allowed out in these grounds. They were specifically for Annette and Claude. A privilege of sorts.

"Do you remember when you and I would have a row over the last tea biscuit?"

Annette laughed. "Every time."

"And you got the biscuit—"

"Every time." She finished with a smile.

"But" – he interjected – "sometimes, you would save me the last bite." He turned to look at her. "Remember?"

Annette nodded. "I had to take pity on you sometimes."

"You did indeed." He nodded, a soft smile crinkling near his eyes. "What does this have to do with anything?" She shifted to face him.

"Sometimes, I miss that side of you," he expressed quietly.

"Excuse me?" Annette barked, immediately defensive.

"Nettey, don't get your back up," he breathed. "I simply mean, I think sometimes you get so invested in the job, you forget to be" – he shrugged – "you." Claude knew exactly what he was doing. A part of him felt guilty about it, but the other part knew the necessity behind it. Charming people was a game he was good at. Even Annette was not immune to his strategies. By blaming it on work and stress he was catering to her, rather than attacking her. *Oh, poor Annette, you are so overworked, you never take time for yourself.* In his own way, encouraging her to take it easy was really a way to get her a little less involved. At least for a little while. Until things simmered down between her and Lana. He just had to plant the seed.

"Are you suggesting something?"

Claude shrugged and leaned back on the bench. He took a sip of his tea, still quiet. He waited for her to draw her own conclusions. Just like she always had to. She had to believe it was her idea. He lined up the pitch and she would be the one to take the swing.

"It has been a lot lately, hasn't it?" Annette said solemnly, staring out at the trees in front of them. Claude bit back his smile. He turned to her feigning surprise. As if he had no idea she would come to that conclusion.

"I wouldn't be against a little vacation," she said, her voice squeaking with the suggestion. "Where shall we go brother? Madrid? Vienna? Tasmania?"

Claude shook his head. "You know I cannot go with you Nettey."

Annette sighed and crossed her arms over her chest in quite a child-like fashion. "Someone has to stay here, you know that," he said softly so as not to stir her. He needed her to keep following this path. Get her away for a bit, and she would come back softer. She might even avert Lana from her crosshairs.

"Fine" – she pursed her lips – "But I'm going to go somewhere incredible."

"Oh, I have no doubt." Claude nodded, smiling.

# Chapter Thirty-Four

Henry went to collect Lana from mealtime, just like he always did. She no longer greeted him with a smile or any chummy side talk. She barely looked at him actually. She brushed past him in the hallway and led the way to her dorm.

It had been a few days since her last practical and any media room homework sessions. She still hasn't resumed her sessions with Dr. Mason. He wondered why Mr. Armstrong had let that slide for now. Maybe, he wanted to give her extra time to recover? Or maybe, he was testing some other tactic to get her to conform. Lana stopped in front of her door. She peeked over her shoulder, her beautiful gray eyes flicking over to him down the hall. She crossed her arms over her chest waiting for him to unlock her door.

"Lana," he said softly, as he approached.

"Don't," she warned, snapping her head around to glare at him. "Don't you dare."

He sighed. "What did you expect, Lana? I'm a guard? Of course, I am going to be loyal to my duty?"

"Your duty?" she mimicked, scrunching her face in disgust.

There was no denying the tension between them. It thickened the air like fog on a spring morning. She could feel it too. He knew she could. There was still an unexplainable electricity between them, even if she wanted nothing to do with him right now.

That was OK, right? She would get used to the island. The

Armstrongs, the way things worked around here. She might even grow to like it. The more well behaved morphers were, the more privileges they would get. Maybe one day she could live a fairly normal life on the island. Maybe, then they could be—*No. Don't go there. Don't give yourself that hope*, he thought to himself. *She is very far from that place.*

"Just try to give it a chance," he breathed, reaching to unlock her door.

"Hmm," she said, sliding in between the barely ajar door. She turned. "Well, I gave you a chance, and look how well that turned out for me?"

She pushed the door closed on him. He stood there a moment. His chest tight with a flurry of emotions. He was frustrated, sad, hurt, angry, and disappointed. Each of them were fighting for precedence in his mind. He locked her door, the familiar click filling the empty hallway. She was still the only morpher in this wing.

"She'll do better with time," he said aloud as if speaking the words would help him believe they were true. Maybe he shouldn't have told her about her aunt. It seemed to be what had tipped her over the edge. Maybe, if he had kept that to himself, she would have assimilated quicker.

"No." He shook his head. "I couldn't do that." He might be a guard, but Lana was also his friend. The two might conflict with one another, but he had to stay true to himself and his values.

"I can be both," he assured himself. "I can be both."

***

Lana stared at her paper in front of her. It was how she spent most of the time in her dorm. Of course, she had her back to the camera and her books out so it didn't look suspicious. There was still one factor she hadn't quite figured out. The Oval was the objective, but how to make it happen. They wouldn't be able to access it at night, and unless they were able to sway Timothy over to their side it would have to be during the day. During one of their mealtimes.

"Dinner," she whispered to herself and scratched it on the paper. She circled all three mealtimes countless times, but dinner carried the advantage of darkness shortly after. They could escape into the woods and have nightfall in their back pocket to aid in their escape. Now, that did make it more difficult for their own movement, as well as the Islanders... but it was just something they were going to have to work with.

- Island-Helicopter
- Reinforced exits
- ~~Don't know where the exits are?~~ Oval
- Don't know how big the island is?
- ~~Todd-Henry no longer an option~~ Bennet, Riley, Taurin.
- Dinner

Everything was falling into place. Now more than ever, the question was *when*. There were only so many oddities that she could plan for, but nothing would match the actual attempt. There would be no way to predict exactly how things would turn out. She would wait for the bags from Taurin, and then after that. It would be time to move.

There was a light knock on the door. "Todd," she mumbled to herself. "Dammit." She smacked her hand on the ground. "Henry, his name is Henry." After a moment the door opened. It was indeed *Henry*. She looked at him for the first time in a few days. His hair was shaggier than usual, a little more unkempt, a slight stubble on his chin making him look a bit older.

She'd avoided him, avoided looking at him and talking to him, everything about him as much as she could. It was less confusing for her that way. As mad as she was at him, her heart still leapt at the sight of him. It was consistently followed soon after by a rush of joyful comfort. He was a source of comfort for her. He had been such a steady ally, but more than that. There was something more than that. The kiss they shared—it was more than that. She couldn't explain it exactly. It was unfamiliar territory. So, it was easier not to look at him, not to speak with him, because she could stay focused on why she was furious with him.

After all the fucked-up things they had done, he was really trying to convince her the island was a good place to be? He was really choosing the Islanders? How could any sane person do that? How could any person with an ounce of a moral conscience do that?

*They wouldn't.*

"You ready for lunch?" he asked.

Lana pushed herself off the ground, cringing at the lingering soreness in her wrists. They weren't fully healed yet. She pushed past Henry and down the corridor.

\*\*\*

She headed straight to the buffet, her mind still sorting through her inner conflict about Henry. Her stomach growled loudly as she approached the table. Her internal monologue and scheming was burning through extra calories. She went through the line almost on autopilot. A small tap on her shoulder startled her.

"Hey," she said, her voice squeaking in surprise at who had approached her. A small bug-eyed boy stood in front of her. His strawberry blonde hair falling into his eyes.

"Are you avoiding me?" he asked, leaning across her to pull a croissant onto his plate. Lana stopped and turned to face him, unable to hide the surprise from her face.

"Me?" She pointed at herself. "Avoiding you?" Her tone breaching sarcasm.

Riley shrugged as if unaware of the irony. "You walked right past me," Riley said, gesturing to the beginning of the buffet. "Right there."

Lana looked to where he was pointing. "Oh," she said, turning back to her food. "Sorry, I'm just a bit distracted," she said, stepping down onto the grass. She didn't need to turn to see if Riley was following her. She could hear the familiar shuffle of his feet hurrying after her as she made her way toward what was now becoming 'their' picnic table.

Before she could even take a bite of her sandwich Riley blurted, "I got them."

Lana's eyes flicked up. "What?"

"The files you wanted from Claude's office. I got them."

"When?" she asked, her voice rising.

"Shhh," he said shushing her. "This morning. Claude was out with Annette."

"Riley." Lana breathed, her heart hammering. "You shouldn't have done that," her voice a firm whisper.

"What?" he stammered. "You asked me to?"

"Yes," she said quickly, "but we needed to plan when!"

Riley's eyebrows drew together confused. Lana leaned forward. "Riley, how long do you think it'll be before Claude notices those files are gone?" Riley breathed a slow breath, understanding filtering into his large eyes.

"Not long—a day maybe."

"Exactly." Lana breathed. "Which means, we have to break out sooner than that and we're not ready yet."

Sweat started to bead on Riley's forehead, "I didn't know," he said, panic in his eyes. "You asked me to, so I got them," he spoke so quickly his words jumbled into one another. Lana imagined her own eyes mirrored his panic. She couldn't help it. This is not what she had expected. She didn't even know he was interested. She didn't know what he was going to choose.

"Where are they?" she asked, peeking under the table, half expecting to see them stuffed in his hands.

"I don't have them here. I'm not a complete idiot!"

"Sorry," he said before Lana could say anything. "I didn't mean to snap at you. I'm just mad at myself—" He wiped at the sweat on his brow. "And scared," he whispered.

Lana leaned forward, her heart aching for the boy. As crazy as this was, this was legitimately Riley's worst fear. He was the typical teacher's pet. Now, not only had he gone against *said* "teachers" but he might have tattled on his classmates at the same time. "It's all right, Riles. We'll figure it out."

"Where are they? In your room?"

"No." He shook his head. "In my practical room. I thought that was a better hiding place."

"I wasn't sure you were in," Lana said.

A long pause. "I wasn't either." He looked around the Oval, slowly turning back to face her. "I thought about what you said. I've been here a long time and I want to see it. I want to see what's beyond these walls."

"And what about—" She couldn't bring herself to say his name aloud. "Your brother?"

He flicked his eyes over to her, a fierceness in them that she had never seen before. "I don't want to talk about it."

She sat back, surprised with the curtness of his answer. This wasn't the right time to push for that information. Clearly something had happened.

Riley dropped his head into his hands. "What are we going to do?" He groaned. She reached across the table and placed a hand on his, pulling them away from his face.

"We're going to have to make it work," she said, scanning the room to find Bennet and Taurin. "We're going to have to fast track our plan."

\*\*\*

Taurin and Bennet were equally surprised to hear the news. They both thought they would have more time as well. "No better time than the present, right?" Lana feigned cheerfulness.

"Should we just go now?" Bennet said. "Fuck being ready? Are we ever going to actually be ready to do this?" he asked, as the four of them huddled together in a spot on the grass farthest from everyone else. They ignored the strange looks from their coupling. Everyone was probably remembering when Lana socked Bennet in the face.

"We can't," Taurin piped, "I didn't bring the bags down. I was going to zip a bunch of them together into one and leave it by the buffet for you guys." She looked over to the buffet.

"I didn't think it would be happening today, they're still in the infirmary."

"The files too," Riley said, "I tucked them away as well." Bennet nodded, knowing it wasn't possible for them to leave in that moment. Lana could see the apprehension in him. He was worried his chance at escape was slipping away. Lana didn't want to let him know how real that fear was. Every moment they waited was a minute Claude was closer to finding out the files were gone. After that it would only be a hop skip and a jump into figuring out what happened to them. Seeing as only Lana, and Bennet's files would be missing, he would zero in on them pretty quickly.

"We have to go tonight, and we won't be able to wait until the end of dinner," Bennet said.

That had been the plan originally. They would wait until the dinner hour was almost over, until most of the morphers had filed out back to their dorms and then Bennet would provoke Timothy in some way and get him to charge the plexi-glass. Lana looked around the room. Around all the other morphers. He was right. They wouldn't be able to wait that long.

"I know," she said, nodding to herself.

"Is that such a bad thing?" Riley asked.

"It puts everyone else in danger, Riley," Lana explained, "not just us."

"Oh—right," he said, pulling at the grass underneath him and making a neat pile at his side. It was okay for them. They had decided to take this risk. This risk against the Islanders, against their lives, but the others had not.

"We could start spreading the word now, that way people will know by dinnertime," Riley suggested.

"No," Bennet interjected firmly, "that is a fast way for the wrong ears to hear it."

Riley seemed defeated by that, his shoulders sank like a deflated balloon and focused again on his grass pile. Lana knew he was feeling guilty and was trying to come up with a way to fix it. She leaned her head back against the plastic wall and closed her eyes. She wasn't sure there was a way to fix this one. At least not in a way that catered to all parties.

# Chapter Thirty-Five

The time seemed to slip away faster than she expected. It felt like only minutes had passed before Henry came to collect her for dinner. The anxious twisting in her stomach had not subsided since lunchtime. It grew angrier with every passing hour, like a sunburn on a hot day. She walked into the Oval almost in a trance. She couldn't even remember getting there. Her mind was so preoccupied, like a state of hypnosis.

She scanned the room slowly. She saw Riley sitting at one of the picnic tables alone. A full plate of untouched food in front of him. He kept his head down, but she could see his eyes watching her. He moved his hand quickly into a thumbs up position.

She kept scanning, she saw Bennet leaning against plexiglass. He tried to look nonchalant, but it was a peculiar position for him. She noticed a few morphers throw odd looks his way and give him a wide berth.

Taurin was behind her, standing near the door of the Oval. Lana could see a bag tucked behind her legs. This was it. She blew out a long breath trying to expel some of the nerves with it. It didn't work. Her stomach was an anxious knot of anticipation and fear. What if it didn't work? What if they got this far, and they couldn't break the glass? What then?

She made her way over to Riley's table, her mind throwing question after question at her. She sat down on the hard wood bench. It was the signal Bennet was waiting for. She closed her eyes and breathed a slow breath, clearing her mind. *Enough. You have to focus on this now. Focus Lana.*

She watched out of the corner of her eye as Bennet sauntered over to Timothy's group. The group consisted of Timothy, a small boy about Riley's size named Adam, and twins Sarah and Sasha. They had already discussed how to provoke Timothy.

The opportunity presented itself faster than they had anticipated as Adam ran toward him chasing a frisbee. Bennet stuck out his leg blatantly tripping the young boy. Adam flew over his leg and crashed hard onto the grass. He turned over onto his back. His eyes bulging with hurt and fear as he turned to see Bennet hovering over him.

Bennet laughed and Lana knew immediately it was forced. It was more just a sound. There was no emotion in his face, no crinkling in his eyes. It was a sound to get everyone's attention and embarrass Adam.

Timothy was there in an instant. "What the hell, Bennet?" Timothy exclaimed helping Adam to his feet, "What is your problem?"

Bennet smiled and shrugged, "Where do I begin?" he sang, shoving Timothy's shoulder hard.

"Just fuck off, man."

Bennet laughed again and ran a hand over his mouth amused. "That's cute," he clipped. "Are you going to make me Tiny Tim?"

A spark lit in Timothy's eyes. Lana sat up straighter, there was an ominous silence in the dome. Every single pair of eyes were on the two boys. Frozen and invested. Timothy lunged. "Just leave us alone," he yelled as he pushed Bennet backward.

Bennet responded, circling around Timothy so he was in the right position, facing the plexiglass. He dodged Timothy's next attack easily and Timothy slammed into the glass. He grabbed his shoulder, wincing in pain. "Nice one!" Bennet egged.

That was it. The Asian boy in front of her started to blur. *Oh my God.* She saw Bennet's eyes widen with surprise as well. He clearly thought it would have taken more than that. Before she could blink a bison stood head-to-head with Bennet. But there was one very big problem, he was not facing the right way.

Bennet would have to reposition him to hit the glass again. She was standing before she knew it. Riley matched her. They both stood breathless, but ready. Bennet looked over to them. He nodded once and backed up. He was crouched and ready for the bison to charge him.

Which he did, the bison dipped his head and charged. Bennet dove to the side, somersaulting over onto his hands and somehow scrambling back onto his feet. There was an audible gasp from everyone in the Oval. Everyone was just as on edge as she was. Bennet ran back toward the glass and Lana inhaled a sharp breath.

He didn't have much of an escape with his back to the wall. *Why didn't we think about that? Why didn't I look into how BIG a fucking Bison is?* It was like the size of a small SUV, and just as powerful. Lana squeezed her hands together, her heart thumping furiously in her chest.

The stagnant silence in the room quickly turned into cries of fear and disbelief. The various groups quickly shuffled themselves to the back of the room closer to the buffet and away from the showdown in front of them. Timothy charged again and Bennet dived again, this time sliding to the side on his stomach like a baseball player hitting home plate.

Lana cupped her hands against her ears, cringing as the impact exploded in her ears like a firecracker in a sealed room. Everyone else around her did the same. So did Bennet, he was lying on his stomach still, his hands covering his ears. Lana caught movement at the corner of her vision. She turned her head slightly and saw Timothy. He shook his head, as if ridding his head of the sound and then dropped it, his eyes level with Bennet still on the ground.

"Bennet, move!" Lana yelled. Her voice acting like a starter gun to a track athlete. The bison kicked back and charged again. Bennet's head snapped up, his eyes widened at the beast tearing toward him. He scrambled to his feet and launched himself over one of the nearby picnic tables. Timothy slammed into the plexi-glass again and this time he went through.

The sound wasn't nearly as bad the second time. Either they had gotten used to it, or because the room wasn't sealed any more it didn't compact it. But somehow the room fell silent. Every single pair of eyes was scanning the room, unsure of how to proceed.

Lana approached the open barrier. She hesitated a moment feeling a fresh cool ocean breeze whipping through the opening. It was just what she needed and helped carry her through. She nearly fell onto the grass on the other side.

It felt like an enormous weight had been lifted from her mind like a bag she had been carrying dropped from her shoulders. A constant worry no longer nagging at her. She spun around a smile on her face and waved everyone else forward, maybe she *could* get them all out. She had to try, right? She wasn't going to tell them, oh you stay there while I run away?

"Come on," she encouraged the sea of shocked faces in front of her. That was all it took. The kids bee-lined toward the opening like schoolchildren for recess.

Lana stepped to the side to allow them some space to come out. She nearly bumped into Timothy. The bison was frozen on the grass, his breathing heavy and labored. "Hey, Timothy." Lana cooed gently as she approached him. "It's all right now," she reassured. He swiveled his enormous head toward her. "It's all right," she said again, reaching a hand out to stroke his nose.

She felt someone standing behind her. "No hard feelings big guy," Bennet's distinctive voice said. She could almost hear the smile in his voice. He reached his long arm over her shoulder offering it to the bison. Timothy pulled his head away and breathed a short breath. "All right." Bennet laughed. "Not friends yet, I get it."

Lana patted him just behind the shoulder blades. She could feel his breathing starting to return to normal. She felt bad for using Timothy like this, but it was the only chance they had. "We need to go," Bennet said, placing his arm on Lana's shoulder. "As amazing as this is." He swept his arm wide, gesturing to the greenery. "The Islanders will have heard that—easily."

Taurin was one of the last to step through the glass. She handed a bag over to Lana. "The other one is stuffed inside."

"Two?" Lana asked, peeking inside the bag. Taurin nodded, "Three, Riley already took one."

Lana's head snapped up. *Riley.* She spun around scanning the crowd for the familiar strawberry blonde hair.

"He's at the buffet," Taurin added quickly, seeing her distress. Lana ran over to the hole in the glass. Sure enough, there was Riley dumping food into his backpack. It was smart, but extremely risky.

"Riley!" Lana yelled, "Get out here."

"One minute!" he yelled back holding a finger up to her.

Lana turned back around and was met by several pairs of inquiring eyes. Everyone was staring at her. She looked down at herself, half expecting to see something on her clothes that was of interest to them. Half hoping that was the real reason. She knew what they wanted. They were all looking for direction.

She took a breath and balled her hands into fists. *I can do this; I've gotten them this far; I can get them a little further.* They needed to move, and quickly. Their window of escape was narrowing by the second. "We don't have a lot of time," she yelled, "everyone will need to split up and hide in the woods. It will be harder for them to find us."

She saw the looks of concern and uncertainty shared between friends. "You don't have to go," she continued, "you can choose to stay. No one is going to force you, but if you want to, you need to go now." Before anyone had a chance to speak, she continued, "Groups of three or four, no bigger!"

There was a moment of hushed collaboration. Large groups of friends huddled together to decide who would pair together. After a moment's hesitation, she was astonished to see the compliance. A few of them glanced back at her seeking approval or reassurance, she nodded to each group as they took off.

A loud bang sounded from inside, Lana jolted and immediately yelled for Riley. She knew that sound. The door to the Oval being opened. *FUCK!* Their time was dwindling fast. "We've got to go now!"

"Yep," Bennet said, grabbing her by the arm and pulling her away from the building at a jog.

"RILEY," she yelled over her shoulder, "get out now!"

"He's coming," Bennet panted struggling to keep his grip on her. "Look he's coming! You can stop squirming now and run!"

Sure enough, she could see a tiny strawberry blonde body flying out of the smashed hole, a backpack swinging dramatically between his hands. His small legs pedaling fast to catch up with them. She stopped at the tree line, planting her feet hard so her arm ripped loose from Bennet. "Come on," he groaned, waving her into the forest.

She turned and looked back at Riley, "Give him a minute," she said. She didn't care how stupid it was. She wasn't going to leave him behind. "Come on, Riles," she said, urging the boy faster. She saw a figure then emerging from the plexi-glass hole. There was no mistaking the blonde hair and crisp black shirt. It was Claude. He stood there alone for only a second and was soon followed by a blur of similarly dressed men, they dispersed quickly into the surrounding woods. Clearly on the trail of some of the morphers.

"Shit!" Her eyes flew back over to Claude. He was holding his arm out, almost like he was pointing, but there was something in his hand. Something small and black and directed at Riley's head. "No," Lana whispered, the breath leaving her body with realization. There was only one thing that size and shape that made sense. One very terrifying thing. She didn't hear a shot, or bang, or any sound at all, but she saw Riley crumple to the ground.

Something flashed in her peripheral vision. Lana shifted to see a large furry beast break through the trees into the clearing. It was Timothy, two of the guards had slung a rope around his neck and were pulling him back toward the building. He must not have made it far into the thick brush.

Timothy bucked and pulled against the rope, the two guards struggled to keep their hold on it. Timothy reared backwards and charged toward the tree line. He probably realized they wouldn't be able to keep their hold on the rope if he ran full tilt.

The two guards were jolted off their feet crashing into one another before releasing their grip on the rope. Timothy didn't falter, the weight of the men had steered him in another direction, but he was steamrolling forward. Trying to get away from his captors. The only problem was he was now running directly in Riley's path.

Lana screamed Riley's name and tore into the clearing.

"Lana, DON'T!" Bennet called after her, but it was too late and there was no stopping her. Lana ran as hard as she could, but she felt like the world was moving in slow motion. Riley was about one hundred yards from her and completely motionless on the ground. Timothy was closing the gap between them fast. She screamed at Timothy to stop, even though she knew it wouldn't stop him. It was an instinctual response. She needed to try everything. *Anything.*

"Riley!" Lana screamed at the top of her lungs, hoping to somehow rouse him. Even if she got him to move a few feet he would be out of Timothy's path. "Fuck!" she yelled. She pushed herself faster pushing her legs harder with each step. She felt an intense warmth spread through her arms shooting toward her fingers and down her legs. It felt as if she was pulling energy from the ground. The very familiar metallic taste shot to the back of her throat. She swallowed hard ignoring it. She had no time for that right now.

A strange tingling sensation coursed through her blood, like a beautiful powerful hum. She could feel it pulsating within her, like the thrumming of a birds' wings. She was close now, but so was Timothy. They were both mere feet from Riley. Lana screamed and jumped. She had no idea what she was doing. What was the plan? To hurl her body across at a stampeding Bison, and hope to make an impact? She didn't know, but it was all she could do.

Her body slammed into Timothy's side, pushing him off track just enough that he missed Riley. The bison lost track of his footing and stumbled sideways falling once before jumping back up and taking off into the woods.

Lana laid on the ground for a second, assessing herself. Nothing felt broken, not yet anyway. There was no immediate rush of pain or spots of blood. In fact, she felt the opposite, she felt strong and powerful and alert.

She slowly pulled herself up, waiting for something to object. Something to be bleeding, broken, or hurt in some way. There was no way she could make an impact like that and be fine. She turned slowly to see Riley in the same spot. She was only a few feet from him now. He was lying on his back, but something was very wrong. His eyes were open and she could see the panic in them. She inched closer, and he made a small squeak. His lips didn't move, no expression on his face, just a small terrified squeak.

She couldn't see blood anywhere. *God Dammit, where is he shot?* She tried to yell to him, but only a gargled gruff came out. She stopped, placing a hand against her throat, confused by the raw tortured sound. Her long thin fingers did not touch her throat. The feeling was in fact foreign to her. A padded softness putting pressure on her neck, like she was wearing mittens and a turtleneck. A thick layer of something covering her neck or maybe her hand.

*Or maybe both* she thought as her mind snapped to the conclusion. She stood up fully feeling perfectly balanced on powerfully muscled legs and shoulders. She looked down at herself to see sandy colored fur billowing beneath from her legs and chest.

She didn't have time to sit and think about this. Riley needed her. She shook her head, feeling its heaviness sway in the air for the first time. She reached to nudge Riley and stopped short with her hand raised mid-air. Except it wasn't a hand, it was a thick furry paw. She felt like she was in a dream, staring at this odd extension of her. She brought it closer to her face, and twinged a whisker. She jumped startled at the twitching sensation that zipped through her face. *You don't have time for this Lana.* She reminded herself again. It was hard to ignore everything she was feeling and seeing. *You can figure this out later.* She reminded herself again. As much as she wanted to investigate every inch of herself, this was most definitely not the time. *Riley is more important.* She glanced over her shoulder toward the building. She could see Claude there, in the same spot he'd been earlier. He hadn't moved. He looked almost frozen where he stood.

She dropped her head back down to Riley, he was staring up at her, but still wasn't moving. Lana bent down and nudged his arm with her nose. Or at least what felt like her nose. She obviously wasn't fully used to its size and had to try it three times before she made contact. His arm fell loosely at his side when she touched it. *Something is wrong.* She scanned him from top to bottom. *No blood? What is this? Why can't he move? What did they do to him?*

"Lana!" She heard someone call. Her head snapped up, snarling instantly, expecting one of the guards to be approaching. She recognized Bennet's dark curly hair instantly and softened slightly. He approached with his hands raised in surrender. "Fucking hell," he said, as she faced him head on. "I guess you were worth the wait," he said, bending down to sling an arm under Riley's shoulder. "We've got to go," he said, nodding over her shoulder. Lana followed his gaze behind her, back toward the facility. Even a hundred yards away she could feel his stare, somehow making the football field length between them feel like only feet. Henry was standing next to him now. She recognized his tall, lean frame. She chuffed at them and turned with Bennet, who was now fully carrying Riley in his arms.

She trotted behind Bennet into the brush. She didn't think too much about that, she let her body lead her. Anytime she thought about the fact that she had to coordinate four legs, and massive paws she stumbled or tripped. She didn't have the mental space for that. She'd let whatever she was lead her, for now.

# Chapter Thirty-Six

They ran for a long time but Lana didn't tire. They needed to put distance between themselves and Islanders. That was her focus. She kept her mind on that because if she thought about anything else, she would unravel quickly. A lot had happened in the last few hours, but the most important thing was they got out. Now, they needed to work on staying out.

Bennet started to slow down. His breaths were coming out fast and short. She could see his arms shaking from carrying Riley. She wished she could say something, but managed a grunt instead, "I don't exactly speak tiger," he snapped at her.

Lana froze, one paw still outstretched. She looked up at him. He sighed, "Sorry." He gently put Riley down, propping him so he was semi sitting, semi leaning against a tree. "I just need a breather."

Lana still hadn't moved and it wasn't because Bennet had just snapped at her. *Tiger.* That's what he said. *Tiger.* That made sense for the sandy, auburn coloring of hair. *Tiger.* She looked at her legs again, there was a slight dappling there, spots like a cheetah or leopard would have. She assumed she was probably one of the latter and Bennet just spewed the first large cat that had come to mind. Still, there was this subtle relief in knowing. Even though she didn't have the full picture. It would be great if she actually *had* a picture like a mirror or any kind of reflection. For now, she would just have to rely on Bennet's words to satisfy her curious mind.

Bennet dropped down next to Riley and bent his head between his legs, still trying to catch his breath. There was a small crunch in her ears. Lana's head snapped up and swiveled toward the noise. Her ears craned forward. Bennet had not moved, nor had Riley. This was something else. Something only she could hear. She growled, something she didn't even know she could do. It was an instinctual reaction. Her throat answered her brain's desire to get Bennet's attention.

He looked over at her immediately, "What?" he asked, his eyes darting from the trees around them and back to Lana. Clearly recognizing a growl meant something bad. Lana looked from him back into the woods where the sound was coming from. He followed her gaze, his eyebrows raised curiously.

Lana picked up her large paw and padded it on the ground to mimic someone stepping. Bennet jolted upright and moved to her side. He looked back at Riley. "Fuck, I would morph with you, Lana, but—Riley," he said, his voice dropping into a whisper.

Lana nodded at him, and nudged his leg pushing him back toward Riley. "Wait, what?" he asked. "Don't, Lana, don't go in there." She shook her head at him, and slowly crept toward the noise. She kept her body low to the ground, carefully stepping over twisted tree roots and dead branches. She moved with incredible precision and softness. She barely made a sound.

She found the culprit of the sound in a matter of minutes. She felt her heartbeat ease up a bit at the sight of them. She knew right away that it wasn't an islander. She stepped out into the person's path, flinching when she gasped loudly.

She fought the urge to shush her, which she wouldn't be able to do anyways. Lana emitted a low growl to signify her displeasure with the volume. It vibrated in her throat in a very satisfying fashion.

"Holy shit!" Taurin squeaked, staring at Lana wide eyed. "There's no way." She breathed, taking a step closer.

A breeze carried through the trees, rusting through the leaves. Lana stilled as it lifted through her fur. It was a wonderfully unique feeling, like the earth was speaking to her. She closed her eyes for a moment and appreciated the connection.

"Oh my God," Taurin said, interrupting her moment of tranquility. She took another step closer, "Lana? Is that you?" she asked, her voice shaking with disbelief. Lana dipped her head to mimic a head nod. She hoped that would be enough understanding for Taurin.

"I-I don't even know what to say? I mean not that you can say anything back."

Lana dipped her head again to show she was listening, or at least understanding her. After another minute, she trotted into the woods. She stopped and looked over her shoulder at Taurin swinging her head back along the path to encourage her to follow.

Taurin stumbled into their momentary camp. She ran to Bennet and Riley immediately, throwing her arms around Bennet's neck. His eyes widened with surprise and he patted her on the back awkwardly.

"Hey Taurin." He breathed into her thick curly hair. "Where did you come from?"

She released him and sputtered, "The guards found my group a few hours ago, but there were only two of them, Mike and I managed to get away, but I lost him in all this and we haven't reconnected yet." Taurin's eyes fell on Riley slumped against the tree. "Riley, are you okay?"

"He can't talk," Bennet said, dropping down to Riley's shoulder. "Actually, doc, it's probably a damn good thing you're here. We don't know what's wrong with him. It's like he's completely paralyzed."

The color drained from Taurin's face, she dropped onto her knees in front of Riley and pressed her fingers to his neck checking his pulse.

"What?" Bennet asked, hovering over her shoulder.

"I need to tell you guys something," she said, slowly pulling her hand away.

Lana took a step forward, she didn't like the sound of that. She growled softly. Taurin looked back at her. "Look, I'm not a traitor or anything, but a few days ago, Claude made me surgically implant a chip into Riley."

Lana blew out an agitated breath and started to pace back and forth, "I know, all right." Taurin threw her hands up in the air. "I know, it's terrible, but I didn't have a choice." She pulled Riley's legs to lay him flat on the ground.

"As far as I know it's meant to act like a sedative," she said, looking at his pupils. "How long has he been like this?"

"A few hours," Bennet said, crossing his arms over his chest. Taurin nodded to herself and checked his pulse again. "His pulse is getting stronger, he should be coming out of it now."

"We should camp here for the night."

Lana exhaled another breath making her disapproval known. They should keep going and put more distance between them and the facility. Bennet seemed to understand each one of her noises perfectly. "I know, Lana," he said, raising a hand to acknowledge her protest, "but I'm beat, I can't carry Riley any more. If he's coming out of it, it's better to rest for a few hours and continue when he can carry himself."

Lana blew out another breath. She didn't like it, but she knew it was their only plan. She couldn't carry Riley like this and

Taurin definitely wouldn't be able to carry him very far.

"Are we going to talk about that?" Taurin asked, nodding toward Lana.

Bennet laughed. "Not right now," he said, laying down beside Riley. "She won't believe us anyway. We'll tell her when she's human again."

Lana huffed in aggravation. "Don't worry about it right now, Lana," Bennet said, pulling the hood of his sweater over his eyes. "We've got lots of other things on our plates at the moment."

That was true. Whatever they were whispering about could wait until morning. For now, they needed to rest and get Riley back up and running. Then they could start on the next part of their plan.

\*\*\*

Lana woke up shivering. Her muscles aching and sore. They throbbed like they were healing from an old injury. She groaned and pushed herself up, the dirt of the forest floor sliding between her fingers.

She bolted upright, pulling her hand toward her face. Flesh, fingers – *yes* it was indeed her hand. "Oh my God," she breathed with relief. She touched her throat happy to hear her own voice again. She examined her bare arms and legs. *Clothes? Where are my clothes.* She looked at the ground around her. Nothing. "What the hell?"

She pressed her hands against her chest, expecting to feel her bare breasts, but felt a soft fabric instead. She leaned back to catch some of the moonlight. It was her spandex uniform. OK, that was great, but that was essentially her underwear, where were her actual clothes.

"Hey," Taurin said, sitting up and rubbing her eyes. "Are you OK?"

"My clothes are gone," Lana hissed, still patting the earth next to her and expecting to suddenly find them.

"Oh," Taurin said.

"Oh?" Lana said, turning back to the girl.

"Lana," she said, scooting closer to her. "Those were probably shredded when you morphed."

"What?"

"I mean, the reason the Islanders make us wear those spandex suits is because they are a microfiber creation that morphs with us." The words brought back the conversation with Claude. She had completely forgotten that was the original purpose of the suits. Well probably because she had never morphed so that information wasn't relevant at the time. A comprehensive training suit that eliminated the vulnerability of being naked after morphing.

Taurin took Lana's silence as incomprehension. "Your fur," she said, "it comes through teeny tiny little holes in the fabric and it stretches or shrinks as you morph."

Lana looked down at her body again. She still hadn't processed the events of earlier. "Here," Taurin said, unzipping her sweater. "Take this, it'll help for now."

Lana shrugged the sweater on, grateful for something to cover up with. She hugged the fabric closer, pulling the hood up over her head to enclose more warmth. She breathed a few quick short breaths to try and warm herself up. Taurin looked up to the sky. "The sun will be up soon, we should start moving." She slid her arm across to give Bennet a gentle shove.

A familiar strawberry blonde head sat up. Lana felt her heart leap with excitement. She ran over to him. "Hey Riles," she said softly helping pull him to his feet. "How are you feeling?"

"I should be asking you the same question," he said, his voice deep and husky.

Lana smiled. "I guess you're right." It was quite an eventful evening. Bennet was watching their conversation intently. Lana peered over her shoulder at him, feeling his looming presence. "What?"

"Oh I'm just waiting for him to tell you."

"Tell me what?" Lana asked, her head swiveling between the three of them.

"Your morph," Taurin interjected quietly.

Lana laughed. "Oh." She pointed at herself. "Some kind of big cat, right?"

When no one answered her, she looked back at Riley. He had a worried look on his face. He smiled sheepishly at her, and gave her a tiny nod, but she could see the hesitation in his eyes. "Yes, technically it's a big cat species but—"

"But nothing, we don't have time to discuss this right now, and honestly—" she threw her hands up in the air. "I think I need time to process everything."

"Then you should probably know what you are," Bennet said, pulling an old bagel out of one of the backpacks. "Because you're gonna need to process that as well."

Lana rolled her eyes and sighed, "All right, out with it, then," she said, waving a hand at the small boy. Riley stood up and glanced between Bennet and Taurin. Almost looking for encouragement.

"Come on, Riles," Lana said, "you're scaring me now."

Riley blew out a long breath. "OK, OK," he said, his hands raised. "You are indeed a large cat. The amazing or strange or unbelievable part about it is, that is not all you are."

Lana raised her eyebrows, confusion clear on her face. *Something more than a cat? What does that mean?* "What? like a hybrid?" she asked, searching for some kind of answer that would make sense. She had seen hybrids at zoos and sanctuaries, like half-tiger half-lion or half-leopard half-tiger. That made sense since Bennet called her a tiger, but she'd seen some spots on her legs. She scanned their faces waiting for an answer.

"No," Riley said, "not a hybrid. A species that, to be frank, is extinct."

Lana's took a step back, she laughed thinking she must have misheard him. "I'm sorry, what?"

"A saber-toothed tiger, Lana." Riley breathed, his eyes boring down into hers. "That's your morph."

Lana gulped the air quickly. Her chest rising and falling rapidly. She stepped back further. *No. A saber-toothed tiger?* "That's impossible." It wasn't possible, right? There was no way that could be possible.

"We descend from an ancient breed that can transform into animals, but this is impossible," Bennet snarked.

That helped refocus her. She could transform into an animal, why was it strange if that animal existed or not. It was all crazy. This was just another ingredient.

"Guess Claude was right about you." Bennet smiled gently. Lana didn't look at him, she barely moved, simply stared at the floor between them. She had spent so long fighting it, fighting every word out of Claude's mouth. About her history and her lineage. It aggravated her that he was right. Part of her had hoped she would never morph. Just to spite him.

Her hand flew up to her mouth, tenderly touching her gums. It made sense now. Her canines, a saber-toothed tiger. They were the cause for her gum pain all these years. She thought back, she'd been on medication for that since she was at least twelve to thirteen years old.

*That long* she thought, *Aunt Alice had been hiding this from me for that long?* She quickly wiped at the tear sliding down her cheek. She cleared her throat and looked to Riley.

"We should go," she said, slinging one of the backpacks over her shoulder and hustling into the brush. She didn't want to think about this. How was she supposed to think about it? A saber-toothed fucking tiger? She couldn't be just a regular tiger. Claude had seen it too. That's what was worse. She'd morphed right in front of him. She might have been able to deny her morph and her value before, but even she knew if she was valuable as a Mùth, she was ten times more with an extinct morph.

She still didn't even know what the Islanders did with Mùths, didn't know how they proved their value, but she didn't need to know that right now. She just needed to hike and focus on that. Just like it was another day of training back at the cabin.

"Wait!" Riley called, chasing after her. "Lana, you should talk about this," he called. She cringed hearing the loudness of his voice and brashness through the wood. They needed to be *way* more quiet if they wanted to go undetected.

She turned nearly colliding with him. "Riley, shush!" she whispered, holding a finger against her lips.

"You have to talk about this," he whispered.

"Not now, Riles. I need a second to process this for myself before I can talk about it with someone else, OK?"

"OK." He nodded. "But then you and me—"

"Yes, Riley" – She rolled her eyes – "then you can be my therapist, OK?"

He rolled his eyes in return. Lana turned back to the rich forest all around them. Bennet and Taurin caught up now, they had taken their time and followed her much more quietly than Riley had.

"Now what?" Bennet asked.

"Now, we get off this island," Lana said, scanning the forest.

# To Be Continued...